The Last Street Novel

Omar Tyree

Simon & Schuster

New York London Toronto Sydney

Simon & Schuster
1230 Avenue of the Americas
New York, NY 10020

First Simon & Schuster hardcover edition July 2007

SIMON & SCHUSTER and colophon are registered trademarks of Simon & Schuster, Inc.

For information about special discounts for bulk purchases,
please contact Simon & Schuster Special Sales at
1-800-456-6798 or business@simonandschuster.com.

Manufactured in the United States of America

1   3   5   7   9   10   8   6   4   2

Library of Congress Cataloging-in-Publication Data
Tyree, Omar.
The last street novel / Omar Tyree.
p.   cm.
1.   African American novelists—Fiction.   2.   Harlem (New York, N.Y.)—Fiction.
3.   Gangs—Fiction.   I.   Title.

PS3570. Y59L37   2007

813'.54—dc22   2007002185

ISBN-13: 978-1-4165-4184-4
ISBN-10:   1-4165-4184-5

This
is for those
who still believe
that feeding the mind
is the most powerful tool
of survival

I was born into this world

with the mind and spirit

of a revolutionary

unfortunately

in the time of my short existence

there was no longer

a revolution

so I walked the earth

for 40 days

and 40 nights

angry

apparently

at nothing.

WASTED
BY SHAREEF CRAWFORD

Contents

Harlem, 2006

THE SMOKE FROM THE CIGARETTE rose to the unblemished young face of a Harlem street general. He took another toke, holding the slim white cancer stick to his dark brown lips in between the fingers of his left hand. On his wrist dangled the overpriced timepiece of a pink gold Rolex, face all broken out with diamonds. His eyes squinted from the smoke while he stared forward. And when he spoke he possessed the full confidence of authority.

"I heard you had a whole lot to say about me. What you got to say about me now? You still got a mouthful you wanna spit out?"

He was real easy with his movements, relaxed like a pool shark who knew he'd win. He was twenty-five, but his baby face and wiry frame made him look closer to twenty. He wore a beige tennis shirt and top-grade denim jeans, held up by a leather belt with a chrome belt buckle with the capital letter G.

When he walked forward, a black semiautomatic pistol, elongated by a silencer attachment, tapped against his right leg. The pistol and silencer were firmly secured in his black leather–gloved shooting hand. Several of his trusted soldiers surrounded him in a lineup to his left and right, leading to their prisoner, who sat in the middle. And a dim light slashed in from the top of the blacked-out windows, good enough for them all to see, while no one could see them.

Their prisoner—a too-late-to-pray victim of disrespectful swagger—was strapped to a wooden chair with duct tape wrapped around his mouth to muffle his screams. The duct tape also served to stop him from ratting out any more information. That was why the man was in trouble in the first place; he knew too much, and he wasn't afraid to say what he knew.

The young general reached him at the chair and smacked the man upside the head with the hard handle of the gun.

Clack!

The man dropped his head and whimpered in pain.

One of the soldiers looked on and grinned. "I bet he ain't gon' talk that shit no more."

They were inside a run-down storefront property off Adam Clayton Powell Boulevard, north of 125th Street, and away from the foot traffic that flooded their popular neighborhood. They were all in their reckless late teens and young twenties, well groomed, all except for the tattered prisoner. He was in his early thirties and nappy-headed, with his last haircut performed by the barber over a month ago.

"Oh, that's no doubt," the young general stated. He backed away from the prisoner, far enough to aim the extra long barrel at his face.

He then took another puff of his cigarette. He said to no one in particular, "You know what I always wondered about these silencers? I mean, if you can't really hear the bullet when it comes out, then how you know if it hurt or not?"

"A knife don't make no sound, but you know that shit hurt. Especially a military knife that got them jagged edges on them," another one of his soldiers said.

"But that's the wrong answer. The right answer is: you gotta read their eyes. Like it said in *Scarface*, 'The eyes, they never lie.' So watch this motherfucka eyes when I shoot 'im."

He aimed the gun at the man's forehead and paused for the reaction, but there was none.

"You see that? He try'na play brave now. He don't even wanna blink. But watch his eyes after I shoot 'im in his toes."

He flicked his nearly finished cigarette away and aimed down at the prisoner's shoes, firing without hesitation.

The silent bullet zipped through the front end of the man's left shoe and sent him into a chair-rocking frenzy.

"*Grrrrrr!*" he growled through the duct tape that was secured around his mouth.

The man's eyes tightened in a flash as if someone had squirted them with lemon juice.

The young general got excited, proving his point. "You see what the fuck I'm talking 'bout? He ain't playing it cool now. Let me see what his eyes look like when I shoot 'im in his arm."

Another silent bullet ripped through the flesh of the prisoner's left arm, which was strapped to the back of the chair. The man shook his matted head and squeezed his eyes shut in excruciating pain.

"This probably how they doin' ma-fuckas in Iraq right now. I'd be a good torturer," the young general joked. "You gotta keep it entertainin' when you do it. Ain't so sense in being mad about it. We got the ma-fucka now. So I could fuck around and shoot 'im in his ear and let him feel his blood dripping down his eardrum."

A few of his soldiers winced.

"You sick, son," a brave one commented, with a shake of his head.

Fortunately, the young general didn't pay him any mind. For the time being, it was kill one mockingbird at a time.

"So what you want it in your head or in your chest, man? You make your choice. I don't mind," he teased the prisoner, who was bleeding from his left foot and left arm.

The unfortunate older man continued to keep his head down, not willing to volunteer anything to the game. That decision forced him to take another bullet, this time to his left earlobe.

"*Grrrrrrr!*" he growled and shook his head hysterically.

The young general became angry, like a psychopath. "Nigga, you listen to me when I'm talking to you! You hear me? Or you ain't gon' hear shit else in here."

Nobody laughed or said a word at that point. Their leader was in psycho mode.

"Shit. Now I gotta talk to you in your good ear."

His wry comment broke the tension in the empty room, compelling his soldiers to laugh out loud again.

The young general walked over to the prisoner's right ear and stopped to address his set. "Ay, ain't nuttin' fuckin' funny in here. I'm about tired of this shit now. And you look at me when I'm talking to you, *Eugene.*"

He called the prisoner by his first name and aimed the gun to his forehead again.

Eugene slowly lifted his head and forced himself not to beg for mercy. He realized that his begging would be useless—it would only add more fuel to an ugly fire.

"Now you got something else to say out your mouth about me on the streets? Hunh? About how I don't know shit. About how I ain't got shit on lock. About who supposed to be pulling my fuckin' strings? You got something else to say now?"

Eugene shook his head and sniffed. Fresh snot ran out of his nose, mixed with tears that ran down his face in a combined slop of terror, while blood painted the side of his neck from the bullet that shot off his earlobe.

The young general snapped, "I thought not." Then he made his whole point of the evening. "Nigga, I'm not no fucking game. So when you hear somebody say Baby G don't take that 'Baby' shit seriously, 'cause I'm a grown-ass man now. And I don't make fuckin' music, but I *will* make a motherfucka dance. You hear me?"

He was speaking more to his set of soldiers than to Eugene. Eugene was a dead man. He was no more than a human blackboard on which Baby G was writing his message. But instead of chalk, he was using bullets.

"Aw'ight, son, so where you want it—in your head or in your chest—'cause I got shit to do?"

Eugene stretched his eyes in disbelief. Baby G read it and frowned at him.

"Aw now, I know you don't think you was gon' live in here. What you think, I'ma let you walk around deformed and crippled? What if somebody ask you what happened? What you gon' say, you got caught up in a drive-by? We can't have no drive-bys in Harlem. That shit is way too sloppy. Somebody fuck around and hit Bill Clinton by accident, and these beat walkers'll fuck up the whole neighborhood looking for niggas. They'll turn us into Jews for a new Holocaust."

He said, " 'Cause Harlem is changing now, B. These adventurous-ass white folks is moving in and running up the property value with these new condos and shit. So now we gotta do our shit underground; silencers, leather gloves, and shit like that."

He looked over to his soldiers and said, "Ay, they even shutting down the liquor store game and puttin' up coffee and cake shops on every corner now; fuckin' bagel and Philadelphia Cream Cheese shops and shit."

His set started laughing again.

"Word up, son. That shit is real. Got me drinkin' coffee and shit now," one of his soldiers agreed, while the rest of them nodded in unison.

Baby G looked back at their prisoner of war and said, "I bet you ain't think I knew shit like that, did you, Eugene? You just thought I was another young, dumb-ass criminal, hunh?"

He stopped and eyed Eugene in his face, stooping down to get his point across with the silencer. "Nah, B. I know shit. So I figured I'd educate ya' ass before I kill you."

His soldiers stopped laughing after that. Play time was over. It was killing season.

"So where you want it: in your head or in your chest?" Baby G backed up and repeated. "Come on, son, let's make it happen. Let's get it over with."

When Eugene failed to answer, the young general wiped his hands of the whole scene.

"Fuck it, it's your head then."

He squeezed off two more shots. The silent bullets splattered through the back of the man's skull and left him limp in the chair. Baby G then tossed the gun to one of his soldiers.

"Do something smart with that and burn the glove . . . or I'ma have to burn you."

"I got it," his soldier assured him calmly.

Baby G nodded. "That's good." He turned and headed toward the back door to make his exit the way they had all entered.

"Yo, somebody give me another cigarette."

When they walked back out into the tranquil night air, bright stars and a half-moon were out. Everything was good. Harlem was an every-night holiday in the summertime. The streets were always flooded with the celebration of life. And there was no other place in the world they would rather have lived.

Baby G continued to nod. A fresh cigarette rose to his lips in between the fingers of his right hand.

"Yo, let's ride in that Mercedes with the top down. I feel like meeting me some new girls tonight. What's going on at Zip Code?"

Somebody answered, "They got that comedy hour goin' on there tonight."

Baby G thought it over. Comedy was good.

"Aw'ight, that's good money. Girls love to laugh. But let's smoke some of that sour diesel first. The laughs come easier with the weed."

"That's what's up," another one of his soldiers agreed. "I'ma go get that."

"And hurry up wit' it, too."

They eased their way down Adam Clayton Powell Boulevard toward the black Mercedes CLK convertible and a Chrysler 300 that were parked a few blocks away.

Times Square

AT SIX O'CLOCK in the morning, throughout the streets of Manhattan, New York, yellow taxis zoom through light traffic, carrying early-bird employees and managers along the empty sidewalks of a thousand high-rise buildings that cluttered the "Big Apple." And on nearly every midtown street corner, newsstands and food and refreshment joints set up shop for another busy day feeding the local patrons and tourists who buzzed in and around the city.

At the corner of 7th Avenue and 47th Street stood the towering Sheraton Hotel, close by Times Square. A simple walk south on 7th Avenue would deliver you right smack into 42nd and Broadway, with all the bright lights, billboards, and attractions, including where the stars hung out—actors, writers, directors, producers, comedians, musicians, athletes, dancers, fashion designers, and your popular business moguls.

The Sheraton Hotel was a centrally located New York hot spot, a place for those who wanted to be close to the action. And Shareef Crawford was one of them, a bestselling author of romantic fiction who was still young and athletic enough to run with the wild horses. As the first light of dawn cracked through the curtains of his luxurious suite, his circadian rhythm began to kick in and awaken him. No alarm clock was needed. The hustle was the hustle, and his body had gotten used to his early rises a long time ago. So he opened his eyes and stretched his dark brown arms over several extra fluffy white pillows in his room up on the twenty-second floor of the west wing.

"Aaaahhhh," he grumbled. "Another day another dollar . . . another fine girl another holler," he rhymed to himself in singsong.

He rolled over on his back in the comfortable king-sized bed and looked up at the ceiling. He was wrapped snugly inside the expensive white quilts of The Author's Suite, and sinking into the bed like a fly in sticky buttermilk. A large, cherrywood bookshelf stood against the wall to the right of the bed beside a tall reading chair and matching footstool. Various first editions, hardback novels by national best-selling authors, filled the shelves, including John Grisham, Stephen King, E. Lynn Harris, Michael Crichton, Terry McMillan, Anne Rice, Nora Roberts, Amy Tan, Dan Brown, and Danielle Steel. Before he checked out of the hotel, Shareef wanted to add one of his own books to the collection. He figured he had earned it.

It was the first day of his seventh book tour, which always kicked off in his hometown of New York, the city that never sleeps. And he was being pampered as requested.

He peeped over at the clock on the nightstand. It read 6:17 AM. His limousine and driver would arrive at the hotel for pickup at 6:45. His first interview that morning was at 7:30. The producers of the morning news at New York Cable Network (NYCN) wanted him at their Manhattan-based television studio by 7:15. And although the interview would last no longer than five minutes, it was well worth it.

African-American writers could rarely count on television time in New York City, but Shareef could. He was special that way. And the ladies loved him. So he used what he had to use, his sex appeal and un-inhibited imagination, to make himself into a millionaire.

"Damn, it's fuckin' time to go already," he mumbled as he continued to watch the clock. He was still feeling a slight hangover from too many drinks at the bar, entertaining old friends at TGI Friday's the night before. He gave himself another five minutes, another three, and another two before he finally forced himself out of bed at 6:27 and jumped into the shower.

AT 6:49 THE LIMOUSINE DRIVER, a light brown black man in his early thirties, wearing a dark suit, white shirt, and bright tie, looked down at his watch and began to wonder if he should call up to his client's room. He stood outside a shiny black Lincoln Town Car, parked at curbside on 7th Avenue. In his right hand he held the itinerary for the day, with Shareef Crawford's name, cell phone number, and the date printed at the top of the first page of three. In his left hand he held a hardback copy of Shareef Crawford's latest novel, *The Full Moon*. On the cover jacket, an attractive couple embraced passionately on a moonlit beach.

The limo driver smiled and thumbed through a couple of the pages. His wife was an avid reader and fan of Shareef Crawford's novels, so he was a little excited to meet the author. The man's books had served to spice up his sex life at home.

"This gon' make Carletta's day," he told himself, grinning while he waited.

After another minute of wavering, he decided to call Mr. Crawford to make sure he was up on time that morning. He pulled out his cell phone and dialed Shareef's number.

SHAREEF SPRAYED Sean John's Unforgivable cologne into his hands and rubbed the scent on his neck, chest, shoulders, and lower torso before he slid his wife-beater tank top over his shoulders.

He stared into the large mirror over the cherrywood dresser and boasted, "It looks like another good day. Damn it looks good!" He took a strong whiff of himself and added, "Smells good, too."

He slid on a white button-down cotton shirt with no tie before his cell phone rang. He pulled his phone from the holder that was attached to the dark blue dress pants he wore and read the 917 area code before he answered the call.

"Hello."

"Yeah, my name is Daryl Mooreland, and I'm your limo driver for the day. I just wanted to make sure that you were ready. We're not running late yet, but . . ."

Shareef cut him off and said, "Perfect timing, Daryl. I'm coming down right now."

"Oh, okay. Good. We got about twenty minutes to make it over to the station."

"Aw'ight. I'll be right down."

Shareef closed the cell phone, slid it back into its holder, and took a seat on the edge of the bed. He reached forward and grabbed his dark blue alligator shoes and slipped them on. He tied "the gators" up, grabbed his camel-colored sports jacket, and stood back up to slide his arms and shoulders in. He looked into the dresser mirror one last time while grabbing his brown, saddle leather briefcase.

"Let's go get it," he told himself in the mirror. He checked his pants pocket to make sure he had his hotel key card. Once he confirmed that he did, he was out the door.

SHAREEF ARRIVED at the lobby floor of the Sheraton Hotel and walked out of the elevator with swagger to burn.

The security guard at the elevators nodded and greeted him.

"Good morning, brother."

Shareef looked like a man of importance. He walked like a VIP, dressed like one, and smelled like one. And he didn't take his good fortune for granted, either. The privileges of wealth were definitely a good thing.

"Hey, you have a good day, man," he told the security guard.

"You, too."

"Oh, you know that. I feel good this morning. It's time to do what I do."

An attractive young white woman looked him over curiously as she walked out behind him. *Who is he?*

Shareef caught her stare and responded accordingly. "Yeah, you look good this morning, too," he flattered her.

She grinned sheepishly. "Oh, thank you."

"Have a good day," he told her.

"Oh, yeah, you, too."

Sometimes recognition was all a person needed to start off their day with a bang.

Shareef strolled out the front doors of the Sheraton in his immaculate attire, with briefcase in hand, and spotted his limo driver at the curb. It looked like a day for bright sunshine in July. And that's what it was, a bright and sunny day in New York City, forecast for a high of eighty-nine degrees.

"Hey, brother, you ready to make this trip to the station?"

The limo driver nodded to him and smiled.

"I've been ready, but I can't leave without you."

Shareef walked down to the curb where the black Lincoln Town Car was parked and said, "Well, let's do it then. We got people who wanna see me on TV this morning."

The limo driver perked up and opened the back door of the car. There was a certain pride in chauffeuring another young black man. Even if he didn't get tipped well, it felt good to see another brown man move up the ladder of American class, and for something positive and intellectual at that. The book business was historically an aristocratic white folks business, and as high class as golf, tennis, and traditional country clubs before Tiger Woods and the Williams sisters broke in.

So as soon as Shareef was comfortably seated in the black leather seats inside the limo, Daryl Mooreland told him, "Now I want to get this out of the way bright and early so I won't have to bother you anymore today, brother . . ."

He stopped and held out the new book in his hand.

"Could you *please* autograph this book for my wife. Her name is

Carletta, she loves your work, buys everything you put out, and after that, I won't bother you no more today. I'm just your driver."

Shareef took the book and laughed. "Naw, man, you're more than just a driver. You got a wife, you probably got kids, you got a job, you doing what a man is supposed to do, and I respect the fact that you respect me and what I'm doing. So it's all good."

Daryl said, "Well, I haven't read any of your books myself. I don't really read these kind of books, but as long as my wife is happy with it, that's all that really matters."

Shareef paused and decided to let the comment slide. Just keep the peace and move on in silence.

"Yeah, you gotta keep the ladies happy these days," he responded. "Somebody's gotta do it. That's who I write for." He then took out a Cartier pen from inside his sports jacket and asked, "How you spell Carletta?"

"C-a-r-l-e-t-t-a," the driver spelled out for him.

Shareef nodded and autographed his latest novel with his favorite pen, a gift from his editor. He was awarded the platinum pen after reaching his first one hundred thousand mark in hardback sales in 2000, for *I Want More*, the sequel to *Chocolate Lovers*, published in 1996. *I Want More* was also the book that landed Shareef his first seven-figure contract. The exact numbers were undisclosed. He didn't like people knowing too much about his income. His grandparents had told him never to reveal that information to the public. "People start thinking they know you better than what they do when they know how much you're worth," his grandfather had told him.

Shareef looked back to his driver and said, "I figured that's how you spell it, but I had to make sure. You never know with our people's creativity. I had a girl get mad at me one time in Detroit for spelling her name J-a-n-e. You know how she spelled it? J-a-i-n, like pain, and she expected me to know that."

They shared a laugh before he handed the signed book back.

"Naw, we don't allow no crazy spellings in my house," Daryl told him. "I got two little girls named Jennifer and Jessica, and their names are spelled correctly."

"Are they twins?"

"Nope. Two years apart."

Shareef's wife of eleven years was named Jennifer, but he decided a long time ago to keep his private family life out of his public affairs as well. So he didn't bring it up.

Daryl said, "Well, let's get going, Mr. Crawford. And thanks a lot for signing this book for me. My wife is gon' flip for this." He climbed behind the wheel and added, "You gon' get me some good love tonight, brother. Thanks!"

They laughed again before pulling out into traffic on 7th Avenue.

A YOUNG ASSISTANT met up with Shareef while he sat comfortably inside the green room at the NYCN television studio.

"You want any coffee or anything?" she asked him.

"Naw, I don't drink coffee. I got a natural high," he told her.

The assistant chuckled. "I guess that's a good thing to have. You're always up and going. I have a few friends like that."

"Are they successful people?" he asked her.

She stopped and thought about it. "Well . . . yeah, I would pretty much say they were successful."

He nodded. "That's the basic rule of life. The busiest worms eat the most apples. And they don't drink caffeine."

She nodded back to him and grinned. She understood that she wasn't on that busiest worm level. So she left his philosophy alone.

"Well, what about water?" she asked him.

He grabbed the white paper cup that sat on the table beside him and took a sip. "I already got it," he told her.

"Oh. Well, you're very low maintenance, I'll tell you that," she commented with a chuckle.

Shareef smiled at her with nothing left to say. He figured he would save the rest of his charm and wit for the morning news hosts and their cameramen.

"I'll be back in a minute to get you," the assistant informed him.

"Okay."

The time was 7:27, and Shareef was scheduled to go on air in less than five minutes. When the assistant returned to the room, they were ready for him.

"Okay, we're ready for you," she told him.

Shareef walked out of the green room behind her, and as soon as they entered the recording room, with all the cable wires, three large cameras, and several colorful background sets, a makeup artist checked the radiance of his skin and touched him up with dark brown powder to take away his shine.

Shareef then looked over at Heather Cooke, the entertainment host. She was a mixed-race, cream-colored woman with long, dark hair and sharp features. Shareef's old friends from the neighborhood had told him about her the night before at Friday's when he told them about his interview that morning.

"That girl Heather Cooke is *bad*. You might want to try and slide her your number after the interview, son. Hooking up with her would be good money," they told him. And they would all be watching, including his grandparents, who had recently moved to Harlem's West Side in Morningside Heights near Columbia University.

Hundreds of thousands of New Yorkers loved to watch the New York Cable Network news in the morning. NYCN gave them a stronger rundown on the local news and events as opposed to the ABC, NBC, CBS, and Fox affiliates, who focused more or national and international news with only a slice of the local. So plenty of urban New Yorkers would see his interview that morning.

The pressures of fame never fazed Shareef Crawford. He was perfectly at ease in the limelight. He craved it, as much as he craved good-looking women like Heather Cooke, who wore a dark gray business suit with a purple blouse.

Yeah, she do look good. She look like a Brazilian or some shit, which means she got black blood in her, he smiled and assumed to himself.

Right before the commercial break, Heather introduced a tease of their upcoming interview.

"Next up in the world of books and publishing is a new hot summer beach read from Shareef Crawford, *The Full Moon*. We all know what happens to our hormones during a full moon. And we'll be back to talk to the author about his latest hot novel after the break."

The key words to Shareef in the introduction tease were "summer beach read." He hated hearing that shit. It made his books sound like bubble gum, pop culture songs from suburbia. However, it was what it was, and he had made millions of dollars writing it. So he had to suck it up and accept it.

"Okay, we're ready for you," the assistant told him again. She led him over to the news set where a sound technician slid a mini microphone under his sports jacket. He didn't have to say much before Shareef had taken care of the microphone and clipped it into place.

"Looks like you've done this a few times before," the technician assumed.

"Yeah, about twenty-five to fifty times on different shows," Shareef joked to him.

The news anchor, James Callahan, a tall, middle-aged and graying white man, stuck out a manicured hand from his dark suit to greet the author before Heather could.

"I've heard a lot about you," he commented.

"Good things?" Shareef asked him, taking his hand.

James hesitated with his grin. "Well, let's just say I hear you have a way of expressing yourself with the ladies."

That meant the man knew nothing about Shareef except what he had heard from women going crazy over his books. However, misperceptions were part of the fame game. Some people heard everything but knew nothing for sure. And again, Shareef was forced to let it slide.

"Well, don't believe everything you hear. But sometimes you can believe it," he joked within earshot of Heather. He knew she had heard it. It was his preliminary flirtation with her.

Finally, he slid into the guest chair next to her. She looked at him, touched his knee and smiled.

"I started reading your book last night and had to stop myself to get some rest for work this morning," she told him.

"That means I was on your mind all last night, hunh? You know we have dreams about the last things we do at night," he told her.

She grinned, shook her head, and faced the cameras. It was the only thing she could do to avoid his advances. Shareef figured as much and backed off. He was there to do an interview and to pitch his new book to thousands of his New York fans, thousands who had heard of him but had never read his work, and thousands more who had never heard of him and never cared. Such was the life of an artist.

"As soon as you see the red lights go off on the cameras, that means we're on," she commented without facing him.

Shareef thought about red lights, cameras, and being on with Heather and began to smile. She felt it without looking at him and continued to grin. But now it was time for business, for both of them. Heather wouldn't allow herself to be distracted by him. She was a professional.

A producer began the countdown, "Five, four, three, two . . ."

The red lights of the cameras popped on, and Heather Cooke went to work with great face, posture, and diction.

"Well, if you haven't heard of him yet, you soon will. His new sexy summer novel is called *The Full Moon,* his seventh in the genre of African-American romance, and he's back home in New York to talk about it, and to sign your personal copies.

"He's the *New York Times* and *Essence* magazine bestselling author Shareef Crawford."

She then faced him with the cameras turning in his direction.

"Well, we're glad to have you this morning on New York Cable Network. Welcome to the show."

He said, "I thank you for having me. I also want to thank you for giving such a great introduction to my new book."

She held up her copy of the book for the cameras and smiled.

"Well, I must say, I started to read it and it's quite engaging."

"Like a good black man should be," he told her.

She laughed and stumbled over her words, the color rising on her flawless cheeks.

"Well, it's, it's your fifth, excuse me, your *seventh* novel, and they just seem to keep getting better."

He said, "Yeah, that's my intention. We all want to keep getting better at what we do in life, don't we? That's how I keep my readers coming back for more."

Heather smiled and couldn't seem to close her mouth. Was he that frank, or was she misreading his comments? She then looked at the teleprompter for something else to say.

"Well . . . I guess, you heard it right here from the author himself, ladies."

Up in the Washington Heights section of Manhattan, above 165th Street, Polo, Shareef's longtime friend from the old neighborhood, watched the interview on his flat-screen TV and screamed, "*Aaaahh-hhh,* that's my nigga! That boy is crazy, God. He got her fucking up her words. She don't even know what to say to this nigga."

Polo was ecstatic and enthused with energy before eight in the morning. He was standing in the middle of his living room in a purple bathrobe and slippers, with only a pair of colorful boxers on underneath. His hairy belly hung out over his boxers, while he absently scratched the side of his balls. Wrapped over his head was a black do-rag.

He hollered, "Yo, Shareef is a pimp, son. Let me call up Trap to see if he watchin' this shit."

A skinny, ten-year-old boy ran out into the room to ask what was going on with all of the racket.

"What is it, Daddy? What is it?"

The boy was still in his tight underwear himself, with a white T-shirt and socks on.

Polo grimaced at his son and snapped at him. "Boy, get the hell out of here and finish gettin' dressed. Ain't nobody call you out here. How many times I tell you 'bout ear hustlin' when grown folks in here talkin'? I dun' told you 'bout that, didn't I?"

The boy nodded, "Yes."

"Well, get your li'l ass out of here and finish gettin' dressed then."

Before the boy left, he looked around the room and mumbled, "I don't see nobody out here."

Polo started in his direction with a stomp. "Nigga, if you'on get your li'l ass out'a here . . ."

His son took off running back up the apartment hallway toward his room.

"Smart-ass li'l nigga. Just like his motherfuckin' pop," Polo grumbled. "He makin' me miss the interview. Let me call up Trap," he told himself with his cell phone in hand.

BACK DOWN in Spanish Harlem, below 115th Street, the slim brown man named Trap grinned at the small color television screen at the foot of his bed and laughed. Shareef was still the cocky, go-for-it cat he grew up with on the East Side, not far from where he lived now.

When Trap's cell phone went off next to a semiautomatic handgun and a large bag of weed on the nightstand, he picked up the phone and read Polo's number before he answered it.

"Hello."

"Yo, B, are you watching this interview?"

"Yeah, I'm watchin' it."

Polo yelled, "Yo, is this nigga Shareef a pimp or what, son? Just let me know."

Trap held the phone away from his ear a few inches and shook his head.

He said, "It's a little too early for this screaming and yelling shit in my ear in the morning, man. I still got a hangover from last night."

"Aw, stop girlin' and get the fuck up. You ain't even drink that much last night. You see Shareef up bright and early. Now don't tell me that nigga can outdrink you and still get up and do a interview in the morning."

Trap continued to shake his head. Polo needed some Ritalin for attention deficit disorder. The man was far too hyper, and he had been that way his entire life.

INSIDE THE LARGE FAMILY ROOM of the Morningside Heights home that Shareef had bought for his proud grandparents, Charles and Wilma Pickett watched their grandson from their twin rocking chairs that sat in front of their forty-six-inch, floor model TV, another gift from Shareef. They were both fully dressed, gray-haired, walnut brown, wearing reading glasses, and ready for their early-morning walk after the news. They had been married for forty-seven years and he had just recently retired from work at the post office. They had been together for two years before marriage when Wilma got pregnant with Shareef's mother, Patrice, and asked Charles if he would marry her. Watching their only grandson, who had become a celebrity author, on the New York Cable Network news was an extra treat for them.

"He sure is a fresh somethin'," Wilma commented with a giggle.

All Charles did was grin. He was fresh, too, once. That was what a vibrant man was supposed to be. After holding his tongue for a minute, he decided to speak up about it.

"If somebody else wasn't fresh, that boy wouldn't have been here. None of us would have been here," he added. "So just let that boy do what he do now."

Wilma eyed her husband through her glasses and grunted, "Mmm, hmm. Sounds like somebody still thinking about his middle age. Well, just don't let me find out you bought no Miagra. 'Cause them wild and crazy days are over for me."

"The word is *Vi*-agra," he corrected her.

"*Mi*-agra, *Vi*-agra, whatever. You know what I'm talking about."

Charles shook his head and grumbled, "You ain't never been wild and crazy. Maybe in your own mind, but definitely not to me."

She continued to stare her husband down.

"Now what you mean by that, Charles? Speak your mind."

He said, "I already spoke my mind. Now cut it out, I'm trying to hear the rest of this boy's interview. You know they ain't gon' have him on there much longer."

"Mmm, hmm," she grunted again. "Well, we gon' finish our conversation as soon as his interview is over with."

Charles decided to ignore his wife and listen to his grandson from the TV. He could fight with her anytime. And he did, every day of the week. But their fights had somehow kept his blood pumping, and his views had done the same for her.

BACK ON AIR at the NYCN station, Heather Cooke had regained her composure.

"So, you were the first recipient of the Black Hearts Book Award."

"Yeah, I won the first three Black Hearts awards for contemporary male romance before I asked the voters to honor someone else. I wanted to give other brothers a chance to show and prove with their writing."

Heather nodded to him. "Well, that's pretty nice of you."

Shareef grinned at her. "Yeah, I try to be nice sometimes, you know. People like you when you're nice, nice and bad," he flirted with her again, and chuckled.

Heather smiled it off and got back to business.

"Okay, so you have a lunchtime signing at the Virgin Records store in Times Square."

"That's right, from twelve noon to two," he filled in.

"Then you have a reading and Q and A tonight in Harlem at the Hue-Man bookstore at seven."

Shareef nodded. "Yeah, that one's gonna be big fun, back to the home turf again in Harlem."

"Well, it's been great talking to you this morning, and we all wish you the best of luck on your new book."

With the red light of the camera finally off them, Heather's co-reporters introduced the next news story and the weather report.

Heather then asked Shareef, "How many cities are you touring to this year?"

"Seventeen."

Her eyes stretched open. "Wow, that's quite a schedule." She expected him to say nine or so.

He said, "A lot of people want to see me. But each city is its own adventure." He then looked her in her eyes and added, "I'll tell you all about it if you're free for dinner after nine."

The man was like an arrow straight to a girl's heart. He wasted no time with it.

Heather looked around embarrassingly to see how many of her coworkers overheard him.

In her hesitation, Shareef pulled out a business card and slid it into the palm of her right hand as he stood to leave.

"All it is is food, drink, and simple conversation on me. Then you get a free limo ride back home. So call me."

She nodded to him quickly and didn't say a word. The faster she acknowledged him, the faster she could get his flirtations over with. As for his business card, she didn't quite know what to do with it. How could she slide it into her purse without it being obvious to everyone?

Shit! she cursed. Shareef Crawford had put her on the spot at her job and had slipped out of the room like Bruce Wayne running to change into Batman.

I wonder how many of his romance stories are based on his own rendezvous, Heather asked herself. However, since she was already involved, she was not interested in finding that information out.

• • •

AS SOON as Shareef exited the building to meet up with his limo driver, his cell phone went off. He looked down at the screen and read Polo's number before he answered it.

"Yeah, what's up, man?"

He knew damn well what his friend wanted to talk about that morning.

"Yo, son, what she say about hooking up? Give me all the details," Polo stated immediately. He said, "I know she was feeling you. I could see it in her eyes. You had her stumbling over her words and shit. You probably got her li'l panties moist this morning."

Shareef smiled while Polo kept going with it.

"You think she wearing a thong or no panties? I mean, did you see 'em, like a line around her ass or anything?"

Polo was a riot. Shareef shook his head and got serious with his answer.

"Look, I gave her my number, man, and pushed up on her the way you're supposed to. She probably used to guys trying to get her on the low because she's on TV every day, so I did mine out in the open to get her to think about it stronger. Otherwise, I'm just another player trying to holler."

Polo disagreed. "Nah, fuck that, she know you more than the average nigga, son. You put it on her way too strong this morning for that. Save that sucker shit for the bill collectors."

Shareef chuckled and spotted his driver parked in front of two yellow taxis that were pulling up to the curb.

He said, "A woman like her got a man already anyway. Ain't nobody letting her roam around out here alone. So I don't expect much from it. If she call she call. But yo, let me hit you back later. I gotta make this radio interview at WLIB, then get me some breakfast, and get ready for this first book signing at Virgin."

He stated, "It's time to go to work, baby. Time to go to work."

"Oh yeah, do your thing, B. I'll just see you up in Harlem tonight at

Hue-Man. But I probably won't get there until eight, to see what kind of fly stunts show up for you this year."

Polo laughed loudly over the phone and said, "You know how I do. You can't have 'em all. So I'ma scoop up your rejects tonight like I always do."

Shareef ended the call with a smile on his face.

His driver jumped out of the car to open the back door.

"I had to move up a bit for these taxis to get in," he explained.

"It's all good, man, it's New York. Nobody stands still here."

Daryl laughed and said, "Now that's the truth." He closed the door behind his client and scrambled back over to the wheel to drive.

THE BLACK LINCOLN pulled up to the WLIB radio tower on Park Avenue at 8:23 AM. Shareef hopped out, made his way up to the top floor, and charmed everyone in the building. He signed copies of his new book for the staff, the hosts, and as giveaways for the lucky fans who called in during the show. It was all part of touring in the publishing world.

By the time he was off the air and back inside the limo at 9:30, the hardworking author was starving for something solid. He hadn't had time to stop and eat that morning, and doughnuts, snacks, and coffee just weren't going to cut it. So he had turned all of those teasers down.

He told his driver, "Hey, man, it's time to get me something to eat at one of these breakfast spots before I fall out in here."

Daryl looked into his rearview mirror and chuckled. "Oh, I got you. You wanna order room service back at the hotel? That way you can get some rest before your signing at Virgin."

Shareef answered, "Nah, man, I'm back in New York. I don't want to be cooped up in no room. I wanna see my city while I'm still here. I can rest when I get to the next city."

The limo driver continued to laugh. He said, "Aw'ight, we'll find you a breakfast spot then. That's easy. What city you headed to next?"

"After New Jersey tomorrow, I hit Philadelphia. Then I hit Baltimore and D.C."

Daryl nodded. "Where you go after that?"

"Atlanta, Jacksonville, Houston, Memphis, Birmingham—"

The driver cut him off, "Birmingham? Alabama?"

Birmingham, Alabama, didn't sound like much of a book-reading city to him.

Shareef said, "Yeah, Birmingham gives me much love, in a whole lot of ways. Ay, don't sleep on the old school, man. Old southern cities like Birmingham are dying for black culture."

The driver nodded. He said, "You learn something new every day."

"Oh yeah," Shareef agreed. "You learn a whole lot when you travel. I'm ready to start traveling around the world. I've seen mostly everything now in America."

"Must be nice to be able to travel like that," his driver commented.

Shareef said, "Shit, man, all it takes is a bus ride. Take your family somewhere on the bus and stay a couple of nights at the Holiday Inn. From New York, you could go up to Connecticut, Boston, the Hamptons, or down to Philly, D.C., Baltimore, just to let your kids see another city."

He said, "I mean, I'm from New York and I love New York, man, but this is just one small place in the world. And it eats up all your money. So if you can get out of here with your family, then do it, and just come back to visit when you need to."

Daryl responded, "Yeah, that all sounds good, but for a limo driver, New York is the place to be. I could move down to Jersey for my family though. But I just never liked New Jersey. I mean, New Jersey just seem like, you got right up to the gates of New York and couldn't get in. You know what I mean?"

Shareef smiled, planning to cut his argument short.

He answered, "Yeah, I know what you mean. New York City seduces people that way."

· · ·

BY 11:00 AM the streets of New York were in full buzz about the new Shareef Crawford novel. First printing hardback copies of *The Full Moon* were being sold fresh out of their boxes in the Virgin Megastore, Barnes & Noble, Borders, Waldenbooks at the malls and shopping centers, and by a hundred independent bookstores and street vendors in downtown Manhattan, Brooklyn, Queens, the Bronx, and of course, on the busy streets of Harlem.

Urban women began to clutch their new craving of romance to their chests like Bibles, reading them on the trains, buses, taxis, and inside the offices, retail stores, and restaurants where they worked. Shareef Crawford had struck gold again and life was good.

As he finished the last bites of his breakfast of pancakes, eggs, bacon, grits, home-style potatoes, wheat toast with butter and jelly, and orange juice at The Hot Spot Cafe in Midtown, he received another call on his cell phone. Shareef wiped his mouth, took another sip of his refilled orange juice, and looked down at the screen before he answered it. It was a 212 number—this time his editor at the publishing offices back up in the Times Square area.

"Hey, Bill, everything's feeling good so far, man," he addressed his editor of the past seven years. William Sorenski was one of the few male editors of romantic fiction at any publishing house, and he and Shareef had formed a successful relationship. They were roughly the same age, in their early thirties, both married, both attended school in the south, and they were both ambitious about their futures in the publishing industry. Bill was itching to become a publishing boss one day, and Shareef knew it. Shareef was prepared for a long career at the top of the bestsellers charts, and Bill knew that. The next frontier for both of them were packaging creative and intellectual rights from their book titles into television, feature films, and stage play deals to acquire an even larger reading audience. A guest spot on the *Oprah Winfrey Show* wouldn't hurt in that capacity, either.

"I hear you were turning up the heat early this morning on the New York Cable Network," Bill commented.

"Yeah, you know how I do. But don't tell me you missed another one of my live interviews."

"I had my assistant tape it for me."

"Yeah, here we go. So now you can play it over and over again and tell me what I said wrong, right?"

"Well, you are still married aren't you? From what I hear, you were getting hot and heavy with Heather Cooke."

"It was that obvious, hunh?"

"Well, as long as your readers respond to it. You never talk about being married anyway. So they all believe they have a chance."

"And that's exactly how you have to do 'em, too. But I am separated."

"Well, if it'll make you feel better, I would probably get into trouble with Heather Cooke myself if I was a guest on the show. Only she would probably have *me* stuttering instead of it being the other way around. And that would only make my wife more incensed."

Shareef laughed and said, "Yeah, I can imagine. 'Why did that mulatto woman have you stuttering, William? I want to know,' " he teased.

Bill responded, "I think my wife already knows why Heather would have a guy stuttering. But I hear you had her stuttering. You think you can do that with Oprah?"

Shareef stopped laughing and paused. He had an image of Oprah Winfrey in his mind. She wasn't exactly his kind of woman, either physically or in age.

He said, "I don't know about no Oprah, man. I mean, my powers can only stretch so far. And I don't really have anything to offer to her audience unless I write a couple of books about down-on-their-luck white women. I mean . . . Oprah just don't deal with that many black books, or with black men in general."

Bill said, "She had Tyler Perry on her show."

"Yeah, because he created that grandma Madea thing. I mean, you want me to write something like that? White women look at that as comical. It crossed over. But, you know, man, I'm already separated from my brothers as it is. I start writing stuff like that and . . . I mean, I played football with guys. I'm a locker room kid. I'm not trying to get that far away from things. I have enough problems explaining what I write about now."

"Shareef, I'm not telling you what to write. I'm just trying to figure out how we can cross over. Maybe you could have a show on Oprah about the disrespect of intellectual black men. You've always seemed to talk about that. And your novels, even though they deal with romance, have had some of the strongest black male voices in contemporary fiction."

"Yeah, because I know how real brothers think. We used to be up at all times of night, debating everything under the sun at Morehouse. So I just know."

"Well, it's just something for us to think about as we attempt to, ah, make our move into television and film. We have to find new ways to engage a larger audience. But anyway, let's save that conversation for later. We have a book tour to do. So, are you just about ready for your signing at Virgin?" Bill asked.

"Come on, man, I'm always ready. I'm about to roll up to Virgin early, right now."

"That's good, because the managers there have been dying to meet you. You could talk them into buying some more books before the lines get started."

"How many books did they buy?"

"More than usual, but they could always buy more."

Shareef grinned and said, "Yeah, that's with every bookstore."

"All right, well, go have fun. I have to take this call."

"Aw'ight, I'll tell you all about it tomorrow."

He ended the call and relaxed in his restaurant booth while his food continued to settle. It seemed no matter how many millions of books he sold, it was never enough. But what exactly was the purpose of it all? Did he want to sell more books about romance just to make more money? Or would he rather write about something that meant more?

Yeah, and then be ignored for it, he pondered the idea. It was a catch-

22. Write serious content and receive awards from the literary elite while never being understood by the popular culture. Or write popular fiction that crosses over and opens up new bank accounts, while never being respected by the literary elite.

Maybe I should write new books under a pseudonym, but that shit never seems to work.

"Would you like anything else?" the waitress in a light blue apron asked. She broke Shareef out of his daydream.

"Oh, nah, I'll just, ah, take the bill." And he gathered himself to leave.

SHAREEF ARRIVED at the Virgin Megastore in the heart of Times Square near West 45th Street. He met with the store managers and staff and was treated like royalty. The line of book readers flooded into the store even before noon, packed with mostly black women and Latinas—young, old, short, tall, light, dark, skinny, plump, domestic, and international. Then there were men, who mostly wanted to write and publish poetry or novels themselves, or were simply buying books for the women in their lives, along with gay men, who dreamed of rendezvous with the author like some of the women did. But there were only a few crossovers in line, supporters from other races and cultures who were curious enough to enjoy the love and literature of black America. And Shareef sold them all, signed them all, worked them all, and smiled to them all, even though he still felt a sense of emptiness. He always felt as if there was more to do, and more ideas to explore in the creation of new literature.

The Proposition

A T 3:47 PM a young male reporter from the historic *Amsterdam News* interviewed Shareef inside the lobby of the Sheraton Hotel concerning his seventh novel and successful writing career.

"So, how does it feel to be able to sell millions of books to a growing fan base each year?" the reporter asked him. He was an eager young man out of New York's Hunter College who dreamed of a career writing Hollywood screenplays. In the meantime, he chose to keep up with his bills and pay off his student loans by reporting and writing for the *Amsterdam News*. Dressed in a blue-and-white-striped button-down shirt, a noncoordinating tie, blue jeans, and brown leather shoes, the young man would win a fashion award from no one. In contrast, Shareef's sharp style of dress, poise, and status was something the reporter could look forward to in the years to come. But at least the young reporter had a sharp haircut. During the interview, however, Shareef was distracted with boredom. He continued to watch guests coming and going from the hotel and imagining what their lives were like. Watching people was one of the many skills he utilized as a writer.

"I mean . . . having a fan base is one thing, but being able to move people in a certain direction is another," he answered.

They were sitting comfortably in lounge chairs with the reporter's tape recorder running between them. And the young man was grow-ing a little confused by his subject's increasingly complicated answers.

The reporter raised his brow and asked, "How exactly do you plan to move people?"

Romance was romance. Did the author actually expect people to learn more about loving one another through his books?

Instead of answering the interviewer's question, Shareef looked into the young reporter's eyes and asked a question of his own.

"What do you read?"

"What do I read?"

"Yeah, what do you read?"

"Ah, I mostly read historical books, nonfiction, or books on screen-play writing."

"And you want to be a screenplay writer yourself, right?"

The reporter had discussed his future ambitions with Shareef be-fore they began the interview.

He nodded and answered, "Yeah, I do."

"But you don't read any fiction?"

Shareef waited for the young man's answer.

"Not really, no."

He could imagine that the author was setting him up for some-thing. But what could he do about it? Shareef was in authority. He had more years of writing and reporting experience and he wrote at a much higher level.

"Well, let me ask you a question. What do you think the best screenplays are? Nonfiction? Historical documentaries?"

Shareef waited for his answer again.

Understanding that he was trapped by a superior intellect, the young reporter began to smile.

"Okay, you're probably right," he admitted.

"I'm probably right? Probably right about what?"

The reporter nodded. "Most of it is . . . probably fiction."

"But you don't read fiction," Shareef stated again for the record.

The young reporter tried to defend himself.

"Well, a lot of good screenplays are based on the truth, though."

"And so is good fiction. You think we're making up shit that never happened before? Have you ever even read any of my books?"

"Well, I mean, I tried to, but—"

Shareef cut him off, "You tried to? Well, have you read any novels at all?"

"Oh yeah, I've read Richard Wright, Ralph Ellison, James Baldwin, Donald Goines, you know, the classic stuff," the reporter answered.

Shareef had read books by those authors himself, along with books from more than a hundred other writers.

He asked, "Do you plan to write screenplays about their kind of books? You know, the old slave days, the forties, the fifties, and the sixties?"

The young man could sense that he was falling into another trap, but he was still useless in defending himself against it.

"Well, I can see where you're going with that—"

Shareef cut him off again and said, "Answer the question."

All of a sudden, he was no longer distracted by the curious human traffic that flooded through the lobby of the hotel. He was giving the young man his undivided attention with the intent of turning him into a pupil.

"Ahhh . . . no, I wouldn't say I plan to write screenplays about what they were writing."

"What are your screenplays about?"

Who was being interviewed now? And there was no easy way for the younger man to regain the upper hand.

He said, "I want to write screenplays about, you know, the things that are happening now?"

"What kind of things?"

"Well, I wrote this one screenplay about these four college friends who graduate from school and then they all go in different directions."

Shareef nodded. "It sounds like a period piece. How many years does it cover?"

"Yeah, it covers about ten years, from college to, you know, their late twenties, early thirties."

"Have you finished it yet? I'd love to read it."

The young man hesitated. "Well, I'm still kind of hashing it out, you know."

"So, you haven't finished it?"

"Yeah, I'm finished, but, you know, I'm not really ready to show it around yet."

Shareef had him sweating bullets. It was getting hotter in that hotel lobby by the second.

The young reporter moved to shut his tape recorder off since he was no longer interviewing. He considered their conversation wasted tape, but Shareef stopped him.

"Don't do that. You gon' need this information," he told him. He said, "Now let me tell you something. From what I understand about black Hollywood, we don't have that many good screenplay writers. And you know why?"

He paused again for his pupil to answer him.

"Why?"

"Because we don't fuckin' read enough," he told him. "So most of our screenplays end up being corny, simple-minded, uneven, copycat shit. Why? Because we don't know how to tell a good story. And why don't we know how to tell a good story? Because we don't take the time to *read* good stories, or to understand what makes a story good. So without reading good *fiction,* brother, we end up writing weak character development, weak dialogue, weak plot points, with a weak buildup, weak chronology, uneven climaxes, and a weak resolution. And now you got all of that on your tape to study. But since you don't read my books, you can't really converse with me about my career, because you have no idea of my skill level. Therefore, without reading any of my shit, if you write anything positive about me, then you're being patronizing. And if you write any negative shit about me, especially since I might be hurting your feelings right now, then you'll end up showing your ignorance, because you didn't read any of my shit to judge me from in the first place."

And with all of that said, Shareef stood up to make his exit.

He said, "So I want to thank you for making your way down here to interview me, but we can't possibly continue this interview until you've finished your homework. I mean, that would be like throwing a rookie into the playoffs without him even having a scrimmage or a basic practice. You feel me?

"And I'm not hating on you, young blood, I'm just showing you tough love right now to get you ready for the real world," Shareef explained to him. "Because when you actually start reading more and studying your craft for real, then you'll begin to set your own mark of excellence to the point where no white man or anyone else can tell you that you don't know what the fuck you're doing. And when you get to that point in your career, you'll be able to pick up your rifle and go to war with me. But right now, you're empty-handed, brother, and we can't go to war like that. You'll fuck around and get both of us killed."

Shareef then forced a departing handshake before he walked away toward the elevators, leaving the reporter dazed, overwhelmed, and speechless. And once he realized that his interview was officially over, the young man looked at the still running tape recorder and shook his head in disbelief.

"Damn! What did I say?"

AT 5:49 PM, Shareef took a deep breath inside the bathroom of his hotel suite and sprayed on a second layer of cologne. His driver would be ready to take him back up to his birthplace of Harlem at six o'clock for a seven o'clock reading, Q&A, and signing at Hue-Man Bookstore. The store was located at the corner of Frederick Douglass Boulevard and 124th Street, right under the Magic Johnson/Sony Theaters.

"One more event for the night," Shareef told himself while looking in the mirror. "But this is the big one."

He brushed his teeth, gargled mouthwash, and before he grabbed his briefcase to head down to the limo, he remembered to call his grandparents.

"Hey, it's me, Grandma."

Wilma got excited over the phone. "Hey, Shareef, how's your busy tour day gon' so far?"

He answered, "You know, same-o same-o. If something happens differently, I'll tell you all about it. But are you sure you guys don't want to come out tonight?"

"No, we don't want to be around you with all them crazy people tonight," his grandmother responded. "We'd rather do breakfast with you in the morning, where we can enjoy our famous grandson alone.

"What time do you need to leave for New Jersey tomorrow?" she asked him.

"My first event is in Newark at noon. So I need to leave by eleven to get there on time."

His grandmother said, "That's perfect. We can do breakfast with you tomorrow morning at nine. And it shouldn't take us two hours to eat."

"Okay, so we'll do that then," he agreed. "Where's Grandpop?"

"Over here stinking up the bathroom," his grandmother answered loud enough for her husband to overhear her.

"Mine don't smell no worse than yours," Charles yelled out with a muffled echo from behind the closed bathroom door.

Shareef shook his head against the phone and chuckled. Real life was stranger than fiction, but it didn't read as well.

His grandmother asked him, "You didn't hear that, did you?"

"Nah, I didn't hear nothing," he lied.

"Good. So we'll see you tomorrow morning for breakfast then. And you be safe out there tonight, Shareef. You know we love you."

"I love y'all, too," he told her.

"Have you spoken to Jennifer and your babies today?"

He paused. "Grandma, they're not babies anymore. Little J turned nine this summer, and Kimberly turned seven in March. You remember? You were at the birthday party."

"Yeah, I remember. I know how old they are. I'm not senile. But at sixty-seven years old, they're still babies to me. Now have you made up with your wife and moved back into your house?"

That was a much longer conversation, and it was too close to six o'clock to have it. Shareef didn't want to talk about his relationship with his estranged wife anyway.

"I'll be calling them shortly," he answered. *Just probably not tonight,* he told himself. He said, "Well look, Grandma, I gotta get going. My driver's downstairs waiting for me."

"Okay, well, like I said, you be safe out there tonight, Shareef. And you make sure you call your family."

WHEN SHAREEF CLIMBED back into the limo, parked curbside at the Sheraton, all he could think about were his two kids. His grandmother had shot an arrow of guilt into his heart. But he still didn't want to call them yet. Tour season was his time to be a man again, and even though he cherished the role of father, there were times where he needed to turn his paternal emotions off and focus on his business with grown-ups.

Yeah, I'll call them, right after the book signing, before they go to bed, he decided.

WHILE SHAREEF was on his way to the Hue-Man Bookstore for his signing in Harlem, a rival author aggressively worked the street corner in front of the Magic Johnson/Sony Theaters with his own new book, *The Streets Keep Calling Me.* He was dressed military style with black boots, black pants, a green camouflage T-shirt, and a matching camouflage bucket hat with a draw string. He looked in his late thirties. He had a box of books on the ground, and four loose books in his hands. He worked every man, woman, and child who happened to walk by him.

"Get the real deal, the truth from the streets, baby, the black man is in a crisis. It's my new book right here, *The Streets Keep Calling Me,* get it now," he announced repetitively.

A couple of young women stopped to take a look on their way into the bookstore. They were both in their late teens, and not quite grown yet.

"Hey, young sisters, they call me The Spear. This is my new book right here," he told them. He handed them each a copy. "Have you heard about it on the streets yet?"

They both looked at the urban jungle cover jacket of the two-hundred-page paperback with The Spear printed at the bottom. Both girls shook their heads in unison. They hadn't heard of it.

"Well look, y'all need to get up on this one. Your boyfriends, brothers, uncles, fathers, nephews, they're all in a crisis in America, and reading them romance books ain't gon' help them. You young sisters need to understand the struggle of a real black man," he explained to them.

He said, "So, here's what I'ma do. These books are thirteen dollars each, but I'ma give them to you both for ten."

One of the girls concentrated, trying to understand his math.

"You gon' give us both these books for ten?" she asked to make sure she heard him right.

He looked her in her eyes to make himself clear.

"Ten dollars for each book," he told her. "That would be twenty."

The girl frowned and said, "Oh." She was immediately disappointed. Two books for ten dollars would have been a great deal. She would have gone for that. But twenty dollars for two books from a street author she had never heard of before was robbery. So she snatched the copy her friend was holding and handed both books back to the man.

"Naw, that's all right."

He said, "You gon' pay twenty-five dollars in the store. What's that, fifty? I mean, do the math, sisters. This book is to help you understand your brothers for real, not just what they look like in the bedroom."

The girl grinned and said, "We want 'em in the bedroom," and forced her girlfriend to laugh before they walked away.

He spoke to their backs as they left him. "That ain't gon' get you nowhere but pregnant. And a pregnant woman can't help no man in the struggle. That's just another burden on him. Y'all need to get y'all minds right."

As soon as the two girls walked into the bookstore with the rest of the crowd, one of the bookstore staff hustled out to have another talk with the man.

"Please, brother, we've already told you, you can't be out here."

"Well, invite me in there then."

She said, "All you have to do is talk to our events coordinator and we'll work out a date that works for all of us. Now please, you have to leave."

She was being as pleasant as she could, but the brother felt slighted anyway. He looked over at the large poster of Shareef Crawford and his latest romance novel that was posted in the bookstore's window, and he frowned at the whole suave, chocolate image of the man.

Fake-ass Billy Dee Williams wannabe, he told himself. *That seventies playboy shit is over.*

The bookstore staff member was still waiting for him to leave the premises.

He looked at her and barked, "Aw'ight, aw'ight, I'm leavin'. And I'ma talk to your events coordinator tomorrow."

"Thank you," she told him, and walked back into the store.

The brother shook his head in disgust, and as soon as he turned to pack up his box, he nearly rammed into a woman.

"Oh, I'm sorry, sister," he apologized. He stepped back and looked the woman over. She wore expensive black heels, a lavender business suit, a black lace top, and was astonishing from head to toe—all five feet six inches of her. She smelled like the most expensive flowers mixed with vanilla and cinnamon spice. She had flawless brown skin, and jet black Caribbean hair with the thick waves swimming through it.

The brother opened his mouth and said "God *damn!*" before he could catch himself. He said, "Sister, you're not going into that book signing, are you? Don't tell me you're going in there."

She didn't even get a chance to answer him. He was all over her.

"Look, these romance books are not gonna get us out of our present crisis, sister. We really need to understand one another in the struggle."

To his surprise, she nodded to him and said, "I agree." Then she extended her hand for a copy of his book.

He handed one right over to her.

"How much is it?" she asked him.

He looked at her again and said, "Thirteen."

She took out a twenty-dollar bill from her small black purse and told him, "Keep the change."

The man was falling in love right there on the sidewalk.

He said, "You want me to sign it for you?"

She opened the pages of his book and said, "Sure."

SHAREEF CRAWFORD pulled up to the curb of 124th Street and Frederick Douglass Boulevard in his black Lincoln at 6:45 PM, so he had a few minutes to prepare himself for the standing-room-only crowd of eager fans. The bookstore was jam-packed with customers with more still walking in.

Daryl looked out into the crowd through the store windows and said, "They're feeling you in there tonight, brother."

The bookstore staff had blocked off room out front for the limo driver to park.

Before they climbed out of the car, Shareef asked his driver, "Are you coming in for this one?"

Daryl hesitated a minute. He still didn't want to get too involved.

Then he said, "Sure, why not? They already got a spot out here for me."

"Okay, well, I might need you to do me a favor," Shareef told him.

Daryl turned and looked him in the face.

"What's that?"

"Well, usually, after the last signings, I like to take a lucky girl out to dinner. But since they're all up in my face inside the store, I usually can't do it by myself. So I always pick out somebody with me to be the one to say something."

Daryl smiled and started laughing.

He said, "You got it down to a science, hunh?"

Shareef grinned and said, "All I need for you to do is tell her that I would like to treat her to dinner if she has the time this evening. And that's it. I'll look at you to tell you which woman to ask."

Daryl nodded to him. "All right. I think I can do that."

Shareef said, "Okay, let's do it then."

Daryl let him out of the car and escorted him through the front doors of the bookstore like a bodyguard.

"There he go, there he go," a single, young woman swooned.

"Hey, how are y'all doin'?" Shareef spoke to them all with humble authority.

"Waitin' for you," someone answered. The room broke out with a ready laugh. That was a good thing. The crowd was loose and bubbling.

The bookstore owners, Rita Ewing and Clara Villarosa, immediately greeted the author and pulled him into a side storage room for privacy.

Clara the older partner with striking gray hair and shorter stature, spoke up first.

"Shareef, we're about to run out of your books."

He looked at her and then at Rita, the younger, taller partner with freckles.

"How many books did you have?"

"We ordered two hundred of the new book, and the other books have been selling out all week."

"So how many do you have left?"

Rita answered, "We have seventeen of the new book left. And I've lost count of the other ones. But it's not much."

Clara added, "It's probably less than that now, since you're here. You know, there are people who won't buy the book until they see the author first."

At that point, there was nothing Shareef could do about it but continue with the game plan. So he shrugged his shoulders.

"Well, when we sell out, we sell out. And we just tell them that we'll have more books in stock tomorrow. Do you have any of those name plates that I can sign to stick inside the books?"

Rita said, "I wish we did."

"Okay, but we don't. So let's just do what we do then," the author concluded. At the end of the day, he would much rather sell out than to sell nothing. So he was ready to rock and roll with the punches.

"Are we ready to do this?" he asked them both.

"We're ready when you are," Clara told him.

"Well, let's go do it then."

They returned to the bookstore showroom where Shareef was led to the front of the crowd. There was a small table covered with Kente cloth, a comfortable reading chair, a bottle of lemonade, and a plastic cup all ready for him to sit, read, drink, answer questions, and sign copies of his latest novel as well as his previous novels.

Clara stood in front of the crowd to make the introduction while Shareef took a seat in the reading chair behind the table.

"Without further ado, the man you've all been waiting to see is here."

"Yeeaaahhh! a few of the women in the crowd cheered before the store's co-owner could finish her introduction. Off to the side, Rita smiled as Clara continued.

"*New York Times* and *Essence* bestselling author of *Chocolate Love, I*

Want More, and several other hot and steaming titles of black on black romance, Harlem's very own, Shareef Crawford!"

Thunderous applause rang out from the standing-room-only crowd of fans. They filled every section of the bookstore, nearly two hundred people, most of whom were women. Only a few men speckled the crowd, including The Spear. He looked unimpressed, but he was there mainly to observe the nonsense voodoo Shareef was able to pull on so many women, including the gorgeous sister in the lavender business suit who stood not far from him in the back of the room.

Shareef stood at the front of the room with a copy of his latest novel in hand.

"First of all, I want to thank everyone for reading and loving my work, because without your kind support, I would have no inspiration to write."

More applause met his humble comments.

"Don't worry about it, baby, just keep doing what you do and we'll keep doing what we do to support you," someone yelled.

Shareef smiled and nodded to the woman. He said, "That sounds like a fair trade to me." Then he raised his new book to eyesight level. "This new book of mine, *The Full Moon*, is all about the power of yes and no. And my whole idea to write a novel about it was based on a magazine essay I wrote last summer, where I explained that 'yes' is the dominant answer for most happy relationships. Now, that doesn't mean that we never say no, but if we're saying no more than we say yes, then there's obviously something wrong with that relationship. Because in a happy relationship, we're eager to say yes. Am I right or am I wrong?" he asked the crowd.

Most of them nodded and mumbled in agreement with him.

He said, "In fact, there is no relationship without a yes." He then looked at several of the women in the audience and asked each of them a specific question. "Can I have your phone number? Will you take mine? Will you call me up sometime? Are you free on the weekends? Can we go out?"

He said, "Now, if every one of these sisters tells me no, then who can I start a relationship with?"

"Who would tell you no?" an older woman sitting in the second row of chairs asked him. There were only six rows of chairs of eight across, and those forty-eight chairs had been filled long before seven. Everyone else had to stand.

Shareef responded, "Oh, you'd be surprised. Everybody gets their share of nos. But let's think about it, without the yeses, there would be no stories for me to tell. So I want to read from one of the hottest chapters of many in this new book of mine."

"Yeaaahhh!" the crowd responded again.

"That's what I'm talking about!" someone else yelled.

The Spear continued to shake his head in the background, joined there by Daryl, who was impressed. From Daryl Mooreland's perspective, any man who could hold the attention of that many women for a book was well worth watching.

As Shareef thumbed through the pages of his novel, the anticipation continued to build in the room. The crowd of women breathed deeply, swallowed hard, readjusted their stances, smiled from ear to ear, and gave the author their undivided attention.

He found his chapter, took a sip of his lemonade, and began to read from his standing position:

Carla looked down at the phone number she had scribbled onto the back of one of her business cards and thought about the man's proposition. Why travel to Bermuda by herself to begin with if she was only there to window shop? She could window shop at home with friends in Houston. But what was the use in lusting for a man through a window? Either she would decide to wear his soft brown skin, aroma, and hard flexing muscles while she was there on the exotic island, or she would only have her moist dreams to remember him by when she left. Still, she could have had her wet dreams back home at Houston.

If she was not willing to indulge herself and become physical with the man, she could have been just as easily served watching the movies of Denzel, Morris, Kodjoe, and Shemar under slippery satin sheets. For what was life if she didn't live it? For how long would she allow herself to continue being a spectator. Every grown woman had been hurt to some degree by love and loss; it was the victorious women who were courageous enough to move on and find new love. Then again, becoming a revolving door of sexual fantasies, a human McDonald's, where every customer was served, and cheaply, was not an option she would allow herself to entertain.

That was Carla's dilemma. How much would she be willing to give of herself? To whom? And at what price to her conscience? Nevertheless, she was an honest woman who craved a man's touch, his words, his comfort, his caress, and his intimacy. Holding out would only build up her intensity and anticipation of release, and indeed, a release was needed. She was woman enough to admit it; "I need what I need."

Suddenly, she became antsy. Normal human lust was winning over. She felt butterflies in her stomach, quivers in her legs, and twinkles in her toes, as fresh blood rushed to her bosom, producing the perfect firmness for foreplay.

Her desires were undeniable. Her cravings were strong. Her will was weakening? Or was it strengthening? For what was the equal balance between yes and no? Was no more courageous than yes? Or was yes more courageous, particularly while Carla held the phone number and her fate in her own hands. A no was as simple as no phone call, but a yes had to be initiated.

Then again, she reasoned that there was room for a series of yeses and nos. For instance: she could say yes to a walk on the beach, but no to a temptatious glass of wine too late in the evening. She could say yes to dinner in a public restaurant, but no to a private nightcap. She could say yes to an afternoon swim in her bathing suit, but no to a skinny-dip after dark. Such was the proper etiquette of a tactful lady.

Nevertheless, at the end of their courting, Carla would still have a pressing question to answer; yes or no, with only three nights left between them for seduction.

So she took a deep breath and boldly decided to pick up her hotel phone and call the number he had given her. She would start with that first yes—a phone call—after that, she would determine how far another yes would lead them.

When Shareef closed his novel and made eye contact with the crowd, they began to exhale and celebrate.

"*Whuuuuww! Give us more!*"

"*Somebody turn on the air! It's hot in here!*"

"*I know you're not stopping on us there!*"

Daryl started grinning from the back. Even The Spear cracked a smile. And the sister in the lavender business suit had been smiling since she walked into the store.

Shareef laughed out loud from the front. He said, "One thing I've learned in this publishing industry is only to read enough to wet your whistle, and let you read the rest. Besides, we still got books to sell and I don't want to bore anybody."

"You're not boring us. Read some more," one woman stated.

"They said your books are sold out tonight," another woman pouted.

"They'll have more in stock tomorrow," Shareef responded quickly. The hustle was the hustle. He said, "And at this point, we'd like to start our Q and A's."

The crowd asked the usual questions about his writing process; his inspiration; how they could become writers; who he liked to read; what was his take on the state of African-American literature, sex, and relationships in the new millennium; books to feature film deals; e-books and Internet dating; science fiction and fantasy writing; how to sell poetry; how to get a publishing deal; how to market your work—the list went on before the sister in the lavender business suit asked her question.

"Have you ever thought about writing something other than romance? I mean, your writing skills are obviously above average. I just feel that you could do so much more by writing more universal subjects."

The Spear looked at her and nodded his head in agreement. The woman continued to turn him on. Someone had to break away from the idolization and bullshit that was going on inside the store.

Shareef looked the woman over and answered, "Yeah, I've thought about it. But ultimately there's no subject more universal than love. Don't you think?" he asked her back.

She was easily one of the finest women in the room. She looked just below thirty, but her smooth, young face could pass for a fresh college grad.

"I mean, we have a million books published about black love, but how many great books do we have about the everyday struggle?" she questioned.

Shareef read her position and liked the woman. She wasn't grandstanding at all, she was simply expressing her mind, just like he would.

Before he could answer her, The Spear spoke up and added, "Yeah, this *Full Moon* book, to me, sounds just like *How Stella Got Her Groove Back*. I mean, what's the difference?"

Shareef backtracked. "Well, let me answer her question first, then I'll come back to yours."

He answered, "I would say, yeah, it is true, we don't have many great books about everyday struggles. But who wants to read those kind of books? We want to get away from struggle when we read. So when those great books are written, how many of us are really willing to pay attention to them?"

He said, "And as far as *The Full Moon* being similar to Stella's *Groove*, I would say that the only things in common between the two is the island romance, and the fact that a woman has to talk herself into saying yes. But this book is not about an older woman and a younger man. *The Full Moon* is about people in their prime years and beyond, having the courage to say yes to love in general."

The Spear mumbled, "Yeah, all right, it's all the same thing to me."

Daryl overheard him and didn't speak on it. Nor did the sister in the lavender suit.

Clara took center stage again. "Well, as everyone can see, Shareef has a gang of books to sign tonight, so we want to limit each person to two books."

As soon as she made that announcement, some of the readers with three books or more to have signed began to grumble.

Shareef spoke up on their concern immediately. "Nah, if they bought my books, I wanna sign everything they bought. I'll just have to sign them quickly. So please forgive my handwriting."

The first young woman in line said, "Thank you." She was holding five of his books to have signed.

So Shareef took a seat, pulled out his platinum pen, and started signing away while thanking the readers.

"Thanks for coming out tonight."

"Keep reading my work."

"Thanks for your love and support."

"Okay, I'll use your name in the next one. I promise."

There were several women Shareef wanted to ask out to dinner, but there were just too many books to sign. He could barely lift his head up to signal his driver in the background to ask one of them. Nor did he spot any of his Harlem homies who had promised to make it out to the bookstore that night. He didn't count on that anyway. Book events were not their thing, so there were single women to talk to everywhere.

When it came time for the sister in the lavender suit to have her four books signed, she made sure she got his undivided attention. Not only did he smell her, remember her look, her question, and her poise, she managed to write her name and a question mark on a piece of paper for him.

"Hey, thanks for the tough question back there," he commented as soon as he spotted her at the front of the line.

She only smiled at him with no words exchanged. Then she slid him the piece of paper on the table in front of her books.

Shareef looked down and read the name.

"Coffee? Your name is Coffee?"

She continued to smile at him. "That's what they call me," she responded.

He paused for a minute, imagination running wild.

"Why?" he asked her.

"I just have a lot of energy."

Shareef was ready to signal his driver for her for sure.

Then he read the question mark below her name.

"What does that mean?" he asked her.

She looked him in the eyes and answered, "Whatever you want it to mean? It's up to you."

On cue, Shareef spotted Daryl toward the back of the room. Daryl caught the look and already knew. He had peeped her out as soon as he walked into the store. She was the one he would have went after himself, just like the camouflage-wearing brother beside him had tried and failed before she stepped up into the line.

Daryl grinned and nodded. Shareef nodded back and went back to work.

He signed her books with the normal messages of "Thanks for your support," blah, blah, blah. Then he told her on the sly, "Stick around for a minute."

The woman called Coffee heard him and nodded. Their understanding of each other was clear. She was reading his real-life book and he was reading hers. Nothing else needed to be said until later.

When she was close enough, Daryl pulled her aside and made sure that his words were perfect.

"Mr. Crawford would like to know if you would be available to join him for dinner this evening."

Daryl wanted the invitation to sound as professional as possible to keep himself out of any trouble. A complimentary dinner seemed innocent enough, and that's all it had to be. If the dinner led to more, then it was none of his business, nor was he responsible for their actions once they were outside of his vehicle.

Coffee looked pleased by the invite. She answered, "Yes, I would love to."

The driver nodded to her and looked back toward Shareef. Shareef caught the nod from his table at the front and nodded back. It was all nonverbal language.

Coffee asked Daryl, "Does he want us to wait in the car for him?"

She was taking the proposition to the next level with confidence and speed. Daryl was stunned by it.

He said, "Well, okay, I guess we could wait out in the car." She was the only woman Shareef had given him the signal to ask, and she had already agreed to dinner, so what was there left to wait for? He led her out of the bookstore and to the waiting limo.

The Spear jealously watched the whole scene, but was powerless to alter the script. Coffee had sent the alley cat scampering away so she could snag the prized lion.

Aw, that fake-ass, wannabe Diana Ross. They deserve each other, he told himself as the woman left with the limo driver.

Let me get the hell out of here. This was a big waste of my time.

And the rival author left empty handed and spiteful.

Another Novel

B Y 9:03 PM, Shareef had signed every book and said his final good-byes to the store owners, staff, and the rest of his dedicated fans before Daryl opened the limo door for him to climb back inside.

"Looks like you had quite a successful book signing tonight, mister," the woman named Coffee commented. She sat on the left side of the limo, behind the driver's seat. She was applying a fresh coat of gloss to her lips for extra shine and sex appeal.

Shareef looked her over and grinned. "Yeah, and I even get to leave with the finest girl in the place. Must be my night."

She chuckled and said, "Must be." Then she asked him, "So . . . are we headed anywhere in particular?"

"It's this place in Times Square that feels like you just left the country and went to Asia. It's called Ruby Foo's. Have you ever been there before?"

"I know where it is, but I've never been there."

"Well then, tonight is your night."

WHEN THEY ARRIVED at the corner of Broadway and 49th Street, Shareef walked Coffee inside Ruby Foo's restaurant and ordered a table in the back for two.

He told her, "I want to square away my driver, then I'll be right back in to join you at the table."

"Okay. I'll be here."

He stopped and joked to her. "You mean, none of these rich white guys in here can snatch you away from me while I'm gone?"

She smiled at him and answered, "Not a chance."

"Good. I'll be right back then."

He ran out to meet Daryl at the curb. He dug in his wallet and pulled out a fifty-dollar bill.

Daryl put his hand up and shook it off. "You know what, I don't even need that. It's just been a pleasure driving you today, my friend. So whenever you're in town again, just call me up on the card I gave you."

Shareef told him, "That's all good and I appreciate the gesture, but you need to take this fifty before I put it back in my wallet. And I'm only gonna ask you once."

Daryl started laughing out loud. "Man, you just too real, brother." He went right ahead and took that fifty-dollar bill, too. He said, "But be safe with that. I mean, I know she fine and everything, but . . ."

Shareef cut him off and said, "That's the only way to be with it. I already know the rules. I got it all covered. I'ma send her right home in a taxi, and it's all good."

The driver nodded. "Okay. If you got it all covered, you got it all covered." He shook Shareef's hand and said, "Again brother, it's been a pleasure all day long."

"Same here, man. Now go on and get that book back home to your wife."

"Oh, you know that's right. It's time for me to go do some book reading together."

WHEN SHAREEF JOINED Coffee at their table toward the back of the restaurant, she was just finishing her cell phone call.

He sat down with her and flirted immediately. "You were just telling your mother that you won't be making it back home to-night?"

She laughed and said, "Mr. Crawford, I don't think I agree with how you're reading me. Do you do this all the time?"

"Would you believe me if I said no?"

She smiled. "I'm just asking to make sure?"

"Well, while we're asking each other these questions, what is your real name? That's first of all."

He hadn't asked her anything personal while inside the limo with Daryl. He wanted to save the detailed interrogation for the restaurant.

"My name is Cynthia. Cynthia Washington."

"And you tell everybody that your name is Coffee?"

"No, only people who I want to know."

"I guess you wanted me to know then."

"Yeah, I did."

He nodded and asked her, "Do you have a lot of energy left over tonight?"

She smiled wide and kept her mouth open.

"Why do you wanna know?"

He told her, "Game recognize game. I got a lot of energy, too.

She grinned and kept her thoughts to herself. She couldn't tell him too much too early. That would ruin the mystique.

She looked around the restaurant and continued to take it all in. She nodded and said, "You're right. You walk in this place and forget you're still in New York. Everything looks so real. And it's so big in here."

He said, "They use every inch of space to make you feel like you're actually in Asia. That's why I like this place. It's like going away with-out really going away."

She nodded. "You get a chance to travel a lot, don't you?"

"Not as much as these rappers."

She asked him, "Do you envy them?"

Shareef stopped and thought about it.

"I think we all do to a degree. I mean, nobody generates attention and income like those guys do. They get twenty G's just for showing up at a party. I think I can do without the police attention, though. I hear a lot of those guys can't travel without being harassed."

Cynthia grimaced. She said, "You just had nearly two hundred women come out to see you with no sound stage, no bright lights, no entourage, commotion, or security everywhere. I mean, if you ask me, that seems a lot more powerful and gratifying. And they were all paying strict attention to you."

"Yeah, but how many brothers were in there? And that guy in camouflage was hatin'. But these rappers, they get the respect from all the brothers."

"Oh, so all the brothers still respect Ja Rule? And the hard-core guys still respect Puffy? And the New York guys still love Jay-Z and hate Nelly? I mean, that stuff is all so campy," she commented. "It's just like professional wrestling. One week they're all over Atlanta, and the next week they're all over Memphis and Houston. That stuff is all high school to me. And then they all try to act like they're gangstas. They're not real gangstas. I know real gangstas, and they're damn sure not thinking about rapping, dancing, or giving concerts."

Shareef nodded to her right as their waiter appeared to take their orders.

"Can I get you anything to drink?"

They both ordered martinis and told the waiter to return a little later for their food orders.

When the waiter, a twenty-something white man with dark hair in a ponytail, disappeared, Shareef joked and said, "That part of the restaurant didn't leave the country. It's still American in here with the service." He figured he'd change the subject and make their conversation a little lighter.

She said, "Well, they couldn't possible have a huge restaurant like this right in the middle of Times Square without hiring the regular people of New York."

"The popular TV shows did it. *Seinfeld, Friends,* a few others," Shareef said, naming two long-running television series that seemed to paint New York as lily white.

"What about the *Law and Orders, CSI: New York,* and *The Closer?*" Cynthia commented.

Shareef smiled. "Yeah, any show dealing with crime, that's when the blacks and Hispanics show up."

However, the woman continued to impress him. She was ready and willing to go point for point with him on every subject.

"You seem to know a lot for a girl," he told her.

She gave him the evil look for that.

"That sounds very chauvinistic, especially coming from a man who owes his career to the women who read his books."

"Yeah, but a lot of those women are only interested in girly issues. That's why I haven't written anything else. I know where my audience is. And that audience is very selective in what they want to read about.

He said, "That answers your question from earlier. But I'm not dumb enough to say it out in public. All that does is piss the audience off. I learned that when I first started my career as a novelist. You keep them happy and they'll keep you happy."

She said, "But it's up to you to take them somewhere different. You have to challenge yourself and challenge them."

Shareef nodded and took a sip of his water. Their conversation was more philosophical than he expected or desired. He respected the woman's intellect. He respected her wit from the moment she opened her mouth inside the bookstore. But she was also a sexy woman, and at ten o'clock at night, less than five blocks from his hotel, he wanted to deal with their ideas of each other as a man and a woman on a romantic night, at a romantic restaurant.

He leaned back in his chair and gave her another good look with his glass in hand.

"So, ah . . . what time do you need to be at work tomorrow?"

She took a sip of her own water and grinned at him over the rim of the glass.

"Actually, I took off from work tomorrow." She left her answer at that.

Shareef nodded to her. That was the kind of answer he wanted to hear.

"What are you going to do with all this extra time on your hands?" he asked her.

"Enjoy it. I'm enjoying it now."

"How much of this night are you trying to enjoy?"

She continued to smile at him mischievously.

"Are you trying to ask me something in particular?"

He leaned forward with both elbows on the table and said, "Maybe I am. Do you know what I'm trying to ask you?"

She stared into his dark, intense eyes and answered, "Maybe I do."

"Are you offended by it?"

She shook her head. "Why would I be offended?"

"Some women are. For some women it's disrespectful on a first date. But I don't judge respect off sexuality. A woman should be allowed to express herself like any man. So I try to keep the two separate."

"So do I," she responded.

He paused and looked into her pretty brown face.

"So I'm allowed to be frank now."

Cynthia paused herself and slowly nodded to him.

"Yeah, I'm a big girl. Be frank."

Shareef asked her, "Are we fucking tonight?" And the man didn't flinch when he said it, either.

Cynthia tried her hardest to match his steely demeanor but couldn't. She started cheesing and hid her face behind her hands, embarrassed that she couldn't take his forwardness.

She said, "You know, I had heard about you, but . . . wow." She shook her head and tried to look him in the face again. "I mean, I thought I could . . . ."

She couldn't get her words together.

On Shareef's end, he had planned to sock it to her with bluntness as soon as she got him interested in her at the bookstore. She wasn't the typical soft-stepping sister. She could take it. So he allowed her a chance to recover from the initial shock before he said anything else.

"Umm . . ." She looked down at the table where her menu sat. Then she looked back up into his eyes. "I'm supposed to say yes now, right? Is that how it goes?"

"You're supposed to say what you feel," he told her. "I'm just trying to make sure we don't get anything twisted."

She said, "Well, it's not twisted. We straight. But . . . I think you could have used a better choice of words. I mean, you are a writer, right? Be more creative."

Shareef shook his head and wouldn't let her off the hook.

He said, "Nah. Understand me for a minute. There are certain kinds of women a guy may feel soft emotions for, and other women where the emotions are stronger. You follow me?"

Cynthia smiled and was speechless. She wanted to hear more, and he gave her more.

He said, "Perfect example are them two white girls; Jennifer Aniston and Angelina Jolie. I probably wouldn't even deal with Jennifer Aniston. She seem soft, boring, and like it would take all night to nut. But Angelina Jolie? Shit, a guy might fuck around and nut just from looking at her too long. So at the end of the day, I can't blame Brad Pitt for leaving. They didn't have any kids, and he got tired of making love. He wanted to fuck. So he broke off from Jennifer and got with Angelina. And then he got her pregnant immediately. So that tells you how strong he was feeling about that nut."

The woman was so floored by his bodacious logic that she couldn't speak. She couldn't even move. She just sat there grinning.

Shareef told her, "So don't get it confused. Like I said, I still respect you. You're a smart woman. But if we're talking about sex, then it is what it is, and you gon' have to take it how I give it to you."

He said, "You're a sexy grown woman. You don't have that little girl vibe no more. So I'm not changing my words. I meant that shit."

Cynthia sat there, stunned into silence, wondering what she had gotten herself into. She opened her mouth and whimpered, "Okay." And that was it. She would lay down and submit to him.

Shareef leaned back in his chair again and was satisfied. He said, "I'm glad we understand each other." Then he looked around for their waiter. "Now where is this guy at? He should have returned with our drinks and taken our food orders by now."

But Cynthia was no longer thinking about the food and drink. She was thinking about his dick, how long it was, how hard, and how strong was his stroke?

AT SEVENTEEN MINUTES after midnight, up on the twenty-second floor, inside the Author's Suite at the Sheraton, Shareef showed the sexy young woman what he meant by fucking. He locked her legs back and over his arms and shoulders while he bulldozed into her sweet spot, enjoying her squeals.

"Uunnhhh! Uunnhhh! Oohh! Oohh! Oooohhh!"

She had no idea the man would give it to her that strongly. Her plan was to romance him, take him to bed, sex him good, get what she could get out of it, and make a strong pitch to him for a new book idea. But Shareef had flipped the script and showed her that he was much more than a mental specimen. He was physical. Extremely physical. And he wanted to prove it to her.

To lessen the impact, she tried in vain to steady his strokes with the force of her arms and hands against his chest. But with his ramrod posture and muscle mass, even her strongest push was like trying to move an elephant. Then she felt herself arriving at full climax and lost it. She tried to scratch his back to help him share in the pain and pleasure that he was giving her. Shareef, however, could not allow the scratches. So he grabbed her hands in his, aware that she was coming, and he allowed himself to settle into her spot until she had released the glory, torture, and toil of heaven, hell, and earth.

When she came, the nut was stronger than words could explain. Only images could explain the bliss she felt. There were flurries of inch-long snowflakes that fell from the hotel ceiling and landed on Cynthia's face, sizzling into perspiration on contact, creating a sheet of soothing sweat that ran into the pillows under her head. And just when she thought it was over, Shareef amassed a second nut inside of her. And then a third.

What the fuck is he on? she asked herself. This writer was turning her out like some new drug that was too addictive to sell to the public. It was for private use only, and at each woman's personal risk. He had taken her to cloud nine and then tripled it to cloud twenty-seven. And the only space shuttle strong enough to bring the sex-induced woman back to planet earth was Shareef's own nut.

He dropped her legs to the bed and pulled their bodies together to tighten their senses, like a human vise, while the burn built up inside of him and released itself through his holy extension. Then he let her know about it.

"Ooh, shit, this pussy, this pussy," he mumbled into her ear as his seed squirted and squeezed and jerked out of him.

Overwhelmingly pleased with his performance, Cynthia calmed herself and spoke back.

"Was it good, baby? Did you like it?"

In his response, Shareef chuckled, with his full naked body trembling against hers on the comfortable, king-sized bed.

"Did I like it?" he asked rhetorically. He pushed his lips into her right ear and said, "I loved it. I love fuckin'. You hear me. I said, I *love* fuckin'."

Cynthia laughed in between her breaths. She had no idea how raw he would be. But she was pleased with him, very pleased, and she wouldn't mind fucking him again. All he had to do was ask her for it.

Instead of lighting up and sharing a cigarette, which he never smoked, Shareef turned over on his back and freed his mind.

He said, "Women have no idea how strong pussy is to a man. Without pussy, I don't know what else we would live for."

Cynthia shook her head, her cheekbones sore from her continuous grinning. The man was just too much for her conscience.

She said, "Um, how many other women know how . . . I mean . . ." she couldn't seem to get her words right.

Shareef cut her off and said, "Look, I am what I am. So if you're asking me how many women can handle my candor, I'll have to say just the ones who feel me like that. If they can't handle it they move on."

She continued to shake her head. She said, "I'm just thinking about your average fan."

He caught her gist and said, "You have to keep those two worlds separate. And your key word is 'average.' You can't invite the average fan into your world, only those who can take it. You feel me? Otherwise, you'll fuck around and get yourself in trouble."

She understood that much. A woman who read the wrong game could holler foul play and blow an embarrassing bullhorn on a man's personal life. So a player had to choose correctly.

She looked into his serious mug and said, "You're a lot more complicated then what I expected."

He looked back at her. "What did you expect?"

She shrugged her shoulders. "I don't know. I guess I thought you would be more of a tight ass. I mean . . . I just didn't expect to have this much fun with you."

He smiled and looked away. "Yeah, everybody expects me to be like that. And sometimes I am. It all depends on how you rub me. But if I'm just being me . . ." He looked into her face again and added, "Then it's all good."

Hearing that, Cynthia leaned up on her elbows and gave him her undivided attention. It was time to get back to business.

She said, "Now, I understand you wanted to give me a quick answer at the book signing when I asked you about writing something else, but now that we're one-on-one and more intimate, I still want to know why you haven't tried it. I mean, your way of seeing things is far deeper than just one genre. Why cheat yourself like that? Why waste your gifts on chick lit, because that's all it is?"

She was asking the right question at the right time for the right answer.

Shareef stared up at the ceiling. He said, "Mos Def on his first solo album, he made the comment that the state of hip-hop depends on the state of the people. He said if the people are doing good, then the hip-hop will reflect it. But if the people are doing bad, then so is the hip-hop. And it's the same thing with books. You can't push something on the people that they don't want and they don't feel. They're not gon' buy it."

She said, "Did you know they would buy Fifty Cent when he came out a few years ago?"

She sure knew a lot about hip-hop. She didn't seem like the hip-hop type to him, or at least she didn't dress the part. And Shareef wanted to ask her about that later. In the meantime, he went ahead and answered her question.

He said, "Eminem knew it. Dr. Dre knew it. Interscope Records knew it. It was all about the story. This guy got shot nine times and lived, and kept rhyming. And he was good at the shit, too. So they rolled the dice on him. And the shit came up seven, eleven.

"But if you notice, we're talking more about hip-hop than literature," he stated. "Music has always been the drug that crosses over to the masses. All they gotta do is listen. But books . . ." He stopped and shook his head. "That's too much work for 'em. And if they do read, they only want to read shit they can swallow. Soul food. The same old collard greens, candied yams, fried chicken, and slices of watermelon on the side and shit. So that's what I give 'em."

Cynthia started chuckling and couldn't help herself.

Shareef continued: "When I went to Morehouse, we used to be up all night long talking shit about everything. But every time I mentioned a book, niggas couldn't follow me. And I'm talking about *college* niggas. But we could talk about music till the fuckin' *cows* come home. So it became obvious to me that the literature of our music had taken over. Only problem is, with an album, you can skip all the songs that actually mean anything. So instead of a girl listening to rev-olutionary shit, this bitch would rather skip to the club song. And ex-cuse me for calling her a bitch, but that's what she ends up being if she only pays attention to the ignorant club shit. So instead of spending so much time with that booty-shaking, Ying Yang shit, she should listen to songs and albums that mean something. Or read a book . . . that means something. But you know why they don't. Because this shit is all entertainment to them. And if they're not being entertained, then they don't want to fuck with it."

Cynthia had finally caught him on something.

She said, "Well, that's contradictory, because you're doing the same thing that the rappers are doing. You're not giving them any-thing revolutionary to read. You're giving them entertaining books. Booty-shaking books. It's all the same thing. Look how you had them hootin' and hollerin' when you were reading your book tonight."

Shareef laughed out loud. He said, "It's all contradictory. But yo, I wrote a poem a few years after college, when I first started writing novels. And it just seemed like the only people willing to listen to that revolutionary shit was broke niggas or people still in college."

She said, "Well, let me hear your poem and I'll tell you want I think about it."

"Aw'ight, it's about the only one I still remember," he told her. He said, " 'I was born into this world / with the mind and spirit / of a rev-olutionary / unfortunately / in the time of my short existence / there was no longer / a revolution / so I walked the earth / for forty days / and forty nights / angry / apparently / at nothing.' 'Wasted,' by Sha-reef Crawford."

She sat silent for a minute to remember it all in her mind, and to sum it up. Then she nodded to him, convinced of her assessment.

"So, you already know your potential," she responded. "You know all the arguments. And you know what you're supposed to do. But you've given up."

He nodded back to her and said, "Yup. Now I'm doing what all the revolutionaries do when they give up. I'm chasing skirts. Go do the research."

She smiled again, shaking her head one last time.

She said, "I got a story for you that they'll read."

Shareef heard her and grinned. He said, "Come on, girl, we in New York. It's eight million stories in this city. And that was twenty years ago. How many stories we got in New York now?"

She ignored him and asked, "You ever hear of Michael Springfield?"

He looked at her and raised his brow. "Michael Springfield? The Harlem drug dealer?"

She nodded. "Yeah."

He said, "Everybody's heard about him if you lived in Harlem during the eighties. He serving life without parole now, ain't he?"

"And he wants you to write his story," she told him.

Shareef studied her face and asked her, "How you know?"

She said, "I know him."

He paused for a minute. Did she run with drug dealers, or was she related to him?

He said, "You know him? How?"

"Writing letters. Visiting. I just know him."

Shareef started to feel uneasy about it. He had to ask her the questions that popped into his head. All of a sudden the conversation became dead serious.

"So . . . did he tell you to ask me that? What does he know about me? Is he just trying to find any writer to write his book, or did you bring me up to him, or what?"

He was asking her questions as if he was conducting his own interview.

Cynthia shook her head and said, "No, he brought you up to me. I didn't know he even read your books. But he said *Chocolate Lovers* touched him. And he started thinking about his first girlfriend before he got into hustling. You made him think about the innocence of young black people in love. Then he read the rest of your books. And once the word spread that you had a new one coming out, and that you always did book signings in Harlem, he told me to ask you if you would consider it."

Shareef said, "But why me? It's plenty of people writing them street books now. I don't even write that shit."

"But you're from Harlem, and he likes you," she answered. "He said the same thing that I said about you. Your books are deeper than theirs. So he respects you more. He said you can tell when people are writing books just for the hell of it. But you don't. Even though it's romance, you actually care about what you're writing."

"But you just told me a minute ago that I was contradictory."

"Yeah, but you don't need to be. I mean, some people can't help what they do. But you know better. And you know you can write other stuff. You *know* it," she insisted.

He said, "Yeah, and I know better than to write a book about a drug dealer, too. That ain't no damn novel. That sounds like bodyguards and security again."

She snapped, "Oh, I'm sorry. I thought you just chased pussy, I didn't know you *were* a pussy."

When she said that, it became obvious where her loyalties were. So she got up and started getting dressed.

Shareef told her, "Yo, I ain't no fucking pussy! But I do feel kind of stupid right now to think that you went through all this just to get me to write some motherfucker's book from jail.

"Was that all this shit was about?" he asked her as he sat up in bed.

Cynthia ignored him and finished getting dressed.

He said, "Oh, so now I get the fuckin' silent treatment. Is that it?"

She pulled all of her clothes on and grabbed her bags before she responded to him.

"I'll tell him that you said you'll think about it."

Shareef sat up in bed and stared at her. This chick was crazy like a fox, as cool as a cucumber, and she had played him that night like a piano. She was all the age-old clichés wrapped up into one.

Then she added, "By the way, if I didn't want to fuck you, I wouldn't have taken the job. So you have nothing to be ashamed about. You worked it. So give me a call about that, all right? You got the number." And she walked out of his room.

Shareef was shocked into silence. He stared at the door after the woman had left him and asked himself, "Do you believe this shit?"

Then he fell back to the pillows and laughed.

"Get the fuck out of here!" he told himself. "This is crazy!"

AT 8:12 THAT MORNING, the hotel phone in his room rang and knocked Shareef out of his sleep. Since he was up half the night thinking crazy thoughts, he didn't actually fall out until nearly five.

After the second ring, he scrambled over the bed to stop the loud noise before it killed him.

"Hello."

"The kids were up all last night expecting your call."

It was his wife. She was the last person in the world he wanted to hear from. Their entire relationship had turned into antagonism.

"My bad. I had the phone on mute from the book signing."

"How come you didn't call us right after the book signing?"

He answered, "I was too busy having fun."

"Whatever. The kids want to speak to you."

She went ahead and put his son on the phone.

"Hey, Dad, we're signing up for football today."

"Oh yeah? Are you scared?"

"No. For what? I know how to play."

"That's my boy. You show 'em what I teach you out there, and I'll be home for good in a couple of weeks."

"Until the next book tour," his son stated.

Shareef said, "Daddy gotta pay them big house bills, right?"

"Yeah, but I wish I could go with you sometimes."

"What, and sit around a whole bunch of women reading books? I'd rather be at summer camp if I were you."

"Yeah, it gets boring sometimes, Dad. I miss you."

Shareef paused and could imagine his son's sad face, along with his bright smile during the good times.

He said, "I miss you, too, J. Now put your sister on the phone." There was no sense in prolonging the sadness that morning. He still had sixteen cities to tour.

"Okay," his son grumbled. "Here," Shareef overheard him handing the phone to his sister.

"Hey, Daddy, we miss you," she piped into his ear.

Shareef was ready to ask her if her brother had given her the phone with an attitude, but decided to let it slide.

"Hey, baby girl. Daddy'll be back home soon."

"To stay?"

Shit! he thought. *It's too early in the morning for this.*

"If your mommy lets me," he answered.

"Mommy, will you let Daddy stay when he comes back home?"

Fuck! What the hell I do that for?

He knew he would get an earful after that. His wife got back on the phone and said, "We're on our way to camp, I'll call you later. Tell your daughter good-bye."

Shareef did as she told him and hung up. He knew he would get that earful later, she just didn't want to do it in front of the kids.

AT 9:43 AM, Shareef was sitting across the table from his grandparents at a booth inside a midtown Manhattan breakfast and bagels cafe.

"Shareef, it's important to keep your family together," his grandmother was telling to him. "Because once all of this fame and good fortune fades away, your family will be the ones who still love you."

Shareef took a sip of his orange juice. He was dressed sharply in another button-down shirt and sports jacket for the second day of his book tour. He took a deep breath before he responded to his loved ones.

"It seems impossible for me to explain how hard it is to have your insides pulled apart while you struggle to keep it together, Grandma. I mean, with all due respect, you guys have always allowed me to express myself. So to be in a relationship now where my expressions are always limited . . . I just haven't been able to handle that. I mean, I've been trying, but . . ."

He stopped and shook his head.

His grandfather looked into his eyes, grunted, and looked away.

"I know exactly what you mean," he mumbled in the opposite direction.

"Charles, if you have something to say, then say it. Don't talk underneath your breath," Wilma fussed at her husband. "I hate it when you do that."

Charles turned to face them at the table. "That's it right there," he said, alluding to her bossiness. "That's what he's talking about. Shareef's now figuring out that no married man is free. Now, we allowed him certain amounts of freedom while we raised him, and as long as he respected us and our house, we gave him the best of love, and let him do everything he wanted to do."

Wilma cut her husband off and said, "His wife lets him do what he needs to do. Jennifer has never gotten in his way. She's done nothing but help him, and she holds down those kids and that gorgeous house while he's away. And I like that girl. Now I admit, I thought she was a little too cute in the beginning, but once I got to know her, she's really grown on me."

Shareef said, "Yeah, well, she's growing on me in the wrong way."

"Well, what exactly is the problem?" his grandmother asked him.

Shareef looked at his grandfather. They both knew, but how could you tell a woman you respected so much?

Shareef nodded and figured out a way. He said, "It's one thing to love a woman because she's a good person, a good mother, and a good wife, but it just seems like another thing to *make* love to a person. And it just don't seem like all of those things are coming together, Grandma."

His grandfather was impressed. Shareef put together a great choice of words.

But his grandmother responded, "Is this all about the bedroom?" right as one of the waitresses walked by.

That's why Shareef didn't like talking about it. It was an embarrassing conversation that needed to be dealt with in private.

His grandmother added, "Your marriage and kids are far too important for that selfishness, Shareef. A wife is much more than just a sex slave. You can get any girl for that. But you married and had kids with this woman. You have a family with this woman. You can't treat her like that. How dare you?"

It was a no-win situation explaining himself to another woman, even if she was his blood. So his grandfather cracked a smile and shook his head. He would have to talk to Shareef one day about a married man's tolerance. But it wouldn't do any good. Shareef had more passionate blood than his grandfather. They both knew it. And the same passionate blood that made him an overachiever as a boy, a student, an athlete, and now as a successful writer was the same passionate blood that got in the way of him being able to control his sexual appetite, while bowing down to the restrictions of a woman. But how could he explain that to his grandmother without her feelings getting hurt? It only made him sound greedy.

His grandmother continued to pour on her woman's wisdom.

She said, "You have a chance with your family to set the example for the next generation of Crawfords, Shareef. Do you understand that? We don't have that many good examples anymore, and people are looking up to you now."

Shareef understood it. He understood it all. That's why he was still married. He also understood what his grandmother was alluding to. His own parents were an embarrassment to her. They didn't talk about them. Shareef never brought them up. They had never been in his life. And his grandparents would never allow their reckless lifestyles to influence him. So it was they who had raised him. It was they who had taken him to the Schomburg Center to feed his appetite for reading. It was they who had bought his sports equipment and had taken him to the practices. And it was they who had sent him to college, helped him through it, and had been there to celebrate at his graduation. So now he owed them a proper family as a representation of their love and of their teachings to him.

Shareef took another deep breath and said, "I know, Grandma. I know."

His grandfather looked at the agony and defeat in his face and knew better. Shareef had a major problem to overcome, and the stress that it presented was not healthy for him.

Florida

THREE WEEKS LATER, at the conclusion of Shareef's book tour, he pulled up to the front entrance of his immaculate six-bedroom home in Fort Lauderdale, Florida, behind the wheel of his black Mercedes SL 600 to take his son to football practice. His son liked to call the car the Batmobile and was proud that his daddy drove it. But when his wife, Jennifer, saw the car pull up from where she waited with their son and daughter on the front steps, she viewed it as another headache that Shareef seemed to induce in her on purpose.

"It's the Batmobile," Little J yelled as soon as he spotted his father's car. He was dressed in his football practice uniform of orange, blue, and white. Shareef liked to call him Little J, short for Junior.

"All right. It's Daddy," the daughter, Kimberly Crawford, cheered. She was dressed in a colorful skirt, top, and tennis shoes.

Their mother wore casual blue denim shorts, a white top, and gold accessories to match her natural golden brown hair, body, and skin.

Shareef hopped out from behind the wheel of the Mercedes dressed in dark blue Rocawear sweat suit pants with a light blue T-shirt and dark sunshades. He strolled over and met his kids at the walkway, picking them both up for hugs and kisses while his wife watched.

"Who's the best dad in the world?" he asked his kids.

"You are," his son and daughter answered in unison. They were a regal family of big shoes and big dreams; the problem was, in the execution of making it all happen, they had somehow gotten off track.

As soon as Jennifer approached them on the walkway, she asked her estranged husband, "Why would you drive that car, knowing you have to take him to practice?" and shot down his celebration of fatherhood.

"Aw, Mom, come on," Little J protested immediately.

It was no sweat to Shareef. He understood how his wife felt about driving the kids around in his sportscar. Sportscars were not built for kids. So he said, "I'll just take him in your Land Rover."

"Can I go, too? I wanna go," Kimberly begged her father, while tugging at his arm.

Jennifer huffed and said, "I have some errands to run."

"So take the Avalon," Shareef said, regarding her second vehicle.

"You take the Avalon," she snapped.

"Say no more, just let me have the keys."

Jennifer used the Land Rover for more upscale affairs, and the Toyota Avalon as her family get-around car. Shareef used the Mercedes SL for his play, and a Ford Explorer for his get-around. However, on that bright and sunny Florida day, he'd missed his Mercedes and wanted to be behind the wheel again. He had also moved out of the house at the beginning of the year and into a condominium on the twenty-seventh floor of a brand-new high-rise near Miami. His family had never been there. The condo was his private place, somewhere to be himself, and to entertain whomever he wanted.

Realizing he would not be riding in his father's Batmobile to football practice, Little J pouted, "She *always* wants to get in our way."

Shareef wasn't sure if his son was referring to his sister or to his mother, but he didn't like it either way.

"Ay, watch your mouth," he snapped sternly to his son.

Little J dropped his eyes to the ground and held his tongue, but his emotions and intent were still legible. A spitting image of his father with lighter brown skin, it was obvious that he would be as driven, as bullish, and as determined to have things his way as his old man was. It was another dilemma that the author, father, husband, and man would be forced to deal with.

As they drove to the Jaguars' football practice for ages ten and under, Shareef felt it important to have a talk with his son about his attitude.

"Shareef," the father addressed the son in the passenger seat.

His son frowned and said "I'm Li'l J, Dad, you're Shareef," with youthful swagger.

The father took a breath and said, "Look, man, you have a very good life. You understand that? There are plenty of kids out here your age who would love to have all the opportunities that you have. Even on your team. But you're walking around here with an attitude like somebody owes you something. Is that how you want to treat us? You don't appreciate what we do for you?"

The son picked up on his father's serious tone and dropped his eyes again with no answer.

"Shareef, you look at me when I'm talking to you."

He waited for his son to make eye contact.

He said, "You don't drop your eyes when someone is talking to you, you hear me? You sit there and you take it. That's what a man does. We don't look away. We don't look into the clouds. We don't count army ants on the ground. We take it eye to eye like men. So if you wanna be a little man, then you take it like a little man.

"Now answer my question. Do you appreciate what your mother and I do for you?"

"Yes."

"Well, act like it then. Stop pouting all the time, stomping around the house, screaming at your sister . . ."

"Yeah," Kimberly interjected from the backseat.

Little J cut his eyes at her.

"Don't do it, you look right back at me," Shareef told him.

His son started to pout again, "But Dad, she . . ."

"I don't care what she does, I'll handle her. You stay focused on what I'm saying to you. And don't drop your eyes again."

Then he focused on his daughter, strapped in the car's backseat.

He asked her, "Did anyone say anything to you, Kimberly?"

She looked him in the eyes and answered, "No."

"Well, you learn to stop instigating then. You hear me?"

She nodded and answered, "Yes, Daddy." She was a perfect mix between her mother and father, and a slightly lighter brown shade than her brother.

Hearing the word "Daddy" from his daughter softened Shareef a bit. He didn't want to come back home and be the heavy knowing that he would be leaving them again. So he immediately changed his tone while paying attention to the road.

He said, "I love both of you guys. And I love your mother, too. We're all just gonna have to get along with each other. We got a good life."

WHEN THEY ARRIVED at the practice field, Little J hopped out of the car to join his teammates. They ran laps, exercised, and began practicing their team plays.

As practice continued, a few of the fathers and coaches had on-and-off conversations about the game of football.

"You think Miami got a chance this year without Ricky Williams?" one of the parents asked an assistant coach.

There were four coaches and seven fathers out on the practice field with twenty-four kids. Five mothers were there at practice as well.

"Yeah, they got a chance. They got Daunte Culpepper now," an assistant coach answered.

"You think he's gonna make that much of an impact?"

"He should. They haven't had a real quarterback since Marino."

"All of the Florida teams should look good this year," Shareef spoke up. Football was his game. Being from New York, he still rooted for the Giants and the Jets, but he didn't mind watching the Dolphins, the

Bucs, or the Jaguars in Florida. Nor did he mind watching Michael Vick and the Atlanta Falcons in his old college town.

One of the fathers looked him over and said, "You write those books, don't you? Romance novels."

The man had kept that knowledge to himself until Shareef had decided to speak up among them.

"That's what I do," he answered. "Why, you read a few of them?"

He knew better than that, he just wanted to back the father up on his heels.

"Nah, I don't read 'em, my wife does. I didn't think you would watch football, though," the father committed.

"Yeah, football and writing don't go together, hunh?" Shareef quipped.

The father said, "I don't know, I figured you'd watch the soap operas or something. The Lifetime channel. Don't you gotta do research for what you write?"

A couple of the other fathers chuckled and grinned.

Shareef said, "Yeah, but I don't get it from watching television. My research comes straight from us."

Right as he spoke, Little J caught a pass, made a couple of dandy moves, and outran his teammates down the sideline for a touchdown.

One of the coaches looked over to Shareef and stated, "Your boy's gonna be one of our best players."

Shareef said, "I know it."

"J practices with my dad all the time," Kimberly spoke of her brother and father.

The other father looked back at Shareef and asked him, "You played some football?"

"Not really, just fifteen, twenty years of my life," Shareef joked with his answer. "Then I started writing romance books after college and somehow lost every one of my football skills."

"No you didn't, Daddy. You can still play football. J gets mad all the time when he can't catch you," Kimberly added. "And he can't throw as far as you either."

"Aw, he's nine years old, he's not supposed to outrun or outthrow me yet," Shareef continued lightheartedly. He said, "But he'll probably run and throw me down once he gets about sixteen. It's already in the genes."

The other fathers stopped their shucking and jiving after hearing that. They already knew what Little J could do. He had been taking the other kids to school. And if father was like son, then this man definitely had football skills, romance writer or not.

"So, who you like to win the Superbowl this year?" the humbled father asked Shareef.

Shareef said, "It's all up for grabs this year. You got Denver, Seattle, Carolina, Pittsburgh, and the Patriots as always. Then you got Cincinnati, Chicago, the Eagles, the Jags, Indianapolis, and the Bucs, Redskins, and Giants all making a comeback. Then you got San Diego, Atlanta, and Dallas still sitting in the mix, especially with Dallas signing T.O. from the Eagles. So take your pick."

The one father nodded and was speechless for a minute. The other fathers looked around at each other and started laughing.

One of them said, "Well, shit, if you didn't play no football, then you damn sure must be reading a whole lot of newspapers or something. You damn near sound like an announcer to me, right off the Sports Network. What's your picks in college football?"

The fathers and coaches all shared a laugh and went back to respecting each other as football fanatics, and they rightfully recognized Shareef Crawford Sr. as one of the group.

ON THE OTHER SIDE of town from the football practice field, Jennifer Crawford attended her annual fund-raiser meeting at Broward County's African-American Library.

"Do you think your husband would be willing to offer an hour or two of his time to conduct a fiction writing workshop?" one of the senior library coordinators asked her at their roundtable in the second-floor office. They sat around a large, oval-shaped table, five women and two men. Jennifer was second to the youngest at age thirty-two.

She took a breath and answered, "One of the things I try not to do is to ask Shareef to participate in too many of our events. I mean, let's be honest about it; if I were not married to him, would we even be so open to ask?"

"I know, I know, but we had to ask you," another member commented. It was only natural for them to ask about the participation of a nationally recognized, bestselling author who was married to one of their supporting members. But every year they asked, and every year Jennifer gave them her time, ideas, resources, and economic support. Shareef had even participated in several of their past events, so how much more could Jennifer offer them?

"We have a budget that is ten thousand dollars more than last year, so we should be able to invite some of the premiere authors and get a great return on our investment," one of the two men in the room stated. He was in charge of the accounting.

"What other authors are we thinking about inviting?" the youngest woman of the group asked. Outside of Jennifer, she considered herself the most knowledgeable on new and up-and-coming authors in the African-American community.

"Well, we like Michael Eric Dyson because his work seems to cross over to a large section of our supporters. But Tavis Smiley also has a new book out this year, we just don't know how much he would ask for," one of the planners explained.

Jennifer had to sit and listen as price tags were thrown around in regards to other writers, knowing that they rarely offered Shareef much of anything. And although she understood that her family could afford to give and not take, the principle of at least offering a person their worth had always irritated her. No one knew how hard her husband had worked over the years to make himself into a brand name more than she had. Nevertheless, she felt it was her duty to help the fund-raising process in any way she could.

Jennifer found pride and usefulness in being able to assist those in need. The middle child of three sisters and two brothers, she had been the most responsible person in her family. That was what attracted Shareef to her, and she to Shareef, when they attended college in Atlanta at Morehouse and Spelman, respectively. They were each able to find their way around obstacles, but they kept running into problems negotiating each other as a couple. Shareef would pull as hard as he could to the right, and she would resist, only for her to pull as hard as she could to the left, and find his resistance. He would rationalize his perspective with his logic, and she would rationalize her perspective with hers. And at the end of a their long nights of battle, they would both be exhausted, with him refusing to submit to her, and her refusing to submit to him.

She thought about their struggles a lot. She didn't speak about them often. It was not her way to complain about her many stresses, she just worked through them in silence. However, she couldn't seem to work through her inability to trust her husband to refuse temptation like she could. And she wondered if that temptation was more attractive than she was; more uninhibited, more enticing. And those thoughts only made her more insecure and unwilling to compete. Why should she be in competition with other women anyway? She was married to the man, and he should respect her more, holding her high on her pedestal. But since he had obviously forced her to compete, with disrespectful bitches, then he would have to live with her wrath and her withholding her affection from him.

Yet, she felt helpless and ultimately at his mercy. Shareef had become a national superstar, where she was only his wife, an aspiring event coordinator who had been only halfway successful in her attempts at big events in Florida, or in her hometown of Macon, Georgia, where her father, Daniel Mason, was a county judge. So maybe Shareef could walk away and do better, or most likely worse. For what woman would work as hard as she had to maintain the peace with her husband when more than half of her friends and family were separated or divorced for lesser transgressions?

Jennifer loved Shareef, his boastful swagger and his achievements, as much as she loved her father's. But submitting her will to her father was natural—he was Daddy. To submit to a husband she could no longer trust was degrading, and she found herself not able to do it. She had pride. She had value. She had self-respect. She loved her husband very much while despising her lack of control over their marriage, and she found herself paralyzed in her emotions. What was the right way to deal with him? Only if the man wasn't so damned thick-headed and impatient, maybe he could find time to relax with her for a minute, listen to her words, and allow her to develop trust in him again.

Jennifer would sink into deep spells of daydreams about her husband and their marriage at any place or time without warning. All it took was mention of his name or a passing of information to remind her of him. And before she knew it, it was close to ten o'clock at night and their library meeting was adjourning. It would take her another twenty minutes to drive home to relieve him of the children. How would Shareef react to that? He reacted to everything. But if she had reacted as much to him, she may have been forced to stab him.

"I'M ON MY WAY to the house now," Jennifer called and told her husband from inside the Land Rover. By then it was well after ten o'clock, and she had spent an extra ten minutes talking to the youngest member of the fund-raising committee about the best location for a new apartment. That's what Jennifer was like. Loyal. And her job was never done until everyone had received her full attention.

"Aw'ight," Shareef grumbled quickly over the phone.

She heard his voice and knew what he was thinking. He had been waiting to leave for more than an hour, and he was now pissed for having to wait that long. But life wasn't about a clock for Jennifer. Life was to be enjoyed and treasured, regardless of the seconds, minutes, and hours. Time should not control you, you should control it.

So when she arrived home, she was still not pressed.

Shareef, however, was waiting outside the house, on the steps, for her, like an overgrown child who could not wait to catch the minutes that could never be recaptured or replaced.

"I'll see you tomorrow," he told her as he hurried over to his Mercedes.

"How did practice go?" she asked him.

"What?"

"I said how did his practice go."

"Oh, it went normal. He had a good practice."

Shareef had already made it to his car, and since he was so eager to leave right then and there to chase eleven o'clock before he missed it, she told him, "All right," and let the hasty man go.

She then entered the house and walked straight up to the rooms of the children to make sure they had been tucked into bed properly. Because sometimes Shareef didn't take the time to get them into their pajamas.

SHAREEF WAS ON THE ROAD back to Miami at 10:34 PM, and was madder than a motherfucker.

"That's the kind of shit I'm talking about," he fussed to himself about his wife. He already knew what had happened. Jennifer had put in more overtime at her meeting at his expense, but he wasn't supposed to be upset about it. Nope. He was just supposed to wait until midnight and then sympathize with whatever story she gave him.

There was a cat stuck in the tree outside the library so I called the police, an ambulance, and a fire truck to make sure they could rescue her safely before I left.

Shareef would then holler, *Fuck that damn cat! Nobody else stuck around for that shit! So why did you have to?* After a few more hours, once he had calmed down, after he had lost three more years of his life expectancy through the unnecessary stress she had caused, he would feel like a fool for overreacting to her good deed.

"Shit!" he cursed out loud as he hurried back to Miami. He had not been with his new mistress in a couple of weeks, and they had made plans to go out that evening.

He dialed her cell phone number through the car phone, and awaited her answer.

"Hello."

"Jacqueline, I'm on my way," he told her.

"You're on your way? You were supposed to pick me up an hour ago."

"Yeah, well, I'll be there in thirty minutes."

"You didn't even answer my calls," she complained. "I called you three times already."

The truth was, Shareef didn't want to talk to her until he knew for certain he was on his way. Otherwise, he would have looked like a henpecked fool to continue telling her that he was waiting to leave. Maybe Jennifer had planned to ruin his night. Maybe her arriving home later than expected was to control his ability to find happiness without her. That's why his travels away from home and away from her had become liberating, with the only drawback being that he missed his children.

Shareef told his mistress, "I'll make it all up to you," only because he knew she would make it up to him later. And if she did not, she would no longer be his mistress. That was the dilemma that every new woman fell into with Shareef. While he continued in his struggle to understand his wife, he remained pressed for time, stressed out for a release, and intolerant of any new relationship that called for his patience. Because he no longer had any. Jennifer had taken it all.

"Oh, you definitely have to make it up to me now," Jacqueline told him. "You're talking about getting out of here at close to midnight. Most of the best restaurants are going to be closing."

Shareef heard her loud and clear through the speakers of his Mercedes, and he shook his head. The last thing he wanted was to owe another damn woman. But that was his reality after his time had been squeezed. He was being pushed out of his cool mode and into an obvious rush again.

He mumbled, "Aw'ight, I'll be there." But he no longer looked forward to it. The hastiness of their evening would only add to the stress he was already feeling.

AT 1:19 AM, Shareef held on to a Corona beer, sitting at a table at Opium, in the heart of Miami's South Beach party district. It was an elaborate place of flashy lights, balconies, waterfalls, artwork, men, women, money, alcohol, and an abundance of sex appeal. In this exotic nightclub, the beautiful women rarely waited for a guy to ask them to dance, they danced by themselves or with other girls who were as attractive as they were.

Shareef sat and watched a few of them, paying attention to those he wouldn't mind having a fling with, or invite into a ménage à trois with himself and Jacqueline. And as he watched the women swaying to the exotic vibe of the music, his mistress was able to sneak in between his legs and stand there.

"Come on, baby, let's dance," she teased him in her yellow silk dress and matching heels.

Jacqueline Herrera, a Dominican and black hybrid, with deep, beautiful brown skin, dark eyes, a curvaceous body to kill for, and long, thick hair that flowed past her shoulders, was Shareef's latest possession.

He liked his women exotic. Why settle for anything less if you could afford it? And he could afford it. So he told her what she wanted to hear.

"You take care of me, and I'll take care of you."

He had only two rules for his women. Rule number one: "You never hold out on me." Rule number two: "If I hear about or even *think* that another man is touching you, then it's over with, like that." He snapped his fingers in her dark eyes to make sure she got the point.

If she was to be his chosen mistress, then there was no room for a compromise. It was his pussy, and his alone.

Jacqueline responded accordingly, "Only my man can touch me. I've *always* been that way."

So Shareef told her, "Well, from this moment on, until you can't stand me, or until I can't stand you, I'm your man."

And that was it. The chick was in the bag.

However, at the club that night, Shareef wasn't feeling much of anything.

Jacqueline asked him, "What's wrong?"

He shook it off and took another sip of his Corona. He didn't even answer her.

She said, "So, you don't want to dance with me tonight?"

"Nah," he told her.

"Well, I'm gonna dance."

"Go ahead and dance then. That's what you're here to do."

She looked down at his dead energy and said, "Well, what are you here to do?"

He looked up into her eyes and said, "I'm here to watch you."

She paused and stared at him.

He added, "Then I'ma watch you dance again in front of the windows at the condo."

She heard that and grinned.

"You're a freak," she told him before she moved toward the dance floor.

Shareef mumbled, "Yeah . . . so are you."

He proceeded to watch his mistress as she teased him with her curves, her dance, her silk dress, her lips, her hair, her yellow heels, her eyes, her smooth shoulders, and her zest for life.

And while Shareef watched her and analyzed how her seductive moves worked in perfect tandem with the exotic music, he told himself, *I remember when Jennifer used to be that fun.* But his wife was now an older woman and a mother of two, where Jacqueline was twenty-three and single with no children. Was it that simple an assessment? And if it was, then no wonder so many passionate older men went crazy for young mistresses. They just wanted to continue to watch the dance, even if they rarely joined in.

AT 7:28 IN THE MORNING, the early waves of the Atlantic swept up on the beaches where joggers ran by themselves or with their dogs. Up on the twenty-seventh floor of his building, Shareef looked east, out into the vast ocean from behind the two-story glass window. He sat in a reclining hammock chair in only a pair of blue boxers. A tall glass of orange juice was set on the floor beside him.

Florida was lovely. And to have a high-rise condo overlooking the Atlantic Ocean was heaven on earth. Shareef had a good life indeed. But the good life was never enough for a hustler. And at the end of the day, Shareef was still a hustler. That's why he was always up so early. He hustled through grade school with his quick wit and ideas. He hustled through high school with athletics and aspirations. He hustled through college with philosophy and the need for a lifelong mission. And now, as a grown man, he hustled his stories. But if the story hustle was no longer an inspiration, what hustle would replace it?

Jacqueline looked down on Shareef's relaxed body from the second level of his condo. She wore only an extra long baseball shirt with the imprint of the cover jacket of Shareef's novel *Chocolate Lovers* on the front. It was a clever marketing idea that had paid off with thousands of fans wearing his book cover jacket to bed at night.

Jacqueline quietly made her way down the spiral staircase and over to her passionate writer, where she stood behind him and massaged his tense shoulders. But Shareef didn't want it, so he slid her hands away.

Reading his thoughtful mood, she looked away into the kitchen to her left, and took a deep breath.

"I hate it when you get like this," she spoke into the silence.

Shareef ignored her. Fortunately, Jacqueline had been around him long enough to know his ways. So she was not offended by it.

Instead, she teased him while on her way to the kitchen for her own glass of orange juice.

"You think too much."

She pulled out a tall glass from a cabinet, opened the stainless-steel refrigerator, pulled out the Tropicana OJ, and poured herself a drink before Shareef bothered to respond to her.

"How you think I'm able to afford all this?" he asked her without budging from the window. He said, "All geniuses think too much. That's what we do. Some of us do it fast, some of us do it slow, but we're always doing it."

His mistress smiled from behind the kitchen counter and returned the orange juice box to the refrigerator. She said, "You're always doing something else, too."

Shareef caught her flirtation and grinned. Like he said, he had a lot of energy for the extracurricular, so she rarely got a chance to sleep much around him. But that was okay, because he gave her body needed release, after she came several times from his hungry strokes.

He chuckled at it and said, "Yeah, that, too."

Then she became curious as she sipped her orange juice.

"So . . . what are you thinking about this morning? Am I allowed to ask?"

He nodded and continued to stare out the window.

"Harlem," he told her. Somebody wanted him to come back home and write a story. And he was still thinking about it.

"Harlem? What about it? I've never been there."

When Jacqueline told him that, eighteen straight years of growing up in Harlem, New York, flashed through Shareef's mind. He saw the buildings, the streets, the cars, the parks, the people, the graffiti, the billboards, the vendors, and the Apollo Theater. He heard the music, the jazz, the rhymers, the DJs, the preachers, the choir, the Nation, the players, the hustlers, the Five Percenters, and the crazy homeless people. He smelled the chicken, the greens, the brown stew, the bean pies, Chinese food, Indian dishes, doughnuts, trash, coffee, bacon and eggs, and the dead cats and dead dogs in the alleyways.

Shit, he could taste Harlem, and the first time he had blood in his mouth from a fistfight—it was outside his building on the East Side, at 121st Street and 2nd Avenue. He could feel Harlem, and the first time he bust a nut—at age thirteen with a fifteen-year-old Puerto Rican girl who thought it would be cute to turn out a wet-behind-the-ears black boy with her hot and ready pussy inside the projects of Spanish Harlem, while her overprotective mother went shopping at the grocery store. How could he put the sights, scenes, history, and emotions of Harlem into words without running outside the lines of the page, punching his pencil through the paper or running out of ink with his pen?

How many real-life stories could he tell about Harlem? Cynthia Washington had it right. Harlem had countless stories. Not just love stories, but everything. Because Harlem was the *truth*. Harlem was love. Harlem was sweat and tears. Harlem was broken dreams. Harlem was dreaming again. Harlem was never stop dreaming. Harlem was never stop living. Harlem was never stop hustling. Harlem was never stop *believing*. Harlem was never stop *achieving*. Harlem was . . . *shit!* . . . It was just . . . Harlem!

Got' damn, this girl never been to Harlem? Shareef asked himself frantically. He was still speechless. He couldn't even move. Harlem had him in a trance. He had fucked around and zoned out while thinking about Harlem. And he had to stand up from his chair to think about it some more.

Jacqueline had asked him the question five minutes ago, and she was still waiting for an answer. When he abruptly stood up from his chair—a mad scientist in thought—she stared at him from the kitchen as if he had gone crazy.

She asked him, "Are you all right?"

He paused, then looked out the window and into the Atlantic Ocean with an idea.

"Come here for a minute," he told her.

Jacqueline was hesitant. Shareef had a delirious look in his eyes.

He repeated "Come here," with urgency.

She put down her glass and walked over to him, but she was still apprehensive. That's just how insane he looked.

When she reached him, he stretched out his hands and pulled her body in front of his at the window.

"Stop," she chirped like a scared teenager. What were his intentions?

Shareef pulled her in front of him anyway. He told her, "You see that big ocean out there?"

The Atlantic Ocean was right in front of them.

She said, "Yeah." What was his point? He was scaring her.

He said, "I want you to imagine buildings coming up out of the water. Red buildings, brown buildings, gray buildings. And lots of them, covering up everything you can see." He started turning her body in different directions with his. "Over there, over there, over there. And they're all different sizes, too. Some of these buildings have twenty-something stories, and others only have ten. So they go up and down like this . . ."

He grabbed her right hand and moved it up and down and from side to side like a conductor at an opera.

Jacqueline started laughing. He was really getting into it.

He said, "And then, once the whole ocean is filled up with these buildings, right. I want you to imagine looking down at the streets, running inside all the buildings. Left, right, straight, back, and all over the place." He showed her with his hands.

"And then you got cars and people on all of these streets, and inside all of these buildings. Blacks. Puerto Ricans. Dominicans. Jamaicans. Haitians. Africans. East Indians. A few lost white people running around. Asians running in and out of the corner stores. And right in the middle of all that, right. Right in the middle." He showed her with a slice of his hand through the middle of the ocean.

He said, "You got a Hundred and Twenty-fifth Street. And on that motherfucker, it's ten blocks of shops, stores, restaurants, and street vendors all trying to sell you shit while you walk by."

Then he pushed her away from him. "All right, now you walk toward me."

Jacqueline looked at him and shook her head, embarrassed by his enthusiasm.

He said, "Come on, walk toward me."

He was so hyper and assertive that she had to walk toward him before he exploded, and blew up the room. And as soon as she began to walk, he grabbed at her like make-believe salespeople.

"Hey, I got some new shoes for you. What size you wear?"

Then he grabbed her from the other side.

"Do you wear hats? Girl, I got the prettiest hats in the world for you."

He jumped to the other side again and told her, "Keep on walking. You can't stop for these people. You don't have no money. You just checking out the block."

Jacqueline did what he told her and was tickled as hell. It wasn't even eight o'clock in the morning yet, and his ass was wide awake on a natural high over Harlem.

"Hey, you, you, you, I have pretty dress for you," he told her.

Then he jumped to the other side of her.

"Hey, baby girl, you need your hair done. I can hook you up good."

Back and forth he went like a maniac.

"Hey, try this new apple pie in here. This is an original recipe, just try it."

"Hey, sis, I got some dope incense for you. Lighters. Dictionaries. Condoms. Tampons. I got everything you need."

Jacqueline stopped again and couldn't stop laughing.

Shareef said, "I told you, don't stop. Because if you stop, they gon' get your money. I mean, it's like walking through a gauntlet in Harlem."

"Wait a minute, I thought you said I didn't have any money?" Jacqueline reminded him.

"Yeah, that's what you tell them. But if you stop, and you really have some money on you, they gon' find it," he told her. "They'll have you digging in your socks and your panties pulling out money."

She laughed and asked him, "What, are they just robbing you in broad daylight?"

"Nah, they're hustling you. And Harlem is the capital of hustle. Hands down. I mean, Harlem is like . . ." He ran out of words to explain and walked closer to the window. He stretched his arms and hands up to the ceiling as if he were holding up the world.

"Yo, B, it's Harlem *world* up in here, baby! This is *Harlem World!*" he shouted and beat his chest like King Kong.

Jacqueline grinned and shook her head again. Shareef was off his rocker—and she liked it.

After he had used up all his energy trying to explain to her what Harlem was like, he had to sit back in his chair. He wasn't as young as he used to be, and even young guys were forced to rest after taxing themselves.

Shareef took a long swallow of his orange juice and said, "Come here. Come sit on my lap," and he smacked his right leg.

She did what he told her. And when she sat in his lap, he was still smiling like an overjoyed kid. But that kid turned into a passionate man again when he started to kiss her lips, fondle her breasts, suck on her neck, and run his hands through her thick, long hair.

Jacqueline got into it for a minute, but then she stopped and looked him in the face.

"What? What's wrong?" he asked her.

She told him, "I think I'm a little bit jealous."

He frowned. "Jealous? Jealous of what?"

She asked him, "You feel that strongly about Harlem?"

Shareef relaxed and grinned at her. He said, "I'll put it to you this way. You know how people talk about Johannesburg and Rio de Janeiro, Paris, Hong Kong and Tokyo. You know how they talk about that? Cairo and Amsterdam and shit? Tel Aviv?"

She nodded her head in silence.

He said, "Well, in America, it's Harlem. You go to New York, and you go to Times Square downtown, and Harlem uptown. And there ain't no uptown in the world like Harlem. That's just all there is to it. It's culture there."

Jacqueline continued to stare at him.

"Are you gonna take me there?" she asked, seduction in her dark eyes.

Shareef nodded and said, "I'ma take you there." He pulled up her long baseball shirt, and added, "I'ma take you there right now." He tugged off his boxers and made her straddle him in the chair. Jacqueline smiled and kissed his lips, and Harlem felt so good, twenty-seven stories up above the Atlantic Ocean in Hollywood, Florida. Harlem felt wonderful; up and down and in and out of her body.

Mortality

AT 10:26 AM Shareef typed the word "Harlem" into his Macintosh G5 computer, which sat on a desk on the top level of his split condo in front of the bed. His computer faced the Atlantic Ocean for inspiration. He looked at the word excitedly before he increased the point size to 72. Then he saved it in a new file titled "Harlem World."

Jacqueline crept up behind him as soon as he had finished.

"What are you doing, writing your book about Harlem already?"

She was butt naked and beautiful from head to toe.

Shareef turned to face her in his rotating chair and grabbed her naked body into his face to kiss and suck on her flat stomach.

"Not yet," he told her in between his kisses. "I'm just saving the idea on file. Then I'll come back to it. That's my process."

She rubbed his head and the back of his neck while he continued to kiss and suck her belly. She moaned, "Mmm, let's go take a shower together."

That's what older men loved about young and sexy women. They were always open to more play.

Shareef smiled and told her, "How 'bout you run the warm water in the Jacuzzi instead. Then light them candles up in there and turn off the lights. And after I make some phone calls, I'll sneak up in there with you like a butt-naked stalker. Aw'ight? Go do that for me."

He spun her around and smacked her on her naked ass to go.

She cracked a baby girl's smile and headed toward the bathroom.

"Don't have me in here waiting too long, either. I don't want to turn into a prune before you get to me."

"Well, put some oils and bubble bath and shit in there with you."

She shook her head and kept on walking.

Shareef turned back to his desk and picked up the cordless phone that sat next to the computer screen.

FICTION EDITOR WILLIAM SORENSKI, a tall, waifish, dark-haired book enthusiast in a button-down shirt, Dockside slacks, and casual leather shoes, sat in his corner office on the eighteenth floor of the Worldwide Publishing Group building in the middle of Times Square. He could see everything right out of his office window; one of the best views in the building, which proved how much the company liked him. Bill had made some great buys for WPG, including signing Shareef Crawford, who had become one of their strongest stars in African-American books.

Bill was leaning back in his extra high, black leather office chair reading through a soft-back copy of a self-published book entitled *The Street Life*. He read a few pages in silence before he grunted and closed the book. He picked up another self-published street book, this one titled *A Game of Hustling*. He seemed to have a dozen of them spread out across his desk that morning.

When his office phone rang, he ignored it and continued with his reading. He read a few more pages of *A Game of Hustling* before he shook his head and closed that book as well. A moment later, his secretary paged him.

"Bill, Shareef Crawford's on line two. You want me to tell him you'll call him back?"

Bill sat up in his chair and said, "Oh, no, I'll take it," and tossed the street book on his desk.

He jumped on the line with his celebrated author and said, "Shareef, how's it goin', buddy? The new book is doing great. We climbed up to number seven this week. Four more spots and you'll break your old record."

"That's good, that's good," Shareef told him. "Let's keep counting them peanuts."

"Ah, they're a little more than peanuts," Bill told him with a smile. "They're more like walnuts."

Shareef laughed and said, "Yeah, as long as they keep adding up. But anyway, man, I got something new I wanna run past you."

"Oh yeah, what's that?"

When you're a star writer, everything is doable. So Bill was open for anything from Shareef.

"Yo, I'm thinking about writing a book about a Harlem gangster."

Bill heard Shareef and paused. How ironic? He wanted to get into the street-fiction game himself, but with his celebrated author of romance titles? He wasn't so sure.

First he asked him, "You can write that stuff?"

Shareef sounded offended. "Come on, man, I'm from Harlem. I know the streets. What, you forgot who you're talking to? This is me."

"Yeah, but I mean, you haven't written anything like that."

"But you've already said I have the strongest male characters, right? So what do you think street fiction is about? More male characters."

Bill paused again to try and figure out how best to break the publishing industry taboo to one of his favorite authors.

He took a breath and said, "Shareef, book readers are extremely loyal to reading the same thing. So if you start off as a romance writer, that's what they expect from you."

Shareef cut him off and said, "Bill, I know this industry as well as you do. And that's the first thing I said when someone mentioned this idea to me. Keep doing what you do. But at the same time, man, a good book is a good book. And *nobody* can outwrite me about Harlem."

He said, "People mail me these street books every day of the week.

And that shit never goes deeper than the surface. Not to mention how terrible half of that shit is written. They're just on their hustle, man. I understand it. But now when the *master* decides to put his pen down on Harlem, it's a *wrap!*"

Bill believed him. He really did. The words and the passion behind them were more than braggadocio with Shareef, he was a skilled professional, and was indeed a standout.

So he said, "I don't doubt that you can outwrite these guys. But as I read through some of this stuff, I really doubt that the audience pays that much attention to how well it's written. I mean, I think most of this material is pure, ah, sensationalism. And it doesn't paint the best picture of the African-American community. So to throw yourself in the middle of that is going to be a more, ah, of an arduous challenge than you believe right now."

Bill was trying to be as logical as possible, picking his words with tact.

Shareef responded, "But if I pulled it off, everybody would be talking about it, right?" He awaited an answer in the affirmative. Instead, Bill took another pause, a deep breath, and came up with a perfect parallel.

He said, "Sure, everyone may talk about it, but it may not mean that they'll give you their support and blessings. I'm quite sure some of them, if not a lot of them really, would view your writing street fiction similar to an R and B singer putting out a gangsta rap album. And I don't think that's the kind of comparison you'd want."

Shareef heard his analogy and broke out laughing.

"Oh, shit! It's that bad, hunh?"

"Well, it's not as if you're some unknown writer who can just up and change directions without anyone knowing about it. You have quite a fan base now. I mean, what will your million women fans think?" Bill asked him.

Shareef fell silent for a spell with no immediate response. His editor didn't like the sound of that. Shareef always had something to say. So Bill gave him a way out.

"Well, if you're that serious about trying to write some of this stuff, then maybe we could come up with a pseudonym or something, I don't know. We could call you The King."

Shareef listened and started laughing again. He said, "You're a funny guy, man. The King, hunh?"

Bill chuckled at it himself. "Yeah," he said, "you know, short for The King of the Streets. Then you can have the best of both worlds. You'll keep your walnuts with the female fan base and get some of the guys with the street lit. You'd be like ah, R. Kelly and Jay Z rolled into one."

Shareef laughed even harder.

"R. Kelly and Jay Z? What do you know about R. Kelly and Jay Z?"

"Hey, man, I'm up on things. I read," Bill answered. "So, what do you think about that idea?"

Shareef paused again. "I mean, I don't know yet, man. I was actually thinking about writing something as a nonfiction, to tell you the truth."

Bill raised his brow. "You mean about a real person?"

"Yeah, that's how the idea came up."

"Well, is this guy still alive or dead?"

"He's in jail. I'll have to go in and visit him."

That changed everything for Bill.

"Well, that may come under the Son of Sam law," he responded.

"Even if he doesn't accept payment for it?"

"What, this guy would give you his story for free?"

Bill seriously doubted that. In America everything was a deal.

Shareef said, "Or, he could donate the proceeds to someone else, couldn't he?"

"I'll have to check on that," Bill told him.

"In the meantime, I'll do a little research trip up in Harlem next week to see what kind of material I'll be dealing with."

Bill heard him and became a little concerned.

"Hey, ah, you be careful hanging out up in Harlem."

Shareef laughed again. "What do you think, these guys who are writing these streets books are any safer than I am? It's just regular research, asking the right people the right questions, like any other book."

"Yeah, but a lot of these guys are still on the streets. I mean, the last time I checked, Shareef, you were living quite comfy down in Florida."

Bill was opening Shareef up like only a professional editor could. To get the right material, you had to push your way into the truth.

Shareef made note of that himself. He said, "That's why I like you, man. You're always honest with me."

"Hey, if an editor can't be honest, then he's not doing his job."

"Aw'ight, well, I'll try my best to stay safe up in Harlem for you," Shareef humored him.

Bill joked back and asked, "You know of any, ah, bodyguard services or anything for while you're up there?"

He had Shareef laughing more than usual that morning. "Bodyguard services? That's the last thing you want to do in research. That only brings more attention to you. And this is my old neighborhood we're talking about. People still know me there."

"Yeah, I was only joking with you," Bill responded. "Unless you really want to use one."

Shareef told him, "Look, man, I will not be walking around Harlem with bodyguards. Okay?" And that was that.

When Bill hung up the phone, he thought to himself for a second.

"I bet Shareef could pull this off," he said out loud. He took another moment to convince himself. Shareef had all the research and writing skills, and like he kept saying, he was from Harlem.

In the meantime, Bill had his own research to do on whether any of the street writers were worth signing. He picked up the next self-published street book from his desk—this one titled *A Hard Way to Die*—and started reading.

BACK DOWN IN FLORIDA, Shareef hung up the phone and immediately went searching through his cabinets for the business card on which Cynthia Washington had written her number. He was not concerned at all about being safe in Harlem. That was ridiculous. Harlem was his people. So he thought no more about it.

He found Cynthia's card and dialed her number on his office phone. Her card said she was a legal secretary for a law firm, Taylor and Scott. Shareef wondered if that's how she met Michael Springfield. She answered his call on the second ring.

"Hello."

"Long time no hear, no speak, no see," he answered.

"Who is this?"

"Shareef Crawford."

"Oh, hey stranger. What a coincidence? I just thought about you today," she told him.

"About writing your jail story?" he teased her.

"Among other things, yeah. So you called me back, hunh?"

"You didn't expect me to?"

"Actually, I was going to give you until August before I started calling you. I figured you would still be on tour until then."

"Yeah, I just finished touring. So outside of your jail story, what else were you thinking about me?" he quizzed her.

"Umm . . . how strong your stroke was. And your strong conversation, of course."

Shareef chuckled and spun his chair around. He didn't want to have Jacqueline walk out and catch him on the phone with another woman talking about his stroke. A mistress was more than a one-night stand. He had to protect his security with her.

"Oh yeah, in what order?" he asked Cynthia, while eyeing the bathroom door.

"The conversation came first."

"But that's not what you said first."

"Well, that's what I meant to say."

Shareef chuckled and said, "Anyway, I've been thinking about this Harlem crime story you asked me about." He figured he could flirt with her anytime, and in person, where he could do more about it. But he was calling her about business.

He asked, "Does Michael Springfield expect me to meet up with him in jail?"

Cynthia perked up. She answered, "Oh, yeah, he definitely wants to see you."

"Can you set that up for next week? I want to see how much of a story he has."

"You're coming back to Harlem next week?"

"Unless it can't happen?"

"Oh, no, it can happen, I just want to make sure."

"Well, yeah, that's what I'm planning."

"All right, I'll set it up then. What day next week?"

"I'm thinking Tuesday or Wednesday. I wanna get back in the city like, Sunday night, and get settled first. I want to take a few days to see what everything looks like now. I hear there're a lot of changes going on."

"Yeah, you'll see. They have new construction all over Harlem now."

"Construction of what?"

"Condos."

Shareef smiled, thinking about his own condo back home.

"Is that right?"

"Yeah, and they're expensive, too. I even asked about a few of them."

Shareef nodded. He figured he would get to all of that once he arrived back home. He said, "So, see what you can set up and get back to me by the end of the week. You need my number again?"

"Is this it on my phone?"

"Yeah, this is my office number. So keep it business."

She chuckled. "I got you player. I won't mess up your game. It's strictly business then."

He said, "I'm just talking about with the phone calls, not when I get up there." And he grinned. He surely wanted to explore Cynthia's vibrancy again. He only got a chance to do her once before she dropped her book proposal in his lap and broke camp on him.

"Mmm, hmm, you want your cake and eat it, too," she commented.

"Don't we all? So call me up later this week and let me know."

"Okay, I'll call you."

Shareef hung up the phone, smiling with stimulating tingles from the conversation and expectations with Cynthia. Then he remembered to join his fine, playful mistress in the Jacuzzi. He stripped his boxers off and moved butt naked toward the bathroom. But the office phone rang and stopped him.

He froze and thought of letting the answering service take a message. But he checked the number to see who it was first.

"Jennifer," he answered. He took a breath and decided to see what she wanted. Their conversations were rarely long anymore. They had only general information calls, mostly regarding the children.

"Yeah," he answered drily.

"I just wanted to remind you that we have that meeting with the marriage counselor set for next Tuesday at ten in the morning," she told him.

Shareef recalled it and responded, "Shit."

"You didn't plan anything else did you? I asked you to put that on your calendar before you went on tour."

"Yeah, I do have it on my calendar, I just haven't looked at it since I've been back."

"Do you have some other plans for next Tuesday morning?"

"I was going to fly back up to New York to start doing research for a new book."

"When? You just got back from the tour. You know Shareef wants you to take him to football practice."

Jennifer got frantic whenever Shareef changed the plans on her, which was often. It wasn't as if he did it on purpose, but he did make new commitments without much regard for previous ones.

Shareef responded, "He has a whole three-month season. This is only one of the first practices."

"Well, how long do you plan on being up in New York?"

"I planned to be there for a week."

"So you won't make our meeting with the marriage counselor, either? When are you leaving?"

"I planned to leave on Sunday, but I can wait until Tuesday afternoon."

He was actually interested in seeing a marriage counselor. After struggling without help for the past three years of their marriage, a professional point of view on their beefs would offer a breath of fresh air. Or at least he hoped. Hearing what his wife had to say about her loss of passion in their relationship was enough for him to want to stay and go through with it.

"Your son is going to be disappointed," she told him.

Shareef thought, *Tell me something I don't know.*

"I'll spend extra time with him this weekend then," he responded.

"And what about Kimberly?"

"She can stay with you. You know how Shareef gets when she starts whining."

"So what? He has to get over it. She wants to be with you, too."

"But you said my *son* was going to be disappointed, not my daughter."

"You know what? You do what you're gonna do."

When Jennifer hung up the phone with him, Shareef responded, "I am."

He placed the cordless office phone back on the charger and marched his naked behind to the bathroom. When he stepped inside, Jacqueline had turned off the lights, lit up the candles, and filled up the Jacuzzi with warm water, bubbled just like he had asked her to.

When he quietly closed the door behind him and crept over to the tip of the tub, she smiled with bubbles on her shoulders, in her hair, and on her nose.

"I was just about to come out there and get you."

"Why, I'm a stalker. Remember?"

Jacqueline started acting with a squeamish look and put her hands out in front of her. "Oh, God! Who are you? What are you doing here?"

Shareef stopped and frowned at her. Then he chopped his right hand into his left palm.

"Cut. That was terrible. Take two."

She grinned and splashed water at him.

"Whatever. I'm not an actress anyway."

Shareef climbed into the Jacuzzi with her and countered, "Yes you are. You've been acting up all night and all morning."

She grinned and kissed his lips, getting bubbles on his nose.

She said, "But that wasn't acting."

He grinned back in a lip lock and said, "Oh."

AT 8:43 AM, Tuesday, August 1, Shareef labored over what he would wear to his first marriage counselor appointment with his wife.

"Do I go casual or professional?" he asked himself out loud. He had pulled out gray sweatpants and an orange I LOVE THE BAHAMAS T-shirt, versus a white button-down shirt, beige sports jacket, and blue denim jeans.

He looked at both outfits laid out on his bed and pondered.

"Nah, I'm a professional, and I need to be respected that way. This counselor needs to see me the way most people see me when they first meet me." And he began to put on his button-down shirt, sports jacket, pants, fine shoes, and cologne. He drove his Mercedes, too.

Halfway to the meeting at a downtown office in Fort Lauderdale, Shareef found himself stuck in a traffic jam on I-95 North at 9:35.

"Shit," he cursed. "Is it an accident or what?"

He had twenty-five minutes to make it to this first meeting on time, so he got off the highway at the next exit and used his navigation system to find another route, only to run into more traffic and stoplights on the streets.

"Shit," he cursed himself again. "This is just my damn luck."

By the time he arrived at the building in downtown Fort Lauderdale and made it up to the third floor office, it was 10:18.

Shareef strolled inside the door and said, "Traffic jam. I-Ninety-five." There was nothing he could do about it, so he decided to keep his cool and roll with the punches.

Jennifer Crawford sat on a black leather sofa with her legs crossed, wearing sheer stockings, a tan tweed business suit, peach blouse, light brown leather shoes, and a matching brown leather handbag. Her golden brown hair was pulled into a perfect bun, and her lipstick and light makeup were perfect. She never needed much makeup anyway. Her skin was naturally tan and radiant. Shareef used to call her "The Golden Girl" in their better days. But that seemed like another lifetime now.

Obviously, Jennifer wanted to be taken seriously that morning as well. Shareef was still impressed by her. He took a seat on the opposite black leather sofa to his right and sat with his legs wide open for comfort. Then he stared into the face of a black woman in wire-framed glasses and a dark blue suit, who sat behind a desk in front of him. She looked in her forties.

Oh, shit, a black woman, he told himself. For whatever reason, Shareef was expecting to see a white man that morning.

"Hello, Mr. Crawford, my name is Dr. Jacqueline Nelling, and your wife, Jennifer, and I have just been sitting here chatting, about nothing in particular, just getting to know each other while we awaited your arrival."

The fact that her first name was the same as his mistress didn't rattle Shareef at all. He planned to stay cool and in control of his emotions.

"Okay, how are you doing? My wife hasn't beaten me down too badly already, has she?" he joked.

"No, she actually spoke very highly of you," Dr. Nelling told him.

"She tells me that you're one of the leading authors in contemporary African-American fiction."

Shareef looked at his wife, and she smiled at him. She still did have a smile.

He nodded and said, "Okay. That's good."

Jennifer told him, "I always speak highly of you. I can't say that he does the same for me though," she informed Dr. Nelling. Jennifer continued to smile, a good, natural, confident smile. She was determined not to be a sour victim, or at least to appear not to be.

Shareef said, "Actually, she's a very intelligent, caring, supportive, and loyal woman. And as you can see, she's also good-looking, sexy, and professional."

Dr. Nelling looked at both of the Crawfords dishing out compliments and responded, "Wow. So, what's the problem?"

The room went quiet for a spell.

Shareef asked, "Is that how we start, just . . . start talking about the problems?"

It seemed a little too informal to him.

Dr. Nelling asked him, "Why not? You two seem quite open with how you feel about each other, or did you just make those comments up for me."

Shareef looked at his wife and said, "Nah, that's how I feel about her."

"That's not what you tell your little flunkies," Jennifer expressed through her smile.

All of a sudden, Shareef didn't like that smile anymore. It was mocking.

Dr. Nelling looked at Shareef and asked him, "What do you tell other people about your wife?"

Shareef came clean with the woman. That's what they were there to do.

He said, "I tell them that she don't give me none. Or I used to. Now I don't even talk about it. But it's the truth. She won't let me touch her. But I don't call her no bad woman or nothing."

"Yeah, and then his little whores would call my job and our house at all times of night, telling me, 'You're gonna lose your husband if you don't watch your back. You don't deserve him. I'm a much better woman. I know how to hold my man down.' And all kinds of other *bullshit* like that, but he's gonna say that he's *not* saying negative things about me."

Jennifer was no longer smiling. She was venting, and venting good.

Shareef responded, "I mean, I can't say what these women are gonna say or do. I told her that already. That's straight-up woman stuff, cat fighting. I don't even know who they are."

"That's bullshit," Jennifer said with her mocking smile again. "He thinks he knows these women so well, but obviously he doesn't know them at all. And he obviously doesn't know what they're capable of. And this is why you don't *cheat,*" she said into her husband's face. "Because it all comes back home, Shareef.

"And if he wants to know why I don't let him touch me, all he has to do is ask himself, 'Where have all of these tramps and whores been?' " she stated. "Where do you find them? You think a woman can't be a nasty whore just because she reads one of your *books*?"

Shareef had to contain himself before he blew his cool not five minutes into their session. His wife was laying into his ass *quick*.

Instead of getting excited, hot, and bothered by it, Shareef smiled.

He said, "She would have you believe that I just ran out here and started collecting women for no reason. That's not how it went down."

Jennifer stopped him and said, "Collecting women? I guess they're his little *trophies* now." She looked at Dr. Nelling when she said it.

Shareef kept his cool, but he was no longer smiling.

He said, "If I may finish. I'll tell you how it went down. We had two kids after marriage, and then all of a sudden, I had to beg for everything. She just cut off the damn well."

Jennifer cut him off again. "He doesn't understand that your body changes after children. I had to breast-feed. I was sore a lot of times. I had longer periods. Longer cramps. And then I had to go back to work. And sure, after getting the kids ready, feeding and clothing them, working all day, cooking when I get home. Yeah, excuse me for being a little tired. Is that a crime?

"Obviously, it is to him," she continued. "So then he starts running out here to sleep with whore number one, two, three, I don't know how many others and I don't appreciate it."

After another barrage of that, Shareef figured he was in a no-win situation. But at least they had already set up estate paperwork and property assets with their lawyer to determine who gets what in case of an untimely death or a divorce.

He looked Dr. Nelling in her eyes through her wire-framed glasses and said, "The only reason we're still married, Doc, is because we both love our kids, and we don't want to see them dragged through the mud in a divorce. Other than that, and the fact that my grandparents and her parents all want us to remain together as a big happy family, the truth is, we've both been miserable for several years now, mainly because of one issue. Sex."

Jennifer said, "That is not the only issue. He disrespects me. He's always second-guessing my decisions with the children or with finances. He doesn't listen. I have to tell him things three and four times, and then he still doesn't do it. And I don't ask for a lot, but he doesn't seem to be able to do any of the small things that I ask of him on a daily basis."

Dr. Nelling looked at Shareef again. They were airing everything without her even asking.

Shareef responded, "All of that, and she still has a house, a car, insurance, security, vacations, perks. She was able to quit her job and maintain her lifestyle two years ago. She had time to take online business courses. And she never has to worry about anything. I mean *anything*. But I'm the bad guy because of small things. *Small things*," he emphasized.

"Well, there's a whole lot of women out here who would much rather have your *big things* than these motherfucking *small things* you keep talking about," he snapped. "I mean, I don't understand that shit," he addressed to Dr. Nelling. "Every couple has small problems that they need to work out, right? But not having sex is a *big* fucking problem. I didn't sign up for that shit."

Jennifer looked at Dr. Nelling and asked her, "You see how he talks to me? Does that sound like a man who respects his wife?"

"Well, if his wife would *fuck him* like she *used to,* then maybe he wouldn't be so fuckin' *stressed out* to talk like this," Shareef finally blasted. "I mean, she knew what kind of man she was dealing with. I always go after what I want. She knows that. I haven't changed. And if I can't get what I want, I get frustrated."

"Yeah, exactly, just like a child," Jennifer concluded. "He acts just like his son, a nine-year-old."

Shareef looked at her and said, "Well, let's talk about the things that you get. You name anything that you haven't been able to get since you've been with me. I mean, what the fuck are we talking? We're talking about a spoiled-ass grown woman who won't fuck her husband for whatever reason, *small things,* I guess, while I'm breaking my ass to give her and the kids everything they want, and I can't ask for what *I* want. Does that sound fair to you? Does that fuckin' sound fair?" he asked Dr. Nelling.

He said, "And excuse my language, but we're all adults in here."

"Adults don't have to use that language. That's language that disrespectful teenagers like to use," Jennifer stated.

"Okay, so now I've graduated from being a nine-year-old to a teenager. I guess I'm getting older by the minute," Shareef joked. "So, how do I become a man? Do every little thing my wife wants me to do, including the small things, while putting my dick up in the closet, because I can't have any more sex after having kids. I may as well give my dick to one of your charity events. Is that it?

"Here's my husband's dick, we can give that away because we don't use it anymore," he joked distastefully. "I've already had my kids, and I'm too tired and uninterested in sex now to use this old thing anymore. Thank God!

"Is that how you want to live now?" Shareef asked his embarrassed wife. "And you're asking me why I'm fucking other women? Because I haven't retired yet. That's why! And if you don't want to use this thing over here no more, then that's *you're* problem. But as long as I continue to wake up with a hard dick, I'm gon' use it for more than chocking it off in the bathroom."

Jennifer was so embarrassed by his words that she sunk her head into her hands.

Dr. Nelling asked him, "Do you think your words make your wife feel sexy? You think they make her feel loved and desirable?"

Shareef looked the woman in her face and said, "To be honest with you, all that old Valentine's Day shit is tired. If you love a person, you love a person. And you show that person through your *actions,* not all that candy, and flowers, and presents and shit. That's cheap love. Real love is about taking care of family and home and all of their needs. And she has not been doing that for me. Period."

Suddenly, the strong reserve of Jennifer's shell began to crack. Her voice broke when she responded, "That's not true. I am always looking out for you. I always have you in my heart. And I am *always* thinking about ways to try and help you."

Fresh tears rolled out of her eyes and down her face as she wiped them away with her hands.

Shareef saw his wife's tears and shook his head. He had witnessed them all before. Jennifer wasn't as tough as she tried to be. But she was certainly his hardheaded match when it came to giving in. Neither one of them seemed capable of full compromises.

So he said, "Okay, now here she goes with the crying game. And she does all this crying, and then at the end of the night, when I'm crying about not getting any, it don't mean shit to her. Does she break me off with a little something? No. She goes the fuck to bed, and I end up in the fucking bathroom like a asshole."

He said, "Now, I tried to live with that shit, Doc, for three years, where I told myself, 'Look, man, you can't have everything in life. And maybe sex is one of the things you'll have to give up.' And even when I tried not to think about sex, I ended up having wet dreams and shit, in my thirties when I have a wife right there in the house with me, who won't fuck me because she's worried about other women.

"Where are these other women at when I'm right there in the house with her, Doc?" he asked rhetorically. "We were sleeping in separate rooms every night. You know why, because I couldn't sleep with her without having a rock hard penis at night that she wouldn't touch. In fact, she would get up and leave the room."

Jennifer cried, "Our relationship is more than just sex. That's all he ever thinks about."

Shareef was able to reclaim his cool.

He said, "Let me ask you a question, Doc."

"That's Dr. Nelling," the counselor finally corrected him.

"Okay, I'm sorry. Dr. Nelling."

She nodded to him to continue.

Shareef asked, "If a human is hungry, and you refuse to feed that human, what do you think is going to be on that human's mind? Going to the circus?"

He said, "I told her that. The more I don't have sex, the more I'm going to think about it. She creates her own monster by denying me."

Jennifer pointed at him and said, "You are *not* gonna blame me for your *cheating*?"

"No, I'll just blame the kids, your job, and your regular household chores for it," Shareef countered. "That's what you blame, right? Like I don't have shit to do. Like I never help out with the kids. Like I never cleaned the house."

"I didn't say that," she snapped at him.

"Well, you sure made it seem like I'm just sitting around doing nothing while you're doing everything," he told her. "And I didn't even talk about how much TV you watch while you're so *tired,* and how many hours you're on the phone. You could be using that time for me. Maybe I'd be listening more if you're weren't watching TV or talking on your cell phone until two o'clock in the morning."

"What about when you're talking to your little *whores*?" Jennifer questioned him.

"Am I talking to them during your time?" he answered. "I don't think so. And furthermore, if I'm talking to anyone, and you walk into the room butt naked, I'm off the phone real fast."

"Well, I can't walk around the house butt naked with children, like your little *freaks* do."

"You used to," Shareef told her. "And what about when the kids are in bed? What are you doing? Still watching TV, right?"

Dr. Nelling was just about to wrap things up and redirect them when Shareef looked at her and said, "She don't love me like that. She don't love me enough to do what she needs to do. She got too much pride. She thinks somebody's trying to get over on her."

Jennifer countered, "And you don't love me enough not to cheat. You love your dick and your whores more than you love your wife. And that's just sad."

"Yeah, but I wouldn't have no wife if she wasn't a girlfriend first who was willing to fuck me. Because I didn't take no *virgin* to the altar, nor did I plan to end up with one."

"Okay, I believe I've heard enough at this point," Dr. Nelling told them both. "We have a double compromise, and a double trust issue here that we need to address, among other things.

"Shareef, Jennifer does not trust you not to cheat. Jennifer, Shareef does not trust you to show him physical love."

Shareef said, "That's right. Physical love, like we started off with."

Dr. Nelling said, "But I doubt, I *seriously* doubt, that you spoke to her in the same tone and disrespectful manner that you speak to her with now."

Jennifer said, "Of course, he didn't. But now he does it all the time. He's even done it in front of my friends and family members."

Dr. Nelling said, "But the compromises that both of you have to make, if you want to hold this marriage together, and it is repairable, are many. First, you must both reestablish your goals for a marriage. What does a marriage mean to you? How should you treat each other in a marriage? How much time do you allot to each other? How much time should you have apart? What is your sexual midpoint?"

Shareef stopped her and asked, "Sexual midpoint? She doesn't want to have sex at all. Ask her."

"That's not true."

"Well, you never approach me about it. What, you got a man on the side?"

That did it for Jennifer. She stood and said, "I'm not gonna take this. I'm not," and shook her head defiantly. She added, "If you were still at home, you would know that I had no one else."

"If you still had a sex drive I would still be at home," Shareef told her. "But if you're gonna tell me that kids make a woman stop wanting to have sex, then no wonder we have so many . . ." and he stopped himself with a deep breath. He realized that he had gone far enough, and that he had blown his cool a long time ago.

Dr. Nelling asked him, "So you're no longer at home?"

Shareef took another breath and answered, "I'm home on and off."

Dr. Nelling nodded and made note of the information. But there was only so much she could do in one session. She gave them both a Marriage Goal Questionnaire to fill out and to think about before she would meet with them again.

"So, we'll sit down again in two weeks, and with the information I've heard and the questionnaires that I'll need you both to prepare, we'll be able to move you both along to a better understanding of what needs to happen to recommit as a couple."

She said, "But I want to warn you, the assessment is the easy part. Given enough information, we can usually find the ailment and prescribe a treatment. The hard part, in my nearly twenty years of marriage counseling, is the actual process of each person carrying out what needs to happen, the actual work of pulling a relationship back together, and being consistent with that work. Because it is work, and it's work that you *both* have to do."

Harlem Research

ON THE FLIGHT from Miami to New York, all Shareef could think about was his failure to stimulate his wife. Despite her claim that having children had nullified most of her sexual desire, he held himself responsible for not turning her on. He felt less masculine because of it, and tainted with a weakness.

Nah, fuck that! There's nothing wrong with my sex game, he convinced himself. *Jennifer's just not interested. Some women are just like that. That's not my fault.*

As for their marriage counseling, he found it interesting to finally get so many of their issues out in the open, but he doubted if it would work. Unless Jennifer turned into a nympho, or he lost as much of his own mojo, he failed to see them as an equal match anymore.

Fuck it, I'm a passionate man, he assessed himself. *Putting down my dick is like putting down my pen. And I can't see that happening anytime soon, unless I'm either dead or crippled.*

WHEN HE LANDED in New York at 7:34 PM, the plan was to have his friend Polo pick him up at the airport and drive him over to a small hotel on Frederick Douglass Boulevard below 124th Street. The hotel was a renovated spot right down the block from the Magic

Johnson/Sony Theaters and Hue-Man Bookstore. Shareef loved that the place was low-key and right in the middle of Harlem. He could do his research on foot while feeling a part of the neighborhood again. It wouldn't feel the same if he stayed at a luxurious hotel in Times Square. Nor did he pack any of his upscale clothing. It was time to feel the roots of the grind and hustle from the street level again in tennis shoes. And Shareef looked forward to it.

Polo arrived at LaGuardia Airport in an old, two-toned Bronco jeep.

Shareef met him at the curb of the pickup area and asked him, "Where you been hiding this eighties ride at?"

"Man, I just got this thing back out the shop a month ago," Polo answered. "I love this truck, man. It takes me back to the roots." He looked like a bear of a man, with a full goatee, rounded belly, oversized blue denims, and a royal blue T-shirt.

Shareef shook his beefy palm and said, "That's just what I was thinking about. That's why I'm staying at this little hotel on Frederick Douglass." He also planned to wear a lot of basic T-shirts with his slacks and tennis shoes to fit into the Harlem scene.

Polo looked at him in his black tee and said, "Yeah, it's gon' be a whole lot of other people in the roots staying at that hotel, too; junkies, Johns, hoes, young hustlers."

Shareef paused and frowned at him.

"Yo, that hotel gets down like that?"

He looked concerned. Not that it would stop him from staying there, but . . . Then again, if he couldn't trust to keep his luggage there . . .

Polo read the concern on Shareef's face and said, "I'm just fucking with you, man, I don't know that place like that. They're doing a lot of renovations up in Harlem now. That place might be nice."

Shareef grinned and grabbed his luggage to toss in the back.

He said, "I guess I gotta get used to everything again anyway now. There's gon' be some junkies, Johns, hoes, and young hustlers up here. That's every day, all day."

He figured he would need to sharpen up on his street lingo as well.

The two men in their midthirties climbed inside the Bronco jeep and headed for the Triborough Bridge toward Harlem.

Shareef took a deep breath in the passengar seat. He said, "This feels exciting, man. I got butterflies all over and shit."

Polo looked over at him, smiled, and kept driving.

He said, "I'ma have to stop and get gas as soon as we make it over the bridge, man. I had to hustle up and speed over to the airport to get you."

"Oh, it's all good, man. I got you. What's the toll now, three, four dollars, right?"

"Yeah, something like that," Polo answered. He wasn't as talkative and as animated as he usually was.

Shareef asked him, "So, you get a chance to read that new book of mine?" He had given Polo and Trap a book each when he was in New York on tour in early July.

Polo chuckled and said, "Come on, man, you know I gave that book right to my girl." He said, "I can't read most of that shit you write anyway. My dick be too hard. But it's good to get her ready."

Shareef laughed with him and said, "I wish my wife would read the shit and get ready."

Polo looked him in the face.

He said, "Your wife be acting up on you?"

"As a matter of fact, we met with a marriage counselor in Florida this morning."

Polo shook his head. He said, "Man, no matter what it is, a woman always finds something to complain about."

"Ain't it the truth. You can't ever please 'em. Pleasing a woman is only temporary."

"Yup," Polo agreed with a nod, " 'cause she gon' act up sooner or later."

Shareef said, "Speaking of women, I gotta call this girl back and let her know I'm here. She's the one who gave me this idea after I met her at my signing that night at Hue-Man."

Polo looked again and said, "Yeah, I apologize again for not making it out that night. A couple things came up."

Shareef shook it off. "Don't worry about it, B. I always do what I do anyway. I had a good time that night."

Polo laughed and said, "Shit, I bet you did. What color panties was she wearing?"

Shareef shook his head and laughed it off without answering.

They made it through the toll at the Triborough Bridge and to the first gas station on Second Avenue in Harlem to fill up, with Shareef paying for everything.

Polo tried to bite his tongue while they stood outside the truck at the gas pump, but he couldn't.

He said, "I bet it feel good to just dig in your pockets and knock shit off like that. I wish I had it like that, son. I be stealing and borrowing from my own pockets to pay for my shit. Rent due tomorrow."

Shareef asked him, "You're not living from paycheck to paycheck are you?"

Polo said, "Nah, I'm living from my *next* paycheck to my *next* paycheck," and laughed. He said, "I'm like two paychecks and four weeks behind."

"On everything?"

"What's everything?"

"Rent, bills, car, health?"

"Health? Nah, my girl got us under insurance with her job. But yeah, I'm behind on everything else, B. It's like I'm writing one of your books from page negative one hundred and eighty-four. And once I get back to zero, then I can start writing chapter one. I just gotta figure out how to get back to zero."

Shareef asked his friend, "How much loot would you need to do that?"

Polo studied Shareef's face to see if he was serious. But Shareef rarely said anything he didn't mean.

Polo told him, "Yo, all I need is like two, three Gs, and I'm straight. That's word to my whole family, B."

Shareef nodded to him as the gas continued to pump into the truck.

He asked Polo, "Well, the streets are always talking, right?"

Polo looked into his eyes and read what he was really saying. The streets didn't need to know their business. So he answered the question correctly, "Not in my house it ain't. I'm like the little pig with the brick house. The wolf ain't saying shit to me. So he can huff and puff all he want to, but he ain't gettin' in my house, B."

Then he quieted down and added, "Shit, if you square me away like that, man, then I'm good on the hush. That's word to my whole family."

Shareef said, "So we understand each other then?"

Polo frowned at him and put his right hand up for affirmation with a shake and a hug.

"Come on, man, this is blood right here, son."

Shareef took his hand in his and they embraced like urban men do with arms and shoulders.

He said, "I got you with five."

Polo froze as if he had been zapped by an ice machine.

He said, "Yo, man, honestly, if you did some shit like that for me, I'd fuck around and wouldn't know how to act, B. I'd be like Antonio Fargas in *Across 110th Street,* when he had that orgy and got castrated. Remember that shit, when we used to watch that movie all the time at my mom's crib?"

Shareef went into acting mode, quoting lines from the movie: *"You was a punk errand boy when you married the boss's daughter, and you're still a punk errand boy."*

Polo laughed his ass off. He said, "Yo, you still remember that shit, line for line."

"Hell yeah, that's my all-time favorite movie. I ordered two copies on DVD, one for watching and one to keep in storage."

"Yo, you was always a collecting-ass nigga. I bet you still got old rhyme books from our grade school days and shit," Polo stated. "I remember you was the first one in our projects with the Treacherous Three, Trouble Funk, and that Micstro shit."

Shareef said, "I was always first. *Arcade Funk* blew ma-fuckers minds up here."

Polo sang, " '*F-U-N-K*' . . . Yo, somebody need to sample that Trouble Funk shit, B."

"If they can still find it."

They finished pumping the gas and climbed back inside the truck.

Polo looked over at his friend in the passenger seat and said, "I'm glad you back, Shareef. You like inspiration to a nigga, man. Word."

"Ay, man, it's good to be back home," Shareef told him.

Polo started up the engine and nodded. He said, "I bet we'll never laugh at your ass again for writing books. Books is the main movies being done now."

He said, "After watching all that *Harry Potter* and *Lord of the Rings* shit with my son, I was seeing that shit in my dreams."

Shareef laughed as they pulled into 125th Street and made a right.

He said, "Hopefully, I can write some bomb-ass shit like that."

Polo looked at Shareef and said, "Shit, B, you 'bout to do that shit now. What you think you back home for? This shit is your mission. We were watching *Across 110th Street* before we could nut, like we was grown-ass men."

Shareef smiled and said, "Yeah, and I heard it was a book first. So now I need to go and find it."

SHAREEF CHECKED into the renovated hotel on Frederick Douglass Boulevard for five nights, and planned to hook back up later with Polo and Trap for something to eat.

The little hotel with five floors wasn't bad. They even had a mini microwave in the room. But they had no king-sized beds, only double twins.

Shareef smiled and said, "I guess I can't stretch out with Cynthia in here. She got her own bed."

Then he called her on her cell phone.

"You just got in?" she asked as soon as she answered the line.

"Yeah. I've been off the plane for about an hour, and I just checked into my hotel."

"Where are you staying?"

He knew that was coming.

"At a little renovated deal down the street from the bookstore."

"You got plans for the night?"

Shareef was used to doing the asking, but a change in format from a fine, assertive woman was okay with him.

So he answered, "Not after midnight."

"That's when you want me to come? That may be a little too late for tonight," she told him. "We have to get up early tomorrow to go up north to see Michael."

"I'm always up early," Shareef responded. "So, you should be more worried about you."

"Well, if I came over there that late, then I may as well bring my clothes for tomorrow so we can leave from there together."

"Aw'ight, so I'll call you once I get back in. I need to meet and greet with old friends."

She said, "Don't have me waiting too long after midnight."

"I'll stay on the clock for you then," he told her. "But the sooner I get out there with them, the sooner I get back here for you."

"Okay, go do what you gotta do. I'm not a blocker at all. I understand."

"Good. I'll call you later then."

Shareef ended the call and laid back on the bed that was closest to the window for a minute. It was therapeutic to hear the noise of street traffic again. The reminder of the 24/7 Harlem hustle was sure to keep him on his toes while he was here. Harlem was no Atlanta or Fort Lauderdale, and Fort Lauderdale and Atlanta were definitely not Harlem.

Shareef looked around at the basic necessities of the modest hotel room and figured he had come a long way. Some folks never had a chance to move up in life. For those who did, it was a mind-blowing experience they would be forced to live with and adjust to, or else suffer the consequences of slipping and falling back down to the bottom.

Shareef sat back and mumbled, "Shit, never that. I never been on the bottom." But he thought about it. Because life had opposites. And if there was a top, then there was surely a bottom, and he realized that most of his childhood friends were now closer to that extreme than they were to his.

BEFORE SHAREEF KNEW IT, he had fallen asleep on the bed, and Polo was calling him on the cell phone from out in front of the hotel.

"Hello," Shareef answered and cleared his throat.

"Yo, don't tell me you up there sleeping, man, on your first night back in Harlem."

"Yeah, I crashed for a minute. So what?"

"So, get on down here so we can get something to eat. We all out here in the truck."

"Who's *we*?"

"Me, Trap, and Spoonie. You remember Spoonie from middle school days and football?"

Who could ever forget a kid nicknamed Spoonie?

"With the teeth?" Shareef asked him subtly.

Polo laughed loud enough to cover up his answer. In their youth, Spoonie was tortured by a slight overbite.

Polo said, "Yeah. He wanted to sit down and shoot the breeze with you, too. I told him what you was working on."

Shareef didn't know if he liked that or not, but it was too late to pull it back. Polo had already made his move.

He said, "Aw'ight, I'm coming down now."

He ended the call, rose up from the bed, checked his face, hair, and clothes in the mirror, and brushed his teeth.

When he strolled out of the building to join the group inside Polo's Bronco, the front passenger door was left open for him.

Shareef looked into the back of the jeep and gave Trap and Spoonie a handshake.

"What's up, fellas? What life look like now?"

"Not as good as yours," Spoonie responded to him. "I see your face on the back of books everywhere now. And I stop people all the time and tell them, 'I went to school and played football with that kid.' "

He was taller and thinner than all of them, wearing all dark blue.

Shareef asked him, "You tell 'em I used to lay your ass out in football, too?"

Trap chuckled and answered, "Nah, he didn't tell them none of that. He just told them the good things."

Trap was dressed in all black, and was usually a sly counterpuncher. No one ever had any idea of when he would speak. So his friends and foes were forced to expect the unexpected from him.

"So, where we off to first?" Shareef asked them as he got in and closed the door.

"Trap wanna take you over to the Native. It's this place on one-eighteenth and Lenox," Polo told him.

"What kind of food is it?" Shareef asked.

"Is like Caribbean, Indian, soul . . . I can't explain it, man. You tell him, Trap," Polo responded.

Trap said, "They got like a mix of everything. I just like the vibe in there."

"Yeah, it's low-key, like you like it, right?" Spoonie offered.

Shareef nodded and waited to see for himself.

They arrived at Native, a dark, red, cultural food corner at 118th and Lenox, and Shareef could see why Trap liked it so much. The place was out in the open yet hidden at the same time. In fact, a person could easily drive right past if they didn't stop to look. There were no bright McDonald's or Wendy's signs out in front. The owners seemed to want it dark on purpose. Inside they used more candles than lights, and the dark, wooden tables and chairs were set close together for more intimacy.

Shareef grinned as the four black men took a seat at an empty table against the back wall of the restaurant near the bathroom and coat hooks.

He said, "This feels like a stake-out joint for undercover cops."

Trap grinned at him from across the table and said nothing.

Shareef announced, "Aw'ight, so, am I the fat pig here, or is everybody paying for their own food?"

Spoonie looked at him while sitting beside Trap and hinted, "Damn, you did put on some weight over the years, son. What you been eatin'?"

They shared a laugh at the table at Shareef's expense.

Trap said, "I got my own shit, man. They know me in here. They got my face on file."

Shareef told him, "Nah, I can't pay for two and leave you hanging. So I'll just take the whole bill and eat it. But I ain't doing this shit tomorrow."

Polo looked offended. He said, "Who told you you was paying for my shit? I'm not homeless. I drove us over here."

"Dig it, I'm a man up in here, too," Spoonie added.

Shareef looked at them all and said, "Aw'ight, well, if everybody wanna pay for their own food, then that's cool with me."

Polo backstepped and said, "I mean, I'm not gon' fight you over it, B, if you wanna go ahead and pay for it, then I'm good with that."

Spoonie said, "That's what I'm saying. We all grown, civil men in here. I know how to accept a gift."

Shareef grinned and shook his head. He looked at Trap again and said, "What about you? You got yours?"

Trap answered, "Like you said, man, if you planned on paying for everything, then just go ahead and put it all on one bill. That keeps it simple."

It was no big deal to Shareef. It wasn't as if he was around those guys every day. So they started ordering drinks, appetizers, and main courses all on him.

Once they began to drink and dig into the sweet and spicy chicken, shrimp, and fish dishes, with vegetables and rice on the side, Trap asked Shareef, "So, what are you trying to do up here with your next book?"

That was what they were all there to talk about. They had celebrated a coming home party for Shareef before, but this was different. He was working on a book about the Harlem streets this time, the Harlem they all knew and that he had moved away from.

Shareef bit into his spicy shrimp with white rice and answered Trap's question with a question of his own. "Who runs the block now?"

Spoonie looked at him and shook his head.

"This ain't the eighties no more, man. Ain't nobody gettin' down like that. You got a million hustlers trying to do what they can, and most of them ain't really gettin' no money."

"Yeah, hustlers got regular slave jobs like we got now," Polo commented. "I mean, them niggas hustling for a flat-screen TV now. What's the use in that?"

Trap said, "Some of these young bloods, they try to do a little something, but it just don't last, man. It's too much heat up here on the streets now. I mean, look around you, man, and see who you see moving in."

Shareef had to look no further than the customers in the restaurant; white, black, Asian men, women, couples, and college students represented a Bohemian appeal. That wasn't the Harlem he knew.

Spoonie said, "I can introduce you to a few guys to tell you how it is now. But they not gon' talk just for the hell of it. I mean, they're out here hustling for a reason."

Shareef wasn't interested in too many small-time players, especially if he had to pull arms and legs and eventually pay them for it. He could see how that would go before he started. He wanted to get a feel for the new heavyweights in his old neighborhood first. He needed to understand the big fish of the book before he could focus on the chapters of everyone else. He didn't plan on telling his friends about his meeting with Michael Springfield in prison the next morning, either. He didn't want any of their opinions to bias his visit. There was a method to his madness, and he planned to stick to it.

"So, you're telling me there's no new Nino Brown in the 'hood? Or somebody trying to aspire to be?"

There was always someone going after the vacated number one spot. It was only natural.

Polo mumbled through his stewed chicken, "You hear about any new John Gottis walking around? Any new Al Capones? I mean, when they're here they're here, but when they're gone they're gone. And them niggas is gone. Ain't nobody gettin' big like that no more."

Trap nodded and picked a piece of steak from his teeth with his fingernails. He said, "I still know a few guys. But they're not try'na let it be known. I mean, you plan on putting any names in this book?"

Shareef said, "I don't know what I wanna do with it yet. I just wanna hear what people got to say at this point. I'll decide what I want to do with the book later."

Spoonie frowned at him. He said, "Well, if you don't know what you wanna do with it, then why should a motherfucka talk to you? That don't make no sense." He looked at Polo and commented, "I thought you told me he wanted to write some top-notch shit."

Polo said, "He is, once he get started. But he don't wanna talk to no regular-ass niggas on the block. He wanna talk to who runnin' the motherfucka."

Shareef relaxed and figured that he would have to do his own thing. His guys were never closely connected to the real street thugs anyway. Only Trap had done any time in the pen. So Shareef asked him about it.

"What about guys you know from jail, Trap? None of them came out and ran with a new plan?"

Trap shook his head. He said, "The old-timers come out and go legit, and young bloods, who are too hot headed, come out and get blasted, or go right back in. That's how it is, man, and ain't nothing sexy about it. I mean, this is real life out here. You don't get ten chances to live like no cartoon."

A twenty-something black woman with braided hair stopped on her way to the bathroom and stared at Shareef for a moment.

"How are you doing?" he asked her.

"I'm fine. Umm . . . are you Shareef Crawford?" she asked him back.

"Yeah."

She said, "I told my girl that was you. You're from Harlem, right?"

"What, you been reading my bio?"

"She been reading your bio all right," Polo joked. He could see the element of surprise in the woman's face.

She said, "No, I just had a couple friends pass around a few of your books and talk about it, that's all."

"Oh, okay, well tell them to keep reading them."

When she left, Spoonie said, "Man, if I had girls on me like that for writing love stories, I wouldn't be thinking 'bout writing no street shit."

Trap said, "You crazy. The street niggas get the baddest hoes."

Shareef sat there and thought about Cynthia Washington. She was obviously into street-caliber men herself, and it was getting close to midnight. Most of the customers were beginning to leave the restaurant, and he wasn't getting too much useful information from being around them.

"So I guess we can hit a couple other spots tomorrow night," Shareef told them while he picked up the bill that sat at the edge of their table.

Polo said, "Tomorrow night? Man, I already told my girl not to expect me back home tonight. I'm ready to hit five more spots *tonight*."

Shareef was still thinking about Cynthia coming to see him and visiting Michael Springfield in the morning. He was leaning toward passing on more time wasted with Polo, Trap, and Spoonie. They weren't the only folks he knew in Harlem.

He said, "Nah, we'll get a fresh start tomorrow night. So after I make a few runs in the morning, I'll see what y'all ready to do by, like, seven or eight. And line up some folks for me to talk to tomorrow. But tonight I'm still a little drained from travel," he told them.

He actually was travel weary, but that had never stopped him before from doing what he wanted to do. He just wanted to retire from his friends and trade them off for a woman.

Polo looked him over and smiled, knowing better. He said, "What, you dun' called up one of your shorties already to meet you back at the hotel? You got a little midnight action set up, B? I mean, I know you, man. You ain't never tired. That must mean you bored with us," Polo assumed correctly.

He said, "But that's aw'ight. We gon' have you set up for tomorrow then. And we can introduce you to some fly street honeys, too. That's word to my whole family. We gon' help you make this book right, son."

Shareef smiled, shook his head, and said nothing. Then he paid the bill.

WHEN HIS FRIENDS dropped him back off at the hotel, Shareef was happy to be alone again. He had spent so much time alone in his thoughts that it became his natural element. Nevertheless, the company of a willing woman was just as pleasing and as peaceful. So he wasted no time before he jumped on his cell phone to call Cynthia.

"Boy, when you say you're gonna make a call, you make a call. I was expecting you to hit me back by one or so," she told him. It was five after midnight.

Shareef asked her, "Does that mean you're gonna be late with your visit?"

She paused. "No."

"Good. Because we both gotta be up early tomorrow, right?"

"Yup."

"So you might as well bring your clothes over."

She paused again. "Do you have your way with your wife?" she asked him frankly. Cynthia had never even asked about his wife before.

Shareef kept his cool about it.

"Why do you ask?"

"Because you seem spoiled. Does every woman do what you want, when and how you want it?"

"I wish," he told her. "I wish I could write every character. But I can't. Not in real life. And ultimately, each person does what they wanna do. So I just try to control as much as I'm allowed."

"Hmmph," she grunted. "Interesting answer."

He said, "Can I ask you a question?"

"Go ahead."

"How long have you known?"

"About your wife?"

"Yeah."

"Since before I met you. And when you never bought it up, I figured you do what you do a lot. Fucking. But your wife probably wants to make love."

Shareef laughed. He said, "So, I see you got a nice pair of ears on you."

"Yeah. Listening is the best thing I do."

After the phone call, while waiting for her arrival, Cynthia's last comment stuck in his mind, *Listening is the best thing I do.* His wife used to be that way. Jennifer used to listen to everything while they were still students together in Atlanta. But after marriage and kids the listening became more compartmentalized. Not now, but later. And not later while I'm on the phone or watching TV, but later when I'm ready to hear it. So Shareef shut down and stopped talking to her, and he allowed his pretty fans to listen. The sex went the same way, and where his pretty fans began to receive more of his energy, his wife got less.

Shareef nodded to himself while stretched out across the twin-sized bed near the window. "I guess she got reasons not to wanna fuck me," he grumbled. "I was supposed to stick in there and ride it out."

Only problem was, he had rarely rode anything out that had stalled on him. When he lost interest, from a lack of response or otherwise, Shareef would simply roll out and move on. That was his way of coping with the complicated book called life. He never got stuck on the pages with writer's block, he just forced his pen to move forward to the next plot point.

"Fuck it, man, that's on her. She shouldn't have switched up on me."

He would tell himself any and everything to take the burden of his failed marriage off his shoulders. Yet they were still married and holding on to something other than the kids, and stronger than the pressures of their extended family. They were holding on to the intimate dream of being there for each other. At one time, they really believed in it. Together forever. Where had that dream gone?

Cynthia arrived ten minutes later and broke Shareef out of his funk. He had to meet her down in the front lobby to let her in. The small hotel had nighttime security that made sure all guests had room keys or were accompanied by someone occupying a room. Those were the rules to keep the place closed to riffraff.

Cynthia climbed onto the elevator with him, holding a stuffed Fendi bag and grinned. She wore a mint green Baby Phat sweat suit.

"I guess this is a major step down from the Sheraton," she commented.

Shareef smiled back at her.

"Yeah, I wanted to feel the true grittiness of Harlem again."

She eyed him and said, "I see."

He looked over to her large, brown Fendi bag. "And I see you brought more than a pocketbook with a makeup kit," he told her.

"That's what you told me to do, right?"

"Yeah, but I didn't know you were gonna do it," he admitted. "Especially after you brought up my wife. I thought that was your prerequisite to check my ego."

She smiled and said, "It was."

When they walked into the room, Shareef crashed right back on the twin bed near the window.

Cynthia sat her bag down on the floor and took a look around the room. She nodded and said, "Yeah, this is a big step down from the

Sheraton. I mean, it's not all that bad with the remodeling and everything, but still . . ."

Shareef asked her, "What, you've been in this place before it was renovated?"

"No."

"So how come you know so much about the remodeling?"

She looked at him and asked, "What are you trying to get at, that I do this often? You better ask somebody. Then you'll find out what select company you're in. Because I don't do this every day."

Shareef didn't want to know that much. Or maybe he did. He had only known the woman for a total of five to six hours and a couple of phone calls. She, on the other hand, knew a lot about him through his books, from internet searches, and through his reputation as a celebrated author.

Shareef finally shook his head and said, "I don't want to fight with a pretty woman. So let's just leave it alone. If you're safe, and I'm safe, then that's all we need to know for now."

"Are you sure?" she teased him.

Shareef ignored her and, using the remote, clicked on the nineteen-inch, color television.

He said, "I don't have to have it every night. I got some discipline. So I'll just leave you alone tonight and rest up for the morning."

Cynthia grinned and repeated, "Are you sure?"

Shareef paused before he mumbled, "Yeah." Then he continued to watch cable television.

Up North

I N THE MORNING, Cynthia Washington was butt naked under the sheets and snuggled under Shareef's left arm in the fetal position. He may have had enough discipline to do without sexing her for a night, but she had not exactly agreed to that. She was eager to find out if their last time together was only a fluke. Turned out it wasn't. The writer of romantic fiction actually knew a thing or two about how to please a woman.

Shareef opened his eyes, thought about their second night together, and grinned. It was the biggest ego boost in the world for a man to turn a woman down, only for her to come on strongly to him. What passionate man would decline to write that real-life story?

Then he leaned forward and looked at the clock on the nightstand to his left. It was 6:27 Wednesday morning.

"Hey," he addressed the sleeping beauty with a nudge of his arm.

"Hmm," she responded meekly.

"You said we need to be out of here at seven-thirty, right?"

She took a minute to answer with her eyes still closed.

"Yeah. What time is it?"

"It's six-thirty."

"Mmmph," she grumbled. "We got another hour left."

Shareef thought about that extra time on his hands and grinned.

His manhood responded to the idea of an early-morning quickie before a shower.

Cynthia could feel him pressing up against her leg under the sheets. She began to smile.

"I must admit, you have way above average stamina," she told him.

He said, "It's a gift. But some people can't just take all that shit."

"I can imagine."

"So . . . what am I supposed to do with it?" he asked her. "I mean, sometimes I got discipline, but other times . . . I just don't."

Cynthia didn't answer him. Instead, she slid under the covers and took his manhood into her mouth.

ON THE LENGTHY TRAIN and bus ride "up north," as New Yorkers called it, Cynthia and Shareef headed toward the state correctional facility to meet the man who had summoned him. And the woman who had set up the date for him had a sudden confession to make.

Cynthia looked down at the floor from where she sat next to Shareef on the bus and said, "You know what?"

She waited for him to answer her. Her confession would be more dramatic that way.

He looked at her and said, "What?"

He pondered if he needed to be alarmed or not. He really didn't know anything about this woman, and there he was taking this trip to a prison with her to meet a man he had only known by name and reputation. Shareef had never personally known Michael Springfield. He had only seen him on the Harlem streets, while living the hustler's life of fast cars, pampered friends, and hot girls, back in Shareef's high school days in the late eighties.

It was one thing to be brave, it was another thing to be stupid. Shareef actually began to question his sanity that morning as he waited for a response from this mysterious woman. He had never even visited his own friends or relatives in prison.

"What?" he asked her again. She was taking too long to answer. He wanted to rush the suspense and get to the surprise.

She glanced into his face and said, "I didn't, um . . . I didn't expect to like you like this."

That froze the writer for a minute. All of that build up for a basic crush. Women were funny that way. Or maybe men were too much on guard. So he chuckled at it and loosened up.

"You think that's funny?" she asked him.

He shook it off. "Nah, I was just, ah, thinking something else, that's all."

She studied his face and felt slighted. Was he playing her emotions cheaply or what? He had to understand that she didn't actually like a lot of guys. Most men failed to meet her criteria. The young, searching girl in Cynthia loved the deep soul of a man. She craved to learn more about life from her men. And a man inside prison walls had been hardened by the truth.

But Shareef was a pleasant surprise who could still teach her something outside the gates of confinement and failure. Intelligent men of the free world had souls, too.

He said, "So, how did you expect me to be?"

She grinned and lightened up again.

"I don't know, I just thought you'd be more . . . *studious* or something."

A Cuban-American woman who sat a few seats away overheard her and grinned. Studious guys rarely scored with women who visited correctional facilities. Shareef was in an odd place considering his academic credentials. He even admitted as much.

He said, "I am studious. I've been an A student my entire life."

"Yeah, but you're cool with it," she told him.

Shareef leaned back in his seat and grinned in sarcasm. "Oh, okay, so a smart guy can't be cool, hunh? I'm supposed to be a geek ma-fucka. Pin the tail on the donkey, right? Nah, fuck that," he told her defiantly.

Cynthia laughed and shook her head at the conflicted reality of urban stereotypes.

She said, "That's sad, ain't it?"

"It's sad that you believe that shit, yeah," he expressed to her. "So the only respected knowledge is street knowledge, hunh? That's why you got me traveling up here in the first place."

"No, that's not the truth," she argued.

He said, "Yes it is. And I bet I'm not supposed to be able to lay it down right, either? That's why you're so damned surprised now."

The Cuban-American woman overheard that and chuckled. He looked good enough to lay herself. She liked intelligent men. Smart men were her type. If only her boyfriend had not tried to outsmart the law, he could have done something legal with his life.

Cynthia spotted the woman eavesdropping on their conversation and fell silent. But she had to respond to that. So she elbowed him in the ribs without words.

Shareef frowned and said, "What's that for?"

She stared into his face and grumbled, "Your smart-ass mouth."

He said, "You shouldn't have brought it up then."

WHEN THE BUS PULLED UP to their destination, twenty-one passengers—family, friends, and significant others of the inmates—filed off into the bright sun to enter the barbed-wire gates and hard concrete of a New York State correctional facility.

Shareef looked at Cynthia and asked her, "So, this is it, hunh?"

She nodded. "This is it."

He looked up at the tall towers surrounding the prison, where armed guards were posted with sniper rifles. A mile-long triple fence of tangled, barbed-wire circles at the top of the gates said one would have to be insane to even think about escaping. Digging under the gates looked to be the only way out. But how long would that take before the sharpshooters popped you, or sent out a goon squad to beat you senseless and drag you back to a cell?

Shareef took a breath as he surveyed things up close. For the first time in his life he could witness a prison facility not from a television or movie screen.

He told himself, *Damn! I'd never wanna be in this place. This is crazy!*

Cynthia snapped him out of his daydream by grabbing his arm.

"Come on. You're not having second thoughts, are you?" she teased him.

"Nah, it just hit me for a minute."

She nodded and said, "Yeah. That's how I felt the first couple of times. But then you get used to it." She said, "But the key is not to think about the gates, the guards, or the concrete buildings. You have to think about the people who are locked inside. I mean, these guys are all human in here. Everybody makes their share of mistakes, they've just made bigger mistakes than the rest of us."

Sounded like she had her rationalization all mapped out. How else could she continue to visit a man in prison? You had to believe they were still men who just happened to be locked away for the time being, and not view them as prisoners who were no longer allowed to be men. So Shareef understood her optimism. It was the right way to think, humane and respectable.

They stepped up to the visitors' entrance together and walked through a metal detector similar to airport security. Any and all dangerous objects would be confiscated, along with a rejection of such a visitor and an imminent arrest. All the warning signs reinforced the rules. However, men and women were sometimes desperate. So every once in a blue moon a visitor would put his or her own freedom on the line by attempting to aid an imprisoned loved one.

Shareef walked through the metal detector behind Cynthia and took a deep breath. The metal detector made him feel guilty about any- and everything he may have gotten away with over the years. Then he stood as still as a statue on the other side of the machine to make sure it was cool.

"You're good," the security guard told him.

Shareef nodded and walked forward.

Cynthia smiled at him. "Are you sure you're all right with this? They're gonna let you back out," she assured him.

He laughed it off. He said, "I know, right? I'm feeling like I'm going into this motherfucker for real."

"Like I said, you gotta get used to it."

"Yeah, well, that's easy for you to say, you've been here before."

She started laughing as they made their way to the visiting area.

When they made it all the way inside, visitors and prisoners were everywhere: black, white, Asian, Italian, Latino, Russian, Aryan—you name it. They could even walk out to the prison yard together. Shareef couldn't believe that part. He was expecting glass windows and phones, or monitored tables like he had seen in various television shows and movies. So he watched the prisoners and their visitors walking out in the yard together and became confused for a minute.

He turned to Cynthia and said, "Yo, we can walk out in the yard with them?"

She grinned and answered, "Yup."

The next minute she was embracing a well-built, walnut brown man in a perfectly clean, white T-shirt, green pants, and state-issued boots. Shareef didn't even see him approach them. Then he backed away and kissed Cynthia on the cheek.

"So, you actually brought him here," the brother stated to her. He was still surprised by it.

"And he was brave enough to come," she responded.

The man faced Shareef with his hand extended.

"Michael Springfield, man."

Shareef took his hand in his and remembered him being taller during his high school days. Maybe that was because of his youth back then, and his adoration for the man as a popular street hustler. But in prison, Michael Springfield was brought down to size, with no jewelry, no fly clothes, no expensive rides, and only one lady. He also had low-cut hair that was even all the way around, no fade.

"Good to meet you, man. Shareef Crawford."

Michael smiled, with good teeth and genuine friendliness.

"I know who you are, playboy. You made a whole lot of lonely nights bearable for a nigga in here. I gotta tell you."

Cynthia overheard him and laughed. She already knew the story.

Shareef chuckled and said, "Well, it's always good to know a black man's reading my work. I don't get a lot of that. It's mostly women giving me love."

Michael said, "Shit, playboy, that's the right kind of love to get. Every nigga in here wish he had that kind of love now."

He looked at Cynthia. She grinned at him and said nothing.

Then he turned back to Shareef. "Let's walk and talk on the yard."

Shareef was still hesitant about walking the yard, but what could he do? He couldn't turn the man down and go out like a scared-straight punk, so he strolled out on the yard following Michael's lead. Cynthia followed them, but not too closely, so that the two men could have a little privacy in their conversation.

As soon as they walked out in front of her, Michael asked his guest, "So, you like her or what?"

Shareef frowned and played the dummy role for a second.

"Who?"

Michael looked him dead in the face. "Come on, playboy, you know who I'm talking about. Me and her cool like that. We talk about everything."

Shareef nodded and said, "I see." Then he paused. He answered, "Okay, well, yeah, she's a nice girl."

Michael nodded back to him. He said, "Did you fuck her brains out?" His tone was so nonchalant that Shareef had to make sure he heard the man right.

"Ask me that again?"

Michael laughed, amused at his own candor.

He said, "She told me you like to speak from the heart, so go ahead and be you, man. I can't hurt you in here. Them days are long gone for me anyway. That's why I like wearing pure white tees now. I surrendered from all the bullshit. Jealousy. Envy. Hatred. Pride. Anger. All that shit'll end up gettin' you right back in here."

He said, "I know better now. But once you got them years on your back, they gon' make you do at least half of 'em. And I got a whole lot of years left on me for the shit I did out there, playboy. Believe me."

Michael still didn't appear that old. Maybe it was the haircut that made him look so young. He had been in prison for at least ten years already.

Shareef listened to his words while watching the men in the yard who were watching them. He even nodded to those who seemed to recognize him. Even though they had only been together for a few minutes, with armed security guards and other prisoners eyeing their every move, the time between them seemed infinite. Their short walk inside the yard was like a mile long.

"So, what kind of book would you want me to write? A book about a surrender from the street life, and call it, *I Surrender?*" Shareef asked his host.

Michael leaned his head sideways toward the sunny sky and nodded while he thought it over.

He repeated, *"I Surrender."* Then he nodded again. "That's a good fuckin' title right there, playboy. She told me you called yourself a genius."

Michael was grinning from ear to ear, proud as hell of his choice of a writer.

Shareef said, "I'm just using your own words, playboy. That's what a good writer does. He takes the information that's right there in front of him and makes it work." But he couldn't recall telling Cynthia that he thought of himself as a genius. Maybe she had read that somewhere. He surely had said it before, just not to her.

His host said, "Well, yeah, I surrendered, but first we gotta start with the war. You know that."

Suddenly, his demeanor turned back into street warrior mode.

He said, "You get caught up in that shit, man, that lifestyle, and you can't fuckin' sleep. I mean, every hour is like the front line. You gotta have ya' guns ready. 'Cause these motherfuckers are definitely shootin' at you. And I don't mean like real bullets every day, but mental bullets. People plottin' to take you down."

He looked straight into Shareef's mug to make sure he was recording his intensity.

He said, "It's a real human chess game out there, playboy. And I ain't even play chess until I got in this place. But now I play it. Playing wit' these Italian niggas. They funny in here, man. Too many of 'em been watching that *Sopranos* shit."

Shareef smiled, but he was focused at that point, and all about the business of reporting and writing. *I Surrender* was indeed a perfect title. Every prisoner understood that statement. Most had not surrendered voluntarily, but once they had been captured, they were forced to deal with that reality.

He said, "So, how do we start this off? We go back to your childhood years or what?"

He could already see the story taking shape. It would be another *Manchild in the Promised Land*, the classic Harlem autobiography by Claude Brown. Or *Down These Mean Streets*, the Spanish Harlem tale of Piri Thomas. But this one would be more up-to-date from Shareef Crawford, using the on-point ghostwriting styles of Alex Haley and Quincy Troupe. It was all about pulling the most truth from your subject. There were no lies allowed, except for the ones that made the story bigger. Such was the truth of all great books. They were recreations of the largest ideas of humanity. The smaller ideas rarely deserved a book, so they were ignored by the public. The public craved the big dreams. Yet how big could Michael Springfield's dream be? That was the question Shareef would soon have to answer for himself. Was the urban dream of Michael Springfield big enough to re-create?

Michael answered, "I grew up on the West Side at One Twenty-eighth and Amsterdam. I had two older brothers who died in the war before I was even drafted. And I ain't talkin' 'bout no Korea, Vietnam,

Iraq, or no overseas shit like that. I'm talkin' 'bout the wars in Harlem. The motherfuckin' street wars. There needs to be a book about that shit."

He said, "And I ain't talkin' 'bout no rap shit, either. Them attention-gettin' niggas be clownin' our history. So if you gon' talk about it, then you need to get the story right."

"And you got the right story?" Shareef asked him.

Michael looked at him and frowned. "Shit, playboy, you ain't in here by accident. This shit right here is a hustler's destiny."

Shareef asked him, "But how many other hustlers in here could tell it?"

It was a legitimate question. The writer was back in his normal position of authority. He needed to know that the man's words were worth the real deal from his pen.

Michael began to smile, understanding the writer's technique. He had him inside the prison walls, now he had to show and prove.

He looked around at some of the clueless prisoners eyeing them in the yard and responded, "Let's put it this way: if half these motherfuckers could have read your books, studied your style, and masterminded a way to get you in here to talk to them, then they deserve to say something. But since it didn't go down like that, then that's obviously telling you something."

He said, "I read somewhere that victory goes to the man who is most prepared to win. Well, I'm prepared to win. But I can't speak for these other guys. You know what I mean? Let each man speak for himself."

Shareef nodded and was impressed with the man. He could hold his own.

By that time they had walked nearly the entire yard and were approaching the gates at the far end. Cynthia was still following behind them, close enough to be in their party, but far enough away to stay out of their business.

Shareef stopped walking and said, "So, if we're gon' make this all happen, then I need you to make notes on your chronology; what came first, what came second, what came third, the whole nine. That makes it easier for us to organize. And we go step by step, chapter by chapter, day by day. It's a long process."

Michael paused and nodded back to him. He said, "Well, all I got is time in this place, playboy. I ain't goin' nowhere. We got years to put this shit together."

No they didn't, either. Shareef was an impatient writer. He would want the story yesterday. Last week. Last year. Then he could take his time with it. That was the major difference between fiction and non-fiction. In fiction, you could create from your own recollections and the recollections of others on your own time. But with this story, he had to wait to hear from his subject first—he was on some one else's time. So how many visits would it take him to get it all?

Shareef extended his hand anyway. He said, "We'll work it out." That's when the reality hit him, inside the far gate of the yard in the New York State correctional facility where eyes were always watching them.

Michael Springfield shook his hand in agreement, while Shareef wondered what would be the final result of all of his time, toil, and research. How many hours, days, and nights would he spend away from his wife, mistress, and kids in Florida to write this story? And how much would he be paid for it? Those were all real concerns.

Michael smiled again and whispered. "You still didn't answer my question, though, Shareef. How did she feel?"

He was back to asking about Cynthia again. Shareef began to wonder if Michael had had private time with her on any of her visits. He assumed that the man had, but he blocked that thought from his mind. How many degrees of connection did he care to confirm?

He answered, "Some things just ain't meant to be talked about like that, man. Maybe I'm just old school."

Michael studied his calm reserve and nodded to him. The man was telling the truth. It wasn't his M.O. to fuck and give names. Shareef was the private party thrower. He only wrote from his ideas, rarely from actualities.

Michael said, "Okay, I can respect that. I don't know nothing either then. That's loyalty."

He raised his fist and pumped it forward.

Shareef grinned and accepted the man's show of respect. Respect was a good thing. They could build from there on equal footing.

WHEN SHAREEF and Cynthia left the state prison and headed to the bus stop to return to Harlem, she asked him, "So, what do you think?"

Shareef was still pulling all the details together in his mind, trying to remind himself where the story begins: *I grew up on the West Side of Harlem at 128th and Amsterdam.*

Then he responded to Cynthia's question.

"It was interesting," he told her. That's all he wanted to say about it. Anything more would tax too much of his concentration. He wanted to slip back into his zone of deep thought. It was the way he worked. The world could all go to hell while he was thinking, because thinking was his heaven—as much a heaven as great sex.

Cynthia read as much from him and left him to his thoughts. But she did grab his hand at the bus stop. She liked him, and she wanted to remind him of that. Michael Springfield had even given her a second okay to fuck him as she pleased. He respected the man that much. And he realized that a private man would not intentionally hurt her.

Back in Harlem

EARLY IN THE AFTERNOON, two brown-skinned East Indian men walked toward a run-down, storefront off Adam Clayton Powell Boulevard, north of 125th Street. The shorter and older man in front, graying hair on the edges, pulled out a ring of keys from his beige khakis as the younger, taller man followed close behind him. They were fifty-something and thirty-something in age, respectively.

"This is a good location here, you know, right?" the older man said to his younger friend.

The younger man, adorned in gold jewelry, was more interested in seeing it all and hearing the price tags of business first.

He nodded quickly and said, "Yeah, let me see, let me see it."

"I'm gonna let you see it," the older man fussed at him. "That's what we're here for."

"Yeah, yeah," the younger man repeated in haste.

As soon as they got the heavy front door open, a whiff of repugnant air rushed into their noses.

"Shit, what is that smell?" the younger man asked immediately. He raised his right hand over his nose to protect it from the foulness. "It smells like a dead cat and dog in here."

The older man was hesitant as he walked farther into the empty

137

store to investigate. Sitting in the center of the open floor was a dead man strapped to a chair with duct tape who had been shot to death.

The younger man saw that and cursed even louder.

"*Shit!*"

The older man was more poised. He slowly raised his right hand to cover his nose.

"Fuck me," he cursed himself. He thought, *This is the last thing I needed right now.*

WHEN THE NYPD ARRIVED at the scene, they had a million questions for the older man.

"When was the last time you were here?"

He answered, "I've been out of the country for three, four weeks. I come back to renovate, sell, or rent out the building. I opened the front door with my key, and I find this . . . this man sitting there in the chair, shot to death, just like that."

Several officers studied the tortured body in the chair as they continued to ask the older man questions. The younger man kept his distance near the front door. He tried to catch the fresh air while he continued to cover his nose.

"Did anyone know you were leaving the country?"

"Yes, all of my employees who work at my dry cleaners down the street."

"You have a list of those employees?"

He said, "Of course."

Another officer inspected the kicked-in door at the back.

"Did you know that this back door was broken?"

"Well, I know it now, but it was not broken when I last left here."

The older man was clearly agitated by it all. The incident could cost him hundreds of thousands of dollars in resale value.

"Is this the only property you own?"

The man became hesitant. He didn't want to answer that question.

He said, "Well, I own a few . . . a few other properties, but not anymore in Harlem. Why?"

The officers became more interested by the minute.

"Are there employees at these other properties?"

"Well, of course," he answered. He said, "I own a few Indian grocery stores, and a restaurant, but not in Harlem."

"Well, where are these other properties?"

"Ah, near Midtown. But what does that have to do with this?"

"Do any of those, ah, employees, know that you have this property?"

"No."

"Are you sure?"

"What do you mean, am I sure? Of course, I'm sure. What are you trying to say, that one of my employees did this?"

He surely didn't want to accuse anyone in particular with black, white, and Latino officers in the room. There were six officers there in all, and more were on their way, including a coroner and a crime scene unit.

"Well, they at least knew that you were out of the country, right? And who's to say that none of them ever saw you walk in here with the keys? You said your dry-cleaning business is down the street, right?"

The case was elementary to the officers. Someone knew he was going out of the country, knew the property would be empty, and they knew no one would find a dead body inside until the owner returned. That line of information was more than just a coincidence.

One of the officers looked toward the younger Indian man and asked, "Is he one of your employees, too? Or he doesn't count?"

"No, he does not work for me," the older man answered. "He was interested in buying this property. I was showing it to him."

"Is that right? Did he know how long you were gonna be out of the country, too?"

That question sounded incriminating.

The younger Indian man decided to speak up and defend himself immediately.

He said, "I had never even seen this place before."

"Did he tell you where it was?"

"No. I just knew it was in Harlem," he answered. "There are a million different storefronts in Harlem. What are you trying to say? This is bullshit!" he cursed the officers as more of them showed up on the scene. A few plainclothes detectives walked in.

"You do not think that we had anything to do with this, do you?" the older man asked them all. "I can not believe you believe that." He wanted to give the officers the benefit of the doubt. He strongly believed in American justice.

The younger man, however, repeated, "This is bullshit! I don't have to take this." He was deeply offended. He said, "I am a legitimate businessman. And I will tell my lawyer *everything*."

One of the detectives told him, "Look, calm down, sir, we're all just doing our jobs in here. Now there are certain questions that we need to ask."

"Well, you can ask the rest of them with my *lawyer*," the younger man snapped again.

The detective shook his head and knew it was going to be a long night.

SHAREEF AND CYNTHIA walked out of the subway station at 125th and Lenox Avenue at close to six o'clock that evening, and into a human flood of summer foot traffic. Folks were everywhere in Harlem—short ones, tall ones, hairy ones, bald ones, men, women, children, foreigners. Shareef hadn't witnessed the carnival-like atmosphere in his Harlem hometown in years. He smiled with his head bouncing left to right to left, as if following a tennis match.

Cynthia took in his glee and grinned at him.

"You haven't been up in Harlem in a while, hunh?"

He said, "Nah, I've only been doing bookstore events up here for the last few years. Either that or taking my grandparents out to eat somewhere. So no, I haven't seen this in a while."

Cynthia looked across the street to Starbucks Coffee at the corner.

"You want some coffee? My treat."

Shareef eyed the coffee shop sitting right in the center of things, but he still wasn't a coffee drinker. He was hungry instead.

He shook his head and answered, "Nah, I want something to eat."

"Sylvia's Restaurant is right up the street," she told him. "But I want to get some coffee right quick first."

As they crossed the busy Harlem street in the direction of Starbuck's, Shareef looked through the glass window and into an already crowded line.

"I don't know how quick you plan to get it, but it looks like you're about to be waiting for a while."

"Yeah, it's always crowded in here."

"Get the real deal, the truth from the streets. The black man is in a crisis!" they both heard at the same time.

The Spear was out in his military garb, selling his books up and down the Harlem streets again.

Shareef caught his eye and nodded to him.

The Spear nodded back, then he looked at Cynthia.

"What are y'all, writing a book together now?" he asked sarcastically.

"Nah, we just hanging out?" Shareef answered.

The book-hustling man doubted that. They were doing more than hanging out. They looked too comfortable together.

Right before The Spear could respond, a group of girls in their late teens stopped right in front of them all.

"Ay, aren't you Shareef Crawford? I just got your book."

"The new one or an old one?" Shareef asked the girl in the middle of her crew of four.

"Um, *Chocolate Candy,* or something like that."

"*Chocolate Lovers,*" he corrected her. "That's one of my old ones."

"Well, I have two of your other books, too. I can't remember all the names."

One of her girlfriends spoke up to help her out.

"*I Want More* and *Man to Woman*," the friend stated. She smiled and said, "We all read 'em. We take turns."

Shareef nodded and said, "That's good, as long as you read it." He would have told them to buy their own books, but not in front of a rival author out there pushing his work on the street. It seemed disrespectful and unnecessary.

The Spear, however, already felt disrespected. He had heard enough. So he butted in and said, "Well, I have a new book right here, sisters. It's about the black man in the real struggle. *The Streets Keep Calling Me,*" he told them.

The girls were barely willing to pay him any mind with Shareef standing there in front of them. One girl picked up one of the books only to look at the cover jacket, nod, and hand it back to him.

"Only ten dollars, sister."

"I don't have it."

"Well, how much did y'all pay for his books?" The Spear asked them.

Now he was being disrespectful to Shareef.

Shareef told the girls, "Well, keep reading," and prepared to walk off with Cynthia into Starbuck's.

"Aren't you from Harlem?" another one of the girls asked him.

Shareef nodded and moved on, "Yeah."

"Well, bye, Shareef Crawford," the girls told him as he walked off.

The Spear shook his head and let it ride. He was poised to move on to the next potential customers who were walking by. The hustle was the hustle.

"Get the real deal, the truth from the streets. The black man is in a crisis!"

As they entered the coffee shop, Cynthia smiled at Shareef and said, "He's jealous of you."

"Of course he is," Shareef told her. "That's just human nature. I'd be jealous of me if I was him, too. But I put in my dues. I'm not just some fly-by-night author. I got a degree in writing."

As Cynthia stepped in line, an old grade school nemesis of Shareef's was just getting his coffee at the front.

He turned with his coffee and cake in a brown bag, spotted Shareef, and addressed him immediately.

"Shareef Crawford, the big-time writer."

The man moved his coffee and brown bag to his left hand to extend his right for a shake. He was so forward in his greeting that Shareef was forced to accept it despite their history of opposition and several fistfights, the last of which Shareef had won.

"Jurrell Garland," he responded, *the big-time hoodlum.* Shareef kept this added thought to himself. The Jurrell Garland he knew from nearly fifteen years ago was more than just a thug and a hustler. The Jurrell Garland he knew robbed and assaulted thugs and hustlers.

Jurrell was pure hoodlum, as sinister a street terrorist as you could get. And Shareef was unfortunate enough to attend nine straight years of school with him, from kindergarten through eighth grade. Now Jurrell looked civilized. He was dressed like an average behind-the-counter retail manager, not too fancy, but more than casual. And he was drinking Starbuck's coffee even.

As they shook hands, Shareef noticed that his nemesis had thickened up in the body since he saw him last on the Harlem streets. Jurrell had also done time in prison for just about everything: assault, manslaughter, narcotics, illegal weapons, bribery—the list went on.

He looked Shareef in the eyes and said, "I'm not involved in any of the stuff I used to be involved in, Shareef. I mean, you just get older and you grow up from all of that, you know."

He said, "I served my time, and I changed my ways. I sell cell phones for a living now."

It was as if he was reading Shareef's mind. Nevertheless, Jurrell realized that everyone who knew him knew his history. His rap sheet was far too long to forget or to ignore. So he had to explain his new way of life often. His speech was even different. There was no more street swagger or slang on his tongue.

He addressed Cynthia with a nod.

"How are you?"

She smiled pleasantly. "I'm fine."

"That's good to hear, sister. You look fine, too."

"Thank you."

He said, "I'm only telling the truth. Shareef always had good taste in women." Then he focused back on Shareef. "So, what are you doing back up in Harlem, man? You got a book event?"

Shareef was still in minor shock. He couldn't believe Jurrell had changed that drastically.

He said, "Nah, I'm up here, ah, doing some research."

"Research on what? You writing a book on Harlem now?"

Shareef was still hesitant to reveal too much. But the man was right in his face and asking him questions with all sincerity.

"Yeah, a little something, you know. I just haven't been up here in a while."

Jurrell nodded to him. He said, "A lot of things are changed in Harlem now. It ain't about that street life no more. It's about moving on up. And if you're not moving on up, then you're moving on out of Harlem. It's a new ball game now. I'm just trying to stay in the game.

"Yeah, so you was down in Atlanta last, right, at Morehouse?" he asked him, changing the subject.

Shareef began to wonder how much they still knew about each other.

"Yeah," he answered, keeping everything short. He needed to decide how much he wanted to trust Jurrell.

"You get involved in that music game at all down there in Atlanta? They're blowing up now, ain't they? T.I., Young Jeezy, Lil John. You didn't try to write any songs for any of those singers down there, little girls like Ciara?"

Shareef said, "I actually did try to write a few songs. But the whole political game just killed my interest in it."

"What, with certain people wanting to write?"

Shareef wondered how many questions Jurrell was planning on asking him as the line moved up.

He said, "Yeah, you got managers in the way, labels that want brand names, singers who want to write their own shit. It was just too much of a hassle, man. So I let it go."

Jurrell nodded to him again. He said, "Well, I don't want to hold you up, man. It's just good seeing you again. Seeing you and knowing how big you've made it, just gives me inspiration. I mean, we were in the same classrooms together for years."

He smiled and stuck out his hand again. Shareef shook it a second time. And before Jurrell left, he offered him his business card.

"Look, if you need any help on your research, or on anything, just call me up while you're here. Because you know I know everything," he added with a grin. "But some of these young bloods I talk to nowadays don't want to believe it. They all wanna find out the hard way. So call me up, man. Let's talk.

"And oh, nice meeting you," he addressed Cynthia.

"Same here."

As soon as he was gone, Cynthia asked Shareef, "You know him?" She seemed surprised by it.

He grinned at her. He said, "I'm still trying to figure that out myself. But like he said, we went to school together. Why? What do you know about him?"

She had already ordered her coffee. They were waiting for it at the end of the counter.

She answered, "I don't know that much about him, but whenever I see him, he seems to get a lot of respect around here."

Cynthia had told Shareef that she was originally from White Plains, and that she had only lived in Harlem for a few years. So she was still figuring out who was who and what was what.

Shareef nodded to her.

He said, "Yeah, well, if you did the kinds of things he did, people are gonna either respect you or want to kill you. So, if they're not trying to kill him, then they're damn sure gonna respect him. And that's all I need to say about it."

Cynthia tested her cappuccino and asked him the next question.

"Was he as popular on the streets as Michael Springfield?"

Shareef shook his head in the negative. "Nah, popular is not the word I would use for him. I would call him more *infamous*. Because you didn't even want to say his name."

She tasted her coffee again as they walked out and said, "But he looks so, you know, *normal*. I would even say he looks handsome."

Shareef had to chuckle at that. He said, "That's what got me so confused. I mean, Jurrell was never really an ugly person in the face, he was just ugly in the mind. Because his mom looked *good* coming up to the school offices. I still remember that. It's just that he never tried to look good on his own. He was too busy being a fuckin' villain.

"So now that I see him all cleaned up and civil-looking, the shit is just weird, man," he told her. "It's just weird."

Cynthia said, "Well, I hate to run while you get something to eat, but I have some things to catch up on. I like changed my entire schedule to make today happen for you."

He said, "Cool, go do what you gotta do. I'm tired of seeing your face for this long anyway," he joked to her.

She stopped him and said, "Watch it now. That's exactly how a guy pisses a woman off, and then he wonders why she doesn't want to give him none later on."

Shareef froze and thought about it. Immediately, she had him thinking about his wife again.

He asked, "Is that right? So, I need to be nice at all costs, hunh?"

"If you know what's good for you."

"Well, what if a woman still won't give it to you even when you're nice to her?"

She took another sip of her coffee and answered, "Either she doesn't like you like that, or she doesn't trust you enough yet to be intimate."

Shareef nodded and sucked up the woman's knowledge.

"Thanks."

"Don't mention it," she told him. "Now run along and get yourself some soul food from Sylvia's, and I'll call you later tonight so we can plan to go back up north on Friday."

"Aw'ight, I'll talk to you later then."

SHAREEF TOOK A SEAT ALONE in Sylvia's Restaurant at 127th and Lenox, where he ordered fish, greens, yams, and rice with gravy. For his drink, he ordered lemonade. While waiting for his order to arrive at his small, two-person table set by the left wall, he went ahead and called his wife and children in Florida.

"Hello," Jennifer answered.

"How was your day today?" he asked her. Civility was the best model of repair.

She said, "We're running late for football practice."

Shareef paused. *It figures,* he told himself. He shook his head at the table with his cell phone in hand and didn't say a word about it. *Even without a job, and with all day to prepare for it, she still manages to run late for everything. I just can't understand this woman.*

Anyway, "Outside of that, how did the rest of your day go? He'll get to practice."

"Do you really . . ." Jennifer started and stopped herself. The kids were still in the car with her. She said, "Shareef, Kimberly, your father's on the phone."

Yeah, leave it alone, Shareef told himself. Their marriage seemed like a lost cause.

"Hey, Dad. We got our first scrimmage next week against the Raiders. Will you be there?"

"What day?"

"Thursday."

"Yeah, I'll be there," he told his son.

"And I might be the starting running back now, Dad. But the coach won't say yet."

Shareef raised his brow. "Running back? I thought you were playing wide receiver?"

"I was, but at practice yesterday they moved me to running back because nobody could tackle me. And I ran for like three touchdowns on eight carries."

"Shit," Shareef told him. "I mean, good. That's real good," he corrected himself. *He'll be a real star at running back. But not if he's late for practice every day.*

"Do you know all of the plays?" Shareef asked him.

"Most of them. But now I have to study them again."

"Yeah, I bet you do. Well, I look forward to that. Are you excited?"

"Yeah. I'll get the ball a lot now. I wish I was at practice now. But um, we're like late all the time."

Shareef could tell that his son didn't want to say it. His mother was probably staring at him, too. But he could hear that the phone call had cheered his son up.

He probably had his lips poked out a mile before I called, Shareef assumed with a grin. But his grin quickly turned into a frown. *And if I'm not around to get him to practice on time, it's only going to make his attitude worse.*

Shit! he cursed his dilemma. *I got work to do. But now I gotta have this shit on my mind.*

He told his son, "Hey, look, J, it'll all work out. Maybe you can start getting a ride to practice with one of your friends."

"But nobody on the team lives near us."

That was probably true. Shareef had gone out of his way to have his son play for the Jaguars just so he could be teammates with boys his own color. He figured it was important for his son to be able to connect to the victories and struggles of being an African American. The earlier he did so in his youth, the better. The memories of a man's childhood were the strongest, even for Shareef Sr., growing up in Harlem.

"Well, we'll figure something out," he responded. "And in the meantime, just try to . . . try to get along, Shareef. Just do what you're told to do."

The words came slowly only because the father felt hypocritical about them. He didn't stick around and just get along, or do what he was told to do. When the going got too tough, Shareef Sr. found a new place to live, breathe, and dream. Now he was telling his son to do the opposite.

When he gets old enough, he'll make his own decisions about life. But for now, he's just a boy, Shareef rationalized. He figured a lot of decisions adults were forced to make for their kids were hypocritical. Hypocrisy was a natural part of parenthood. You couldn't have your kids knowingly doing what you did in your own reckless youth. That would be insane. What if Shareef had been involved in the same destructive nonsense that his biological parents had been involved in? He still never even talked about them. And he wouldn't.

"When are you getting back from New York?" his son asked him.

"Early next week."

"You wanna talk to Kimberly now?"

"Of course I do."

His daughter answered the phone. "Hey, Daddy," and her voice melted him. What was it about his girl that made his heart flutter so much? For the son he felt proud, boastful, authoritative, and protective. He wanted nothing to happen to his little boy. He wanted the world for him. But for his daughter, the world just stopped moving and stood still when she spoke.

"Hey, baby girl. You miss me?"

"Yeah, I miss you. I love you," she told him.

He said, "I love you, too. And I'll be back home to see you next week."

"Will you spend the night?"

Shareef paused and took a deep breath. Separating from a loving family was hard to do.

What the hell, he told himself. *She only gets a chance to live once. But what if she gets spoiled by it and wants me to do it all of the time?*

"Yeah, I'll spend the night," he told his daughter anyway. Jennifer never denied him visitation rights. He could stay as long as he wanted to. It was still his house. And they were still officially married. He just couldn't bother her until whatever differences they had were settled.

"Daddy said he's spending the night," his daughter announced to her mother and brother in the car.

Shareef overheard her and shook his head again. He was spoiling his daughter the same way that millions of other daughters were spoiled. He only told her yes because he knew it would make her feel good. It was a decision of emotions over reason. But the reality was that Shareef and Jennifer were only living on borrowed time as a couple. Only a miracle could hold them together in peace, a miracle that Kimberly and Shareef Jr. prayed for every night.

When Jennifer reclaimed the phone from her daughter, she said, "We'll need to talk." That's all she needed to say. Shareef knew the program. He would have to explain why he continued to make spontaneous decisions that created more family confusions.

"Yeah, I know," he mumbled as his food arrived.

A spontaneous life was what he wanted sometimes. As a professional writer, he had enough planning, plotting, and scripting in his life as it was. Spontaneity was that added spice that kept his blood pumping. It was the reason he was back in Harlem in the first place. A return to Harlem was something brand new, exotic, and different.

Jennifer needed some spontaneity back in her life. And he would tell her so when they talked again in private.

Shareef ended the call with his wife and family and dug right into his food, like he had never eaten before.

"Excuse me, I hate to bother you while you're eating, but could you sign my book before you leave?"

Shareef looked up and smiled to a black woman in her thirties with his mouthful of food. Then he nodded to her.

"Oh, thank you so much," she told him. "I just missed when you were up here last month at Hue-Man."

He mumbled, "All right. I got you when I'm finished eating."

"Thank you, and I'll just leave you alone to finish your dinner."

As soon as the woman left and returned to her table, Shareef had an incoming call on his cell. He looked down and read the Miami area code and phone number of his mistress.

Should I answer this now or call her back? he pondered. Then again, Jacqueline had the keys to his condo for the week, and there may have been an emergency that he needed to handle, or at least know about right away.

"Hello," he answered.

She said, "You know I haven't heard from you in more than twenty-four hours. I mean, you could have at least called me to say that you had made it to New York safely."

"Or, you could have called me."

"Well, I didn't want to seem like I was bothering you, but still . . ."

"You know what? I love you, too," he told her out of the blue. Be nice at all costs was on his mind. Cynthia had just taught him that less than an hour earlier.

Jacqueline said, "If you loved me that much, you would have taken me with you."

"But that's *why* I didn't take you with me this time," he told her. "I had to visit a damn prison this morning. I don't want you around that. And tonight I'll be around old thugs and street criminals. I'm even staying at a run-down hotel."

He said, "I don't want you coming to New York with me like that. I want you to have all the best when I bring you here. And I want to have time for you."

Jacqueline paused and asked him the question that had been lingering on her mind since the moment he left for New York without her.

"Do you have a woman up there in Harlem?"

"What? Look, I'm not up here to do that. I'm up here to do research for a new book. In fact, when you asked me about Harlem that morning, you were the one who solidified the idea in my mind."

"Yeah, and you also told me that you would take me there. Or were you just talking about the fucking part?"

Shareef had to pause for a moment.

He said real calmly, "I'm eating dinner right now, Jacqueline."

"With who?"

Right as she asked him that, one of the waiters was walking past his table. Shareef reached out and tapped him on the arm to get his attention.

"Yeah, you need something?"

Shareef immediately handed him his cell phone.

"Could you tell the woman on the phone who I'm sitting with."

The man in short dreads and a long white apron held the phone up to his ear and smiled.

He answered, "Hello."

Shareef said, "Just tell her who I'm sitting with, man."

"Actually, he's dining alone."

Then he listened.

"This is Sylvia's Restaurant on Lenox."

He listened again as Shareef waited.

"Yeah, I would say so. I love working here."

He looked down at Shareef sitting in his chair and grinned. Shareef went right back to stuffing his mouth with his food.

The waiter said, "Yeah, he's pretty cool." Then he shook his head, "Nah, I'll have to pass on that. But I have to get back to work now."

He handed Shareef the phone back and whispered, "She asked me to blow you a kiss for her, but I don't get down like that, brother."

Shareef shook his head and mumbled, "I don't either. But thanks, man. These women be trippin' out here."

"Hey, man, hold it down however you have to. That's all we can all do."

Shareef swallowed his food, got back on the phone, and asked Jacqueline, "Are you happy now?"

"You're crazy," she told him with a chuckle.

"And you asked him to blow me a kiss?"

"Well, if you're gonna act crazy, then I'm gonna act crazy."

"Oh, so if I jumped off a bridge, you're gonna do that, too, right?"

"Only for you."

She froze him with that answer. Shareef thought about how exotic Jacqueline was and how great it felt to be up inside her, and he started getting hard under the table.

"So, are you still wet for me?"

She laughed and said, "You know I am. But you're all the way up in New York."

He said, "Well, put it in the icebox for me. You know where that is, right? It's inside the kitchen."

She laughed again and said, "You know I'm gonna get you when you get back home. I'm gonna buy some tropical-flavored Popsicles, too."

Shareef had food in his mouth when she said that and almost choked on it. He coughed and had to catch himself before his fish with hot sauce and yams went down the wrong pipe.

He mumbled, "Can you take something like that?"

"I'll try it," she told him.

"Well, shit, I can't wait to get back home either then. But let me finish my dinner, because I haven't eaten anything all day."

"Okay, well, I love you, too, Poppi."

Shareef grinned and said, "Now you know I love when you call me that."

She giggled. "That's why I don't say it too much. I don't want to ever wear it out. I feel like it's a woman's job to keep things fresh, you know."

He nodded, in full agreement with her. "Yeah. I know exactly what you mean. And that's exactly how I want it. Fresh."

When he finished the call with his mistress, after just hanging up with his wife, Shareef thought, *There's no way in the world I'm going back to Jennifer with girls like Jacqueline around. Unless they don't want me no more.*

Crossing Paths

THE YOUNG HARLEMITE known as Baby G sat absent-mindedly in the passenger side of his squad's black Mercedes CLK convertible. It was parked on the sidewalk at 122nd Street beside Marcus Garvey Park. He and his bodyguard/driver were simply enjoying the summertime. And while he appeared lost in thought, Baby G actually knew everything that was going on around him, like a super villain with super senses. So as he felt his street soldier approaching the car from behind, he casually looked into the sideview mirror to confirm it.

"What, you trying to assassinate me, man? Fuck you sneaking up beside the car for?"

His beefy bodyguard/driver reached for his pistol tucked deep under his seat.

Baby G looked at him said, "Man, I would have been dead already if I waited that long to tell you. Fuck you reaching for this late? Put that shit back down and be ready next time. You need more practice pulling that shit out quickly anyway."

He looked back at his soldier, who was standing at attention outside the door of the car and said, "What's up, man? What you got to tell me?"

The boy couldn't have been more than eighteen, but he was loyal. Loyalty was written all over his stern, young face. He loved being part

154

of a unit. And when he could speak to the young general, Baby G, in person, with valuable information, it made him feel valuable. He felt like a Green Beret with a special mission to bring back information from the enemy's front line.

He said, "They finally found that body today, son. I saw like thirty five-ohs and detectives all up in there."

Baby G nodded to him and took the information in calmly.

He asked, "Don't nobody know shit, right?"

His soldier shook his head, "No, sir. We don't know nothin'."

"We don't have nothing to worry about then. Just keep ya' cool."

Baby G then dug into his roll of green cheese and pulled out a hundred-dollar bill.

He said, "You doin' all right today?"

His young soldier saw the money and answered, "I'm good. I don't need that from you. It's just love for the team."

Baby G paused and looked his young soldier in the eyes.

He said, "That's the right answer. It's always about love for the team. And why is that?"

"Love for the team is the only way we win," his soldier answered.

"That's right. Now take this money and know that I'm good to you."

The soldier remained hesitant.

Baby G said, "Look, man, don't make my motherfuckin' arm fall off. Take the money."

His soldier finally cracked a grin and took the hundred-dollar bill.

Baby G told him, "That's ya' bonus for good work. When you work hard, you should be paid for it. But if you don't, then don't expect shit back. Does that sound fair to you?"

The young soldier nodded. "Yes, sir."

"Good. You dismissed now. Go on back out there and do some more work."

"Aw'ight, son," the soldier commented and started to move.

"Ay," Baby G called him back.

The soldier hustled right back over to the car and stood at attention again.

The general told him, "You still young, man, but I like you. So here's what I'ma do. I'ma give you something extra. A little bit of wisdom on ya' dome."

He said, "All that little money you get from me. It's nothin'. And when you spend it fast, it get even smaller. So what you do, right, is keep that shit. And you let it stack up. Then you start looking at setting bigger goals for yourself. *Always* have goals. 'Cause if you out here spendin' up money with no goals, then it's like sand blowing out your fuckin' hand in the wind. You dig me?"

The soldier nodded his head to him.

Baby G continued. He said, "You got a big advantage while you still young. You don't have no babies, do you?"

The soldier shook his head and frowned. "Naw."

The general said, "Me either. So while you don't have no kids, no bills, no car, no credit, that's the best time for you to stack ya' cake. And *please* don't let your family know you got no money. They the last people you want to know. 'Cause all of a sudden, they sick on the job and shit, and lookin' at you for health benefits. You know what I'm talkin' 'bout?"

He said, "They start coming up with all kinds of emergencies and shit. And they be needin' exactly how much you got in your pocket. So if you got four hundred dollars in your pocket, ya' sister'll need three hundred and ninety. And if you got a thousand, your mom'll be late for rent and need groceries. But you know you can't turn your mom dukes down. So you gotta get in a habit of saying you broke."

The young soldier started laughing, but Baby G wasn't finished with him yet.

He said, "Let me hear you say it."

"I'm broke," the young soldier told him.

The general looked at him and frowned. "Nah, man, you gotta say it like you mean it. I wouldn't believe you with that shit. You gotta say it like, 'I'm *broke*, man, I ain't got it.' And then you raise up your hands like Jesus, and pull at your pockets. Let me see you do it."

The young soldier did a better job of it. He said, "I'm *broke*, man, I ain't got it." He raised up his empty palms, pulled at his pockets and everything.

Baby G smiled and said, "That's more like it, B. That's why I don't like my family now. I wish somebody taught me this shit when I was your age. Now I feel like I'm everybody's daddy. And shit, my name ain't Puffy."

The young soldier started laughing again. But he was taking every word of it to heart. The general was spending extra time with him. That was special in itself. So he planned on heeding the wisdom.

Baby G asked him, "You hear me on this, man?"

"Yes, sir."

They looked each other in the eyes before the general nodded him off.

"Aw'ight, you can go now."

"Are you sure?" the soldier asked him.

Baby G said, "Yeah, I'm sure, man. Now get on out of here."

The soldier chuckled. "Yes, sir, thanks for schoolin' me."

When he walked off on his way toward 123rd Street and beyond, Baby G stared at the boy's back for a minute.

He looked over at his bodyguard/driver and said, "You see how he looked at me, man?"

His beefy driver nodded. He said, "Yeah. He was taking you to heart."

"That's the way it should be. But everybody don't take it like that, man. But that boy right there, I'ma call him The Truth from now on. T for short. And I'ma see if he live by what I just told him."

His bodyguard said, "He will. I can see it in him."

Right then, Baby G's cell phone went off. He looked down at the screen and noticed the undisclosed number.

"Hello," he answered.

The caller said, "I read the Harlem newspapers today. Did you get a chance to read them?"

Baby G asked him, "Was it something about a month ago?"

"Yeah, that's what it was. And I don't like that shit. But it's done now. But I'm a tell you what . . . I don't wanna read no more shit like that. You hear me? Let me write that shit my way."

Baby G smiled at it. He said, "I got you. Thanks for the call. It's always good to hear from you."

The caller responded, "Ditto," and that was the end of the conversation.

Baby G closed his cell phone and asked his driver, "So, what's poppin' off tonight?"

"Anything you want. This is your world," his bodyguard/driver told him.

"Well, we gon' need that bigger car then."

"The Chrysler three hundred?"

"Yeah, 'cause I wanna pick up some more girls tonight."

"Aw'ight, let's go get it."

The driver started up the Mercedes engine, backed up, turned the wheel, and pulled out into the street.

As soon as they made it to the first traffic light, another phone call came in. The second call was from a regular Manhattan street phone with a 212 area code.

Baby G answered, "Hello."

"Yo, I got news for you, B," the caller announced.

"Is it old news?"

"Yup."

"Well, you late already. I already got that news a month ago. So, bring me something new."

The caller paused. "Aw'ight," he responded dejectedly.

Baby G heard the disappointment in his voice. He said, "You did good, son. You just a little late with the info. So, you stay on your grind and keep your eyes and ears open. You don't need no hearing aid or glasses, do you?"

The caller chuckled and said, "Nah, I'm good."

"Well, keep up your exercise and stay healthy. That's all you need to do," the young general advised him.

When he ended this call, Baby G told his bodyguard/driver, "A hustler's job never ends, B. You always on ya' toes."

His beefy driver nodded from behind the wheel.

He said, "Donald Trump's job ain't never done, either. Nor is that Martha Stewart chick's. She even ran her shit from jail."

Baby G got excited and said, "Yeah, she did, didn't she? Martha Stewart went to jail, started making quilts and ponchos, came right back out on TV, and sold that shit."

He said, "Now that's a fuckin' hustler, B. Word up."

BY NINE O'CLOCK THAT NIGHT, Polo and Spoonie had scooped Shareef up from his hotel. They were more prepared to run that night.

Shareef asked them from the front passenger seat, "Where's Trap?"

"He had some other shit to do tonight," Polo answered, wearing an oversized blue velvet cool cap. He said, "But you know how that nigga is. He get on his own little missions and he don't talk to nobody about it. He always been that way."

Polo thought about it for minute. He said, "Matter of fact, you again get like that yourself sometimes, Shareef. You did that shit to us last night."

"Yeah, but you knew where I was goin'," Shareef responded with a grin. His friend had read his mission correctly the night before.

Polo told him, "You damn right I knew. But it wasn't like you was trying to volunteer the information to us."

Spoonie was in the backseat checking messages on his BlackBerry.

Shareef asked him, "Why you so quiet back there, man?"

Spoonie didn't answer. He was that much into his messages.

Polo glanced to the back and said, "He back there on that Black-Berry."

Spoonie continued not to respond.

Shareef said, "Modern technology is something else, ain't it? It won't be long before we're talking to each other face-to-face on like, mirror phones. You just dial a number, hold the shit in front of your face, and talk right into it."

Spoonie said, "Yeah, then I can show a broad how hard my dick is on those late-night booty calls. I'll tell her ass, 'Look, my dick don't get much harder than this.' "

Polo laughed and said, "Oh, he heard that shit, hunh? Perverted ass nigga."

"That ain't perverted. It's just personal porno," Spoonie responded.

Shareef grinned and said, "Aw'ight, so where we headed to first tonight?"

"We just wanna show you all the different little spots up here now. Some of 'em you already know, but others are like new hangouts," Polo told him.

They pulled up first outside The Lounge on Adam Clayton Powell.

"This place still open?" Shareef asked them. "I remember the old-timers used to swing up in here when we were still too young to use the bathroom."

"Well, we the old-timers now," Spoonie told him as they climbed out of the Bronco.

Shareef said, "Shit, we ain't that damn old. They were listening to disco up in here."

Polo said, "Yeah, that's what they listened to in the seventies. But they were in their twenties and thirties back then, just like we are now."

"Yeah, I guess your right," Shareef conceded as they walked in.

The old establishment was lit with neon blue light and had silver wall panels. A mix of new wave jazz and funk was pumping out of the stereo system, while customers in their thirties, forties, and fifties drank at the bar, shot pool, and talked shit to one another. A few of them even utilized the small dance floor to twist hips, dip shoulders, and vibe to the music.

"If you ain't drinkin', you can get the hell out," one of the bartenders snapped from behind the counter. She was a tall, heavyset woman in her early fifties, with short, honey-blond hair.

Polo chuckled and looked at Shareef. Shareef smiled back at him.

"Ain't nobody playing up in here," the bartender continued. "I'm at this bar ready to take your drink orders right now. So what are you drinking?"

Spoonie made it over to the counter first, "Give me a rum and Coke."

"Now that's what I'm talking about. I like you already," she told him. She went right to work on his drink order.

Polo and Shareef slid up to the bar next.

"And what are you two having?"

Polo looked at Shareef and said, "Give us two Long Islands. You still drink that?"

Shareef nodded to him. "Sweet and powerful, that's all I drink."

They started sipping their drinks, digging the old-timer scene, and getting their early swerve on before Shareef overheard Spoonie tell someone, "Yeah, my man over here writing a book on Harlem. He from here, but he ain't been here in a while. So he coming back to check out all the hot spots and talk to the people again about the new Harlem."

"You mean how they try'na move us the hell out of here again," the bold bartender spat. "They try that shit every ten years."

An older black man dipped in Shareef and Polo's direction and asked, "What you writing a book about, young brother? You writing about the real history of Harlem, or that young, black bullshit."

Shareef could tell the older man was already inebriated. His thin, frail body was already leaning from an overload of alcohol.

Shareef decided to engage him anyway.

"What do you consider young black bullshit?"

The older man explained himself patiently. "Well, it seems to me that . . . a lot of younger guys, when they talk about Harlem, they always wanna talk about the pimps, the hustlers, prostitutes, crime . . . you know, shit like that."

He said, "They never wanna talk about the honest, hardworking families, the mothers and fathers, who make up the vast majority of Harlem. No. They wanna talk about . . . excuse my French here, the fuckups. Basically."

Polo started laughing, but Shareef was giving the man his full attention.

Shareef asked him, "And which book would you read; the book about the fuckups, or the book about the honest, hardworking folk?"

The older man said, "Well, when I get a chance to read . . ."

One of his lady friends at the bar had heard enough already. She said, "Aw, nigga, you don't read nothin'. Stop lyin' and leave that man alone."

Polo thought the whole shit was funny. Being at The Lounge on a good night was better than a comedy show.

The older man argued, "I do read. I've read a lot of books on Harlem. I read about the jazz. Be-bop. Poetry. The Harlem Renaissance. The civil rights movement. Marcus Moziah Garvey's Negro Improvement Organization. The migration from the south."

He said, "See, what a lot of people fail to understand is . . . a lot of the black folks living in Harlem, are actually from the south."

His lady friend interrupted him again. "Well, that ain't shit new," she said. "Everybody know them damn slave ships ain't park in Harlem. We were dropped off in South Carolina, North Carolina, Virginia. Everybody know that."

"No they don't," the brother argued. "This is what they're not teaching in these schools. Furthermore, a boat cannot *park*. A boat *docks*. See. So you need to get your facts right before you open your fat mouth in here."

Polo was laughing his ass off. It was all hilarious.

The lady friend said, "I'll open my fat mouth whenever the hell I please. Unless you gon' pay for another drink to put something in it," she told him.

The man ignored her and went back to his teaching.

He said, "Now . . . the original idea of Harlem, was actually created for wealthy white people. Harlem was Uptown Manhattan, a place where white folks could leave the downtown area."

One of the other brothers at the bar said, "Well, while you in here alcohol-preaching, won't you tell him something he didn't know."

"I'm trying to get to that point if y'all would just shut the hell up. That's exactly what you did in grade school. You interrupted the class, so you ended up failing . . . or dropping out. And then twenty years later, when you don't know shit, and can't get no job, you turn around and blame the white man."

"Aw'ight, Bill Cosby, sit ya' ass down," his lady friend joked from the bar.

That only fueled his fire. He said, "Bill Cosby is *right*. He is *right*! It's up to *us* to change things."

Polo was wiping fresh tears out of his eyes he was laughing so much.

Spoonie told him, "Goddamn, Polo, you only had one drink. Get yourself together, man."

Polo shook his head and ignored him.

Shareef stayed on point. He was focused about his work again. He asked, "So, Harlem was set up for white folks?"

"Yes it was. But mostly West Harlem," the older brother answered. "But what happened was, a lot of white folks bought property farther north and upstate New York, and then out on Long Island, and that left Harlem open. So then black folks started moving in. And once the word got out that Harlem was the place to be . . . well, you know how black folks are. We all wanted to raid the picnic."

All of a sudden, the customers at The Lounge were all in agreement.

Another older brother added his two cents. He wore a tight, black cap plopped on his bush of hair.

He said, "Yeah, and once the new blacks starting moving in who couldn't afford the real estate in West Harlem, they started building homes and the first projects in Central Harlem, and overpricing them."

"They still doin' that shit now," the bartender spoke up again.

"They don't know if they wanna keep us or get rid of us in Harlem, but we ain't goin' nowhere," the man's lady friend at the bar added. "Harlem is home now."

The older brother got back to his point. He said, "Right, so Harlem became the new home for black people. Then you had your Spanish and West Indians moving in, and that created East Harlem."

Someone stated, "But we still have crime here. They found a man tortured and shot to death right up the street in one of those empty storefronts today. It's gonna be in the newspapers tomorrow, if it's not on the news already tonight."

"Is that why they had all those cops out there today?" the bartender asked. She softened up her tough stance behind the bar and looked concerned for her own storefront job and property.

Spoonie heard that and looked at Shareef for his response.

Shareef didn't have one. People got killed every day, and everywhere around the world. It was no shock to him. Friends were shot and killed when he was growing up in Harlem, and he expected those who lived the fast life to continue to die.

Instead of asking about the murder, Shareef asked, "And what about what's going on with these new condos in Harlem now? What are your views on that?"

Shareef had heard about the new Harlem condominium homes from several sources.

The older man answered, "They're going back to their original idea now; Harlem is Uptown for Manhattan white folks. And former president Bill Clinton is leading the movement."

He said, "The average black family around here can't afford no million-dollar condos. So if we don't get our act together, protect what we got, and prepare our kids to compete for the property, they're gonna build right overtop of us, and we'll be scrambling around on the ground while they living up in the sky. Right here in Harlem."

Shareef said, "Well, if we can't afford it, then how are we gonna stop it?"

The bartender answered that question. She said, "Look, we got enough rich black folks with money right now to buy up everything in Harlem, but they too busy chasing around white folks to live where they live. In the meantime, these white folks are turning right around and buying up where you used to live and making it better."

She said, "So, in ten more years, I'm still gonna be here, and I'm gonna have them white folks buying *five* drinks. 'Cause see, they like to *drink*. We like to *talk*."

The older man said, "Well, if ain't nobody talkin', then what kind of lounge you expect to have up in here? I come in here to hear us talk." He said, "Without us talking that talk, walking that walk, and doin' what we do, Harlem just wouldn't be the same.

"That's what makes Harlem special," he commented. "Black people. And don't you ever forget it."

AFTER A COUPLE MORE DRINKS and plenty of conversation about Harlem, Shareef, Polo, and Spoonie made their way out of The Lounge.

Polo said, "You hit the jackpot in there tonight, B. You got all the Harlem history you need. I didn't know half of the shit they were talking about." He chuckled as he opened the doors to his Bronco.

He added, "I guess I was one of them fuckups who didn't get what he was supposed to get out of school."

Spoonie smiled and said, "You and me both."

As they climbed back into the Bronco for their next destination, Shareef was deep in his thoughts again. How big of a book could he write about Harlem? And how did he feel about writing the criminal perspective instead of the historical? Could he do both?

This shit is gonna get complicated, he imagined. *There's just too much to write about in Harlem.*

"What you think about that, Shareef?" Polo asked him from the driver's seat.

"What I think about what?"

"What they had to say in there?"

Shareef said, "I'm still wondering how many of them are gonna read a book, to tell you the truth."

"If you write about them they'll read it," Spoonie commented from the back. It made sense to him. Add as many people to the text as possible and let them know the book is about *them* specifically.

"Yeah, but how many of these people can I write about? It just seems like having one or two sources is stronger, and I'll use all the other information as background to make sure the book stays on point."

His idea was to use Michael Springfield as a story arc guideline, while he directed the path that he wanted the book to follow.

Polo said, "If we get more people talking to you like that, son, you'll fuck around and have *three* Harlem books to write."

"That's what I'm afraid of," Shareef told him. "Then again, all I have to do is ignore the extra shit and just use what I need."

"Dig it," Polo agreed. "Throw the fat back to the dog."

Spoonie said, "Sounds like the right plan to me. How do you write your other books?"

He was back there checking his BlackBerry again.

Polo noticed it and said, "Man, you using that BlackBerry shit like a high school white girl or something. Get off that shit while we rollin'. What, you checking up on the lottery or something?"

"Nah, man, this ma-fucka just keep sending me messages."

"Who?"

Spoonie paused and said, "You don't know him."

"Well, I know he ain't in the car wit' us. That shit is rude, man. Show Shareef some more respect than that."

"Aw, you sounding like a bitch now. Shareef ain't thinkin' 'bout my ass. He be in his own fuckin' world half the time anyway, him and Trap."

Shareef only smiled at it. He and Trap were the thinkers of the bunch. Polo and Spoonie were the idle talkers. And Spoonie had not been around them enough for Shareef to know that much else about him.

"So, where we off to next?" Shareef asked.

"The Harlem Grill, right down the street," Polo answered.

Spoonie said, "Well, hell, we could have walked down the street then. What we get back in the car for?"

"Because we already in the car, motherfucker!" Polo snapped at him.

Sure enough, they were parking again.

Spoonie shook his head and said, "That was a waste of gas."

Polo climbed out and responded, "What, a half a fuckin' pint? Nigga, shut up."

Spoonie put his BlackBerry away and faced Polo on the sidewalk, standing tall but slimmer than the man.

He said, "Don't get out here frontin' for your boy, man."

Shareef leaned up against the Bronco and watched the action with an amused grin.

Polo said, "Now you know, I wouldn't even fight you, son. All I'd do is body slam you and stomp you." He said, "You better get ya' heater fuckin' wit' me, kid. You better get ya' heater."

Spoonie said, "Nigga, you too slow to body slam me," and faked a left-hand jab.

As soon as Polo moved forward to grab him, Spoonie bounced to his right and faked five more punches, while Polo continued to pursue him.

Spoonie spun him around in a full circle and called out to Shareef.

"You see that, man? You see that? I'm on my bicycle, son. He can't touch me."

Just then Polo got a piece of his shirt and pulled him into a bear hug.

"Now what? You goin' down," and he faked a body slam.

Spoonie said, "You would have already been down. I would have hit you like eight times already."

"Yeah, wit' li'l girl punches. I would have walked right through all that shit," Polo argued.

They gathered themselves and began to walk toward the Harlem Grill with Shareef following.

Spoonie complained, "Now you dun' wrinkled my shirt all the fuck up, try'na make me look like you. Sloppy nigga."

Polo froze and said, "What? Hold up now, I know you ain't riffin' on my gear. Why you think they call me Polo?"

Spoonie looked him up and down, from his velvet hat to his shoes, and said, " 'Cause you a big, roly-poly-lookin' nigga. That's why. It ain't got shit to do wit' ya' gear."

Polo said, "Aw, B, you always been hatin' on my style. But I see what it is now. You'd like to have some of my fly clothes, wouldn't you? You'd like to have some of the fly women I got, and do the things I do."

Spoonie said, "Aw, nigga, stop the fuckin' cameras. You ain't *The Mack,* you's a regular burger, with no lettuce, no tomatoes, no special sauce. You straight off the fuckin' family picnic grill with grease and ketchup runnin' out the side, fuckin' up your fingers and shit. You sloppy-ass nigga. Cancel that fuckin' order and let's go up in here and get something else to drink."

He said, "And Shareef, you payin' for the shit, nigga, 'cause you got money. Now let's go."

Spoonie walked forward and slipped into the restaurant without another word. Polo and Shareef were still standing outside.

Polo asked his boy in confusion, "Who the fuck this nigga think he is, B?"

Shareef shook his head and smiled, taking it all in stride.

He said, "He's a Harlem nigga. That's what makes Harlem," and he slipped inside the restaurant behind him.

Polo was the last one in. He told himself, "That nigga's crazy, that's what that is. Straight up and down."

The Harlem Grill was a more ritzy establishment, with wooden panels, reddish brown earth tones, and small private booths that were situated low to the ground. It gave customers a more intimate feeling. They even had dark curtains inside for added privacy.

Spoonie was stopped at the reception booth up front. As soon as he saw Shareef walk in, he said, "Yeah, I got my man, a *New York Times* bestselling author right here. He's writing a new book on Harlem now. You ever heard of Shareef Crawford? He's out of Harlem."

The older male receptionist, dressed in a button-down shirt and a nice sports jacket, the uniform Shareef generally wore, nodded to him and extended his hand.

He said, "My wife and daughter read your books."

Shareef shook his hand and nodded back to him.

"That's good."

Spoonie said, "So, yeah, he just wanted to see the place. I mean, we know we don't have reservations, but we just wanted to walk through."

By the time Polo made it inside, a curvy waitress noticed Shareef standing at the front as well.

"Shareef Crawford," she called out like she knew him. "I love your stuff."

Polo eyed the woman from the back as she breezed on by with drink orders in hand.

He mumbled, "Damn, I love your stuff, *too*."

The receptionist smiled at him and asked, "How many are in your group?"

Shareef said, "It's just us three. We just wanna look around and give you some more bar money, that's all."

The brother leaned his head forward and said, "Come on in. But we don't have any tables available."

Spoonie said, "That's cool. We'll just stand with our drinks."

"And nice meeting you, brother," the receptionist told Shareef as they walked in.

"Ay, no problem, man. And thanks."

As they walked through the restaurant and past the low tables toward a larger area to the back right, Spoonie grinned and said, "Shit, I can use you like a black card, Shareef. You need to move back up to Harlem."

Polo told him, "Stop leechin', nigga. Hold ya' own weight."

"What, like you hold yours?" Spoonie responded to him.

Shareef finally asked them, "Y'all gon' riff all night long? Cut that shit out and let me enjoy this for a minute."

Spoonie looked at Polo and stated, "The money has spoken. Time to shut the fuck up."

Shareef cracked another smile and shook his head.

When they walked into the larger room to the back right. It was more wide open, well lit, with more furniture, no curtains, a giant, projection screen TV toward the front, and a raised platform where at least ten, flashy-dressed men played a game of cards. They all looked important: fresh haircuts, attention-getting clothes, jewelry, expensive caps, and plenty of swagger. They played their game of cards as if no one else in the room existed. A steady stream of food and drinks were rushed to their table.

Shareef looked them over. He told himself, *Now this is what I'm talking about, the insider's club.*

He asked Spoonie, "You recognize any of 'em?" Harlem always had new people. The place was a magnet for opportunists from all over New York and beyond.

Spoonie nodded and said, "Yeah, but they ain't talkin', I can tell you that."

Just then Spoonie nodded to a few of them who were facing him. But it was only a nod of recognition. It wasn't as if they wanted to talk to him. Spoonie knew the rules. When they wanted to talk, they would call you over to their table.

"What about you, Polo? Who you know over there?"

Polo said, "Man, I don't be hanging out like that no more. I go to work and go home. I stay up in Washington Heights more now anyway."

Shareef was thinking, *What good are they? How can they still live in Harlem and not know anyone well enough to speak?*

But it was only his ego talking. Harlem had always had a strict class system. If you were not a part of a certain class, you could see a person every day of your life and never be invited to really know them. That's just how the place was. There were too many people there, representing far too many cliques, for many of them to invite you in.

Millionaires socializing with beggars was dangerous. It only caused more envy. So unless you could keep up and keep it moving, Harlem would turn its head and leave you behind in a heartbeat. Life was less complicated that way. So Harlemites had learned to stick with their own and stay with their own for their safety, and for their emotional well-being. Because if you couldn't keep up with your group of friends, family members, or neighbors, you could easily get your feelings hurt and slip into a social depression that was ripe for addictions to drugs, alcohol, sex, and general crime.

Technically speaking, Harlem, New York, was the most significant microcosm of American economics, culture, and social status, and it all sat right there in front of you, in a square radius of less than five miles.

Shareef knew all that himself. Or maybe he had forgotten. But while he stood there with no table or chair inside the cozy restaurant, he was surely reminded of Harlem's community status. At the same time, that out-of-reach status was what made Harlem so alluring in the first place. Everyone wanted to get in, be in, and stay in, and they were all that close to it, like having a lottery ticket with one more number to go for a big hit.

Shit! Shareef stood there and cursed himself. *I'll look like a straight-up asshole if I just walk over there and introduce myself. And I bet none of them guys read much, especially not my kind of books. So what do I have to say to them?*

"Can I get you something to drink, Mr. Crawford?" a second waitress asked him. Obviously, they had shared information on who he was.

Shareef wasn't that interested in drinks at the moment. But once he thought about it, he figured, if the waitresses were ready to serve him on a name basis, then maybe he could use that to make himself feel more valuable in the room. After all, he was a somebody himself now, and deserved respect.

So he said loud enough for seated customers to overhear him, "Yeah, take my friends' orders, and I'll just order last. This a nice place y'all got up in here," he added with swagger of his own.

He was making it known to everyone that he was important enough to be served while still standing. Sure enough, a few of the guys at the card game gave him notice. *Who is this guy?*

After Spoonie and Polo had ordered, Shareef said, "Give me an extra large Amaretto sour."

The waitress smiled and said, "Okay."

"You read any of my work?" he asked her before she left.

She continued to smile and said, "Of course."

He said, "That's good, that's a good thing. If I get to know you a little better, I'll put you up in the next one."

She stopped and asked, "For real?"

She wasn't originally from Harlem. The young woman had only moved there a year ago from Ohio, and she was still looking to break into something special, like a thousand others who moved there. But she wasn't exotic enough for Shareef's usual taste. She was only a seven. He was just testing his status in the room with her, while using her as a pawn in the game of social chess.

He said, "You give me your number before I leave, and you know, we'll talk about it."

She nodded and said, "Okay."

Polo and Spoonie giggled their asses off as soon as she left them.

"Yo, you gon' have that girl wet up her panties in here, son. She gon' have to change her underwear in the back," Polo joked.

Spoonie said, "If she wearing any."

Shareef only smiled at it. He knew what he was doing. The waitress was not his focal point. He continued to notice the reactions to his power move.

A woman to his left looked on from her table, where she sat with her date, and asked, "Excuse me, but are you, ah, who I think you are?"

Shareef nodded and asked her, "Do you read books?"

She immediately smiled, snapped her fingers and said, "Shareef Crawford."

"In the flesh," he told her smoothly.

She said, "Aw, I wish I had my book on me. I was just reading that new one today?"

"*The Full Moon?*"

"Yeah. That book is good."

"Thanks."

He was thanking her for plenty of reasons actually. She was really causing a storm of interest in there. Half of the room began to eye Shareef, and mostly the women. That only made the guys look harder.

He told himself, *Now this feels a little better,* as the drinks arrived. He took his off the tray, took a sip of it, and the waitress slid him her number on a business card all out in plain view.

"Don't take it if you're not gonna call me."

She smiled, and went to the next customer.

Polo grinned with his own drink in hand. He said, "Shit, you better call her up, son."

"And get your dick sucked," Spoonie whispered. "You see them perfect lips on her?"

Shareef chuckled at it. He was working the room just like a novel. Everything was falling right into place. All he needed now was an available table.

"Hey, look what the cat brought in," someone stated right beside him.

Shareef looked and locked in on Jurrell Garland, his old neighborhood nemesis again. Jurrell looked jazzy in a wide-collar oxford shirt. It was cream with thick vertical stripes of orange and brown. He wore dark blue jeans, sharp brown leather shoes, and smelled good, too, with a great choice of cologne.

He held his right hand out for a shake, while his left hand embraced the light-brown fingers of a lady friend.

Shareef was stunned and speechless.

"You gon' leave me hangin' over here, Shareef?" Jurrell asked him about the handshake. He smiled, good-heartedly.

Shareef finally snapped out of his daze and shook his hand after switching his drink to the left.

"My bad, you caught me off guard."

Jurrell said, "That's twice in one day now. That must mean something." He added, "Oh, Meesha, this is Shareef Crawford, a bestselling author. We went to grade school together in East Harlem."

Meesha nodded with a slight grin. She said, "My girlfriend has all of your books. Wait till I tell her I met you here tonight."

She had an easy way about her and was a sure nine. She actually reminded him of Jurrell's mother at about the same age. Shareef had always had a boyish crush on his nemesis's mother. And with Jurrell getting into trouble at school as much as he had, all of the kids had seen plenty of her.

Jurrell asked him, "You got a table in here?"

"Ah, nah, we were just ah, you know, passing through."

Jurrell looked at Spoonie and Polo and spoke to them.

"What's up, fellas?"

"Yeah, what's up?" they both mumbled.

Jurrell then eyed the drink in Shareef's left hand and said, "You gon' drink that standing up in the middle of the floor? I'll let you share my table."

"What table?" Shareef asked him. There were no tables available.

The next thing he knew, a group of four walked past, and a waitress gave Jurrell the signal to move forward, while she quickly wiped off a small table that was up front near the large-screen projection TV.

"This table right here," Jurrell answered slyly.

Shareef paused and looked at his friends. They were as stunned as he was.

As Jurrell began to move toward his reserved table with his date, the flashy, unapproachable men in the card game responded to him.

"Ay, it's Mr. Cell Phone. What's up, Rell?"

"Yeah, it's ya' world now. It's your world," he responded to them. He sat at his table with his lady friend and faced Shareef and everyone else inside the room.

"Ay, Rell, what I need to do to get a new one from you if the phone breaks?" one of the guys at the card game asked him.

Jurrell told him, "Just call me up on it."

Then he looked back at Shareef and motioned for him to join them. They had two extra chairs at the table.

Shareef looked back at Spoonie and Polo for comments, but they both seemed frozen.

Polo finally uttered, "Yo, man . . ." and never finished his sentence. He acted as if he was afraid to speak his mind.

And Spoonie didn't say anything. So Shareef was forced to make his own decision.

He said, "I'ma go over here and talk to him and see what's up."

When he walked toward Jurrell's table at the front of the room, Shareef could feel every set of eyes that cut to him.

So, he's been selling these guys cell phones, hunh? he mused as he approached. *I wonder what other kinds of business they're doing.*

Shareef still didn't trust the man, but he sat at the table to the left of Meesha anyway. As soon he sat down, Jurrell brought up their history to his date.

He said, "Do you believe that me and this guy were enemies from kindergarten to eighth grade? I was terrible back then, and this guy was the only one brave enough to keep standing up to me. We had like, what, five different fights, Shareef? And you won the last two, right?"

Meesha shook her head and commented, "I have no idea why guys must fight so much. I just don't get it. Is violence that much a part of manhood?"

She sounded educated, like a college grad asking philosophical questions about life.

Jurrell answered, "Obviously, it must be. But I guess we'll all calm down when we get to be old men. I've already calmed down. I can't take this stuff that's going on out here now."

Shareef said, "Actually, I didn't even know we were keeping score." He was still thinking about the five fistfights they had as boys, and how Jurrell still recalled who had won each of them.

He said, "I mean, with everything . . . and all these years, I'm still wondering how you remember them fights with me."

He didn't want to bring up too much of Jurrell's crazy past without knowing how much his lady friend already knew about it.

Jurrell understood it from his pause and nodded, recognizing Shareef's show of respect for the lady between them.

He said, "Nah, no matter what, I still remember you, Shareef. You know why?"

All of a sudden, there was no one in the room but Shareef Crawford and Jurrell Garland.

Shareef said, "Nah. Why?"

Jurrell answered, "You kept it movin', man. A man gotta respect that. You finished high school. You went away to college and finished that. You became a popular writer. People know you for that. And I asked myself each time, 'What am I doing?' You know what I mean? 'What am I doing?' "

He said, "See now, a lot of guys would hate in the situation. And at the high school level, I did. Because I wasn't really around you anymore and I stopped going to high school anyway. But every once in a while, I would miss being behind you, right. And I would ask myself, 'Yo, where Shareef at?' "

Shareef failed to follow him. He frowned and said, "You missed being behind me?"

Jurrell cleared that up quickly. "Crawford, Davis, Evans, Garland, Harper, Kelly . . ."

Shareef caught on and laughed. "Oh, you're talking about roll call."

Jurrell said, "Man, after all them damn years of hearing my name called behind yours, I went to detention centers and even jail, thinking, 'Where Crawford at?' Ain't that some shit?"

He said, "But you wasn't there anymore. You were out there taking care of your business. And I gotta respect that. So I remember. I damn sure remember you."

At that moment, it appeared to Shareef that Jurrell had always passed into the next grade to stay behind him. He was no underachiever until high school, when they were no longer together.

Shareef even joked about it. He smiled and said, "Maybe if you had gone to Manhattan Center like I did, you would have graduated from high school behind me, too."

Jurrell laughed and said, "I thought about that shit myself. When you on lockdown every day you think about a lot of different shit. But I doubt if we would have been in the same classes in high school. That would have been a little too crazy. And Martin Luther King was where all the action was, the action that got my ass right into trouble."

The waitress finally made her way over to their table to take their orders.

"Oh, are you sitting here with them?"

It was the same waitress who had given Shareef her number.

"Nah, I was just about to leave," he told her.

Jurrell said, "Well, look, call me up, man. I mean that. We grown men now."

Shareef stood up and looked him in the eyes. They were grown men. They were both in their thirties now. Why not let bygones be bygones?

So he nodded and said, "Aw'ight, I'll call you."

Jurrell said, "Now don't tell me that if you don't mean it, man."

The waitress looked at Shareef and grinned. It was the same thing she had told him. Don't lie about it.

Shareef nodded, thinking about them both. He said, "If I say I'ma call, then that's what I gotta do, right?"

"That's a man of his word," Jurrell told him.

Shareef stuck out his hand to shake on it.

"It's a done deal then."

By then, some of the card players were anxious to know who the hell he was. Shareef was generating a whole lot of attention in there.

"Ay, Rell, who 'dat, man?" one of the flashy card players asked him.

Jurrell said, "Shareef Crawford, a *New York Times* bestselling author. He's working on a book on Harlem now. So I'ma have to line y'all all up to talk to him."

They all started to pay attention after that. The name rang a bell.

"Shareef Crawford? My girl reads your books. That's good money, man."

"Yeah, my sister read your books."

One of them said, "Shit, everybody's girl reads his books. Moms, sisters, aunts, little cousins. So, what are you writing about Harlem?"

Shareef faced all of them at the same time and backed down.

He said, "I'm still working on it."

Another one of the card players said, "Well, yo, if you need some updated movie shit, we'll talk to you. Now, we can't tell you everything, but we'll tell you enough. You know, we still got rats running around."

"And the rats end up in the alleyways," they warned him.

Jurrell said, "Yo, when he call me, I'll set it up. I'll let y'all know what it is then."

"Aw'ight, Shareef, keep writing them books, son. I might have you write my life story one day," another one of the card players boasted. They were all with Harlem swagger, but you couldn't talk to them unless the right person spoke for you.

Obviously, Jurrell Garland was the right person.

Baby G

AS SOON AS SHAREEF walked out of the Harlem Grill with Spoonie and Polo, Polo said, "I don't know about that nigga right there, man. I mean, I know we know him from back in the day and everything, but he ain't never been friends with us."

Shareef admitted it. He said, "I know. He was my main enemy."

Spoonie said, "Yeah, and the only reason he talkin' to you now is because you're Shareef Crawford. You see he didn't invite us to his table. And how he know you writing a book about Harlem?"

"I bumped into him earlier at the Starbucks on Lenox," Shareef answered. "And he don't know y'all like he know me."

Spoonie shook his head and said, "Man, when guys like him pay attention to something, it's usually for the wrong reasons, B. Believe that."

Shareef heard them out, and he understood their caution. But at the same time, didn't Jurrell deserve a fresh start like any other man? He didn't appear to be breaking any more laws, jaws, or into stores and cars. Couldn't he have grown up to sell cell phones, and have a girlfriend, a wife, and a family outside of the street life? And sure, he still knew guys out in the streets, but that didn't mean he had to be involved with the things they were involved in anymore. So Shareef decided to speak up for him.

"I mean, who's to say he's all bad like that still. All he's asking me to do is call him. I mean, what's wrong with that? It ain't gon' hurt me to call him."

Polo said, "Aw'ight, so, what if the police have him on surveillance? If he say anything under code to you, that automatically makes you a suspect, especially since you got money."

He said, "That's the new game around here, son. You got a lot of old hustlers and vics, lookin' for somebody like you to leech on to to help them go legit. They ain't lettin' hustlers buy up shit around Harlem like they used to. I'm tellin' you, B, that's the new fuckin' game. I mean, you gon' make your own decisions anyway, but just watch that nigga, man. The streets is never sleepin'."

Shareef didn't want to hear any more of it. He started walking toward the Bronco jeep and said, "Aw'ight, so where we headed to next?"

Polo turned around and looked down the street.

He said, "Zip Code is right there, so ain't no sense in me wasting another pint of gas trying to find a new parking spot, right, Spoonie?"

Spoonie was back on his BlackBerry again, and was not paying attention.

He looked up and grunted, "Hunh?"

Polo frowned and said, "Yo, man, what the hell is up with you and that BlackBerry tonight? For real?"

Spoonie ignored him. "Hold up a minute."

Polo waved him off and started walking toward their next destination down the street. Shareef followed him.

"So, what kind of spot is Zip Code?" he asked.

Polo said, "It's like a combination club. Some nights they'll have a regular party, other nights they'll have comedy and music showcases. Then sometimes different people'll throw their events there."

"Is it big?"

Shareef had gotten used to the bigger, fancier clubs of Atlanta and Miami. What did Harlem have to match that?

Polo said, "It's big enough. They got upstairs, downstairs, a third-floor area."

"A third floor?"

"Don't get excited, man, it's just a small area to catch some breathing room when it's packed in there, that's all."

"What age group?"

"Oh, you'll get some young bucks in here. That's like the only place for them to party in Harlem. I mean, you know downtown ain't having it, unless they're ready to spend forty dollars. And ain't nobody try'na party that hard."

"How much does this place cost?"

"You can get in for ten, twenty. It ain't bad."

When they approached the basic-white-and-black nightclub called Zip Code, a line of younger Harlemites in their early twenties were trying to get in.

"Come on, man, why y'all always make us wait out here?" a young man in all dark brown complained to a doorman dressed in all black.

The doorman answered, "You'll get in when we let you in."

"But y'all ain't moving the line, man. We been standing here ten minutes. What we waiting for?"

There was a solid line of young men and women held up at the door behind him. He had made it to the front and was getting anxious.

As soon as Polo and Shareef made it to the vicinity of the club and stood out on the sidewalk to watch the interactions and energy of the younger Harlemites, a gang of seven marched up to a second door of the club to the far right near a parking area.

"Yo, it's Baby, man, I'm paying for my whole squad."

"Awi'ght, hold up," another doorman in black addressed them.

The young man in brown began to fidget in the main line, while he looked back and forth at the front door versus the side door.

A minute later, the crew of seven marched inside through the second door.

Polo said, "Come on, man, let's go with them."

The doorman stopped them, along with a bunch of other anxious Harlemites, who scrambled along the sidewalk to get in.

"What are you doin'?" the doorman asked Polo.

"This my man, Shareef Crawford, a bestselling author. He just wanna check the place out, man. He writing a new book on Harlem."

The thick doorman looked Shareef over and didn't budge.

He said, "That's nice, but what that got to do with me? The line is over there."

Polo said, "You gon' make him stand in a long line like that, B. That's disrespectful. You can show us more love than that. He from Harlem."

"I don't care if he from Africa, he not on the list."

A few of the younger guys around them began to laugh.

"Aw, he said he don't care if he from Africa."

Shareef asked him, "What's the charge, man?" He just wanted to get the hell in the place. He had more than a hundred dollars still left in his pocket from hitting the ATM machine earlier.

"Gimme forty dollars," the doorman told him.

Shareef said, "Each?"

Polo said, "Hell naw, he mean for both of us."

"Nah, it's all good, it's all good. They my people," Spoonie announced from behind. He said, "This Shareef Crawford right here. You know who he is?"

The doorman answered, "A bestselling author."

Spoonie looked at him and said, "Damn, everybody know."

"Your man just told me."

"Aw'ight, well, they wit' me," Spoonie told him.

The doorman nodded and let them in without another word. That only caused more people to hustle up to the second door behind them.

"Aw, man, see, that's what I'm talking about," the young man in all brown complained again at the front door. "That ain't even fair."

SHAREEF WALKED into the dimly lit club of tall ceilings, white walls, and white furniture behind Spoonie and Polo.

Spoonie said, "I do know people up in here. I can even get us a couple of free drinks."

Shareef smiled and said, "If you can get drinks for you and Polo that would do me just fine. How many free drinks they gon' give us?"

"I can get what I want in here. These my people."

Shareef nodded and looked around the bottom floor of the night-club, where they had tall, white, circular lounge chairs, with white curtains hanging from the ceiling. He studied all the young faces and bodies that populated the place.

He nodded to Polo and said, "Yeah, this is a much younger crowd in here. I feel like I'm back in school in Atlanta."

"I told you," Polo commented.

Spoonie had already disappeared to the bar area to the left.

As they continued to walk through, Shareef took a second, third, and fourth look at the young women. Which one would catch his eye?

After a few more minutes of looking around, he finally shook his head and said, "Damn, Polo, these girls look as hard as the guys in here."

Polo laughed at it. He said, "That's how these girls like to get down nowadays, Shareef. They not fly and feminine like our girls used to be back in the day. These new school girls wanna be thugs like their boyfriends. That's why I deal with nothing but older women. These young girls ain't got no style to me."

Shareef had to agree with him on that. He wasn't used to bullish, young women either. He nodded his head and mumbled, "Dig it."

Spoonie called them over toward the bar area.

"Yo, come get these drinks!"

"I guess he was serious, hunh?" Polo commented.

Shareef smiled and followed him over.

When they arrived at the bar and collected their drinks among the young hustlers, playboys, and thugs, draped in jewelry and designer clothes, Shareef studied them all and then stopped at a gold mine.

"Got' damn," he mumbled to himself.

Polo caught it and said, "What?"

Shareef told him, "Look straight ahead and then to the left."

Polo followed his lead and landed at the same spot.

He nodded with his drink to his lips. "She the flyest girl in here," he commented.

Shareef said, "You know what's crazy about it? She reminds me of my wife when she still loved me."

Polo looked at his boy seriously. He said, "Cut that shit out, B, your wife still love you. How she not gon' love you? You doin' everything a nigga supposed to do. Shit, I'd marry you my damn self."

Shareef laughed it off and said, "Nah, man, she . . . she love the *idea* of a man now. 'Cause she damn sure ain't treatin' me like flesh and bone no more. I can barely touch the girl now."

Polo nodded and said, "Yeah, that's how women get once they got you." He took a sip of his drink and added, "That's why I always gotta keep two or three backups."

Shareef laughed again and coughed on his own drink.

He said, "I'm 'bout to make this girl my backup plan right now. I'm still alive, ain't I?"

Polo said, "You don't look like a zombie to me. So go get her, tiger."

Shareef walked straight through the crowd like a man on a mission. When he arrived at his destination, he leaned into the woman's ear and said, "You're about the finest young thing in here, hands down. What's your name?"

She wasn't dressed like eighty percent of the other young women—hard-core jeans, masculine tops, and mad grills. She wore a netted gold top with a white half jacket and matching white pants. She wore gold, Asian-design earrings and her hair straight down with a bang. She carried a gold, sequin purse, and her skin and eyes were light brown and golden like the rest of her. And she looked approachable and pleasant.

"Tiffany," she answered him.

He reached out his hand to hers and said, "Shareef. You're not from here, are you?"

She didn't have the Harlem edge, look, or swagger. She had the mellow demeanor of a sophisticate who was dressed to get attention, and she was getting it. Shareef would have guessed that she was from the West Coast.

She said, "I'm from California," and confirmed it.

He smiled. "Oakland?" She didn't have the Los Angeles swagger, either.

She smiled back at him. "San Francisco."

He nodded. "That's what I figured. So what brings you all the way to Harlem?"

She answered with no hesitation, "It was something different. I just wanted to get away." She sounded as if she had practiced her answer for a frequently asked question.

He said, "I can dig it. Harlem is like a tourist city for a lot of people. So how long have you been here?"

Before she could answer, an energized girlfriend grabbed her hand from out of the crowd.

"Come on, girl, I want you to meet somebody."

Shareef said, "Whoa, hold up that horse for a minute. I'm talking to her."

The girlfriend looked at Shareef as if to say, *So.* But she didn't need to. Her hard eyes said everything for her. And of course, she wasn't half as good-looking or as stylish.

"She'll be back," the girlfriend told him.

Shareef didn't want to chance it.

He said, "Yeah, well let me get her number before she leave then."

Tiffany declined. "I'll give it to you when I come back."

He was too old and experienced for that shit. Just hearing the corniness of it all made him wonder why he was even in the club. But it was all needed research to understand the new Harlem. So he had to deal with the scene regardless. They had even turned him into a young, spurned, and bitter man for a spell.

Aw, fuck her then, he told himself as the girlfriend dragged her away toward the stairs.

Shareef returned to his friend dejectedly.

Polo was already laughing. He said, "What happened, B?"

"Now I know why you called me tiger," Shareef answered. "Them young girls make you wanna pounce on 'em."

Polo said, "That's why I don't fuck with them young girls, man. If they not already up on your shit before you talk to 'em, you ain't gettin' 'em. Not the fine ones like that."

He said, "Them fine young girls are like bumble bees in the springtime, man, buzzin' around to every nigga that's got a fistful of money in his hand. I can't keep up with that shit, nor do I want to. So, what you should have done is sent me or Spoonie over there to prep her for you first. We would have told her who you are, and had that girl fantasizin' before you ever said a word to her. That's how you get 'em."

Shareef asked him, "Well, how come you didn't say that then?"

Polo grinned and said, "To be honest with you, man, I just wanted to see if my theory was right," and he started laughing harder.

BABY G SAT UPSTAIRS in the main ballroom in a plush lounge chair like a young prince, with twenty soldiers surrounding him. He had the audacity to wear a huge, platinum crown medallion on his link chain, too, with a matching platinum belt buckle. And he smoked a well-rolled blunt in plain view as thunderous, Harlem rap music blasted through the giant speakers, forcing the bodacious, young crowd to move to it.

"I was born and raised in Harlem / had my birthdays in Harlem / walked with a sway in Harlem / got my first lay in Harlem / the place where I stay is Harlem . . .

"I was born and raised in Harlem / learned how they play in Harlem / stacked major pay in Harlem / smoked my first jay in Harlem / what can I say, man, it's Harlem . . ."

The rest of the world didn't exist to the people in that room. It was all about Harlem, and the crowd was losing their young minds.

"Ay, Baby, them girls wanna see you, man," one of his soldiers told him.

The young general didn't want to hear it, not while he was nodding to his favorite song.

He said, "Yo, make 'em wait till this song over wit'."

And that was it. His soldier went back to bring the word.

"Yo, y'all gotta wait till this song ends."

The ringleader frowned at him and snapped, "What? Wait till this song ends?"

"That's what he said. What you want me to do? Y'all ain't gettin' over there till he let you."

The girlfriend looked at the thick crowd of soldiers standing and sitting in a full circle around the prince named Baby G. No one could get anywhere near him from any angle without being touched first.

The girlfriend sucked her teeth and said, "Come on, Tiffany, we don't have to wait for this shit. Who he think he is?"

The soldier looked at the girl named Tiffany and lightly grabbed her arm.

He said, "He would want to see you. But if you leave . . . he not gon' wait for you. If you slow, you blow."

The girlfriend overheard him and said, "Oh, he won't wait for you, but he want you to wait for him. Fuck that."

The soldier let the girl's arm go and said, "Whatever then. I'll tell him y'all changed ya mind."

Tiffany looked through the crowd at this prince of a young man, with all these dedicated guys crowding around him like a fortress, and she figured he was worth waiting for. She didn't move to Harlem to turn down opportunities to meet the biggest fish in the pond. That's what she was there to do. So she told his soldier, "I can wait."

Her girlfriend went ballistic. "What? Girl, don't go out like that. That's the wrong way to do it. I'm tellin' you."

The soldier said, "If he like you, you VIP for the rest of the night."

"Don't go for that shit, girl," the girlfriend warned her.

"Look, stop fuckin' hatin' and run along somewhere," the soldier beefed at her. He was tired of the cock blocking already. Tiffany had made up her mind, so he held her hand to make sure she waited.

"Aw'ight 'den, be a dummy," the girlfriend snapped and ran along.

When the song was over, the soldier returned to Baby G without the girl. He wanted to make sure he had the okay first.

"You want me to bring her now?"

Baby G looked up at him from his position on the lounge chair and asked, "What she look like? Is she hot like a video model?"

His soldier nodded to him. He said, "Exactly."

The young general studied his face and slowly nodded. "Aw'ight, bring her over here then. And don't bring her ugly-ass girlfriend, either."

"Oh, she left already."

Baby G took another toke of his blunt and uttered, "Good."

When the soldier brought the California girl over, all eyes were on her. She camouflaged her nervousness with an air of confidence and a swagger she didn't really possess.

Baby G read it from her bold stance and knew he could go as hard as he wanted to with her. If she had something to prove, then he would give her the opportunity to prove it.

He held his blunt away from lips and told her, "I only got one open seat over here, and that's my lap. You sit down first and then I can talk to you. If you don't, then you can walk back by yourself and I'll see you in the after world."

His soldier stood there and thought, *Shit! Baby gangsta as motherfucker!* right before the general dismissed him.

"Aw'ight, son, you can go now. She here. Good work."

Tiffany moved right in between his legs to take a seat below his platinum crown belt buckle.

"Right here?" she teased him.

He didn't expect that from her. He liked her boldness immediately, but that didn't mean he would go soft on her.

He held up his blunt and asked her, "You ever smoked this before?"

She answered, "Yeah."

"Where at?"

"Out in California."

"California? What part of California? L.A.?"

"San Francisco?"

"Was it strong?"

She paused and shrugged her shoulders. How strong was strong?

"I mean, I guess so."

"You guess so? Did you get high? Shit, you ain't smoke this if you ain't get high."

She said, "Yeah, I got high."

"Aw'ight, so if you gangsta like that, let me see you hit this shit," and he passed her the blunt.

He did it so fast she didn't have time to catch herself and slow things down. And everybody was still staring at her. What would they think if she ran scared? And what would they think if she smoked it?

But fuck it, she was in Harlem, thousands of miles away from home, with some exotic nigga who was calling her bluff. And she was not willing to give him the benefit of punking her. So she held that blunt up to her lips and inhaled it deeply.

"Oh, shit," the young general expressed to her. "You high now."

Tiffany tried to laugh and choked on the weed smoke. That only made it worse. Choking got the weed in her system faster. Then the room started moving.

"You want some more?" she heard the young prince of a man ask her.

She nodded and took another puff, holding the smoke in her lungs better the second time. And when exhaled, the room started floating real slowly.

"Yeah, you a gangsta bitch all right," Baby G told her and laughed. "And I mean that in a good way. I trust you know," he told her. "But if you ain't smoke it . . . I wouldn't have trusted you. You could have been a detective's daughter or something."

He said, "You ain't no rich girl like on *ATL* are you?" Before she could answer him, he added, "I would'a worked that situation if I was Rashad. I would'a had that rich girl giving me some money."

It seemed like he was talking forever, an expert conversationalist. Then he squeezed her gently in his arms. And she felt protected within his circle.

"You want something to drink?" she heard him ask her.

She nodded and didn't know if she said anything.

"Yo, man, somebody get her some orange juice or something. Not alcohol, just orange juice. You do drink orange juice, don't you?" Baby G asked her.

"Yeah," she spoke up.

He said, "So, what's your name?"

Tiffany thought about that in her altered state of mind and started laughing.

She said, "You didn't even ask me my name yet?"

"I mean, how important is a person's name, if you really think about it?" he asked her. "A name is just what they call you. But do you like a motherfucker because of what his name is, or what his game is? You tell me."

She nodded to him. He made perfect sense. She said, "His game is more important."

"That's what I'm talking about. I got *game,* shorty. That's why everybody in here surrounding me. And now you sittin' right in the middle of it. You know what that mean?"

She looked at him and grinned, floating on his lap. "I got game, too," she answered.

Baby G laughed loudly at her response. He took another toke of the blunt, which was getting smaller, and muttered, "You see that? You smart. Now me and you, we gon' have a good time together. Is that all right with you?"

She nodded and was pleased to be with him. He was a perfect gangsta gentleman, just what a girl had always hoped for.

She answered, "Yeah . . . I'm glad I waited for you."

• • •

SHAREEF HAD A CALL on his cell phone back on the bottom level of the club. He looked down and read the Fort Lauderdale number of his wife.

How ironic, he thought. He figured she was calling back from earlier, and she was doing so a bit late at that. It was nearly one o'clock in the morning.

"Damn, time flew tonight," he mumbled to himself, while heading toward the restrooms to hear better.

Polo asked him, "Where you goin'?"

"To the bathroom to take this phone call."

Shareef followed the restroom arrows down to a basement area where he answered his wife's late call.

"Hello."

"Where are you?" she asked him. There was still background noise from the club, even in the downstairs bathrooms. But at least he didn't have to strain to speak or to hear. Jennifer simply had a great pair of ears.

She hears, smells, and thinks everything, he assessed. *But she can't see that she needs to love her husband unconditionally.* Then he thought deeper about his assessment. *Then again, do I love her unconditionally? Not without sex I don't.*

He answered, "I'm at a club in Harlem called Zip Code," but he wasn't obligated to answer her. As far as he was concerned, he was out of the house and out of her hair, and therefore, he no longer had to answer to her.

"Zip Code? Why?" she asked him.

"I'm doing research."

"At a nightclub, Shareef?"

"What, there's no nightclubs in books?"

"Well, you didn't tell me what kind of book you were working on."

He said, "At one o'clock in the morning, I'm not. I'll just let you know that it's about Harlem."

Amazingly, Shareef had rarely touched on his hometown of Harlem in his previous seven novels. He was struck by revealing love stories in the southern regions—Georgia, North and South Carolina, Florida, Louisiana, and Virginia. Or exotic locales, like Jamaica, or the new book set in Bermuda.

His wife even alluded to it. "Oh, so now you finally want to write about Harlem." She had wondered about a Harlem story from him years ago after visiting several times and loving his grandparents new home in Morningside Heights.

He answered, "Yeah, I'm finally gonna write a book about Harlem," and was a little short with her.

Jennifer noticed it and decided to get to the point of her phone call before he would ask her.

"Well, anyway, you told Kimberly that you were going to stay over?"

"You know that already."

"Well, when are you supposed to do that?"

Shareef grimaced as if the answer pained him. It was all irritating small talk that was taking him away from his research. She could find out that information from him during the daytime, especially since she didn't work anymore.

He said, "I told her already, when I get back home, early next week."

"You didn't consult with me about it."

That was a bigger argument waiting to happen. After all, Shareef still paid all the bills at the house.

He said, "I don't have to consult with you to sleep over with my daughter. Don't even go there. I'm not gonna be in your bed. Or am I?" he wondered out loud.

Was calling him at nearly one o'clock in the morning to discuss an issue she could take care of at noon the next day her way of showing that she still wanted to be involved in his life? Shareef waited for her answer.

Finally, she told him, "No." With that as her thousandth rejection of him, Shareef was more than ready to move on.

"Aw'ight, well, I got shit to do. And like I said, I'll be back early next week to see my kids as usual."

"All right," she told him with a pause.

Shareef promptly ended the call. And once he was off the line, he stared at his cell phone for a spell and shook his head.

"The Lord will find your equal match, man, I *swear.*"

A younger brother overheard him on his way into the bathroom and laughed.

Shareef looked at him and said, "Laugh now, and cry later, brother. Watch."

The younger man said, "Oh, I already know. These girls are all crazy out here. That's why I do what I do and keep steppin'."

Shareef nodded to him and said, "Dig it." Moving on from her seemed to be the only way of keeping a woman in check.

SHAREEF JOINED Polo and Spoonie back on the first floor.

Spoonie said, "Yo, let's go upstairs and check out the second level. This only one part of the club. The main shit go on upstairs anyway."

Shareef said, "Let's go then."

Spoonie led the way with Shareef second and Polo last. They ascended the stairs and arrived at the second level of the club, where there was a small stage area and a DJ booth against the wall to the right. A dance floor was in the center of the room with lounge chairs and small tables spread around the corners. In the back left of the second level was a curtained-off VIP section.

Spoonie said, "This is where all the live entertainment and dancing goes down."

Shareef and Polo looked around at the obvious. The young twenty-somethings were enjoying their youth through dance, alcohol, weed, and music.

Shareef then zoned in on Ms. California from downstairs, who he had met less than thirty minutes ago. She was sitting on some young player's lap in plain view.

He tapped Polo on his broad shoulder with his fist and said, "Yo, you see what I see?"

Polo looked through the crowd and spotted her. Tiffany wasn't that hard to find in her bright gold-and-white outfit. She stood out like a lightbulb compared to all the dark blue and black gear in the room.

"That's just what I'm talking about," Polo responded. "She walked right up here and jumped on the biggest yacht in the water."

Shareef said, "Yeah, who's that?"

Spoonie overheard him and answered, "That's Baby G. He's like one of the most popular young bloods in Harlem now. They love that fuckin' kid."

"Yeah," Polo agreed. "They treat that motherfucka like he the second coming of Tupac or some shit."

"Does he rap?" Shareef asked them as he continued to study the young man with envy. He had bottled up the girl.

Polo said, "Nah, that kid don't rap. He like a minor hustler. But it ain't really about the hustle to him. He just like showing off for a crowd. He the type that'll do some wild shit just to get attention for it."

"Do all the other young guys know him in Harlem?"

Spoonie nodded and said, "Yeah, they know him. Half of 'em want to be down with him. He roll up with like thirty thick sometimes."

Shareef said, "He got it like that, hunh?"

Polo said, "Yeah, you'll see it at the basketball games. They got games up here tomorrow."

Shareef nodded and continued to stare at the young man through the crowd, while his California interest sat on the man's private parts like a showpiece. Shareef couldn't get over that part. He was a man who wanted everything.

"Does he get girls like that often?"

Polo answered, "Come on, son, you already know. He got your girl, didn't he?"

"She's not my girl. I only spoke to her for a couple of minutes, if that," Shareef commented.

"You wanted to make her your girl," Polo argued with a smirk. He said, "But it's all cool, man. Nobody wins them all. I bet he can't get half of the girls who read your books."

Spoonie overheard that and said, "Are you crazy? All girls love gangstas now, even the smart bitches. Trap told you that last night. Matter of fact, I need to check in with him and see what he's up to right about now."

Spoonie pulled out his BlackBerry again.

Polo shook his head and said, "Here he goes with that shit again."

Spoonie grinned and said, "It's the new world, man. You don't have that Nas album when he talked about the future? That's one of my favorite albums. Now I don't have to yell through all of this music and shit. I can just hit Trap up with a text message."

Shareef finally looked away from the California girl. He had enough women in his life to juggle as it was. Adding one more wasn't that big of an issue. He was just testing out his mojo with the younger crowd. And apparently it wasn't worth as much there. No one bothered to pay him any mind.

After standing under better lighting to send and receive text messages, Spoonie walked back over to Shareef and Polo with a face of concern.

He said, "Yo, Trap wanna meet us outside."

Polo frowned at the idea. "Meet him outside for what? Tell him to come in here. You can get him in, right?"

Polo was already feeling comfortable in the club just watching. He didn't have to be involved with the young bloods to enjoy their brash energy. Besides, he cradled his third drink in his hand and he had barely sipped it down yet.

Spoonie said, "He don't wanna talk in here. It's too noisy and chaotic. And he mainly just wanna talk to Shareef anyway."

All eyes were on the writer for a second.

"Talk to me about what?"

Spoonie told him, "Look, man, I don't type out paragraphs on this thing, just short questions and answers. Now he said he was in the area, he asked if you was here with us, I said that you was, and he said he wanted to meet you outside when he got here in like five minutes. And that all went down in like four text messages."

Shareef nodded to him.

Polo thought about it and smiled. He said, "That sounds like an old-school fight or some shit, son." He changed his voice to imitate a young bully, " 'Yo, meet me outside the schoolyard in five minutes.' "

They all shared a laugh about it.

Shareef looked around at the party and said, "Shit, as thick as this place is now, it'll take us five minutes just to get out of here."

"Dig it. Let's start moving out now then," Spoonie agreed.

Polo moved last, starting to hurry up with his drink.

"Shit," he cursed. "Trap try'na fucked up a nigga's wet dream." Polo's glassy eyes were wandering the room frantically as they headed back toward the stairs. He still wasn't ready to leave.

Shareef said, "I thought you told me you don't deal with these young girls in here."

Polo had made that point several times that night.

He said, "Yeah, but that don't mean I don't like to watch them."

Spoonie laughed and said, "Okay, so who the pervert now?"

"Ain't shit perverted about watching fully dressed girls. How you figure that?"

"It's perverted when you watch how they dance and start talking about wet dreams and shit."

"That was just a figure of speech."

"Yeah, aw'ight, I got your figure of speech."

Shareef shook his head. The two grown-ass men were at it again. And before he descended the stairs with them, he snuck one more look to Ms. California sitting on Baby G's lap, and he wondered if the young man had enough game to take her all the way home.

The Heat Is On

TRAP DIDN'T LOOK TOO FRIENDLY when he arrived outside of Zip Code to talk to Shareef. He pulled him aside and said, "Yo, man, let me ask you a question right quick."

Shareef thought about Polo's joke concerning a grade school call-out, and he figured it wasn't that far-fetched.

"What's going on?" he asked, concerned himself. Had he offended Trap in some way? Shareef was baffled by the sour tone. He didn't have a clue.

Trap looked him in the eyes and quietly asked him, "Did you make a visit 'up north' today?"

Shareef exhaled and mellowed out. "Oh, yeah," he answered. He had nothing to hide about that. And why would that anger Trap?

Trap said, "Who did you visit up there?"

Shareef paused. Now it began to hit him. Who was Michael Springfield connected to and who were his enemies?

He answered cautiously. "Why, is it enemy grounds?"

"Tell me who you saw first."

Shareef figured Trap already knew, so he went ahead and confirmed it.

"Michael Springfield."

Trap eyed him another second in silence before he nodded his head to accept his answer.

He said, "Do you know him like that?"

Shareef shook his head. "Nah, I don't know him like that. He just wanted to meet me."

"I heard more than that. But we gon' get to that in a minute. So who took you up there?" Trap asked next.

Shareef said, "Some girl I know." He wasn't sure how frank he should be with his information. He would have to wait it out to see what Trap's angle was first.

"Some *girl* you know? Do we all know her?"

"I don't think we do, but I don't know."

"Well, how well do you know her?"

"I mean, I know her, but I don't really know her like that. Why?"

Shareef continued to play hopscotch with his answers. He still wanted to see where Trap was going with it all.

Trap studied his face with intensity. He said, "Look, this ain't no make-believe bullshit you gettin' yourself involved in, man. If you don't really know this girl like that, then why would you go up there and start talkin' to a ma-fucka you don't really know about some book you writing. That shit ain't safe. The fuck was you thinkin'?"

Trap's violent tone and intensity got the attention of Spoonie and Polo, who were having a conversation of their own while watching the crowd and the passing cars that were still pulling up outside the club.

Polo asked, "What's going on, B? Is there a problem?"

Trap backed away from Shareef and answered, "There may be a problem."

Spoonie looked at Trap for an explanation. "What? What happened?"

"Shareef went 'up north' this morning and met up wit' a ma-fucka that he didn't tell us shit about. If he would have told us that shit last night, I would have told him not to do that shit. But he went and did it already."

Polo and Spoonie both looked at Shareef for his explanation.

Trap said, "Go 'head, Shareef. Tell them who you visited."

Shareef asked, "I mean, what's going on with him? What's the deal?"

He still didn't know any of the particulars from Trap.

Polo asked, "You went 'up north' today? You didn't tell me that."

Shareef said, "That's where I got this whole Harlem book idea from, this girl who knows Michael Springfield."

Spoonie repeated, "Michael Springfield? You visited Michael Springfield in jail today? What is he trying to talk about?"

Shareef answered, "He was only talking about his life story, and how he surrendered from all of the bullshit that got him there in jail."

"Yeah, and he may just surrender a bunch of fuckin' names of niggas who still out here in the game, too. You don't know what that nigga's intentions are" Trap stated.

He shook his head and said, "I still can't believe you did that shit. I mean, I'm sitting there bragging about you in the barbershop, talking about how you working on writing a book on Harlem, just to see who I could get to talk to you, and these motherfuckers start looking at me like I'm stupid. It was like, you already had your story, a story about Michael Springfield, who may be ready to rat ma-fuckas out, while using your dumb-ass to do it."

Shareef didn't like the sound of that, nor did he like being called a dumb-ass.

He said, "What the fuck makes you think I'm gonna allow him to name drop, and then actually use those names? That's slander, in the first place. I can be sued for that shit."

Spoonie added, "You can be *shot* for that shit."

"But why would you talk to that motherfucker anyway without asking us about it first?" Trap asked him.

"Dig it," Spoonie agreed.

Polo was still stunned by the whole line of questioning. He was stuck on the fact that Shareef had visited prison and hadn't said anything about it.

Shareef answered, "Look, I didn't want too many opinions when I went up in there. I just wanted to see what he had to say, and if it turned out to be something, I would deal with it. If not, I would move on. It's as simple as that."

"Well, it ain't that simple to these other motherfuckers," Trap told him. "They gon' wanna know what he said to you. And then I heard you walked across the fuckin' yard with him."

Polo looked at Shareef again. He said, "You walked across the yard with him?"

Shareef was stuck on that one. He answered, "I didn't even know you could walk on the yard. I mean, I was caught off guard with that."

"Did he want you to walk across the yard with him?" Trap questioned. "Was it his idea?"

The charades were over. Shareef understood he needed to give full and straight answers.

He nodded. "Yeah, it was his idea. But it wasn't like he asked me about it, he just started walking forward and told me to follow him."

"And you did exactly what the fuck he told you to," Trap summed up. He shook his head and said, "Well, your Harlem story is over with, B. So pack up your shit for tomorrow, and go on back home. It ain't safe for you up here now."

Polo was still speechless. Spoonie didn't have anything to add, either. But Trap continued with plenty on his mind.

He said, "All you had to do was ask me, man. But now you got me looking like an asshole, too, 'cause niggas know I know you like that. So they're asking me what's going on. And where the fuck is this girl you talkin' 'bout?"

All eyes were on Shareef again. He didn't know what to say. He thought about calling Cynthia on her cell phone to ask her a few questions himself. She hadn't called him back at all that night. Was it all a setup to get him in hot water with the streets? And if so, why? Did Michael Springfield have a story to tell or what?

He answered, "I don't know where she at right now, man."

"You know where she live?" Spoonie asked him.

Shareef shook his head. He was feeling more ridiculous by the second.

"She always visits me at my place and gets her own transportation back home," he answered.

Trap said, "So you don't even know where this girl lives."

Polo commented, "He don't know where a lot of these groupie-ass girls out here live, B. That shit ain't unusual."

"I'm just saying, you see how bad this situation is when you deal with people you don't know?"

Trap seemed to have calmed down a bit.

Shareef nodded to him and admitted, "You got me there. I guess I fucked it all up then."

Polo wasn't so sure. He said, "Just because he met with the ma-fucka don't mean he gotta write shit about him. Just say you're not gon' do the shit. All you gotta say is you didn't know what time it was. But now you do."

Trap started shaking his head already. He said, "It's too late for that, man. He need to get the hell out of Dodge. I heard about the shit today; how many people you think gon' know about it by the weekend?"

Shareef was actually surprised that news of his visit "up north" had traveled back down to Harlem that fast.

"I mean, who knew about me being up there anyway?" he commented.

Trap looked at him as if he was insane. "Nigga, are you crazy? They know who you are. They may not all read your books, but they know your fuckin' name. Shareef Crawford. And they know that the women know you. So they gon' fuckin' talk about it.

"The streets is always talkin'," he said. "And now they talkin' about you."

Trap had already tasted the strength of the venom within a few short hours. Nervous and connected criminals had made note that he needed to handle his boy's curiosity or suffer the consequences himself.

"Let your man know what time it is and tell him to leave that shit alone, B. That's for his own good health . . . and yours," Trap was told by unnamed faces.

On one hand, Shareef felt a tingle of fear that the wrong types may be thinking about him in the wrong way. But on the other hand, he was curious about how fast word on the street traveled about him writing a Harlem book. Was the street life that alluring? Men had never been concerned about any of his books before. So he was tempted to see just how big of a deal a book on the Harlem underworld could be. It felt adventurous, like writing about a war zone from the middle of the war.

He said, "So you think Harlem would be that pressed to read something that I put out on the street life?"

It was a challenging question, and one that would imply that Shareef was willing to ignore Trap's warning and write a Harlem book anyway.

Trap said, "The point is, if you're gonna write something that they don't want people to read about, then they're not gon' want you to write it. Period."

Shareef asked him, "But is that for the few or for the many?"

Trap became alarmed again. He said, "Look, man, if he got a whole gang of niggas against him, then you'll have that same amount against you."

And me! Trap thought to himself. But how much of his own fears or his own participation in the Harlem streets was he willing to let Shareef know about? The man had pride, more pride than Polo and Spoonie combined. So he had learned to guard his life's interests.

"But I thought you said Harlem don't roll thick like that no more," Shareef asked him.

"I'm not talking about one crew of niggas, man, I'm talking about this kid droppin' names on people who don't want their names out there. I mean, you not gettin' me, man. This ain't some script meeting. This is real life."

Polo asked, "But what if he don't write shit about the dude? What if he just write about the game in general."

Spoonie shook his own head. He said, "Man, don't nobody wanna read about no game in general unless you droppin' names. That's how the magazines do it. And that's how that video chick, Superhead, sold her book. She was droppin' real names. You know that."

Trap figured he had said enough, but he wanted to give his friend one final warning.

He said, "Shareef, I know you, man. You can be a hardheaded nigga sometimes. That's just how you are. But I'ma tell you right now, you gon' play with this Harlem fire, and you gon' get yourself burned the fuck up."

He said, "So if I was you, I'd go back to writing what I've been writing, living how I've been living, and just call Harlem home. Because the stakes is too high out here to be playing fuckin' Columbo. You feel me?"

Shareef listened but he remained unmoved by it. He didn't get to be a writer in the first place by ignoring his instincts. His peers had told him before that he would never make a living writing books. But not only had he made a living from it, he had accumulated millions from his writings. In less than ten years, he had proven the naysayers wrong and had them lining up on his side now while celebrating his name. And it all felt good to him.

There was something there to write about in Harlem. Shareef wasn't willing to let it go that easily. There were thousands of people he could write about at home. He didn't need Michael Springfield's story. Nor was he willing to allow street talk to scare him into running away from doing his research. He hadn't written a word yet. How did they know what he was willing to write?

Trap studied Shareef's unfazed mug for another minute before he finally gave up on him. "Aw'ight, I'm gone, B. You gon' do what you gon' do, and it's gon' be all on your head like a red egg."

With that, Trap left them and walked down the street away from the crowd.

Spoonie looked at Shareef and said, "Are you sure you still wanna do this Harlem book, man?" He wondered if Shareef would be shaken himself. It wasn't as if he had to write about Harlem. He would still be rich and popular without it.

Shareef looked back at him. "I still haven't made up my mind yet," he answered. "I need to think more about it."

Spoonie shrugged and said, "Aw'ight, well, y'all going back in this party or what?"

Just as he spoke, Shareef looked past him and saw that Baby G, the young street celebrity, was guiding Tiffany, the California girl, to a black Chrysler 300 that had pulled up and parked in the street in front of the club. They had a protective line formed out of his young followers, like a red carpet affair.

I guess he do have game enough to get her, Shareef told himself. And in his loss, he had no more desire to reenter the party.

He shook his head and answered, "Nah, I'm good for the night. I need to think a little bit more about all of this anyway."

Spoonie said, "Aw'ight, well, I'ma stay at the party. And Polo, you drive Shareef back home to safety." Then he stopped and asked, "You need my gun?"

Polo looked at him and chuckled. "Nigga, you ain't the Godfather. Fuck are you talking about?"

"I'm just trying to make sure my boy get back home safely, that's all," Spoonie joked. "You need me to send a goon squad with you?"

Shareef smiled it off himself. "Nah, I'm good, B. Harlem don't scare me like that. I grew up here."

Spoonie eyed him and said, "Shit, so did ten thousand other motherfuckers who died of bullet wounds in Harlem. That don't mean shit that you was born here. What, you think that gives you a force field? Nigga, you betta' wake up and get off that high horse. Anybody can be touched in Harlem."

• • •

WHILE POLO DROVE Shareef back to his hotel room on Frederick Douglass Boulevard, not that many words were exchanged between them until they arrived out front.

"So, what do you think about all this, man?" Shareef finally asked his friend.

They sat in the jeep outside the hotel entrance.

Polo nodded and continued to look forward out of the windshield. He said, "First, I want to thank you for helping me out of my jam like you did with them five Gs, son. That's first of all."

He turned to Shareef and gave him a handshake for it.

"Yeah, just try to stay up above water for yourself and your family, that's all," Shareef advised him.

Polo joked and said, "Yeah, that's easy for you to say."

Shareef stared at him. He said, "You know what? A rich man actually has more to lose than a poor man, B. And if I fall behind on my shit, five Gs ain't gon' cut it. 'Cause see, between me and you, it takes me and my family about twelve Gs a month to live."

He said, "And some people may say, 'Well, you can do without this,' and 'You can't do without that.' But the reality is, I'm a goal-oriented person. The challenge of life is what I thrive on. That's what keeps me up and going. So I can handle what I got as long as there's a new goal in front of me. And this right here, this Harlem shit . . . it's a new goal, B. A big one. I can feel it."

Polo looked into his boy's eyes in silence for a minute.

He said, "I just hope you not try'na bite a bigger piece of pie than you can handle right now, Shareef. Like you said, you got a lot on your plate already. I mean, my kids only see a hundred dollars a month from me, if that. But how much your kids gon' miss each month if something happens to you?"

Shareef blew him off with a smile. "Shit, man, I got life insurance. They'll be all right. They still gon' see it."

Polo didn't budge. He said, "That shit ain't funny, son. That ain't nothing to joke about. The last thing in this world I would want is for you to come back home to Harlem and lose your life over some bullshit. I wouldn't be able to take that shit right there, man. That's word to my whole family."

He said, "You an inspiration, B. You a shinin' light in the dark for niggas around here. And not only that, but who else can I count on next time I fall five Gs behind the eight ball?"

They shared a laugh about it.

Polo said, "But seriously, man. You need to really think about this shit, Shareef. I mean, Trap know them street niggas better than all of us. So if he say to leave that shit alone . . . then leave that shit alone."

Shareef looked away from him and stared into empty space. He said, "You can't get nowhere in life by being afraid of it, man. And I'm not gon' sit here and lie by saying I'm never nervous about shit, but I always find the courage to stand up for what I believe in."

Polo said, "Yeah, you gon' stand up until you get blown the fuck down. Like Spoonie said, all that Superman shit is gon' get you in an early grave. I mean, you sound like one of them old-school boxers who can't take his gloves off, B. And what do they end up doing; they end up fighting the next great nigga in his prime, and get themselves beat the fuck up and embarrassed in the ring. I mean, let it go, Shareef. Just let it go."

Shareef took a deep breath and had no more to say about it. Everyone was against his Harlem masterpiece now. Or at least his friends were.

Shareef nodded and went to grab the door handle. "Aw'ight, man, so I guess, um, I'll just go ahead and visit my grandparents tomorrow before I decide when to take a plane back to Florida."

Polo said, "Yeah, if you fly out by like, eight, then I can drive you back over to the airport after work."

Shareef continued to nod to him as he climbed out.

"Aw'ight, I'll call you up."

As he walked to the entrance of the hotel, Polo continued to stare at his friend's back, knowing better. He shook his head and mumbled,

"That nigga ain't gon' listen. That's just what makes him Shareef."
Then he started his jeep back up and drove off.

SHAREEF CLOSED and locked the door to his hotel room and fell out
across the bed near the window. He looked up at the ceiling and pondered his fate. His decision had already been made. He couldn't leave
Harlem. The streets would have to force him to leave. And it didn't
matter what his friends had to say about it. Because Harlem had a
story to tell, and a good writer had to write it.

Walking the Walk

THE FIRST THING THAT MORNING, Shareef called up his grandparents over in Morningside Heights.

"Shareef. What are you doing up this early?" his grandmother asked him.

It was just after seven in the morning.

He grinned and said, "Come on, Grandma, I'm always up early. I've been up early my whole life."

"So what are you trying to say? I'm getting senile already? Is that it?"

"No, I'm not saying that at all. I'm just stating the facts. I've always been an early riser. But anyway, I'm just calling to say that I'm on my way over there to visit you guys at the house this morning."

His grandmother became hysterical.

"What? You're back in New York? And you didn't tell nobody?"

"I'm telling you now," he argued.

"Well, how long have you been here?"

Shareef chuckled, knowing that he was in for it.

"Come on, out with it," his grandmother pressed him.

He said, "I got in Tuesday night."

"And it's now Thursday morning. That's just my point," she told him. Then she called his grandfather. "Charles, Shareef's on his way over here! So get yourself together!"

Shareef shook his head and couldn't wait to see them.

As EARLY AS at 8:32 that morning, Shareef was dressed, groomed, fully alert, and already walking west on 122nd Street toward his grandparents' brownstone home off Amsterdam Avenue. When he reached Morningside Park, he analyzed how the natural boundary and height separated Columbia University from the rest of Harlem. The school and the established neighborhood that surrounded it sat way up on the hill.

Shareef loved walking through Morningside Park because it felt like a nature hike right there inside the urban jungle. Central Park gave him that same feeling, but Morningside was closer, and his grandparents lived there, which made it more relevant to him.

Once he had made his way through the park and up to Morningside Drive, the economics of Harlem became crystal clear. The City College of New York was separated from the lower parts of Harlem in the same way, divided by St. Nicholas Park. And so was the celebrated neighborhood of Sugar Hill, up above Jackie Robinson Park. Was it all by accident? Hell no! It was aristocratic architecture. The civil engineers of America had always taken such natural boundaries into consideration. In the game of housing and property value, prime land was tagged with prime prices.

So Shareef paid extra attention to all the fabulous brownstone homes he passed that morning before he reached his grandparents' home, a place that had cost him close to seven hundred thousand dollars on an absolute steal. The seller had decided that he loved Charles and Wilma Pickett so much, and with them coming so close to being able to afford the place with the help of their famous grandson, that he was honored to let them buy it for less than the asking price, knowing they would treasure the home and maintain its value. And they did, becoming the sweethearts of the neighborhood with their morning walks.

Shareef rang the doorbell that morning and was proud all over again of his decision to move his grandparents up on the hill to Morningside.

His grandfather answered the door in a tan jogging suit and soft tennis shoes. He said, "Are you sure you weren't in the military in your past life, Shareef? Because you're always on time."

Shareef laughed and said, "Maybe I was," and stepped inside. He wore gray sweats and athletic kicks himself.

The tall ceilings, crown moldings, and hardwood floors of the foyer were all reminders of old-world design, and made the brownstones more valuable.

Shareef said, "I forget how nice this place is."

His grandfather responded, "We don't. We thank the good Lord every day for you and for all the good fortune you've brought us."

"Aw, you know how I feel about that, Grandpop. It was what I was supposed to do. Any thankful grandson would have done the same if given the chance," Shareef told him.

His grandfather said, "Well, it don't matter how *you* feel about it, I'm just telling you how *we* feel. And every grandson wouldn't have done what you did for us. Some of them out here are ungrateful bastards. And they end up doing the opposite of what their parents told them. So you've been a dream of a grandson to us."

Shareef wondered how his grandparents' assessment of him would change once they learned of the Harlem underworld story that could put his life in danger. Would they think it too risky as well?

"Wil-ma! Shareef is down here!" his grandfather yelled up the stairs.

She yelled back down, "I know! I heard the doorbell!"

Shareef smiled and took a seat in his grandfather's tall, comfortable chair inside the large living room to the right of the foyer. He picked up a copy of *Uptown* magazine, a new Harlem life publication that sat on the reading table beside him. The actor Terrence Howard was featured on the cover.

His grandfather mumbled, "No matter how much time they have in advance, you always end up waiting for a woman to get ready. That's exactly why I got that chair sitting right there next to the door. So I can sit there and read while waiting for her."

"I heard that!" his wife yelled down the stairs again.

Charles looked at his grandson and shook his head in silence.

Shareef figured he would have snapped *Well, do something about it then!* to his wife. But that was the difference between him and his grandfather. Charles Pickett had a lot more patience.

Shareef asked him, "Did you always have this much patience, Grandpop?"

His grandfather looked at him sideways. He said, "Are you kidding me? I was as impatient as you are at your age." Then he whispered, "But I didn't have as many options as what you got to *stay* impatient. You know what I mean? So I just had to deal with what I had to deal with."

His wife trotted down the stairs dressed in a light blue jogging suit with a white stripe up the side, and a matching light blue visor hat with her own tennis shoes. They were all dressed appropriately for casual walking.

Wilma Pickett told her grandson, "Don't let this man tell you no lies about what he had to put up with from me, Shareef. Because if I didn't take that man, he would be old and lonely right now."

She said, "I'm one of the last surviving women of our neighborhood. Them other women were droppin' like flies. Harlem living was just eatin' them up."

She looked at them so comfortable inside the living room and asked, "So, are you two strong black men ready to take this neighborhood walk or what?"

Shareef set the *Uptown* magazine back down and stood up.

"Hopefully, I can get the cover of a magazine like that one day. I'm from Harlem," he commented. It was a prelude of what he planned to talk about with his grandparents that morning, rediscovering his Harlem roots.

His grandmother looked at the magazine and said, "Well, I'm gonna write them a letter, and give them a few phone calls to put you right up on the next one then."

"Uh oh," his grandfather looked away and grumbled.

"What, he said he wanted to be on there. And if you want something, you gotta learn how to ask for it."

"Exactly," Charles responded sarcastically.

"What are you trying to say?" his wife asked him. "That I don't know how to ask for things?"

"You said it, I didn't," he responded.

"Yeah, but that's what you're getting at."

Shareef followed his grandparents out the front door and continued to smile. Between their friendly bickering and what he had been around the night before with Polo and Spoonie, he realized how much he had missed the wit of his Harlem family and friends.

"SO, WHAT ARE YOU up here researching, Shareef? Because I know you're always researching something," his grandfather asked him as they walked through the campus of Columbia University—even campus security knew the couple. They had often visited the school libraries and attended various campus events.

Shareef's grandmother listened for his response as well.

He answered, "Well . . . I've just been thinking a lot about home lately, you know. And I just feel like I need to be able to do something special for Harlem."

His grandfather nodded. He said, "That's good."

But Wilma was listening more intently. She said, "What do you mean by 'something special'?"

"Well, I've been pretty much writing . . . you know, romance stories so far. But with Harlem . . . I mean, I just want to flip the script for a minute and write about the realities of this community, you know. Harlem got a lot of history that shouldn't be taken lightly."

His grandfather asked him, "So you're trying to write a more historical book on Harlem?"

"Well . . ." Shareef hesitated, looking for the right words to use. He said, "I wouldn't call it historical, it's just more . . . dramatically based than it is romantic."

His grandmother read through all of that and said, "So you're planning to write a book about Harlem crime and the street life, like that last film about Sugar Hill, starring Clarence Witherspoon as a drug-addicted father?"

His grandmother didn't miss a beat. So Shareef decided to humor her and throw her off track.

"Actually, I was thinking about writing a book about a cute older couple who fight the elements of the streets to maintain Harlem as the classy, cultural, significant place of their youth."

Wilma looked at her grandson and smirked. "Bullshit," she told him. "Who's gonna read a book like that unless Oprah says so? I mean, I know what you gotta do, Shareef. You gotta write about the real. I listen to what's goin' on out here today with the youth. That's why we attend a lot of these campus events up here. And they need a good lesson every once in a while."

Shareef was surprised to hear that from her. He expected to have to defend himself with her. Instead, he got excited.

He said, "Yeah, Harlem could use an updated story that could stand the test of time. And I figure I'm good enough of a writer to do that."

"Sure you are," his grandfather agreed. "As long as you present the whole story with balance."

Shareef frowned and said, "That's the biggest problem. The youth don't like balance too much. They just like action and drama. They don't want no backstory and details. And then the elders typically only want to read who they've been reading.

"Then I got my romance audience who only want more of that," he commented. "So my editor wants me to write this Harlem street story under a pseudonym, called The King."

His grandmother eyed him sideways. She said, "The King?"

"Yeah, short for King of the Streets," Shareef answered with a grin.

"Hey, how are you guys doing today?" a student asked as they approached him on campus.

Wilma said, "Hey, Arthur, this is my grandson, Shareef Crawford, who writes the books I was telling you about." She looked to Shareef and said, "Arthur is a journalism major and an aspiring writer himself."

Shareef shook the dark-haired white student's hand. He reminded him of his editor, Bill Sorenski, before corporate America got to him and refined his image. Arthur was still rough around the edges in his choice of wrinkled clothes, tumbling hair, and loose posture like a college student would be.

He said, "Yeah, I read one of your books, *Chocolate Lovers.*" He nodded and said, "It was pretty good. I'd loved to interview you one day for the campus paper, on your work."

Shareef put a professional bug in his ear for the future.

"Yeah, we can call it 'The Revival of Harlem Writing,' " he told him.

Arthur nodded and said, "Hey, I like that."

"Yeah, I'm working on something right now that I think the school might be interested in," Shareef added.

"All right, well, let's trade numbers and talk sometime."

Since the young journalist had already done some homework by reading one of his books, Shareef figured he had nothing to lose. So they traded numbers and email addresses.

When they all separated, Shareef's grandmother told him, "You see that? You even have a white America college boy reading some of your work."

Shareef grinned, knowing better than her hype.

He said, "Yeah, after you've talked to him about me several times already, I'm sure. In fact, you probably gave him a copy of that book of mine he read."

He hugged his grandmother and added, "But it's all good, Grandma. I wish I had a million people like you working the college campuses for me."

They all shared a chuckle about it before Wilma got back to their conversation.

"But anyway . . . now, what was I thinking about before he walked up and interrupted me?" she asked herself aloud. "Oh, yeah, this pseudonym thing your editor was talking about. I don't like that idea."

She said, "If you have something to say, then you should be brave enough to say it. I don't like people hiding behind these anonymous names and things. That's just cowardice."

Charles spoke up and said, "I don't believe that's the reason he's doing it though. I believe he's trying to keep Shareef's romance audience while at the same time gaining him a new audience."

"Well, that didn't work when Stephen King tried it," she argued. "It just confused people. So if you want to separate the work you've been doing from this new book, then all you have to say is 'Shareef Crawford Presents, Harlem Nightmares' or whatever, and then explain that it's a different kind of book. That way you don't do all this work only to confuse an audience and fail at what you're trying to do."

She said, "I still believe that honesty is the best policy. So if you want to do something different, then you tell the people, and you make sure you explain why."

Shareef nodded and liked the idea; "Shareef Crawford Presents . . ." It held the illusion of a more dramatic creation, which was exactly what he wanted from the book.

He said, "Thanks, Grandmom. I might use that. Shareef Crawford Presents . . ."

Wilma grinned from ear to ear. She told him, "And you make sure you tell people where that idea came from, and that'll help you to sell more books to the older crowd."

She even stopped walking and asked him, "You need me to go with you on your book tour for this one? 'Cause I'll let 'em all know. 'You *read* my grandson's new book. It's good spiritual medicine for you. *All of you.*'"

Charles heard that and shook his head. "Aw, you dun' did it now, Shareef. You've created a book-pushing monster."

As a wide smile stretched across his lips, all Shareef could think about was the show of support his grandparents were giving him to be brave enough to finish what he planned to start, a cutting-edge book about the underworld of Harlem.

BY THE TIME Shareef made it back to his hotel room, it was three o'clock in the afternoon and he had four messages on his cell phone to return. Two messages were from Cynthia, one was from Polo, and the last was from Jacqueline back home in Florida.

Shareef called Jacqueline first.

"Are you still having fun in Harlem?" she asked him.

Her tone sounded antagonistic. Shareef pushed her buttons on purpose to see if he was reading her attitude correctly.

"Oh, yeah, I'm having big fun up here. It couldn't be better."

"I know how it could be better," she commented.

"Oh yeah, how's that?"

She said, "If I was up there with you."

Shareef decided to go for broke with her, especially since he no longer trusted Cynthia.

He said, "Well, come on up here then."

Jacqueline paused. "So, you can buy me a plane ticket for tomorrow?" she asked him.

Shareef answered, "Nah, you get the plane ticket yourself and I'll reimburse you for it when you get up here."

She said, "You not gon' buy the plane ticket for me?"

"If I was there with you, I would. And when I'm ready to bring you up here with me, I will. But if you insist on coming up here before I'm ready to bring you, then you gotta get your own plane ticket and fly yourself up. And I'll reimburse you like I said."

Jacqueline was silent for a minute. Then she said, "You told me you would take care of me if I take care of you, Poppi. Then you told me you would take me to Harlem with you. But now you're telling me to take care of myself."

He said, "I'm not telling you that. I'm just saying, if you wanna come up to Harlem so bad right now while I'm still doing research, then you gon' have to get yourself up here, because I got other things on my mind to worry about right now."

"You can't make one phone call to the travel agency and get me a ticket to fly to New York tomorrow?"

She was persistent.

"What about your job?" he asked her.

"I'll take a sick day. Then I can stay up there in Harlem with you for Friday and Saturday, and we come back together on Sunday. Come on, I miss you, Poppi," she whined to him.

Shareef felt like hurling his cell phone out of the hotel window.

Why did I even call her the fuck back? he asked himself. *These women are all fuckin' crazy. Why do I even deal with them?*

He finally said, "Look, Jacqueline. I'm up here doing work right now. Okay? This is not fun and games time. I'm on the clock right now with new book business."

Jacqueline said, "Well, why would you tell me to come if you really didn't want me to?"

"I was just being sarcastic when I said that. Okay? So I apologize for that. And I'll make it up to you when I get back home," he added.

She said, "You're always making something up to me, Shareef. I don't like that anymore. I thought you were gonna treat me right."

She was wearing his ass out. Shareef took a deep breath and ran his left hand over his face in frustration.

If it ain't one thing, it's another, he mused.

"What do you want me to do?" he asked her in surrender.

She said, "I'll think about it and call you back. I'm just really upset with you right now. I'm horny, and you don't want me to come see you."

He said, "It ain't like that at all, girl. Now you know, if I was home, I'd be all over you. But how do you think I get to afford the things that I have? I have to work for it. I'm not out here picking dollars off trees."

"Are you being sarcastic again?" she asked him. "Because I don't like that, either."

Well, what the hell do you like? he screamed to himself. But he kept his cool like his grandfather instead of voicing it.

He said, "Well, all I know is that I like you a lot. And I miss you. But if I don't get things right while I'm up here, then bye-bye condo, bye-bye Mercedes, and bye-bye dinner at all those fancy restaurants."

She said, "Well, those things are all fun, but that's not why I like you, Poppi."

Shareef took that to heart. He slowed down a second and said, "Okay, why do you like me then?"

"Because you get so excited," she told him. "I mean . . . you're just so real. And I've been around guys with money before. That's not a big thing to me. I can pick up a guy with money any day of the week. All you have to do is go where they go and look good. And I look good naturally."

Shareef chuckled and said, "Yeah, you damn sure do. You wake up looking good."

"Then why am I sitting here alone without you?"

Shareef stopped in his tracks and thought, *Damn! . . . I'm gonna lose this girl. And I'm gonna miss her like crazy when I do.*

He realized that he could never match her intensity for him. He just wanted a good-looking woman he could keep and chill with. But now he understood that it would never be an equal match between them. And as many men as there were out there who would give everything for one night with Jacqueline, Shareef wasn't willing to give her one night away from his job.

All he could tell her was, "I'll be home Sunday afternoon. And I'm gon' eat you on the kitchen table like Thanksgiving dinner. So keep that turkey cold in the refrigerator and fresh for Poppi for when I get back home."

"Hmmph," Jacqueline grunted. "You lucky I like you so much. So I guess I'll read another one of your books tonight. And tomorrow. And Saturday."

She stretched it out on purpose, to let Shareef know how long it would it be.

But he had already put out the fire. So he was satisfied with that.

He said, "Yeah, you do that. Read *I Want More,* and then you get ready for me on Sunday."

When he finally ended the call, Shareef took another deep breath and told himself, "I dodged another one." But how many of Jacqueline's emotional bullets could he hope to escape from before she would land fatal shots of frustration to his heart and kill him? It was only a matter of time before that happened. However, for a goal-oriented man, it didn't matter. Because he still had shit to do.

Shareef realized as much and mumbled to himself, "That's probably how I lost my damn wife, too."

The Kingdome

SHAREEF GATHERED HIMSELF TOGETHER and pumped his heart up enough to venture down to Martin Luther King Jr. Housing Towers at 115th and Lenox for the summer league basketball games with no crew, no friends, and no protection. If the hard rocks of the Harlem streets were desperate enough to make an attempt on his life over a book he wanted to write, then so be it. But they would have to kill him out in the open, because he definitely wasn't going into hiding to avoid any of them.

As he hit 115th Street from where he walked on St. Nicholas Avenue, he could already see the crowds of basketball addicts who double parked all over the streets and inside the housing parking lots, as they made their way into the playground area to watch the games.

Fuck that! I'm from Harlem, Shareef continued to tell himself as he approached what was referred to as The Kingdome Tournament. The Kingdome Tournament was the people's response to what they viewed as the overcommercialization of the Rucker League in North Harlem, which had been turned into a corporate-sponsored athletic event that the Harlem public could no longer enter comfortably. The tournament at the MLK Housing Towers, however, represented purity, getting back to the essence of basketball itself.

Yet basketball purity did not mean the Kingdome Tournament was without its own sponsored hype machine. Where the corporate pow-

220

ers of Reebok, And 1, Pepsi, and the like were absent, there were the urban dignitaries of the music industry and professional basketball association, the likes of Sean Combs, Damon Dash, Cam'ron, Stephon Marbury, Rafer Alston, Sebastian Telfair, among others, who gave their financial as well as physical support, while parking their Rolls-Royce Phantoms, Maybachs, Ferrari Spiders, and custom security vans all around the court as was their due as urban royalty.

Shareef saw all of that, where the general public of Harlem—from the youngest ice-cream-eating kids to the oldest denture-wearing grandparents—were all invited out to watch the games on a first-come, first-serve basis. And from the tall, cement bleachers that enclosed the basketball court, Shareef let go of his concerns about security and was happy just to be there. Spectators were sitting in trees, on car rooftops, leaning out of apartment windows, and generally enjoying the games from whatever angle they had available to them.

"Shit," Shareef mumbled out loud while grinning. "This is Harlem."

And what would that Harlem be like without the sounds of new music, pumping from every car sound system? There were food vendors selling hot dogs, chips, candy, water, Gatorade, and soda. Sampler mix tapes were spread throughout the crowd, featuring up-and-coming rap artists as well as old stars with new hits. The Spear was out there hustling his books again. Brand-new clothing lines were being rocked for the first time out in public, along with brand-new jewelry designs, car rims, sunshades, and signature basketball shoes. There was enough urban ritz and glitz to die from an overdose of commercialized culture. And with so much to openly strive for, no wonder the less fortunate could stand it, and not stand being without it.

The overdose of Harlem was the American way. It represented the near delusional hopes and dreams of the red, white, and blue better than any other neighborhood in the country. Where else in America but in Harlem would millionaires be so regularly involved and approachable to the common people who could barely find a daily job?

And where else but in Harlem would the common people feel so connected to those millionaires, to love them for their success, or to hate them for it?

Shareef took it all in while he looked for an open seat on the cement bleachers in front of the basketball games.

"Yo, Shareef!" someone called him.

Shareef turned to find the voice and spotted Spoonie, who was walking toward him. Spoonie was as glam as the other players, spectators and hustlers in the crowds. He wore a pair of dark blue designer sunshades in the bright sunlight.

"You decided to stay up here anyway, hunh?" he asked Shareef while grinning.

"Like I said, man, I'm from here. I'm not running. What that look like?"

Spoonie answered, "That look like a smart man to me, but . . . whatever, son. To each his own out here.

"*Damn!*" he shouted suddenly. Spoonie was reacting, along with the crowd, to a monstrous dunk that Shareef had missed. He turned too late to catch it, and at a playground tournament with no view screens available, there were no replays.

"Aw, you making me miss the game already, man," Shareef joked.

"Shit, this game over wit' already. You late. They up by like thirty."

"Yo, son, your name Shareef? Shareef Crawford?" someone else asked.

Shareef looked and didn't recognize the young man. Was the game of intimidation about to begin? If it was, they would have to send someone a lot more intimidating than this guy. He looked like a straight-laced honor-roll student to Shareef, with bright, trusting eyes. But maybe that was the trap, to send the message through an errand boy who wasn't intimidating.

Shareef looked him in the eyes and said, "Yeah, who wanna know?"

The young man smiled and pulled out a pen and piece of paper. "My friend wanted you to sign an autograph for her. She was scared to ask you."

Spoonie started chuckling. From the look on Shareef's face and the question that he asked, Spoonie knew Shareef had been thinking the worst.

Shareef smiled back at the young man and took the pen and paper to sign it.

"What's her name?"

"Talisha."

Shareef signed his name on the paper first and said, "Spell that for me."

"T-a-l-i-s-h-a. And thanks, man."

He held out his palm for a handshake.

Shareef shook his hand and felt good about it. And as soon as the young man began to walk away from him and back into the crowd, a young woman asked, "Who is that?"

"Shareef Crawford, the writer."

"Oh, hey, I read your books. Can I get an autograph, too?"

And then it began. Shareef's name got tossed around in the crowd like an errant Ping-Pong ball. It wasn't as if they could readily place his face with his name like they could with athletes and rap stars, who received plenty of media coverage and camera time. Shareef was only covered for minutes at a time on local news channels, and usually only during the three to four weeks of a book tour. So his name was twenty times more popular than his face. Such was the case with most authors. Just because a person wrote a great book didn't make him or her a recognizable celebrity.

Nevertheless, Shareef started signing autograph after autograph and bringing more attention to himself in the crowd before Spoonie pointed something out to him.

"Ay, Shareef," he said, and nodded his head forward.

Shareef looked across the basketball court and spotted twenty-five to thirty Harlem street soldiers all gathering in black T-shirts, with one lone orange tee.

"That's how Baby rolls," Spoonie commented.

Shareef nodded back. Everyone in the crowd could clearly see the young general's grandstanding, even the national rap and basketball stars who were present. Baby G was marking his territory in bright orange, while surrounded by a small army of black.

Shareef said, "I thought y'all told me Harlem don't have any more big cats like that."

Spoonie frowned at the notion of Baby G being considered a big deal.

He said, "Man, that's just pure charisma. All those guys he's with are young. They're mostly teenagers just looking up to him."

"They may be young, but they got numbers," Shareef argued.

Spoonie said, "You can find that in every neighborhood in America. But it's still just small-time shit. He ain't really running nothing. He's just gettin' attention."

Shareef thought about it while he continued to sign autographs.

"And Harlem lets him get that attention with no beefs?"

Spoonie thought about that himself.

He said, "He knows who he can get away with shit with. Plus, a lot of the old-timers like him. They figure he can keep a lot of bullshit off the streets with all the younger bloods who follow him."

Shareef stopped signing autographs and said, "He sounds more interesting by the minute."

He stared out across the court and watched the young general in his orange T-shirt interacting with everyone around him.

Spoonie said, "I know you not planning on trying to interview him."

He was jumping two steps ahead already.

Shareef smiled and confirmed his thoughts.

Spoonie shook his head and said, "B, you up here just *asking* for trouble."

"You already told me he likes attention. What you think a book gon' give him?"

"It's gon' give him a meaning to worry about your ass misquoting some shit from him. And the older guys he know wouldn't like him talking no shit in no book, either."

"Yo, you Shareef Crawford?" an older, more intimidating man stepped up from the crowd and asked him.

Shareef looked him over with more courage than earlier and answered, "Yeah."

"You writing a book about Michael Springfield?"

Shareef hesitated. "Who told you that?"

"It's on the wire, son. Is it true?"

Shareef didn't know what to say. It was the moment of truth, and he was choking on it.

Spoonie butted in and said, "That shit's just a rumor, man."

"But you writing some shit about Harlem, right?"

When Shareef looked past the man, he could see two or three more pairs of eyes cutting in his direction.

Spoonie said, "He from Harlem."

The man looked into Spoonie's grill and said, "Yo, man, I already know that. But won't you let him answer his own questions."

Shareef finally spoke up and asked, "Would you read a book about Michael Springfield?"

The man didn't hesitate. "It depends on what he got to say," he answered. "But if ain't got nothing good to say, then I wouldn't write it."

Spoonie couldn't help himself. He said, "He not."

The man looked him in his grill again and kept his silence. Then he looked back at Shareef.

"Aw'ight, be safe out here, man," he warned him before he walked away.

That wasn't that bad, Shareef told himself. In the meantime, his heart was pounding like thunder. Then he looked across the court again and spotted Trap slipping through the crowd on the other side. Or he thought it was Trap. But he didn't get a close enough or long enough look to confirm it. So he decided to ask Spoonie about it.

"You seen Trap today, man?"

"Nah, but he around somewhere."

"In the crowd?"

"Nah, I'on know. Why, you lookin' for him?"

Shareef shook his head and continued to look forward.

"Nah, I was just asking."

"Hey, Shareef, you're writing a book on Harlem?" a young female fan asked from the crowd behind him. She had overheard some of the conversation, and Shareef still hadn't found an open seat to sit down and relax.

He answered, "Not yet. I'm still trying to decide on it." Either way, it was obvious that the word on the streets about a new book from him about Harlem would travel at lightning speed.

When the next game was ready for tip off, Shareef's cell phone went off. He looked down and read Cynthia's number. He had ignored her calls long enough, so he went ahead and answered. He had to figure out what he wanted to do about the Michael Springfield situation anyway.

"Where have you been? I've been calling you all day," she told him.

"I've been running all day," he answered.

"Well, you still going back 'up north' with me tomorrow, right? We can start putting this book together for real now."

Shareef looked right into Spoonie's face as the next game started. Spoonie was close enough to overhear parts of his phone call.

"Yeah, we'll need to talk about that. Can you meet up wit' me tonight?"

She said, "You not gettin' cold feet on me now, are you?"

"Nah, I just need to see you, face-to-face."

"When?"

"Anytime tonight."

"Where are you? It sounds like you're in the middle of a crowd."

The Harlemites were getting excited about the next game.

Shareef said, "I am. I'm at the Kingdome Tournament."

"Oh, yeah, I've been there before."

Shareef was ready to ask her with who, but he figured he would save all of his questions for later.

He said, "We can meet back where we said good-bye yesterday at like ten o'clock."

"On One Twenty-fifth and Lenox?"

"Yeah."

"In front of Starbucks?"

"Yeah, that's good."

"Aw'ight, don't have me waiting there."

"Why would I do that?"

"*Oooohhh!*" the crowd moaned after a crossover and three-point shot fell through the net.

"I'm just letting you know," Cynthia told him jokingly.

"I'll see you there then," he told her. "You're getting in the way of the game now."

"Whatever."

Shareef ended the call and went back to watching the game. He hadn't made up his mind what he wanted to tell Cynthia about Michael Springfield. He still didn't know what he wanted to do himself. But he did want to ask more questions about everything, questions he should have asked her before.

"Shareef Crawford. We just keep bumping into each other. That must mean something. It gots to mean something."

Shareef looked to his right and spotted Jurrell Garland again. He was in blue jeans and a light blue tennis shirt.

Spoonie backed up to give the man room to shake Shareef's hand.

Jurrell commented, "You're checking out all the new Harlem culture spots now, hunh? You been to the Rucker?"

Shareef shook it off. "Nah. I hear this is what's happenin' now."

"Yeah, pretty much. Things change, you know, like people."

Jurrell looked and nodded to Spoonie.

"What's up, man?" Spoonie addressed him.

"Just takin' it light," Jurrell told him.

Then he turned back to Shareef. He said, "I'm still waiting on that phone call, man. And you still here. Call me up, let's get some coffee or something."

Shareef happened to look across the basketball courts and spotted

Baby G eyeing him. But as soon as he noticed it, the young general looked away.

Are these motherfuckers all watching me on the low out here, or is it just me? Shareef was forced to ask himself.

He decided, *Fuck it, go for the jugular.*

He tapped Jurrell on the arm and said, "Yo, you know this kid across the court in the orange T-shirt? They call him Baby G."

Jurrell looked over, spotted him, and nodded. He chuckled and said, "Yeah, I know him. But that Baby G shit is for them young guys. I just know him as Greggory."

He said, "I did time with his older brother Samuel. He ended up getting killed in there. Somebody got to his throat with a flat head."

"A flat head?"

"Yeah, that's like a flat razor, a piece of metal, or a sharp glass that you use like a blade."

Shareef wondered if he should leave the information alone. But on the other hand, his old nemesis probably knew the most about everything. Jurrell was still his best connection to the streets, especially since Trap wasn't willing to help him.

Shareef looked back and noticed that Spoonie had disappeared, so it was just him and Jurrell in the crowd now.

"Yo, ah . . . what you know about Michael Springfield?" Shareef asked him apprehensively.

Was he getting himself deeper into trouble or what?

However, Jurrell answered the question with no hesitation.

"He's part of the old guard. He been off the streets since the late eighties but he still know what's goin' on out here."

"Is he safe to talk to?"

Shareef was actually warming up to Jurrell. What the hell, they practically grew up together. They ran on opposite sides of the streets, but they were still familiar with each other, *very* familiar.

Jurrell said, "What, to ask him questions for your book?"

Shareef became cautious again. "Is that a bad idea?"

It was a good question to the right person.

Jurrell said, "It depends on what kind of information he give you. If he just give you a straight hustler story, then you just determine if it's gangsta enough to package and sell like a rap album."

He said, "But if he start naming names in the game like that Superhead shit . . . I mean, you ain't dealing with people who can afford to ignore it, you dealin' with street niggas. And they just struggling to stay alive out here. So, they not gon' take no rat lightly. They can't afford to. That's what all these rappers already know. So they don't snitch."

Shareef took all the information in and nodded.

Jurrell smiled at him and squeezed him on the shoulder. He said, "I got some more folks to talk to out here, Shareef. But give me a call, man. If you really want to write a gangsta book about Harlem, then I know everybody. All we need to do is sit down and talk about it."

Shareef told him, "Aw'ight."

Jurrell stopped before he walked off. He pointed his finger, smiled and said, "Stop bullshittin', man. Call me up."

Shareef chuckled and repeated himself. "Aw'ight, I got you."

Jurrell told him, "I hope you do."

As soon as he walked away, Shareef felt incredibly alone, which was weird. He had walked there by himself and planned to be alone, outside of the crowd, of course. But there was a community relevance and energy that Jurrell brought to the table that seemed to disappear when he left. The brother was like the missing link.

Shareef nodded his head and realized that he had to call him. Then he finally found a lone seat on the bleachers and watched the rest of the game, while everyone else seemed to be watching him.

Action!

"SHAREEF, what is your problem, man?" Polo asked his friend. "You need to be out of here." He said, "All this hardheaded shit with you, man . . . look, we not kids no more, B. This should be your last night here. Go back home and kiss your wife and kids."

It was close to ten o'clock at night, and they were standing out in front of Starbucks on 125th and Lenox, while Shareef waited for Cynthia to arrive.

He smiled at his friend's warning and said, "Y'all exaggerating a little bit, man. Ain't nobody sweating me over no book I haven't even written yet."

Polo looked at him incredulously. He knew exactly how his friend thought.

He said, "Shareef, I understand that you think you a genius and all that, but I'ma tell you something, man. These streets don't care about that. Now, you out here asking people you don't really know all these questions about the wrong shit, and it ain't sexy. I know you may *think* that shit is, but it's *not*."

Then he whispered, "This ain't no fuckin' game, man. This is real life, Shareef. Close the chapter on this book and move on to another one."

It was Polo's final warning to his childhood friend, and after that, he planned to stay away from him like Spoonie and Trap had decided. Spoonie was convinced after hearing Shareef ask Jurrell too many questions at the basketball tournament earlier. The man was asking to be murdered. He was begging for it. But Shareef refused to budge.

He said, "I understand your concerns, man. I do. And if something happens to me, it's nobody's fault but my own. But I feel like this shit right here is a *calling,* man. And if it's a calling for my death . . . then that's what it is."

Polo stood there and thought, *This nigga's crazy! What the fuck is wrong with him? I mean, am I dreaming this shit or what?*

Polo didn't get it, but Shareef refused to believe that street soldiers, who rarely read any books, would be willing to kill him over one. It just didn't add up to him. So the streets would have to prove that a book was that important to them, not just by threatening him with stares and intimidating questions, but with real actions.

Cynthia popped up from the subway station before Polo could get another word out. He didn't have anything left to say anyway.

"Right on time," Shareef greeted her with a hug. He stepped back so he could take a good look at her. She was all dolled up for the evening, with flowing hair, in a bright floral, wraparound dress, and gold heels, all sure to make a man stare with a hard one. And she carried a large bamboo bag over her shoulder.

Shareef said, "Damn, you make me look like a bum tonight." He was still wearing his gray sweats and basketball shoes from the morning walk with his grandparents.

He turned to Polo and said, "This is Cynthia. Cynthia, this is my man, Polo."

She smiled and extended her hand to him. "Nice to meet you."

Polo left her hand hanging. He grilled at her and said, "If something happens to my boy out here, now I know what you look like," and he walked away.

Cynthia looked back to Shareef in confusion. "What was that all about?"

Shareef stared at Polo's back and shook it off. He said, "I'll tell you about it in a minute. Let's walk down here and get something to eat in the Lenox Cafe."

They walked across 125th Street on Lenox and stepped into the historic cafe on the other side, while Shareef watched everything that moved around him. Just because he didn't believe the hype of danger didn't mean he shouldn't be prepared for it.

The Lenox Cafe was one of the last establishments still standing from the Harlem days and nights of decades ago. Much of the interior was unchanged, with old, cafe stools at the bar, a serving line rail, record machines, and autographed celebrity photos on the walls of Billie Holiday, Miles Davis, John Coltrane, Louis Armstrong, Joe Louis, Muhammad Ali, Sugar Ray Robinson, Redd Foxx, Dick Gregory, Harry Belafonte, Diana Ross, Chaka Khan, Minnie Riperton, Aretha Franklin, Michael Jackson—and the list went on. Smooth R&B music played in the background.

Shareef sat at a small table near the wall to the right and immediately ordered buffalo wings and drinks.

"You want some shrimp, too?" he asked Cynthia who joined him at the table.

She grinned and turned him down. "I already ate, but thank you."

He nodded and looked her over again. She was a dangerous plate of curves and sex appeal. No wonder Michael Springfield was so eager to know what he thought of her.

Cynthia got right down to business. "So, what was up with your friend?"

Shareef took a breath and asked her, "What's up with *your* friend? I seem to be getting a whole lot of flack for this book idea."

"From who?"

"From people who got the word off the wire. Them guys in there been talking already . . . unless you did it."

Cynthia shook her head and told him, "You need to get used to that. They always talk. They talk and they write letters. I mean, they're in prison. What else can they do?"

"Well, how many enemies does he have out here?"

"What?"

"You heard me. How many enemies does he have who are still out in the streets?"

She shrugged. "I don't know. Why would I be concerned about that? He hasn't been out on the streets in years."

Shareef said, "Well, I'm concerned, because people on the street are starting to ask me about it."

"Asking you about what?"

"About this book I'm supposed to be writing."

"So. That just means they're interested. That's a good thing, right?"

Cynthia was blowing the danger off faster than Shareef had.

He smiled and then chuckled at it.

"It's just that simple, hunh?"

"What's so hard about it? People talk."

She took a sip of her drink as soon the waiter put it down in front of her.

"So, people never threaten you about your relationship with him?"

"I mean, they may ask me about it, but they don't threaten me. For what?"

"Yeah, well, you weren't writing any book about him, either. That changes everything. He can become published now. And that's different from your everyday gossip. A book is the gospel. It's permanent."

Cynthia summed things up and said, "I thought you told me you didn't have cold feet?"

"I'm still here, right? And you heard what my boy Polo said. They're all against this shit."

"And you told them all about me?"

"I didn't know it was a secret," he commented. "I didn't tell them anything outside of this book idea, but they can assume everything else. They know how I get down with fine women."

Cynthia smiled and sat silently for a minute.

She said, "You're stronger than that, Shareef. You're the one. That's why I like you, and that's why Michael chose you."

I just don't know if I chose him, Shareef thought to himself. *Or you.*

And he held his tongue as he continued to think it all over. He figured maybe he would go in his own direction with his own Harlem story. So he ordered drinks and ate to think on it.

WHEN THEY HAD FINISHED THEIR MEAL, Shareef paid the bill as they stood up to walk out. Chicken wing bones were left on the plate, along with celery sticks and ranch dressing in a small plastic cup. Shareef had downed three drinks to Cynthia's two. He had a lot on his mind to think about.

"Hey, come back anytime, Mr. Crawford," one of the bartenders yelled out as he and Cynthia headed for the door.

"Yeah, I'll do that," Shareef responded, loaded up on the alcohol.

"What's the next book you working on? Any movies?"

They always asked Shareef about the movies. Movies seemed to be the next logical step for successful authors.

Shareef answered through the frankness of the alcohol, "This is still America, brother. And white folks are surprised that we're even reading books. So they're not quite ready to do the full Hollywood thing with us. And we still ain't got enough brave money to do the shit ourselves. So it'll take me a while to work on that."

When Shareef walked out of the cafe behind Cynthia, he was glassy-eyed and walking gingerly.

Cynthia noticed it and giggled. "You can't even hold your alcohol. I know you're a square now," she teased him.

Shareef grilled at her. "Yo, you gon' stop talking that square shit." Then he stuttered, "That's, that's for real."

She was caught off guard by it and stumbled in her laughter.

"Shit. You got me tripping over myself now."

Right as she regained her balance, a young man dressed in all black reached out and snatched her handbag clean off her shoulder and dashed down the block.

"Shit! Somebody grab him!" Cynthia yelled.

The young man had too much momentum for the slow-reacting

folks who were still out that night. He made a swift left turn on 124th Street and was out of sight in a flash.

Shareef and Cynthia ran to the corner of 124th and Lenox and saw the boy halfway down the block already.

"Damn, that ma-fucka movin', ain't he?" Shareef commented. "How much was that bag worth?"

Cynthia said, "I had all my shit in there. My keys, every damn thing. God!"

Shareef thought about taking off after him and mumbled, "Shit, I can't catch that motherfucker. He look like Carl Lewis from here, wit' a big-ass head start on me."

Cynthia looked at him and said, "You couldn't run now even if you wanted to. You'd run right into the back of a car or something. Shit."

Shareef looked at her and asked, "You want us to call the cops? All I gotta do is push you out in the middle of the street. They'll show up."

"Yeah, very funny," she told him. "But I can't even call the cops."

He looked at her confused. "Why not?"

Cynthia ignored his question and walked away from people who could help them. Some of them had cars parked at the curb who could chase the boy down.

"Come on, let's get back to your hotel before something else happens," she suggested.

"Why you don't wanna call the cops?" Shareef repeated to her as he followed her across Lenox and 124th. His hotel was in the opposite direction from the purse-snatcher.

Cynthia grumbled, "I'll tell you in a minute."

Shareef still wasn't getting it. The alcohol had messed up his sharpness.

He said, "You'll tell me in a minute?"

When they made it across the street where there was much less pedestrian traffic, Cynthia revealed quietly, "Don't get all loud about it, but I had a gun in my bag."

Shareef studied her face as he continued to follow her up the street.

He said, "For what?"

"What do you mean, for what? For protection."

"From who?"

She stopped and faced him. "From assholes like that one."

It all made sense to her.

Shareef said, "So you had that on you the whole time?" He was perplexed by it.

"I always have it on me unless I'm going to the prison," she told him. She started walking along 124th Street toward his hotel again.

Shareef asked her, "You had it on you when you met me?"

"Yeah, I didn't know you like that."

"But you fucked me," he told her. It didn't add up for him.

"After I got to know you a little bit," she responded.

"You mean, after you got to *talk* to me a little bit."

"Whatever, same thing. How do you get to know people?"

She sounded like a guy to Shareef. Getting to know someone through conversation alone, and no time spent, was a sure way of collecting the most panties while out on the road. That only got him thinking again about how much he really didn't know about the girl.

"So what other surprises you got for me?"

She blew him off and answered, "None. I just have to figure out how to get my shit back."

He said, "Well, what else you want me to do? You know I ain't in no shape to be chasing nobody. And then you didn't want me to call the police because you had something in there.

"So how are you gonna get back in your apartment tomorrow?" He asked her. "And how will you prove that it's you? Did you have any money in there?"

Cynthia shook her head and said, "Those drinks got you talking a mile a minute. But I'm gonna have to deal with all of that tomorrow."

She stopped walking and snapped her fingers. "Shit! What about going back to the prison tomorrow? Now I don't have any ID."

"They already know who you are at that prison anyway, don't they? It's not like you gotta be put on no list," he told her.

Cynthia calmed back down. "Yeah, you're right. So are you going with me tomorrow or what?"

Shareef continued to ignore that question.

He told her, "A smart man has to think on it more; weigh the pros and cons." Truth was, he didn't want to go. She would have to convince him again.

She grimaced and said, "Whatever. It sounds like you're just bitching now to me."

Shareef grunted and smiled at her. He said, "I've figured out your M.O. now. You like to challenge me to do what you want. But I'm not falling for that shit no more. So if I write anything about your boy Michael Springfield, then it's gonna be for me and not because somebody dared me to do the shit. This ain't grade school."

Cynthia smirked at him. She thought about how far she had gotten him to go along with her program already and kept quiet. But there he was, a bestselling author, back home in Harlem, hanging out with her instead of his friends and family. So she grabbed his hand and continued to walk with him.

He looked at her and said, "Yeah, now you wanna try and get close to me, hunh?"

He may have had more drinks than he could handle that night, but he still had his wits about him. He knew what a girl's intentions were. He had been writing about them for years. And he planned on dropping this one like he had done with several others. The curious charade was over.

However, Cynthia continued to smile and remained speechless as they made it to 124th and Adam Clayton Powell. She would allow her body to do the talking once they had reached the room on Frederick Douglass, another block away. A drunken man was a long-lasting man. And she had plans for the rodeo that night.

As they got closer, Shareef began to grin to himself, thinking about another roll in the hay with her. It felt good for a man to be able to take care of his needs when he needed to.

This is what my wife needs to learn to do, he insisted to himself as he walked with Cynthia in his inebriated stupor.

"We're almost there now," he looked over at her and joked. "We're almost there."

INSIDE A DARK SEDAN parked on Frederick Douglass Boulevard near the corner of 123rd Street, two black men in their late twenties sat up front with a younger man in the back.

The man in the passenger seat looked forward to his right and spoke.

"Yo, that's him right there with the girl."

The driver looked and studied the woman more than he did the man. "Damn, she a bad ma-fucka, son. He got 'em like that?"

The passenger nodded. "Yeah."

The younger man in the backseat didn't care about any of that.

He said, "Yo, B, you want me to pop him right now?" He already had his gun out.

The passenger snapped, "Look, man, I don't want you to do shit but watch. Just know who he is, all right. That's all you're here to do."

The passenger then jumped out of the car and walked toward the couple on the sidewalk. The young man in the back put his gun away and watched from inside the car.

SHAREEF BEGAN TO DIG in his right pocket for his room key as he and Cynthia approached the hotel entrance.

"Yo, you Shareef Crawford, ain't you?" someone asked him out front.

Shareef looked to his right and spotted a slightly younger man in dark summer clothes. They were about the same height and build.

He joked and said, "What you want, an autograph?" He was still thinking fast. He knew that a well-placed joke would catch an enemy off guard, especially while he had a pretty woman with him. Black men loved to keep their cool around sexy women.

And it worked. The man smiled and responded, "Nah, maybe for my li'l sister or something, but I'm here to ask you a few questions."

"About publishing and writing?" Shareef joked again.

The smile left the man's face. Enough bullshit was enough.

He answered, "Yeah, you can say that. I'm here to ask you about a book you're supposed to be writing."

Cynthia squeezed Shareef's hand to keep his composure.

"What book is that?" Shareef asked.

The man seemed to be getting more irritated by the second.

"Look, man, you know what fuckin' book I'm talking about, that Michael Springfield shit you 'sposed to be writing."

Cynthia spoke up and said, "What about it?"

The man looked in her face and responded, "Excuse me, miss, but I wasn't talking to you."

"Well, I think it's a little too late to be out here talking about some damn book," she told him. "Y'all need to do that at another time."

The man got ready to speak, only for Cynthia to cut him off.

She said, "I'm standing out here tired, my feet are hurting, my back is bothering me, and I need to get up in this room, take off these clothes, and lay down and get my medicine, if you know what I mean. And all this shit right here is just slowing up the process."

Shareef looked at her and giggled. "Lay down and get your medicine, hunh?" he repeated.

He was impressed with her perfectly timed speech.

"Yeah, come on," she told him, dragging him toward the entrance by his hand.

The man in front of them looked on and said, "Aw'ight, we gon' do this another time then."

He also noticed the security guard standing behind the entrance of the hotel.

"Aw'ight," Shareef told the man as they parted ways.

. . .

THE PASSENGER RETURNED to the car.

"So, what he say?" the driver asked him.

The man shook it off. "It ain't the right time. We'll catch up to him," he commented.

"It ain't the right time?" his young triggerman questioned from the back.

"Yeah, it ain't the right time. I don't want to be out here forcing it. We'll catch up to him."

He figured he wouldn't want another man messing up his pussy, either. That was bad karma. So he let it ride.

The triggerman grunted from the backseat and mumbled, "If you say so."

The driver started up the engine of the car before they drove off into the Harlem night.

UP INSIDE THE HOTEL ROOM, Cynthia was incensed. She paced the floor and blasted, "These motherfuckers! Let me use your cell phone."

Shareef gave it right up to her.

He said, "I told you they've been asking me about it." He smiled and added, "I like how you got us out of it though."

"But how do they know where you stay?" she asked him before she used his phone.

Shareef had to think about that. Outside of the other guests who stayed there, Polo, Spoonie, Trap, and Cynthia were the only people who knew.

Before he could respond, she concluded, "You're gonna have to move down to a hotel in Times Square in the morning. Because you can't let them know how to get to you."

"I thought you told me it was no big deal?" Shareef reminded her.

Cynthia ignored him and dialed a number on his cell phone.

She continued to pace the room while she spoke into it, "Yeah, this is Coffee. What's up? I need a favor from you."

Shareef had a seat on the bed near the bathroom. He thought to himself, *Did Trap tell these guys where to find me? Is he still trying to warn me to get the fuck out of here? Maybe I need to call his ass after she gets finished.*

"I need two more heaters," he heard Cynthia say into the phone. That got Shareef's undivided attention.

Who the fuck is she talking to? How deep in the streets is she? he was forced to wonder.

She said, "My fucking pocketbook got stolen out on Lenox . . . I don't know, some little boy just ran past and snatched it off my arm and kept running down One Hundred and Twenty-fourth Street . . . Less than an hour ago . . . I had the heater in there with my house keys, my IDs, every-fuckin'-thing. I gotta get all that shit back tomorrow."

She looked Shareef in his face and answered "Yeah" to whatever question was asked of her over the phone.

"It's on Frederick Douglass, right down the street from Magic Johnson's movie theater."

Shareef stared at her. She must have been telling somebody to come there.

"How you gon' get them guns past security?" he asked her calmly.

Cynthia ignored him again.

"In about an hour?" she asked over the cell phone. "Aw'ight, just call me back on this number when you get here. And oh, bring another bag for me to put it in."

When she ended the call, Shareef was all over her.

"Yo, who you all dealing with up here?"

The seriousness of his concerns began to snap him out of his drunkenness. He could feel a headache coming on from thinking too hard. A thousand thoughts were zipping through his mind all at once.

"I know a few people," Cynthia answered.

Shareef continued to stare at her.

"So now you're gon' carry *two* guns?"

"No, one is for you."

Shareef looked bewildered. Now he really felt a headache coming on.

He shook his head and said, "I'm not carrying no gun. I don't trust myself with that shit. I mean, you got some people who bluff with guns all day long, but I'm not the bluffing type. So if I gotta gun . . ."

He shook his aching head. "Damn, all this shit is making me need some Tylenol or something," and he grabbed the front of his head, massaging both temples with the thumb and middle fingers of his right hand.

Cynthia told him, "You gon' have to carry a gun. You don't have no choice now."

Shareef refocused and asked her, "Well, who the fuck is his enemies?"

Cynthia shook it off again. "Look, I don't know. All I know is that you need to protect yourself no matter what."

"Protect myself from what, thug niggas who don't want me to write a book? I mean, come on, man, this is crazy. Half these niggas don't even read."

Shareef attempted to deny the urgency again. He even chuckled at it. But that only increased his throbbing headache.

Cynthia told him, "You can believe that if you want. But they know how to read what they want to read. They read that damn *Feds* magazine. *Don Diva. XXL. King.* They read all that. And some of them even read your novels, like Michael does. What you think, he's the only one 'up north' who knows about Shareef Crawford? I mean, think about it. They have your books in the prison library. *Requested.*"

The last thing in the world he needed was an argument with her.

"Ah, shit," he complained, sinking his head down into both of his hands.

Cynthia immediately became motherly. She sat down beside him on the bed and hugged him around his shoulders.

"Aw, man, and all my aspirin and stuff was in my bag. Let me call downstairs to see if they have a vending machine or an all-night gift shop or something."

"This ain't the Sheraton," Shareef looked up and reminded her. "Why don't you call your boy with the heaters back and tell him to stop off at an all-night drugstore to buy a box of Tylenol for you? Tell him you got a headache."

Cynthia smiled and picked the phone up. "Men," she stated. "Y'all can have headaches, too. Obviously."

Shareef only wondered what he was doing with that girl up in Harlem in the first place. He figured he deserved a headache.

She dialed the number again and spoke into the phone, "Yeah, it's Coffee. I need you to do me another favor . . ."

The Plot Thickens

EVEN AFTER A HANGOVER, Tylenol, and all-night thoughts about guns, friends, loyalty, street life, and the personalities of Harlem, Shareef was up bright and early at slightly after seven in the morning. And while Cynthia remained asleep in the bed near the bathroom, he sat on his bed near the window and searched the Yves Saint Laurent handbag she had placed on the floor.

He slid his hand inside the bag and quietly pulled out a black Beretta handgun that he refused to keep. It was a perfectly sized gun to conceal inside a waistband. It fit so well inside of Shareef's right hand that he found it hard to ever imagine missing the target with it.

He aimed it at the small television set and thought, *Shit! I would have to be a terrible shot to miss with this.*

Realizing how easy it was to become attached to a gun, Shareef shook it off and returned it to Cynthia's bag on the floor. He then stretched out across his bed and spoke to the ceiling:

"Call me a fool, but if I'm gon' go out, I'd rather go out without using a gun. So which one of you ma-fuckers wanna fight me with your hands? Old School style."

Out of the blue, Cynthia started chuckling. She said, "People don't fight with their hands anymore. So you can forget about that. Unless you're in a boxing ring."

244

She faced him from her bed and added, "Either you're gonna use that gun I got for you, or they're gonna shoot you without one."

He said, "All this coming from the same woman who told me at dinner last night that I was safe. Funny how things change once somebody gives you a reason to fear something.

"It looks like you're the one with cold feet now," he commented.

Cynthia mumbled, "Yeah, well, some of us have to live and die here. We all don't have a big old house out in the suburbs somewhere that we can run back home to."

Shareef said, "You wasn't born in Harlem. You got somewhere else to run to. But I was born here."

"So what's that supposed to mean?"

"That means that anybody can get up and leave if they want to," he told her. "We got all these new people moving to Harlem every year, and just like they came, they can leave."

He said, "You're not stuck here. Harlem's not a prison, it's a community. So if you can't handle it here, then relocate, just like you told me to do."

Cynthia raised her head from her pillow and looked at Shareef with concern.

"I hope you're not planning on staying here, especially with no gun. Is that what you're saying? Because I hope you're not."

He said, "I haven't made up my mind yet."

"Well, you need to make it up fast, because check out is in what, three, four hours?"

"What about your prison visit? Are you going up there with these guns?"

He had a good point.

She said, "I told you, I don't take guns up there. But now I have to get all of my IDs and keys and everything back. So . . ."

"So you're not going?"

She shrugged her shoulders. "When are you coming back? Are you still willing to write the book or what?"

Shareef stared at her and asked, "Just out of curiosity, what do you think I should do?"

She looked at him for a minute before she dropped her eyes to the pillow.

She said, "To be honest with you . . . I wouldn't blame you if you just walked away." She looked back into his eyes and added, "I mean, you have a whole lot to lose, and I think your friend Polo realizes that. And I can't let myself be selfish about it. That would be wrong."

Shareef chuckled and said, "Yeah, 'cause Polo would hunt your ass down if you got me killed."

Cynthia remained silent for a minute. She said, "Look, I'm sorry for getting you involved in this. But like I said, I don't know who his enemies are, and Michael doesn't even talk about specific names and stuff, just what's going on in general. So I don't even know why they're trippin'. He's not a snitch. He's more like a street philosopher, that's why I started dealing with him as friends. I just felt like he had a lot to say in all the letters that he wrote me."

"That's how you met him, through letters?" Shareef finally asked her.

"Well, I had a friend who knew him before he went to prison, and started writing me letters, but yeah, that's when I first started to get to know him."

"And then he came up with this book idea?"

"It was both of us actually."

Shareef nodded. "So, what's in this book deal for you? He plans on paying you for it?" In his excitement over a project about Harlem, he had been slipping on his research.

Cynthia seemed uneasy with the question. She took a breath and frowned. She said, "Well, of course he's gonna try and take care of me for my part in it, but that's not why I'm doing it. I'm doing it because he has an important message to share about the streets. And it's not just about the money, it's about trying to get people to see what's going on out here. And we both felt that you would be the best writer to do it."

Shareef had heard the rationalizations for publishing street literature before. And adding his expertise to the equation was indeed a plus. Nevertheless, he was tempted again to ask Cynthia the more personal question of whether she and Michael had been involved in any conjugal visits in the time that she'd been associating with him, and did that push her over the edge of reason. But he still wasn't ready to know that answer.

He said, "Well, somebody thinks he has something to say that they won't like, and it looks like they don't want me to hear it."

They were both silent for a period. What was there left to say? Would Shareef still pursue the Michael Springfield story? Was Cynthia serious about letting him walk away from it?

"So . . . you wanna go get some breakfast?" he asked to break the awkward silence between them. He was hungry.

They both laughed at it.

"What, in the same clothes I wore last night, with no deodorant and no new underwear?" Cynthia answered him. She said, "I can't even brush my teeth this morning. And you want me to go to breakfast with you. I don't think so."

"So, what are you gonna do?" he asked.

"*You're* gonna pay for me to catch a cab back home, then I'll get a new key to my apartment, get myself showered up and situated, and start pulling together everything I lost in my handbag last night."

Shareef nodded. Her plans all made sense to him, but he had no idea what he was planning to do that day. He figured he'd start off by calling Trap to see what he had to say about the man who questioned him outside of his hotel the night before.

"Are you still gonna try and stay here tonight, or are you going downtown?" Cynthia asked him.

Shareef remained undecided. He could stick it out for two more nights up in Harlem, or punk out and check into a Times Square hotel. That's how he viewed it. It was a simple choice of courage or cowardice.

Cynthia insisted. "I mean, you're only here for two more days, right? Why chance it? Just go on downtown and enjoy yourself, Sha-reef. You've earned it."

He nodded and began to see her point. Two days didn't make much of a difference in bravery, but staying just an hour too long could end his life.

"Yeah, aw'ight, I'll make the move," he grumbled. He added, "But that don't mean I'm scared. I ain't never scared," he joked.

Cynthia shook her head and chuckled at him. She said, "I'll give that to you. For you to walk around like you do with no posse, no bodyguards, and no gun, you gotta be one of the bravest guys in Harlem."

"Or the dumbest, right?" he questioned.

Cynthia shook his comment off. She knew better than to believe he thought that. It was only his sarcasm.

She said, "No, you're hardly dumb. You're a man of strong princi-ples who's willing to stand up for something. And they don't make a whole lot of guys like you anymore."

Shareef responded, "Strong principles, hunh? What do you think about me breaking out on my wife then?"

Cynthia was caught off guard by the question. She studied his face and took another deep breath before she answered.

"I can tell that it bothers you, otherwise you wouldn't think about it so much. And if it bothers you, then you have a conscience about it. But . . . I'm just gonna keep it real with you, Shareef. There are a lot of women out here who get involved with wild men, thinking they can tame them, and that just doesn't work all the time. So they end up fooling themselves and getting their feelings hurt."

Shareef cracked a smile. He said, "Are you calling me a wild man?"

"Oh, I am *definitely* calling you a wild man. And I know you know that already. So don't even try to act like you haven't heard that before."

She said, "But at the same time, you know what's right from wrong. It's not like you're out to hurt her on purpose, you're just doing you. And if she can't handle that, then . . ."

She shrugged her shoulders again.

Shareef asked her, "Well, how come she could handle it in the beginning?"

Cynthia began to laugh out loud.

She said, "Haven't you written about all of this, Shareef? When a woman gets involved with an untamed man, she loves it at first. She wouldn't have it any other way. But she has in her mind that he's gonna grow out of it soon. And when it takes longer for that to happen than what she expected, all of a sudden she has a problem with it. So you end up with men who still want to have fun and get down spontaneously, and women who want to prepare for a week before they feel up to it."

Shareef broke up at the reality of her comment. He said, "Do you know how tiring that is for a man? I mean, I don't understand that shit."

She said, "A woman's maturity clock ticks way faster than a man's. We grow up faster. You know that. But you guys are hyper for like, what, the first *fifty* years. Especially the creative types. The athletes. Businessmen. Hustlers. All the men women really want. You guys feel like you're never gonna get old. So you go from one young woman to the next, or you find a loyal girl who can keep up. And that's a whole lot of keeping up to do."

Shareef had to agree with her. He had always been a fast mover. But why should he be punished for that?

He said, "But she knew that about me when she met me."

Cynthia could hear the stress and tension in his voice. She felt for him. The man was vulnerable.

She said, "Shareef, honey, look . . . women have no idea what it feels like to be a man. We think you're gonna run out of all that energy and settle down like a pet or something. We're ready to pat you on the head and tuck you into bed at night. But a man doesn't want to be tucked into bed. He wants some pussy. He wants his dick sucked. He wants to watch ESPN. He wants to catch the stock exchange. And a lot of women just can't understand that."

Shareef chuckled and was impressed again with her logic. He said, "You sure know a lot for . . ." He stopped and said, "I don't even know how old you are."

Cynthia smiled. She said, "I don't like telling people my age. I like the unpredictability the lack of that knowledge gives a girl."

Shareef nodded to her. "Yeah, you're right. Because you sound like you're about forty."

"Well, I'm not," she told him. "I just know a lot about life, just like you do."

SHAREEF GOT HER A CAB, gave her five twenty-dollar bills, and sent her on her way home before nine. Then he took a shower, got dressed, and went out to get something to eat. Check out from the hotel was not until noon. He figured he had time to eat and get back to gather his things before then. And while eating breakfast at a small cafe on Frederick Douglass, he finally got around to calling his friend Trap on his cell phone.

"Hello," Trap answered.

"Yo, was you at the Kingdome Tournament yesterday? I thought I saw you over there," Shareef told him. He wanted to warm up the stove before he cooked his meal.

Trap turned the stove on high.

"Why you still here, man? Didn't I tell you to leave?"

Shareef paused for a second. He said, "So, you know who wanna talk to me about this?"

"It don't matter, man. I can't stop it. Just like I can't tell you to leave, right, 'cause you too fuckin' hardheaded. But if you just leave the shit'll go ahead. You don't need to be here, man."

Shareef took the information in and nodded. It seemed like he had nothing left to fight for. All of the clues were pointing him in the direction of abandonment. He finally admitted it to himself.

"Yeah, you're right. I might as well scrap this idea."

"That's what you need to do, and *quick*," Trap warned him again.

Shareef didn't like the sound of that, but he had no choice.

"Yeah, aw'ight. That's what it is then."

After he ended the call, he stared into space for a minute and threw in the towel with a shrug of his shoulders.

"Fuck it, let me get out of here tomorrow then." He thought about it further and added, "Hell, I can probably fly out of here today."

He started thinking about making his son's Saturday-morning football practice and spending the night with his daughter. Then he thought about making up with Jacqueline at his condo.

Harlem may have been home, but it was no longer where his heart was.

Shareef finished his breakfast, drank his orange juice, and paid his bill. Just as he was pushing away from his table, he got a call on his cell phone.

He read the number on the screen and saw that it was Cynthia calling him from a house number.

He answered her call and asked her, "Are you pulling everything together that you need to get? I see you break in the house."

Cynthia didn't answer him immediately. In fact, she didn't answer his question at all. Instead, she choked up over the phone and said, "They killed him, Shareef. They killed him."

Shareef looked around the cafe to make sure he didn't overreact and say something to pull the other customers into his conversation.

"Who are you talking about?" he asked her.

"Michael. They killed him in prison this morning. Those motherfuckers!"

She began to sound hysterical.

Shareef asked her, "How do you know that already?"

She mumbled, "I called, and people called me back to confirm it."

"And they know this already."

"Yeah, they know," she barked at him.

He sat silently at his table and didn't know what to say.

"Damn!" he uttered. "So . . . how, um . . ." He wanted to ask her questions but he needed more privacy for that.

Cynthia read where he was going and answered, "They shanked him in the back and in the chest when he walked out of his cell this morning." She added, "It was a setup."

Shareef had no idea of prison rules and regulations outside of what he watched on television and in movies. So more questions popped into his head.

"Hold on," he said as he stood from his table. He heard her sniffing over the phone as he hustled out of the cafe to walk and talk outside.

"So they get to come out of their cells in the morning? And they don't know who did it?"

There were so many questions to ask.

Cynthia mumbled, "Look, just go on home, Shareef. It's over with. I'm sorry for getting you involved," and she hung up on him.

Shareef stopped and stood still on the sidewalk. He was stunned. Outside of a whole lot of questions he didn't have answers to, he began to think a thousand thoughts.

Did I get this guy killed by talking to him about writing a book on his life?

He shook his head and denied it all.

"That's crazy," he told himself. *This shit is all crazy!*

Shareef figured he'd make sense out of it all by calling the only person he was sure would know. Jurrell Garland. So he hustled back to his hotel room to find Jurrell's number on the business card he had taken from him.

"Harlem Mobile," Jurrell answered.

It threw Shareef off a second. How much had Jurrell really reformed himself? He still had obvious questions about that. Prejudice was a hard ailment to cure.

"Hey, man, this is Shareef. What are you up to for today?"

He didn't want to talk to him about everything over the phone. They needed another face-to-face meeting.

Jurrell cheered up and said, "Shareef. What's going on, man? It's about time you called me. I figured I was gonna have to bump into you three more times first."

Shareef smiled it off. "Nah, I said I would call you. I've just been busy running around."

"Yeah, I can understand it. Harlem'll make you do that. Ain't that many fat people in Harlem; we work it off."

Shareef chuckled to keep things light. He said, "But I wanted to talk to you about something, man. What are you doing for lunch?"

Since Jurrell had gone legitimate, a lunch date seemed normal to ask for.

He answered, "You know what, I can take you with me today. I got a few appointments to check out condos and business locations starting at one. What you got to do after that?"

Shareef answered, "My day is wide open, man. Let's do it."

"Aw'ight, well, meet me out at the Starbucks in an hour."

"You got it."

Shareef ended the call and thought it over. How safe would he be while hanging out with Jurrell? Did Jurrell still carry a gun? Did the streets respect him enough not to? It was all a new series of questions to answer.

"I guess I'll just have to find out," Shareef told himself.

He didn't have enough time to check into a hotel downtown and make it back to Harlem in one hour. So he packed up his things and left his luggage down in the front desk storage office until he could get back to it. He hadn't packed anything for this trip that was ultra valuable, so he wasn't that concerned with theft. And he headed out to Starbucks.

It was only natural for a sane man to become more alert with his life on the line. That two-block walk on 125th Street became the longest two blocks Shareef had ever traveled in his life. Every male eye and brown arm that strolled by caught his attention as if he had radar.

This is ridiculous, Shareef said to himself. It may have been, but he couldn't ignore his instincts, and his instincts told him to watch his back. Other brown men from his hometown were out to get him.

"Ay, Shareef," someone yelled out from behind him.

Shareef turned in a panic, expecting to duck, run, fight, or dive to save his life if needed. But instead of an enemy out to beat him, slice him, or gun him down, it was only The Spear with his box of books about street life.

"Oh, what's up, man?" Shareef addressed him. It was better to have The Spear than a murderer calling him. Shareef would never have smiled as wide for his competitor in the publishing world otherwise.

The Spear walked up close and stated, "I heard you got some serious content you working on, brother."

"Not anymore," Shareef responded. "I'm out of here tonight."

He wanted to get the word out that he was done with the Harlem book idea and leaving town immediately. Only he wasn't gone yet. And that reality was bothersome and dangerous.

The Spear told him, "Well, I don't know who advised you on this, man, but whoever it was wasn't thinking straight."

"Yeah, well, it's over with now," Shareef repeated.

"Are you sure?"

He stood still and pondered the question.

"What do you mean, am I sure?" What did the brother know.

He said, "If they think you know something, you just can't leave town and think it's over with. They're gonna want to know what you know no matter where you are."

Shareef didn't sweat that idea. He knew enough about the 'hood to know that most of the criminals there rarely traveled. And if they did, they were traveling to relocate, not to make a hit. It was unsafe to make a hit in a place you were unfamiliar with. Thugs generally terrorized familiar terrain only. The Spear, however, seemed to know something. So Shareef inquired about it.

"What have you heard?"

The Spear searched around to make sure their conversation was only between them. Then he mumbled, "I heard you were talking to the wrong guy."

"What was so wrong about him?"

The Spear looked around before he spoke again.

He answered, "Brother, you gotta ask yourself the question, 'Why now?' He could have tried to tell his story a long time ago. You feel me?"

Shareef shrugged his shoulders. "He didn't have a way to get to me until now."

The Spear shook his head, knowing better.

"Nah, brother. He tried to get other writers to tell his story too, and nobody would go anywhere near him. Until you came."

Shareef nodded. "So, I'm the sucker now, hunh?"

"That's what it looks like from here." Then he slighted him. "You should have stuck to writing romance."

Shareef took the diss on the chin and said, "Well, you tell whoever you know that's involved that I don't know nothing. I barely started talking to him. I was only there once."

"Yeah, and *once* is all it takes to find out something you ain't supposed to know."

Shareef had heard enough already. He snapped, "Aw'ight, whatever, man. Just tell the *streets* what I said."

He walked off for his destination thinking of "the streets" as one big earpiece. It seemed that the men of the inner city spread the word on criminal activity as strongly as their women spread the word on bedroom gossip.

As Shareef moved rapidly toward Starbucks, he noticed a dark car trailing him from the street to his left. He looked and noticed a young brother leaning out the open window, appearing to sneak looks at him.

Shareef slowed his pace and prayed that the young man wasn't crazy enough to try and get to him on a crowded sidewalk. As soon as he slowed his pace, the car sped up the block. Shareef waited for the vehicle to make a right turn on Lenox before he crossed 125th Street for the opposite side. He was less than half a block away from Starbucks.

SSSKRRRTT!

A white sedan jammed its brakes behind him.

"What the hell are you doing?" an older man yelled out of the driver's side window. His adolescent son sat in the passenger seat with wide eyes, terrified that his father had nearly run a man over.

"Yo, my bad, man. My bad," Shareef apologized to them both. He was so busy looking ahead to the corner of Lenox that he didn't even see the car.

"You damn fuckin' right it's your bad!" the father cursed him.

Shareef's nerves were too shot to argue. He made it across the street and continued on his way to Starbucks. When he arrived at the corner in front of Dunkin' Donuts, he glanced south down Lenox to his right, looking for the dark sedan that had turned there. Once he saw that it was out of sight, he hustled across the street and into Starbucks to meet up with Jurrell.

Shit, them guys are probably going back to wait for me at my hotel, he assumed. *And I still got my stuff there.*

Through the shop's window he spotted a taxi pull up right out front. He thought about leaving for the airport right then and there. To hell with his luggage! He could buy it all back again in Florida. But someone jumped into the cab before he could make up his mind.

"Damn," he mumbled as the taxi took off with another customer.

"Shareef," someone called from behind him again.

Shareef turned and looked. It was the young reporter from the *Amsterdam News* with a small coffee in his hand. He was wearing another pair of slacks, a button-down shirt, cheap tie, and a fresh haircut.

"Hey, what's happening, man?" Shareef addressed him.

The young reporter seemed overjoyed to see him there.

He said, "I heard what you're up here doing. That's real brave of you. Now that's a book I would read."

Shareef studied his face and couldn't believe his ears.

He repeated, "That's a book you would read? Why?"

"Because it's real, brother. This is Harlem. And you would do a great job writing a book about Harlem. I know it."

Shareef said, "But you won't read none of my other shit?"

He didn't even care who overheard him at that point. He was expressing himself with raw emotion.

The young reporter said, "I started reading your new one. I'm halfway through it. But I mean . . . it's not like what you're about to write now. If what I hear is true."

Shareef eyed him. He said, "So let me get this straight. You won't read none of my books about positive black relationships and bringing black love back, but you'll read all this crooked, gangsta shit, while I'm out here running for my life now from some motherfuckers who don't even read. What, you think that shit is cool? You think it's a fuckin' game? And you a damn college student, gettin' caught up in the same bullshit these young rappers get caught up in."

He said, "This is real life, man. Learn to follow shit that keeps your mind alive. 'Cause this other shit is just poison."

Customers in the coffee shop looked at Shareef as if he had lost it. And he had. A few of the women even recognized him, but they weren't willing to speak to him after witnessing his outburst. And the young reporter was tired of being dissed by Shareef.

He spoke up and said, "Look, you need to get off that high horse you on, brother. If gangsta books are so wrong, then why you up here working on one?"

"Because it's the only way to get your fucking attention, obviously."

The reporter was no longer impressed with Shareef. He was damn near ready to defend himself. They stood chest to chest and were ready for anything.

"Is there a problem here?"

Jurrell Garland walked into the store and couldn't help interjecting himself. He eyed the young reporter until he looked away.

Jurrell leaned into his view and asked him again. "I said, 'Is there a problem here?'"

The reporter saw there was no way around him and shook his head.

"No, there's no problem."

Jurrell leaned back up, nodded his head, and said, "Good. You can go now."

The young reporter walked off without another word.

"Sorry I'm a little late, Shareef," Jurrell commented. "But when you gotta chase that dollar, you gotta chase that dollar. You know what I mean?"

He was all suited and tied up, but still gangsta with his swagger.

He said, "Well, let's roll. I'm parked right up the street."

The two men headed up Lenox toward 126th Street, with Shareef still cautious of his surroundings.

"So, what was that all about?" Jurrell asked him.

Shareef grinned. "Actually, I think I was in the wrong on that one. I screamed on that kid twice now. But does he know who you are?"

Shareef was impressed with how easily Jurrell had silenced him.

Jurrell answered, "Nah, I just have a way of talking to people. You know me, man. I size a nigga up, and know just how I can get to him."

"Yeah, you got that right."

They made a right on 126th Street and reached Jurrell's car parked close to the corner. It was a dark blue Lexus GS 400. Jurrell popped open the doors with his remote key.

"I never would have thought of you as a Lexus man," Shareef commented as he climbed in on the passenger side.

"Exactly," Jurrell responded. "You gotta keep 'em guessing. So I left the Mercedes, Beemers, and SUVs alone. They're too much of a target."

He made it sound as if he was still illegal.

Shareef asked him, "You still doing things you need to stay under the radar for?"

Jurrell started the ignition and pulled into traffic.

"Nah," he answered. "I'm just trying to stay under the radar from people who know me from my past life." He said, "That's why I was so happy to see you back up in Harlem. You're like reinforcement for me to stay on the straight and narrow. You a brother who made it

from here, you know. In fact, you need to start thinking about invest-
ing up in Harlem."

As he spoke, one of his three cell phones went off. The one ringing
was red. He also wore a black and a blue phone, all laced to his black
belt.

"Hold on a minute," he told Shareef. "Harlem Mobile," he answered. He listened and responded, "Yeah, I got the new ones. The LR
oh-two and oh-three models, right? They added a couple more features and made 'em sturdier. The previous model was breaking too
much . . ."

He stopped and listened again. "Yeah, I got them, too. But they cost
twice as much as the regular phone. I'm just letting you know that up
front. 'Cause I don't want no surprises with my money."

Shareef was surprised with how safe he felt while riding inside of
Jurrell's car. He seemed to have forgotten all about the street goons
who were after him at the moment. Would they still be after him
while he was with Jurrell, or was that only a false perception?

"So, where are we headed?" he asked.

"I'm checking out these new condos on Madison, Park, and Lex-
ington. They got storefront property available on the bottom."

Jurrell looked Shareef in the eyes and said, "Harlem is changing,
man. Harlem is changing."

Shareef said, "You still got your hard rocks on the streets though."
He wanted to lean their conversation toward his current predicament.

Jurrell smiled as he waited in traffic to make a right turn onto Park
Avenue.

He said, "You're never gonna get rid of that. Getting rid of criminals is like getting rid of poverty. And that ain't gon' happen in America. Poverty keeps things in order. It's like the slow lanes and the fast
lanes on a highway. The broken down cars stay to the right, and the
sports cars and limos do their thing on the left."

"I should just stay in my lane then, hunh?" Shareef asked him and
grinned.

Jurrell looked at him and said, "Nah. You still gotta exit sometime, right? The rich and the poor are both on the same highways. So we still have to cross paths."

Shareef nodded. Their conversation was nowhere near what he wanted to talk about. He figured Jurrell had indeed traveled a long way in his life. He sounded like another street philosopher, how Cynthia had explained Michael Springfield. And that gave Shareef the idea to go straight for the jugular.

"Yo, you hear about Michael Springfield this morning?"

"Nah, what about him?"

Before Shareef could respond with more information, Jurrell's black cell phone rang. He looked down at the number on the screen and pressed mute to let it ring.

Shareef said, "I heard somebody set him up and shanked him today. Did you hear that?"

Jurrell nodded and said, "Now I have." He added, "But you should have known that. When you get involved with inmates, you don't know what their situation is gonna be. That's why I always told my mother to pray for me and don't expect to see me again. And she didn't like me saying that shit, but that's what it was. On any given day you can die in prison."

He said, "They're not reforming anybody in there. You reform yourself, and you stay out of other people's business."

"So, what do you think happened with Michael Springfield? He got in somebody else's business?"

"Or they just got in his," Jurrell answered. It was that simple to him.

He said, "You still gotta remember the crabs in a barrel syndrome with our people. Maybe Springfield hooking up with you was too good a thing for somebody else in there to handle. And it go down like that sometimes. It's old debts and old enemies. That's what I mean by staying low out here. You can't be too flashy with people who know you. But if you act too broke, you can't get no business. So you have to work a happy medium."

Before Shareef could respond, Jurrell parked the car and hopped out for his first appointment. Shareef followed him out and thought about his attire. He wasn't dressed as professionally that day as Jurrell was in his sharp suit. Shareef wore blue jeans and a tennis shirt.

"You sure you want me going in here with you?" he asked to make sure. "I mean, you look like the pro, and I look like the scrub today."

Jurrell looked him over and laughed. "Don't worry about that. I got it."

Shareef followed him across Park Avenue and into a new building of burnt-orange brick and gray cement that was twelve stories high. The first level was all storefronts that were mostly empty.

Jurrell pointed to them.

"This right here is a gold mine, but most of us can't afford the rent."

Shareef looked and nodded. He agreed with Jurrell's assessment. The right business on the ground level of Park Avenue was sure to draw an easy crowd.

They walked into the entranceway and security area, where there were key entry sensors, a room intercom system, a video camera, and a security guard station inside to the right. Jurrell punched in five numbers for the sales office.

"Harlem's Park Avenue Number Three," a receptionist spoke through the intercom system.

"Yes, this is Jurrell Garland. I have a one o'clock appointment for a walk-through."

"Oh, yes, Mr. Garland. When you enter the building, you want to turn to your right; we are halfway down the hall on the left."

"Thank you."

Nnnrrrrrkk!

The glass door buzzed open for Jurrell and Shareef to walk inside. They spoke to the security officer and headed on their way down the hall toward the sales office. When they arrived, the receptionist got their full attention. She was a college-educated dime-piece wearing a tailored peach suit. She stood from her desk and introduced herself to Jurrell immediately.

"Hello, Mr. Garland, my name is Meredith. Welcome to Harlem Park Avenue Number Three. If you'd like to have a seat, I'll let our sales manager, Barbara Cunningham, know that you're here."

"Okay," Jurrell responded and took a seat.

There were comfortable sofas spread around the office with coffee tables filled with magazines. Four architecture models of the Harlem Park Avenue condominiums were displayed on four-foot-high stands.

Instead of taking a seat next to Jurrell, Shareef took a look at the models. The first element that struck him were the outdoor swimming pool and tennis and basketball courts placed inside the condominium walls on the roof of the fourth floor.

Jurrell followed Shareef's eyes and chuckled. "That's the same thing that got me. I saw it on the Internet. Now we'll see it in real life."

Shareef couldn't help himself from thinking, *I wonder how much a two-bedroom costs here.*

Meredith walked back out from the sales manager's office. "Barbara will be right out to see you."

Jurrell repeated, "Okay." He seemed at ease there. He even crossed his legs, wearing black leather shoes and dress socks. On a hunch, he asked Meredith, "Do you know who this guy is?" in reference to Shareef.

Meredith sat back behind her desk and looked Shareef over.

When it took her too long to respond, Jurrell filled her in. "You ever heard of the author Shareef Crawford?"

Meredith's eyes stretched wide. "Get out of here." She pulled a hardback book from out of her desk. She flipped it over—*The Full Moon*—and felt embarrassed when she stared at his mug on the back jacket.

She then covered her face with both hands. "Oh, my God. Like, I never really thought about meeting an actual author before." She held the book out and asked, "Can you sign this for me?"

Shareef felt as awkward as she did. Jurrell had put them both on the spot.

"Sure, I'll sign it."

Meredith hustled back out of her chair to bring it to him. By the time she reached him, the sales manager, Barbara Cunningham, a white woman in her forties, walked out from her office, followed by a gray-haired white man in his fifties.

She shook his hand and said, "Welcome again to Harlem Park Avenue Number Three."

Shareef signed Meredith's book and asked her how she spelled her name to personalize it.

"So you're a writer, are ya'?" the gray-haired man asked him. He peeked to see what name was on the front of the book jacket.

Shareef nodded to him. "We all don't play basketball," he joked.

Jurrell stood up from his seat and laughed. "That's for sure," he agreed.

Barbara Cunningham asked him, "So, you two know each other?"

Jurrell answered, "Do we know each other? We did the first nine years of grade school together. Now he lives down south, and I'm try'na get him to see what Harlem is up to now."

Barbara jumped on it like a true businesswoman. "Oh, we have a two-for-one deal then. We have condos available that are right next to each other if you're interested."

Shareef caught on and didn't want to ruin Jurrell's game, so he went along with the program.

"Well, you know, I have to see what you're offering first."

Barbara chirped, "Okay, well, let me get the keys."

They followed her out of the office and around the bottom floors of the building, where Barbara showed them the fitness center, the media room, a reading lounge, a grand ballroom with three sections, and several conference rooms with long tables and tall business chairs.

When they reached the fifth floor and walked outside into the courtyard area, Shareef and Jurrell both felt like kids in a new playground. The recreational area was elevated on a two-foot-high platform, with two full basketball courts, three tennis courts, and an Olympic-sized swimming pool with a diving board at the deep end.

Shareef said, "Impressive."

Barbara chuckled at him. "Oh, it's lovely, isn't it? Physical fitness and family recreation is the way of the new world. And at Harlem Park Avenue condominiums, we want to make our residents feel as though they can get away from home without having to leave the premises."

"I heard that," Jurrell spoke up.

They stepped onto the platform before the sales manager pointed out the two-foot drainage system that surrounded the elevated courtyard.

She said, "We have a drainage system for rain and snow that surrounds the courtyard. That way the elements of the Harlem weather will never settle on the roof. The rain and snow empty right into a drain system connected to the plumbing of the building. There's even heated pipes to help melt the snow and ice of winter."

Shareef nodded. "So you thought of everything in advance."

"Oh, yes. We've had this Park Avenue design since two thousand and one."

After a few minutes of looking around and admiring it all, Barbara said, "Now we can go look at some of our availabilities."

As she walked forward in front of them, Jurrell whispered, "This shit'll make you forget you're still in Harlem."

Shareef grinned and chuckled.

Once they were shown the first three-bedroom condo on the sixth floor, it all began to come together.

"We have hardwood floors, large living and dining room areas, walk-in closets, stand-alone showers, Jacuzzi baths, a washer and dryer room, state-of-the-art stoves, microwaves and refrigerators—all from General Electric—ceiling fans, large bay windows available on the upper floors, a central-heating and air-conditioning system, a maid service . . ."

Jurrell finally stopped her rapid delivery and said, "A maid service?"

"Yes, we have a maid service and a dry-cleaning service, both available by call, or by scheduled appointment," she answered.

"So, how much would this one cost?" Shareef asked her.

Barbara squinted her eyes and answered, "I believe this one is one point six million. And the three-bedrooms on the penthouse level go for two point four. But we only have one of those left."

She ran off those prices if they were professional basketball players with millions to burn.

Neither Jurrell or Shareef flinched.

Nevertheless, Shareef stated, "Let's see what else you got in the small-man's price range."

Jurrell laughed and agreed with him. "Dig it. I gotta put on another hundred pounds before I can fit in this one."

The second condo they saw was a two-bedroom for eight hundred sixty-seven thousand on the ninth floor. Then they viewed a one-bedroom for six hundred thirty-five thousand on the tenth.

Shareef asked her, "Do you have any split-level lofts?"

A split-level loft was what he owned in Florida.

"Yes, we do," she answered him. "And all of our split levels are located on the east side of the building, facing the Harlem River. Would you like to see those next?"

Jurrell nodded. "Yeah, let me see what that looks like."

They walked over to the east side of the building and took one of the elevators back down to the fourth floor. When they entered the loft, it was the smallest square-foot area they had viewed so far.

Barbara told them, "This is the smallest loft we have, a one-bedroom at eight hundred seventeen square feet."

Jurrell walked inside and liked the floor plan immediately. It was small, but not that small. It was small enough for intimacy, but large and open enough to move some nice furniture around with a large flat-screen television set. And since he didn't have a family to worry about, he figured he didn't need that much room anyway. Then he spotted the stairs to the right of the room and took a walk up to see the bedroom.

"Oh, yeah, I like this one," he commented from the stairs. "You just keep everybody downstairs unless you give them private admittance for up here."

Shareef and Barbara smiled at it. Shareef figured Jurrell would like a split-level. There were few people who didn't like them, especially for bachelor pads. The split-levels seemed to be a real turn-on with women. They always wanted to see what's upstairs.

"What's the price on this?" Jurrell asked from over the bedroom rail.

Barbara squinted her eyes again. "Ah, I know it's in the four hundred thousand range, but I'll have to check back in the office to make sure."

"How many of these do you have available?" Shareef asked her.

"I believe . . . three or four. But I have to check again in the office."

Jurrell walked back down the stairs. He said, "I don't need much more room than this. This size right here is perfect. And this whole split-level thing is sexy, like you got a house inside of an apartment."

Shareef chuckled to see Jurrell so excited by it.

"So, the down payment is ten percent, and twenty percent to bypass the mortgage insurance?" Shareef asked the sales manager.

She nodded. "That's correct."

Shareef did the quick math and said, "So that's about forty-five thousand to get in and ninety thousand to bring the monthly mortgage down."

Barbara looked at Shareef and told him, "It sounds like you're a pro at this."

"Yes, ma'im, I've gone through the process a few times now."

Jurrell looked at Shareef and nodded. He was very pleased that he had brought Shareef there to help with the negotiations.

Barbara said, "Now, of course, you know the owners association has dues payments every six months, and the final say on new resident applications. But you guys should pass that with flying colors. A phone company entrepreneur and a bestselling author—they would love to have the both of you here."

Jurrell and Shareef eyed each other. The owners association was definitely something they would need to discuss.

"We'll both take home a package with the floor plans and prices that we're interested in and get back to you," Shareef told her.

"Well, the Harlem Park Avenue condominiums have been rated number one in affordable luxury, occupancy, overall service, and in equal employment hiring. So while you two shop around for a new home in Harlem, just remember that we are one of the best," the saleswoman concluded.

JURRELL LEFT THE APPOINTMENT with Shareef and was ecstatic.

"Damn, Shareef, we worked the shit out of that. But do you think they'll do a background check on me or something?"

"A credit check," Shareef told him. "You have to qualify for a mortgage loan." And honestly, he didn't see how that was going to happen unless Jurrell had built up an excellent credit record since being released from prison.

As they crossed the street and headed back to Jurrell's car, Shareef asked him, "Have you built up any strong credit since you've been out?"

"Yeah, I got credit. I got phone bills, credit cards, electricity bills, utilities, rent . . . How much credit do they need?"

Shareef looked at the Lexus and asked him, "What about car payments?"

Jurrell looked at his car and shook his head. "Nah, I paid for this with cash. This is a used car. I only paid ten Gs for it."

Shareef thought about it. He said, "You probably gonna have to have bigger payments than phone and utility bills. The rent is good if you've been in one place for a while. But how much are your credit card balances? I mean, I don't mean to get too personal . . ."

Jurrell blew it off and said, "Oh, it's cool. You've been through this before. But my credit cards are only for like, two, three thousand dollars each. You know, they start you off low and you have to build your way up."

Shareef nodded, still thinking about Jurrell's predicament as they climbed into the car.

He said, "The main thing they're going to wonder about is the gap in all the years where you had no credit history. You have to come up with a reason for that other than your being in prison. I mean, you're not fresh out of college or anything."

Jurrell paused behind the wheel of the car. He said, "I'll just tell them that I recently woke up to how important a credit record is and that I used to work from paycheck to paycheck doing odd jobs, you know.

"I mean, that's what most guys are doing in the 'hood," he explained. "We not all bestselling authors, either."

Shareef told him, "They're still gonna ask you what odd jobs you've held and want a record of it. But you did work for a phone company before you broke off and started selling your own phones, right?"

Shareef was assuming as much. How else would Jurrell know so much about the phones?

He said, "Yeah, I worked for Verizon for like, eight, nine months. But you gotta put references down on the application, too, right? How much does that count? That's how I got my job at Verizon."

Shareef figured all along that it would come down to his references, and maybe even fronting ownership to get Jurrell what he wanted. Polo and Spoonie were probably right all along. Jurrell needed a legitimate connection with real money to help clean up his own money. But if his money wasn't really clean, and Shareef vouched for him, he could put his entire reputation, family, and career in jeopardy. So he found himself on dangerous ground again, just when he was beginning to feel a real level of comfort with Jurrell.

Jurrell started up his engine and said, "I know what you're thinking, man. You're thinking, 'Why should I get involved with this nigga like that? We ain't never really been friends. I don't know what he really up to.' But I'll tell you like this, man. Just walking up in there in that condo today and seeing how you worked it taught me a hell of a lot. I mean, I had the suit and the tie to play it, but you had the real experience and recognition. I mean, that lady was ready to jump out of the penthouse window to get a bestselling author in the building."

He laughed and said, "She showed us one of the most expensive condos in the whole fuckin' building just because you was there. She wouldn't have done that shit for me, I don't care what kind of suit I'm wearing. This ain't Armani."

He said, "So if you do nothing else for me, man, I just want you to know that I thank you for going up in these condos with me. 'Cause this is where Harlem is leading to now. So let's head to the next one. We running late."

Whose Side Is Safe?

AS THE SUN BEGAN TO GO DOWN, Baby G sat outside the black Mercedes CLK parked by Marcus Garvey Park, one of his favorite hangouts, with his bodyguard/driver, interrogating the young soldier he began to call T, short for Truth.

"So, detectives were questioning your sister at the dry cleaners today about what went down at the storefront?"

"Yeah," T answered him. "Then she told me about it. But she said she didn't want to know nothing. So, she didn't even ask me."

Baby G nodded and said, "Smart girl. I see the apple don't fall too far from the tree. Because the less she knows, the less she got to lie and feel nervous about. That's how they get you on them lie detector tests. The more you know, the more your emotions tell on you."

"We don't have nothing to tell," T commented with conviction.

Baby G nodded again. He said, "See, that's why I like you, man. You know just what time it is."

Over his right shoulder, at least fifteen of his followers watched or played a game of basketball until they could hardly see in the dark, while others hustled their pharmaceuticals on the side.

The bodyguard/driver shook his head. "Them niggas gon' run ball until they're blind."

Baby G paid it no mind. Then his cell phone rang with a restricted number again. He answered it as he walked away.

"Yo, what's up, young blood? What's the weather look like today?"

270

He listened and said, "Is that right? The writer dude? It's serious like that? . . . Yeah, I heard about that. But he wasn't gettin' out no time soon, right? So what he have to talk about that was so important?"

He continued to listen and build his understanding of the new situation.

"That's what you want us to do? . . . Aw'ight. Say no more."

Baby G hung up the phone and spoke to his driver. He said, "We gotta get that other car again. Something came up."

His beefy driver nodded to him. "Let's go get it."

"Aw'ight, gather them up," he told his driver.

His driver turned and whistled loud through his fingers.

Wheeett! Whheeeett!

The soldiers heard the call and all came running. They quickly gathered around their leader for their orders.

Baby G looked them all in the eyes and said, "Yo, we got something we gon' need to do that I'm gon' tell my snipers to handle in a minute, once I find out what the details are. Aw'ight?"

They nodded and mumbled, "Aw'ight. We got you."

He said, "Now, how many of y'all ever heard of the book writer Shareef Crawford?"

They all started to nod their recollections of the name.

"Yo, my sisters read his books."

"Yeah, my girl read him."

"My mom read his books."

"Ay, I read a couple of his books myself. They aw'ight. They good to beat your shit to."

Baby G frowned while a few of his soldiers responded to that.

"Nigga, you need to get a fuckin' girlfriend. Fuck readin' them books."

"Yo, that was too much information, man," the young general told him. "Anyway, have y'all seen him around here and know what he look like? Y'all know he from East Harlem, right?"

"Yeah, I've seen him around. He was at the Kingdome yesterday signing autographs," one of the soldiers stated.

"Aw'ight, well the rest of y'all need to find out what he look like and keep your eyes and ears open whenever you see him."

"Why, what he do?" someone asked.

"I heard he was writing something about that kid Michael Springfield in jail."

Baby G said, "Look, I'll tell y'all all about it in a minute. Now don't rise up on him, and don't let nobody else rise up on him until I find out what the deal is. Y'all hear me?"

"Yes, sir!" they answered in unison.

He said, "Aw'ight, now let me find out somebody's deaf out here and see what happen."

"No, sir!"

He nodded to them and said, "Aw'ight, recess is over. It's paper time now. Go get that."

But before they began to disperse, he added, "Yo, and five of y'all who know what he look like, follow us in a second car. Matter fact, I need a couple of shooters, too."

IT HAD BEEN A LONG DAY for Shareef, and he was still with Jurrell Garland at close to nine o'clock at night. They were riding around in the Lexus, reminiscing about the Harlem of ten, twenty, and thirty years ago. By then, Shareef had told Jurrell all about the trouble he had gotten himself into over Michael Springfield, and that he still had his luggage at a Harlem hotel that he no longer considered safe.

"So, you want me to drive you over there and get your luggage or what?" Jurrell asked him.

Shareef had still not made up his mind. As much as he talked about the nonsensical lure of urban street life, the danger of it all was compelling him to stick around and prove that something could happen. And if he left without anything going down, then he still wouldn't believe. It was like taking a drug to prove it could produce a high. Shareef wanted to have it, while the logical side of his brain told him not to chance. *Just leave the shit alone and go home.* But he couldn't. He wouldn't allow himself to. He was from Harlem.

He asked Jurrell, "What would you do in my situation?"

He wondered if Jurrell would think differently about it. They had been on the opposite sides of the law for most of their lives.

Jurrell smiled and shrugged his shoulders. He said, "You know me better than that, Shareef. If you know anything about me, you know I never ran from shit. I had motherfuckers running from me, twenty-four/seven. And I'm not the most dangerous-looking nigga in the world. I still look good," he commented. "But when I say I'ma fuck you up . . . I'm not playing. I'm gon' fuck you up for real, and real niggas know that about me.

"So what would I do in this situation?" he asked himself. He said, "I'd walk outside that hotel building, hold my gun out and say, 'Who the fuck got a problem with me writin' this book? We can settle this shit right now.' And I'd get the beef over with."

He said, "But that's me. I mean, you got a wife and kids at home, Shareef. I don't have no wife and kids. You a million-dollar nigga with no ball or microphone in his hand. I'm out here selling fuckin' cell phones. And you turn women on through their minds without them even seeing you. I always had problems with women. Outside of my mother, half of these girls are still fuckin' scared of me."

He said, "You remember all them girls I had crying in grade school and getting their fathers and brothers and uncles and shit on me? And I still didn't run. But you, man you got girls fantasizing and they don't even know what you look like when you in the same room with them. I mean, that's some special shit right there, man. These girls sweat you and never even get a chance to see you."

Shareef didn't want to hear all of that. He said real calmly, "But you know what I honestly feel like after you say all of that shit to me, man?"

"Nah, what you feel like?" Jurrell asked him.

Shareef said, "I feel like the guy playing jump rope with the girls, while all the guys are playing football and slap boxing. And then I walk over to y'all and say, 'Yo, let me play.' And y'all tell me, 'Nah, nigga, go back over there with the girls. This a boy's game.' "

Jurrell could see the image in the schoolyard. So he broke out laughing. Then he said, "Yo, Shareef, seriously . . . do you think Hugh Hefner cares about playing football and slap boxing? I mean, if the women love you, then use that shit, playboy. What's wrong with you?"

Shareef frowned and blew it off. He said, "Man, that don't really do it for me. I got a mistress waiting for me in Miami right now, a bad, half Dominican girl with the brown skin and long, jet black hair, but sometimes I don't even want her. It's like you can't really talk to women, man. I feel like I'm talking at 'em half the time. It's the same thing with my wife. She's not gettin' me, and I'm not gettin' her. But with us guys . . . when we talk, I mean, the shit is real. So why can't I talk to other guys about the shit I do as a writer, like an athlete would, or a rapper would, or a thug would? You feel me? That's why this shit right here is so important to me, man. I'm just trying to make a connection to y'all."

Jurrell drove silently for a minute. Shareef didn't know if he felt him or not.

Then Jurrell nodded to him. He said, "Yo, that's some deep shit right there, man. We all try'na make a connection, Shareef. You try'na do it with books and intelligence, I was trying to do it with fear and intimidation. I just figured that . . . if another man was scared of me, then I must have connected to him by reaching down and snatching his fuckin' heart out of his chest."

Shareef grinned at Jurrell's honesty.

He said, "But then, like . . . at the end of the day, if another kid had a toy or something, and I wanted to play with him, the motherfucker was still scared of me. And I felt like telling him, 'Look, nigga, don't be scared. Play with me.' But they never wanted to because I was never their friend. And I didn't know how to be no damn friend. So I'd punch the kid in his fuckin' mouth, take his toy, and then play with the shit by myself, but it never satisfied me, because that wasn't what I really wanted to do. I mean, I wanted to have friends, man, I just didn't know how to."

He looked Shareef in his eyes and said, "But then when it came to you, you was like the one guy who would always fight me. And I secretly admired you for that. I mean, I didn't like you for that shit, but I admired you."

He said, "Now here we are, twenty years later, still in Harlem, riding around telling each other how we want to connect as men."

Jurrell shook his head and repeated, "That's just some deep shit right there, man. Now I'm gon' have to get high and sleep on it tonight."

Shareef chuckled and said, "You got some on you now?"

Jurrell looked at him. "Nah, not on me. I can't get caught with shit out here, man. It ain't safe for me. But if you wanna smoke one with me back at the crib . . ."

Right as he spoke, Shareef noticed that they were crossing Frederick Douglass Boulevard.

"Yo, my hotel is right on Frederick," Shareef told him.

"So, you goin' back?" Jurrell asked.

Shareef decided that he would. Out of the blue, his entire body felt heavy. That happened to him sometimes after going several nights without a solid rest. And he had only slept for three hours at a time since he had been back in Harlem. A man had to rest sometime, no matter how energetic he was.

He answered, "Yeah, man, I'm tired as hell now. Just drop me off right in front of the door."

Jurrell asked him, "You sure?"

It wasn't quite ten o'clock at night yet and Shareef still had a squad of unknown goons after him.

Nevertheless, he answered, "Yeah, I'm sure. I'm just a li'l tired now. Ain't nothing gon' happen to me. I'm getting in here and going to bed."

So Jurrell turned down Frederick Douglass toward the small hotel where Shareef had been staying.

• • •

THE SAME DARK SEDAN, with the three men from the night before, was waiting on Frederick Douglass Boulevard, right down the block from the hotel. They had been waiting hours for Shareef to arrive.

The ringleader sat in the front passenger seat and patiently smoked a cigarette. He watched everything that moved on the sidewalk up ahead to his right.

"What if he checked out already, man. We're spending all night fucking with this nigga," the young triggerman huffed from the back.

He said, "I knew I should have jumped out and stepped to him when we saw him earlier. Now he ain't coming back here."

"No you shouldn't have, either. You did exactly what you was supposed to do, call me," the ringleader told him.

"Well, look, man, are we gonna kill this nigga or what? I still don't even know what we after 'em for," the triggerman responded.

The ringleader chuckled and said, "Exactly. You don't even know what the hell is going on, but you already set to kill somebody. Just let me ask him a few questions first."

He was told to be tactful and efficient, and that's what he was going to stick to.

"About what?" the triggerman asked him.

The driver wanted to know more about it himself.

"What he do, man?" he questioned.

The ringleader figured they were not there to ask any questions. That's why he picked them to tag along. They were both obedient. Still, he didn't want them bothering him all night with questions, so he answered, "He ain't do nothing yet. It's what he *might* do."

The driver listened and said, "Is he a rat? A snitch?"

"Exactly," the ringleader answered, "that's what I'm trying to find out. And don't ask me what the fuck he know, either. 'Cause I don't know yet."

They were all silent in the car for a minute. Then the triggerman let out a long sigh from boredom.

"Wake me up when you see something," he commented. "We might even get questioned by the cops or something waitin' out here this long. This ain't no stakeout."

"Yes it is, too," the ringleader corrected him.

"Well, we ain't got badges for this shit."

The ringleader pulled his cigarette from his lips and snapped, "Look, man, shut the fuck up. Aw'ight? Just shut the fuck up a minute. Got' damn!"

The car went silent again as the driver shook his head and grinned.

WHEN SHAREEF and Jurrell approached the hotel from the opposite side of the street, Jurrell stopped the car and waited for traffic to clear to make a U-turn.

"That's it right there, right?" he asked Shareef.

Shareef nodded to him. "Yeah, that's it."

BACK INSIDE THE DARK SEDAN, the driver watched a Lexus stop in the middle of the street out in front of the hotel and wondered.

"Yo, you see that Lexus? Look like he 'bout to drop somebody off."

The ringleader moved his cigarette out of the way and looked forward. The triggerman looked forward as well. And they all watched in silence as the Lexus made its U-turn.

When the car came to another stop in front of the hotel, they all leaned forward to get a better look.

SHAREEF CLIMBED OUT of Jurrell's Lexus and said, "Thanks, man. We had a good day today."

"Yeah, let's do this shit again," Jurrell told him. Then his black cell phone went off. He said, "Be safe, man. And call me back once you in there good."

"Aw'ight, I'll do that," Shareef responded and closed the door.

• • •

"YO, THAT'S HIM," the triggerman responded from inside the parked sedan. The ringleader wasted no time before he jumped out. He tossed his still-lit cigarette to the sidewalk, and hustled up the block to catch up to his mark.

"Yo, Shareef?" he hollered as he approached him. He hadn't done anything to the man as of yet, so there was no reason to play it like a hardened enemy. He only wanted to talk to the writer, and he told him so.

"Yo, I just wanna talk to you, man, that's all."

SHAREEF RECOGNIZED the man from the previous night jogging toward him on the sidewalk before he reached the entrance of the hotel. He looked to make sure the man was unarmed before he stopped and thought about it.

I can run and irritate him more, or I can stand my fuckin' ground and get to the bottom of this, he pondered. *I'm already tired, but fuck it. I'll sleep a lot better when I get this over with . . . if I'm still alive.*

He took the brave approach anyway and stopped in front of the hotel entrance to talk. There was still a security guard inside the door to report a murder attempt if it happened. But what would that do if the man succeeded in shooting or stabbing him fatally? Nevertheless, Shareef was ready to hear him out and ask some questions of his own.

"Aw'ight, so what's this all about, man? What's really good?" Shareef opened up and asked him with some Harlem slang attached.

The man said, "All I want to know is everything he said to you in jail, and please don't leave nothing out."

Shareef eyed him and grimaced. He said, "Come on, man, I'm not a fuckin' tape recorder. I was in there *one time* for a few hours, and all we talked about was how we would tell *his story* of growing up on the west side of Harlem."

He said, "Now, if anybody got a problem with Michael Springfield trying to snitch on some shit, well, you can put that to rest. He didn't talk about nothing but himself, and if you heard the news on the streets, somebody killed him this morning in jail anyway, so he can't tell me shit now even if he wanted to."

The man looked confused. He said, "Somebody killed him this morning? I heard he was transferred."

After that, Shareef was confused. "Transferred? Who told you that?"

"Who told you he was killed?"

Shareef said, "Everybody on the streets know that by now."

"Everybody like who? Who did you talk to today, somebody on Michael Springfield's side? That don't mean shit. That's game," the man argued.

Shareef thought about it and had to admit that his information was one-sided. He had been told about the prison hit through Cynthia alone. And she hadn't called him back all day.

Shareef shook it off and said, "Nah, it sound like your shit is game. So you check your sources and I'll check mine."

The man said, "Aw'ight, go ahead and call 'em then."

"Call who?"

"Whoever told you he was murdered in jail this morning. 'Cause that ain't what I heard."

Shareef thought fast and said, "Well, where did you get your information from? Are you gonna call *him*?"

The man pulled out his cell phone immediately. "Let's do it then," he challenged. "You call yours, I'll call mine."

Shareef thought it over and said, "Aw'ight." He pulled out his cell phone and found Cynthia's home number to redial. When her phone began to ring, Shareef looked back at his stalker to make sure he was doing the same, and he was. In fact, his informant came on the line first.

"Yo, man, I'm standing out here with this kid Shareef Crawford right now, and you know what he tried to tell me? He's trying to tell me that somebody told him Michael Springfield got killed in prison this morning. You believe that shit? He got transferred, right?"

Shareef didn't hear the answer, but the question surely didn't seem objective. The man was obviously biased toward his side of the story. So by the time Cynthia answered her phone, Shareef realized that it was a mistake. They wouldn't get anywhere by calling each other's sources. That would be similar to a plaintiff and a defense agreeing to the other person's story in a court of law. It was not going to happen. Admitting to fault in a courtroom was not the American way.

"Hey, Shareef, you're not still in Harlem, are you?" she asked him. She sounded calm and relaxed, and she was assuming that he had left already. Or at least had relocated in the Times Square area.

Shareef went right to business. He said, "Yo, man, you told me Michael Springfield was murdered in prison this morning, right? 'Cause I'm standing out here with this guy who says that he was transferred."

Cynthia responded, "What? Who said that?"

"I don't fuckin' know his name, man. He showed up at my hotel asking me shit last night about it, too," Shareef hinted. He wanted the conversation to sound like he was talking to a guy. At the same time, he was giving Cynthia the information she needed to assess what was going on.

She said, "Oh, my God. He's standing out there in front of you right now? So, you *are* still in Harlem."

"That's what I just said," he told her. "Now what's the deal with this transfer shit? Who got their information wrong?"

He was allowing Cynthia plenty of room to solidify her side of the story. And she followed his lead like a seasoned pro.

She took a breath and said, "Of course that ma-fucka's gon' say something else. He's lying."

Shareef cut her off and said, "Yeah, that's what I figured, too."

Then she continued to help him out. She said, "Now why would they up and transfer him out of the blue? He ain't do shit wrong. Do they know something we don't know. Ask him that shit?"

But before Shareef could say it, she added, "They're trying to set you up, Shareef. They're trying to set you up," and her voice began to break.

"Get the fuck out of there, man," she broke down and told him. "Shareef, get the fuck out of there. I told you to leave."

He didn't like the sound of that. Cynthia was losing her poise. That wasn't part of the script. So he told her, "Aw'ight, I'ma call you back in a minute then."

He quickly ended the call and faced his stalker with full zeal.

"Aw'ight, this shit ain't goin' nowhere, man. My guy is sticking by his story, and your guy is sticking by his. So let's cut the bullshit. I'm too tired for this. Just tell me what you need to know. 'Cause that's all this shit is, a seek and find mission, and I don't have shit for you. So, what do you need?"

The man seemed stuck for a minute. And he was actually still on the phone.

"Hold up, I'ma call you right back," he told his informant. He ended the call and looked at Shareef with fire his eyes.

He said, "First of all, you don't fuckin' disrespect me like that, son. I was still on the fuckin' phone. Now I don't know who you deal with on the regular like that, or if you scream on your women like some kind of pimp or some shit, but I ain't no fuckin' ho, and you don't talk to me like that. That's first of all."

As the man got irate on the sidewalk, Shareef noticed another black man step out of a car parked down the block and begin to walk quickly in their direction.

Oh, shit! This is it! Shareef panicked. *I shouldn't have said that shit to him. I should have kept my cool. I should've kept my cool,* he repeated to himself.

But it was too late for regrets. It was time for reaction. He wondered how quickly he could run into the hotel, while hoping they wouldn't try and shoot him in the back through the glass.

Do I push him away from me first to give myself more room to slip inside the doorway? I gotta move fast, he thought.

Realizing he had to create space for himself to get away, Shareef charged out like a football player and pushed the man with his extended arms. But the man reacted quickly enough to grab him and pull him forward as he fell backward. Shareef kept his balance and shoved him to the pavement, but by the time he turned to get away, the second man was moving fast up the sidewalk with a gun out in plain view.

"Shit!" Shareef cursed himself. Trying to make it back to the hotel doorway didn't appear to be safe anymore. There wasn't enough time to rush inside without becoming a sitting duck for bullets. So Shareef went to plan B and ran out into the middle of the street.

"Aw'ight, kill that nigga!" the man on the ground hollered to his helper.

Shareef was already hustling up the street toward 124th when the second man started to shoot at him.

Pop! Pop! Pop!

"*Shit!*" he continued to curse as he ran and ducked bullets. Where were the police when you needed them?

Shareef zigzagged and cut away from the street, slipping in between cars and headed back to the sidewalk to his right. He wasn't brainless enough to run straight down the block with shooters after him. All it took was one straight bullet to hit him.

As he made it to 124th Street with the two shooters still in hot pursuit, three to four more men with guns, all dressed in black, jumped out of a car coming from the opposite direction.

What the fuck? Shareef panicked. He had planned to make it to 125th and turn right, putting him in the middle of Harlem's busiest traffic and police. He figured the shooters would have held back on 125th. But when he spotted the second team of triggermen in front of him, Shareef made a quick right turn down 124th Street and picked up speed.

These motherfuckers are gonna have to catch me to kill me. Fuck that! he told himself. *So I'll just hit Adam Clayton Powell and turn up to 125th Street then.*

Making it to 125th Street was the goal. Shareef was sure there would be police out and a thick enough crowd to make the killers pull back, unless they wanted him that damn bad, which he doubted. So he continued to run for his life while looking back to see where the shooters were and zigzagged across the street in between cars again.

Pop, pop, pop-pop-pop, pop, pop!

It sounded like the fourth of July behind him. People were screaming, yelling, and running every which way to avoid the bullets. But at the same time, it didn't seem like any of the bullets were headed in his direction anymore.

They're shooting at each other, Shareef told himself. So he pulled up from running, ducked behind a car, and watched for a minute.

The new shooters in black were obviously not after him, and they looked to have superior numbers.

"Who the fuck are they?" He wondered. He was confused, while his heart continued to beat through his chest.

Then he spotted a black Chrysler 300 that turned violently onto 124th Street and raced down the block toward him.

He hesitated before running again.

Is that car for me?

He studied the oversized grill and headlights, while not wanting to waste energy trying to outrun a car that had nothing to do with him. But when the car slowed down for no reason, that was all he needed to see. Whoever was inside was looking for something.

Fuck! Shareef continued to curse. There was only one way for him to go. So he took a deep breath as the car got closer to where he hid.

I could just hide under this car for a minute, he pondered. With all the shooting they were doing, he figured the police were bound to show up eventually. Then again, all it took was one stray bullet to hit him while he was trapped under a car, and the police could do nothing to save him. So Shareef thought about his life as a young athlete and repeated, *Fuck it. They gon' have to catch me to kill me.* And he took off running again.

Sure enough, the car sped up the block behind him.

Motherfucker! Now I gotta outrun a car. I should have just kept running, Shareef mused as he sprinted full speed down the block.

He thought, *I would have been at Adam Clayton Powell already.* And he couldn't zigzag in the street anymore with a car chasing after him.

"Yo, Shareef, it's cool, we got you!" someone hollered from the window of the car.

Shareef slowed up and looked back to see if he could see who was inside. He didn't notice the driver. Or did he?

This guy look familiar, but I don't know the motherfucker.

Then he looked to the passenger seat window behind the driver.

"Yo, I know you feel a little crazy right now with niggas shooting at you and everything, but it's cool, man, we the good guys."

Shareef recognized the young, charismatic Harlemite, Baby G, sitting in the back passenger seat and he froze.

Baby G raised his empty hands outside the window and said, "I'm not after you, player. I just want to meet you and get you out of this obvious shit your in."

"Meet me for what?" Shareef asked him.

"We ain't got a lot of time for this Q and A shit right now, but like I said, you good. We just want to get you out of here."

Shareef said, "Aw'ight, well, let me walk to the end of the block, and I'm good. I don't need no ride. My legs work just fine."

Baby G smiled and said, "Yeah, I can see that. I saw them moves you made on them niggas back there. You looked like Curtis Martin from the Jets or some shit, breaking out for a touchdown."

They all chuckled inside the car as if Shareef's life was a joke. He wondered how many young guys were inside.

"Come on, man, I just want to meet you," Baby G insisted. "I mean, you a writer, right? I got some stories to tell you."

Another car pulled up behind their Chrysler in the street, while they held up traffic.

Baby G persisted, "Look, I'm not gon' hurt you, man. Stop acting like that. Everybody know me. I mean, I know you saw me at the game yesterday. My young buck said he spoke to you and got your autograph for his girl."

Shareef remembered that. And he had spotted Baby G at the game, and at the party on Wednesday night at Zip Code. The young charmer had snatched the California girl away from him. Shareef still wondered if he had slept with her that night. But he was still hesitant to trust the young guy.

"Yo, show him your face, man," he said to someone else in the front seat of the car.

Shareef watched as the same pleasant, young man he had signed an autograph for at the Kingdome Tournament stood outside of the car with his empty palms out.

"Yo, Shareef, he just wants to talk to you, man. That's on my grave. And I'm too young to die."

Shareef heard the young man out and didn't budge.

These motherfuckers are clever, he told himself. He wondered if Baby G had told his follower what to say.

The young general continued to stare at Shareef through the opened window. He remained patient and poised. He said, "Come on, man, writers are supposed to be brave. Y'all 'sposed to be the first ones to investigate shit. I don't let people ride with me every day like this, man. Consider this a privilege."

The cars behind them began to blow their horns. Baby G didn't respond to them. He was still waiting for Shareef. He had a quiet reserve about him that was unusual for thug types. Nothing seemed to faze him, not even the gun battle less than a block away.

Shareef took a long breath and made his final decision. He told himself, *I'm a fucking asshole. I deserve to die.* And he began to walk toward the car.

Baby G opened the door for him to get in and slid over in his seat. There was another young man who hopped out of the car on the other side to make room.

"Y'all know how to get home from here. Just call me up when you make it back in safe. Me and this man got some talking to do," Baby G told both of the younger men who stood outside of the car.

They nodded, "Yes, sir," and moved on.

That left Shareef alone inside the car with Baby G and his driver as they zoomed down 124th Street.

Shareef had no idea what to expect from the man. He didn't even know what to say to him.

"Aw'ight, so you met me, now what?"

Baby G looked at him and nodded himself. He calmly extended his right hand and said, "Shareef Crawford, my government name is Greggory Taylor. But the streets call me Baby G. And I don't know what it is, but ever since I was a kid, whenever I spoke, people liked to listen to me. They felt like I was an old soul out here, you know. So once I figured that shit out, I just told myself, 'Well, since people love listening to me like that, let me make sure I always got something for them to do. And after that, all my uncles, cousins, and the old-timers on the block started calling me the Baby Gangsta. You feel me? That's how I ended up who I am."

He said, "But what about you, man? How'd you become a writer?"

Shareef shook his hand and was more concerned about where they were driving him. They headed straight down 124th Street with no turnoff.

"Where are we going?" he asked.

Baby G told him immediately. "Downtown. I don't want you being nervous up here in Harlem, thinking I'm gon' kill you or nothing. So if we ride downtown, maybe you'll feel safer." He said, "We need to get away from all this heat you just caused up here anyway," and chuckled.

His thick driver smiled at it, too.

Shareef asked him, "You spend much time downtown?" He doubted if the young man spent much time downtown at all. Going downtown wasn't a Harlem thing to do.

Baby G shook it off and answered, "I don't. You know better

than that. Harlem and Manhattan is like two different places. Did you go downtown when you lived in Harlem? And I'm not talking about for plays and concerts and shit. I'm just saying to hang out down there."

"Nah," Shareef told him. "We were too proud of Harlem to go downtown."

Baby G nodded and said, "Exactly. Now downtown is coming back up to us. They know what time it is. Harlem is what's up."

Once they made it to the FDR Drive and headed south for downtown Manhattan, Shareef began to relax, just as Baby G had figured.

Then the cell phones began to ring. Shareef answered a call right after Baby G had answered his.

Baby G dealt with his call first.

"Yeah, I got it. We headed downtown right now. I'll call you back later and tell you how it went."

Shareef couldn't trust everything he heard, but he didn't have much of a choice at that point. He was already inside the car with no intentions of jumping out, or at least not yet.

Then he dealt with his own phone call. It was Cynthia again.

"Hello," he answered.

She exhaled and said, "Thank God. You're not out there with them anymore are you?"

"Nah, I'm safe," he told her. Then he looked at Baby G to make sure. He said, "Or I think I'm safe."

Baby G nodded his head with a smirk. He said, "You are safe, player. Just relax like you got a pen in your hand."

On the line, Cynthia was confused. She said, "You *think* you're safe. What are you talking about? Where are you?"

Shareef didn't want her getting hysterical on him again. He wanted to get down to business with Baby G anyway. What were they there to talk about?

"Look, I'ma call you back. Just relax your nerves right now, I'm safe," he repeated to her.

He closed his cell phone and smiled. It was personality time.

He said, "Women . . . when they love you they don't know how to act. And when they hate you they don't know how to act."

Baby G and his driver both started laughing. The subject of gender psychology would always be a hit with men. The need to feed with sex was a constant hunger of masculinity.

Baby G added, "Yeah, they only know how to act when they don't give a fuck about you. They be all strict with their rules and shit. And that's generally when you care the most about them, right? That's why I never let no girl know how much I like her," he commented. "And if she even start off like she don't care about me, I drop her immediately with no phone calls or nothing."

He cracked a smile and said, "That's when they come the fuck back."

Shareef nodded his head in agreement. "Yeah. That's the game right there. And it don't change with these girls. That's why they gotta learn how to be women, and take care of their man no matter what. Just like a real man gotta take care of them."

Shareef silenced the air with that comment. He was the only married man with children inside the car.

Baby G looked for his ring finger and nodded. He said, "What does that feel like, man . . . to be married? I see you not wearing your ring no more."

Shareef looked down at his left hand and asked him, "How you figure that?"

"I can see how skinny your ring finger is. And you old enough to be married, ain't you? Writers always got women, them pretty smart girls who read."

He said, "I had a couple of them. They good and nasty, too. They get all creative on a nigga."

Shareef grinned and told him, "Don't assume everything in this life, man. Just when you think something would never happen . . . it will. And when you think you know everything you need to know, life'll throw your ass for another loop."

Baby G grinned and started laughing. He said, "That's what I heard about you, player. My peoples told me you a old-school nigga. You speak from what it is. A man gotta respect that."

Shareef asked him, "But what about you? I mean, it's obvious to me that you know more than the average 'hood. You a old soul, right? You got the charisma. You got the gift of gab. You got the looks. Fuck you wanna waste your life in this shit for?"

Baby G had not been around a strong straight shooter outside of the street life since his high school days. There were a couple of male teachers who always told him the same thing. But once the next class had moved up and his grade had moved on, the influence was lost.

He thought about it and had a story to tell. He said, "I remember this one time, man, when my mom bought me this new bike for getting good grades in school. And I didn't have that bike for one week before somebody stole the shit from in front of the house. And I went around asking people with tears in my eyes if they had seen anybody with it or knew anything about it, right. And nobody knew shit. So then when I got pissed off and rounded up the thug niggas, we started roughing people up like the cops, and sure enough, man, my bike popped back up in two hours. Motherfuckers were apologizing and all kinds of shit. I even got some new wheels out the deal. And after that, I just knew it, man. Niggas don't care about no smart shit."

He stopped his conversation and said to his driver, "Yo, give me that up there, man. Pass it back."

His driver passed him back a black pistol. Shareef watched the transaction and his heart rate increased again.

Baby G looked and told him, "Don't worry about it, man, it's on safety. But this is what niggas respect in the 'hood, B, raw power. This shit right here. It's just like how Tupac kicked it; '*Once I got that Thug Life across my chest . . .*' That was it, man, niggas respected it. Now maybe if I grew up in the suburbs or some shit it would be different. But you know how it is in Harlem, man. The strong eat the weak. That's in every 'hood. And that's why you still standing right now, Shareef. I gotta bigger squad than them niggas who after you."

He said, "So, you try'na show them the right way. You try'na record history. You try'na do something positive. But when you deal with the wrong niggas, what do you get for it? They out here trying to kill you, that's what. So you gotta take care of them first, then you can do what you need to do."

Shareef couldn't argue with that. How could he? He was still in the middle of the storm and had the young general to thank for bailing him out.

Another cell phone call hit Baby G on his hip before Shareef could get out another word.

"Yeah, y'all all safe? . . . Anybody get caught? . . . Any losses? . . . What about on they side?" He nodded and said, "Good. Spread the word though. Get out the street for the night. Sleep tight. And I'll see y'all tomorrow."

When he hung up the phone again, he said, "First problem solved, Shareef. We got them niggas for you. But the bigger problem is finding out who sent them and gettin' to that nigga. But that's homework time. We'll work on that for you tomorrow."

Imagine that? Shareef was blown away by it. But at the same time, he wondered what Baby G's price tag was. He wasn't protecting him for nothing.

Shareef said, "So . . . what's up with this, man. Why you doing this for me? I mean, you don't know me to look out for me like that."

"Because I'm interested in what you doing," he answered. "But why you writing a book about Michael Springfield? You think he the most interesting nigga in Harlem? I mean, come, man. He been over the hill a long time ago. Like my man Biggie said, '*Things done changed* . . .' That's classic. You gotta get with the new school now. So I want a book on me. Fuck them old-timers."

Shareef couldn't help but smile at it. He said, "I didn't know you young guys even cared about books like that."

Baby G looked at him and said, "Come on, man, books make you famous. That damn Malcolm X book is the most famous book in the 'hood. But everybody ain't gon' read everybody book. You gotta be one of them special niggas for people to read you. And I'm one of them special niggas, not Michael Springfield. You need to make me famous, not him."

Shareef nodded and said, "You know he got killed in jail today, don't you?"

He still wanted to test how many people knew or didn't know.

"I heard about it," Baby G answered.

"Who from?"

"The same place you heard it. On the streets."

Shareef responded, "I didn't hear it on the streets."

"Well, what fuckin' difference does it make, man? If he dead he dead, right?"

"Yeah, but who did it and why is the question," Shareef stated.

Baby G looked at him and said, "Actually, I had him killed in jail so you can write my book instead. It was all mapped out."

Shareef looked at him and froze. Was he bullshitting or what? Shareef even looked up front to see how the driver would respond to it. And the man didn't budge at all from the wheel.

Baby G read the horror on Shareef's face and started laughing. He said, "Yo, I'm just fucking with you, man . . . unless you really wanna believe that shit."

On cue, his driver laughed with him.

"Yo, that shit ain't funny, man," Shareef warned him. He could get himself in major trouble with the streets taking credit for things he didn't do. Shareef knew that much for a fact. Real killers took their work seriously, and he doubted Baby G was a real killer. He had too much charisma to kill.

The young general blew his warning off. He said, "That's the best jokes, man, the ones where you don't know if you should laugh or not. It's like . . . sadistic humor."

He waited for Shareef to respond to it. When he didn't, Baby G continued.

He said, "I bet you ain't think I had a vocabulary like that, did you?

But like you said already, I'm an unusual guy, player. And people gon' like me when they read my book . . . well, the real niggas will," he corrected himself.

Shareef told him, "The only problem wit' that is, the real niggas don't read too many books. What was the last book you read?"

"*Mary Had a Li'l Lamb.* I read that one yesterday," he stated with a straight face.

His driver couldn't wait for that laugh. He broke out immediately.

Shareef grinned himself and said, "That's not even a book. That's only a nursery rhyme."

Baby G asked him, "For real? Damn, man, all these years, and I didn't even know that. Well, *Snow White* wasn't no nursery rhyme, was it?"

His driver continued to break up laughing as they made it to the 49th Street exit.

"Yo, get off right here, man, and head to Times Square," Baby G told him.

Shareef decided to cut the bullshit. He looked into the young general's eyes and asked him, "Yo, seriously, have you ever killed somebody before? I mean, like, you actually pulled the trigger?"

Shareef still doubted it. He believed that Baby G gave the orders and looked away. But all the laughing and joking stopped after that question. The tension was all in the air. And the driver turned into a statue again.

Baby G stared at the writer and thought about it. He still held the black pistol in his hand. He spoke with it and said, "You know what I love about being called 'Baby'? A lot of dumb niggas never take me seriously. They hear that Baby shit, and they think I'm fuckin' jokin'."

He paused and said, "I love that shit. So if I point this gun at your face and you think I'm fuckin' playin', then I got a psychological advantage, 'cause I know I'm *not* playing. And when that shit go off, you shocked then a motherfucker. But it's too late by then. For you. But for the motherfuckers who know me . . . they *know*."

He said, "But am I gonna sit here and tell you some shit like that? For what?"

"Because the readers would want to know," Shareef told him.

Baby G said, "Well, you tell them then. You know how to write it without writing it, right?"

Shareef said, "I know how to do it, but our people don't respond to the hints. They want to see the blood."

Baby G studied his face and said, "Well, give them blood then. That's what they want, right? I figured that, too, about our people. You gotta be willing to die for 'em. And if you ain't ready to die, they don't choose you."

He nodded his head and smiled again. He said, "Like you, you ready to die, player. That's why you jumped into the car. And if you would have stayed on the sidewalk like a bitch, then I wouldn't have respected you."

He said, "Fuck it, I would have shot you myself. But I knew you wasn't no bitch. I could see it in your eyes. That's why I was so patient with you. You wasn't scared of me, you was just being smart. Somebody was just try'na kill you out here."

When they got close to Times Square, Baby G put the gun away by hiding it under the seat.

He said, "We gon' hang out a minute down here, man. I'ma show you that I'm universal. I got range. I can fit in when I need to."

They found a parking spot and climbed out of the car for a walk. Baby G talked with his driver pacing in front of them.

He said, "I can understand where you coming from, man, when you tell me not to waste my life in this shit. I mean, that happens to a lot of people in everything. How many writers out here never get shit published? How many so-called rappers never get no record deal? How many ballers never play in the NBA? You got actors who never act. Singers who never sing. And a million local thugs who never get a rep. But I already got a rep. Niggas in the 'hood know me. So does everybody else who come up to Harlem. If you in Harlem, you in my territory."

He said, "I even made Bill Clinton stare at me. He was at the Rucker Tournament one time when I came through with seven of my best riders all G'd up with jewels and shut shit down for a couple of minutes. And I saw him asking folks about me. But that's how I get down, player. I'ma make a fuckin' scene when I'm alive *and* when I'm dead. But your average thug nigga can't say that shit. That's just how life is, man. Everybody can't be Shareef Crawford, and everybody can't be Greggory Taylor. So you make your mark where you can make it. And this where I'm making my mark. But for all them other niggas who follow . . . what else you expect them to do?"

He stopped walking on 42nd Street and looked straight up at a giant-size billboard of American icon Sean "Diddy" Combs raising a power fist in his award-winning designer clothes.

Baby G stated, "Either you special or you not, man. And that nigga up there is special. But a lot of people wanna act like they hate P now. You know why?"

Shareef grinned and correctly answered the question. "Because they can't be like him."

Baby G shrugged his shoulders. He said, "But I figure, fuck it, he can't be like me. Now I can walk down here every weekend with one man, and have people looking at me curiously, and never touch me. Then I can come back down with fifty Harlem strong and have the whole Times Square walking around us, while the police try and break us up. And I'll have motherfuckers stop, go, turn around, drop, and do push-ups out this bitch. But Diddy, he couldn't even make ma-fuckers on his reality show go and get him cheesecake at night after he fuckin' put them up in that house."

He looked at Shareef and grimaced.

He said, "Man, shit, niggas know me better than that. I'll make a motherfucker run to *Canada,* buy me some ice cream, 'cause I didn't eat cheesecake, and I'd tell them to keep that ice cream cold on the way back. You feel me? Now that gangsta shit. But Diddy gotta pay for it, and they *still* won't do it. *And* I look better than him," he added.

Shareef couldn't help himself. He was smiling from ear to ear. You talk about a vainglorious ego. Baby G was making Muhammad Ali sound shy.

Shareef joked and said, "I hope we got a big enough book cover that can fit your picture."

The driver overheard him and started giggling nervously in front.

Baby G caught on and grinned. He said, "You see that? I like that. You got a sense of humor. You a real nigga. That's why I'ma let that ride. But if I ain't like you . . ."

He paused real long for effect. He said, "I'd have to kill you for that shit. And you'd be standing there surprised that I shot you."

The Morning After

SHAREEF AWOKE at the Hudson Hotel off 8th Avenue and wondered if he had only dreamt the events of the previous night. But he couldn't have been dreaming if he was waking up at the Hudson near Times Square instead of at his hotel room in Harlem. The room at the Hudson was not all that much bigger or nicer, but how did he get there?

He rolled over and eyed the digital alarm clock on the nightstand. The time read 7:49 AM.

"Damn. What a night," he mumbled. Then he remembered, "Shit, I still got my luggage up in Harlem."

He flipped open his cell phone for missed calls and text messages. Once Baby G began to run his mouth nonstop in Times Square, Shareef had clicked his phone on silent to give the young man his undivided attention. And when he looked at his cell phone that morning, he saw that he had missed six late-night phone calls. His wife, Jacqueline, Polo, Jurrell, Cynthia, and Spoonie had all called him late-night in that order.

"Damn. When was the last time I answered this shit?" he pondered. "Cynthia."

He dialed her number to let her know that he was still alive and well.

"Hello? Shareef?" she answered, still sounding alarmed.

Damn, did she even sleep last night? he asked himself.

"Yeah, it's me. I'm alive. Okay. I'm alive," he told her.

She took a deep breath and asked him, "How come you didn't call me back last night."

"It's a long story, and I'm not gon' try to explain it right now. I'm basically just calling you back to let you know I'm all right. But I still need to get some rest."

"You don't need any rest, you're always up," she teased him.

He smiled and mumbled, "Yeah . . . I know. But let me try and get some rest anyway."

Shareef hung up with her and took a deep breath himself. What was there left to do in New York? If Cynthia's information was correct, then there was no more Michael Springfield story to be written, at least not told from the man himself. And was Shareef prepared to start from scratch with a braggadocios life story from Baby G, aka Greggory Taylor? What would be the purpose of that? There was no cautionary *I Surrender* tale to be written about a young, celebratory gangsta in his prime on the streets. Covering Baby G's life now was the wrong story to write. Or maybe it was the right story. The streets loved to celebrate their own. A couple million gangsta rap songs from New York to LA proved it.

Shareef thought about it and shook it off. "That would be just like everybody else's book," he told himself. But how could he write something different about the streets and expect it to be successful? The streets wanted what they wanted, blood and glory. Stick to the script.

For the moment, he didn't have the answers. He stretched out across the bed, buffered by four, comfy white pillows and continued to contemplate. What was the purpose of his writings in the first place? What was the use in the research and the meticulous thoughts that went into it; and the long hours, days, weeks, months, and years developing meaningful characters, plots, motivations, and conclusions? Who really cared about the shit? And what exactly were readers supposed to do with it all?

Shareef answered his own thoughts and said, "Learn something from it." But then his conscience argued from the other side. *Nobody wants to learn shit. Baby G told you that last night. And you agreed with it. They want blood. They want violence. They want death.*

The counterargument paralyzed the rest of Shareef's thoughts. And if it was valid, then what use was attempting to write to teach? He had it right all along; you write to be successful. And if success meant readership, and women were the ones who read, and they preferred to read romance over crime, then writing about crime meant no readership, and ultimately . . . failure. So why was he up in Harlem to fail by writing a true-crime book that no one would read? He had even put his life on the line for it? And for what?

Shareef nodded to himself and mumbled, "Dig it. I got a pot full of money and a whole life waiting for me back down in Florida, and I'm up here fucking with this shit. For what?"

He picked his cell phone up to call his wife and kids in Fort Lauderdale.

JENNIFER CRAWFORD stood inside the large, open-area kitchen of her luxurious "mini-mansion," dressed in long, light-blue cotton pajamas and slippers. She cooked scrambled eggs and turkey bacon at the stove with a white silk scarf wrapped around her head. She listened to sentimental soul music that played from the stereo system in the nearby family room. Her daughter, Kimberly, in pink pajamas, played with two oversize Bratz dolls at the kitchen table. Jennifer's husband Shareef Sr., and son Shareef Jr., were nowhere in sight. Nevertheless, the music soothed her and made their absence bearable.

"Kimberly, go tell your brother to get down here. Breakfast is almost ready."

The daughter set her dolls down on the table and ran for the staircase. Before she could make it halfway up, Shareef Jr. scrambled down the stairs in full football gear and nearly trampled her.

"Watch it, boy," she complained.

"Well, get out of my way then."

"Mommy told me to get you for breakfast."

"All right, I'm down here already."

Jennifer overheard the commotion on the staircase and shook her head. She'd wait to see her son's face before she commented.

As soon as he walked out to the kitchen table she asked her son, "What is your problem, Shareef?"

"I just want to get to practice on time," he told her.

Jennifer stared at him. "Shareef, it's eight o'clock. We have plenty of time to make your practice. It's not until ten."

He took off his helmet at the table and said, "Yeah, but once you start getting dressed, we always end up late."

"Excuse me? Who do you think you're talking to?" she snapped at him. "You say something else like that and you won't go to practice today at all."

Shareef Jr. looked shocked and crippled by it. His faced opened up wide. He asked her, "But why?"

"Why? Because you don't talk to me like that. I keep telling you about that, Shareef. You need to check your attitude."

He responded to her with tears in his eyes, "But it's true, we always end up late."

"Yes, after I cook, clean, wash, bathe, help you and your sister with your clothes, and then hustle to get my *own* clothes on . . ."

Shareef Jr. cut her off and said, "But Mom, you don't have to be all fancy, just drop me off." Then he mumbled under his breath, "Or let somebody else take me to practice."

Jennifer overheard him just as she popped out wheat toast from the toaster. She buttered the toast and made their plates with orange juice in small glasses. And when she marched her son's plate of food and orange juice over to him at the table, she told him, "You know what, you can take everything back off after you eat, because you're not going to practice."

Shareef Jr. pushed himself away from the table in his chair and cried, "Why?"

Jennifer stood in his face with her finger extended to make her point.

"Boy, I will smack you upside your head. You know why? You keep running your damn *mouth,* and I just *told you* about that. So now you're not going to practice."

That was it for the boy. Tears ran out of his eyes, down his face, and he immediately lost his appetite. Kimberly watched the whole scene and studied it without saying a word. She was learning from it. The best way to get to a boy was to take something away from him that he wanted. It worked with her brother every time. But he deserved it for being mean.

In the heat of the action, the kitchen phone rang, a cordless that sat in its charger on the countertop. Jennifer composed herself before she answered it, especially once she saw who it was on the Caller ID. She figured she had another heated argument coming.

"Hello."

"Y'all getting ready for football practice this morning?"

She heard his words and took a deep breath. Like father, like son. The man didn't even say hi to her.

Jennifer brought that up and said, "Hi to you, too, Shareef."

Her son and daughter both looked toward her on the phone.

"Hi," her husband responded to her.

"Mmm, hmm," she grumbled. "Well, you need to talk to your son about practice," she told him.

"Why?"

"Here he is." Jennifer handed the phone to her son without another word to his father.

Shareef Jr. took the phone and mumbled, "She won't let me go." He listened to the obvious question and answered, "Because I had an attitude. But Dad, I just don't want to be late all the time."

Jennifer jumped in and said, "Boy, you've only had a *week* of practice. You're not gonna be late all the time. Don't even try that."

"Let me talk to your mother," Shareef told his son.

"Okay. Mom?"

Shareef Jr. extended the cordless phone back to his mother.

"Hey, Daddy," Kimberly hollered into the phone as her mother reclaimed it.

"He'll talk to you in a minute, honey," Jennifer told her daughter. She expected an extended conversation with her estranged husband about football practice, running late, and aggravating their son. She expected to counter with an argument to respect her as a mother, respect her as a wife, respect her as a woman, and respect all of the damn work she continued to perform around the house and outside of the house to keep their family together and to protect their name regardless of his transgressions. But Shareef changed the whole subject on her.

He said, "You used to be a lot more fun than this, Jennifer. I didn't call you the Golden Girl for nothing. You used to have a shine. I miss that. In fact, I wouldn't have married you without it. But you lost it, man. And you need to get it back."

He said, "You need to get that excitement back in your life and learn how to have fun with your family again."

Jennifer couldn't believe her ears. How could she concentrate on "having fun" with bitches disrespecting her marriage, her kids, her family, her home, her womanhood, and her ability to think straight after *he* had allowed them to through his cheating? How dare he say some shit to her like that? And if the kids were not around her, she would curse his ass out for it. But since they were, she simply refuted it.

"I do know how to have fun. But the problem is, you never want to participate in anything I like to do. It's always about what *you* want," she told him.

Shareef paused over the line. It was the same old argument; his way or her way, his thing or her thing, his idea or her idea.

He finally said, "Look, I wish I could be the man you need me to be for you, but I am who I am, and you knew that when you married me. I haven't lied to you in any way."

Jennifer was ready to jump out of her skin. He hadn't *lied* to her in any way? Who the hell was he talking to? He was a bold-faced *liar*! He had been lying about his commitment to their marriage *for years*! Had he lost his fucking *mind*! But instead of cursing him out in front of the children, Jennifer smiled at the ridiculousness of his charge and walked away from the kitchen with the phone in hand. She was walking toward the front door where she could step outside, shut the door behind her, and speak frankly.

"Hold on," she told her husband as she made it to the front door. She couldn't wait. And as soon as she reached her destination outside the house, she repeated, "You said you haven't *lied* to me in any way? Is that what you said? So, you didn't *lie* to me whenever I asked you where you were and who you were with whenever you went out of town on your little *book* events."

Shareef paused again. He said, "Every single time, I went and handled my business, just like I'm doing right now."

"Yeah, and then you went and handled some little *freak*, too. And then you wonder why I don't want you to touch me. Probably had some little ho in New York with you. Didn't you?"

Shareef was at a moral crossroad. What came first, the chicken or the egg? If Jennifer had simply taken care of her business as his woman like she used to, he would have had less need to chase and capture. He would still look and wonder. Every man looks and wonders. But the chase and capture game was all about the frustration of unused energy at home.

Shareef wasn't a liar. He was too transparent to lie. He wore his heart on his sleeve for everyone to see. That's why people respected him. He told them what the truth was every time, even when he was a young Harlem snot nose. But he had energies to deal with; energies that Jennifer knew about firsthand. Energies that had attracted her to him. Energies that had given her a beautiful life, home, family, children, and lovely vacations. But his energies meant nothing to her without his loyalty. A man's loyalty to his woman was pivotal, but what about her loyalty to him as his wife? What did that loyalty mean? And how did loyal people act to one another?

Shareef finally blew his lid and spat, "You don't get shit in this world for free, Jennifer! You gotta *pay* for the shit I give you. That's just the way life is. Grow the fuck up and stop thinking somebody gon' *give* you something without *work*!"

He said, "We all gotta fuckin' work in this life, girl. So if your job as a wife is to fuck your husband for all of the things that he does for you, then you fuck your husband! Is that so hard to do? Am I an ugly-ass man now? I didn't used to be. Other women don't think so."

He said, "And don't tell me no shit about no cooking, cleaning, washing, and all of that. Because I've never sweated you about that. I can hire a chef, a maid, and a housekeeper for that. I know you're an educated, working woman. But I can't have no wife I can't touch when I come home. What I gotta make a fuckin' appointment for you? Mark the shit off on your little calendars? Well, fuck that! I'm not living like that. And if you thought you married a man who would just sit there and stand for that shit, then you got me wrong. But you *know me* better than that. You knew I wasn't gonna go for that shit. So what the fuck was you thinking?"

Jennifer took all of his heat and responded to him calmly, "I was thinking that you would treat your wife with respect and honor, that you would cherish your wife and stay committed to her. I had no idea that I *owed you* anything for loving me. But obviously, I was *wrong*, Shareef. I was wrong for ever marrying you. Because it's obvious to me now that you don't really want a wife. You want a live-in whore you can do what you want to with and have your way with, and I'm sorry to disappoint you because I'm not that kind of a woman."

She pressed the off button on the cordless phone and hung up on him. But then she realized that Kimberly had not had a chance to speak to her father. And what about Shareef Jr. and his football practice? She wanted to teach him a lesson on how to act to make sure he was never rewarded for disrespectful behavior, but at the same time, she never wanted to stop either of her children from doing what they wanted to do and enjoying themselves in life.

But there's a right and a wrong way to do things, she argued to herself.

And Shareef is not right, she insisted. Nevertheless, it hurt her that her son and husband were so deliberate in having things their way. If only boys and men would learn to just . . . *behave.* But since they didn't, and she couldn't seem to win either of them over without bringing so much pain to herself in her forceful attempts to maintain dignity, she took a seat on the front steps of her home and began to cry.

Being a smart, respectable wife; a good, responsible mother; and a mature and honorable woman seemed to be a torturous affair. But Jennifer was determined to maintain her stature. And no matter how much the struggle seemed to hurt her, she was no man's doormat and would never allow herself to be walked over.

SHAREEF STOOD UP from his bed at the Hudson Hotel in Times Square and was pissed. He looked at his cell phone after his wife had hung up on him, and he thought of throwing it up against the wall and breaking it. But instead he threw it down against the soft pillows.

"Mother- . . ." he began to curse and caught himself. He was breathing heavily and pacing the small room from the window next to the bed, all the way to the front door and back.

"Fuckin' girl gon' change up on a nigga," he mumbled to himself. "She's the one who lied from day one. I thought she loved me. But now she don't wanna touch a motherfucker after all I gave her. After *all* I fuckin' gave her!"

He couldn't understand how his wife could live in a million-dollar home and not honor his passion for her. They had dreamed about their lives together. They had discussed it before marriage. And Shareef just assumed that their sex life would remain as it was when they were dating, a heated, passionate, spontaneous romp.

He burst out and screamed, "Why you fuckin' lie to *me*?!" to the hotel walls. Then he sat on the edge of the bed with tears building in his own eyes. He even felt his chest tighten up.

He put his right hand over his heart to calm himself down from the stress.

"Okay . . . now she's try'na kill me," he stated. He stood back up from the bed to pace the room again with his hand still placed over his chest. He said, "Well, you know what? Since it's all about me, that's how it's gon' be then. I'm not gon' be respected for writing no fuckin' romance shit just to pay for your ass. So I'm gon' do me now, all the fuckin' way. That's what I'm supposed to do, right?"

He continued to pace the room with angry energy, while going over his thoughts and decisions out loud.

"Richard Wright wrote about the streets. Chester Himes wrote about it. Langston Hughes. Eldridge Cleaver. Iceberg Slim. Donald Goines. James Baldwin. Ishmael Reed. Claude Brown. They *all* wrote about the streets. And their shit *lasted*. And not one of them is famous for writing some romance shit. None of them!"

He mumbled, "I can't even hold down my own fuckin' romance, so how the hell I'm gon' write about that shit for other people? It's hypocritical. It's all about the money."

Then he stopped in his tracks and stood still in the room. He said, "Well, you know what? Thank you, baby. Thank you for lettin' me see what I need to do. It's a clear picture now. I'm right where I'm supposed to be. I'm a street nigga. I was *born* to the streets. *Harlem!* I don't even know my parents. So if I die fuckin' with this book, then that's my legacy. But I'm not running from shit. And if you don't want to be a part of my life, then that's *your* fuckin' problem. You can stay your ass out in the fuckin' suburbs."

Just as he got all the ranting out of his system, his cell phone rang from the bed. He walked over and picked it up to view the number. It was his wife calling him back from home.

Shareef exhaled and shook his head. "What she got to say to me now?" he grumbled. He answered her call anyway. "Hello."

"Your daughter wants to speak to you," Jennifer told him. She put Kimberly on the line.

"Hey, Daddy."

Shareef went soft again. "Hey, baby girl. Did you have a good breakfast this morning?"

"Yeah, but I don't like eggs."

"Yeah, I know. You like cinnamon toast with butter. And a glass of milk."

"Yup," she confirmed with a giggle.

Shareef listened to his daughter and smiled. Family was family, no matter what. And he would never forsake his children. But at the same time, he had a job to do in Harlem, and he remained focused on getting that job done.

Your daddy ain't no punk, he thought to tell his seven-year-old daughter. *For nobody!* So after a brief conversation he told his daughter that he loved her, ended the call, and prepared his mind to get back to business in Harlem, USA.

FIRST SHAREEF CALLED BACK his friend Polo. And as soon as Polo answered the call, he went into overdrive.

"Yo, where you at, B? The cops are looking for you. Don't go back to that hotel, man."

"The cops are looking for me for what?" Shareef asked him.

"Them killas who were after you got shot up last night. Only one who got away was the driver."

Shareef said, "What does that have to do with me?"

"What does that have to do with *you*? The cops feel like you hired them. They think they were part of your crew."

Shareef thought about that and said, "Even so, it would be self-defense, right? I mean, them guys were trying to kill me, man. It wasn't like they got shot for no reason."

Shareef was already siding with Baby G and his team. It was old-school loyalty. The kid had looked out for him in a life-and-death crisis, and Shareef had to respect him for that.

Polo paused a minute. He said, "Yo, you don't want to tell the cops that. Just say you don't know who they were. I mean, you didn't know who they were, right?"

Polo already knew more about it than Shareef felt he should. He wasn't even there. So Shareef listened to his instincts and commented on it.

He stood deadly still in his hotel room and asked, "Polo . . . you know what's going on, don't you? I mean, don't bullshit me, man. This is serious. They were straight up trying to kill me last night. So who the fuck is after me, man?"

Polo took a deep breath over the phone line. That's all Shareef needed to hear to know that he was right. His friend had been holding out on him.

He said, "Yo, son, I tried my best to get you to leave Harlem and go on back home to your wife and kids in Florida, man, but like . . . I'm sayin', you just about the hardest-headed nigga I've ever known in my *life*, Shareef. I mean, you smart, man, but sometimes you fucking *stupid*. I told you, just leave that street shit alone. Make your book money, go chill out on an island somewhere, and stay away from these streets. They don't care about you out here."

He said, "But you just keep pressing for this shit, over some damn girl at that. I mean, you don't know her like that. What's wrong with you?"

Polo was getting sidetracked, but Shareef went back to his initial question.

"So who the fuck is after me, man?" That's all he wanted to know.

Polo said, "Come on, man, you know who it is. This ain't no damn mystery book. What, you been off the streets too long?"

Shareef was puzzled. He had no idea what Polo was talking about.

He said, "Come on, man, if I knew who it was, I would have stopped this shit. I would step right up and ask what the problem is to get this shit over with."

"That's what I told him," Polo commented.

Shareef froze in his tracks. "That's what you told him?" he repeated. "You know who it is then?"

• • •

OVER AT POLO'S APARTMENT in north Harlem, he was dressed in a long bathrobe, purple with gold trimmings. A black pistol hung heavy in his robe pocket.

He grimaced while listening to Shareef's ridiculously naive responses. He shook his head and walked toward the hallway bathroom to get away from his young son, daughter, and their mother, who were playing video games and eating the last crumbs of breakfast on the living room sofa.

Polo walked inside the bathroom and closed the door.

He said, "What the fuck, I gotta spell it out to you, man? Who was the first one who said something about you talking to Michael Springfield in jail?"

Shareef paused and answered, "Trap."

"Exactly," his friend told him. "And y'all just alike, man. Hard-headed. So his whole thing was gettin' you to drop the idea, and your thing was still trying to fuckin' do it."

Shareef said, "Well, how come he just didn't come out and tell me that?"

Polo got excited. He said, "He did tell you that shit. How you just gon' sit here on the phone and say that? He told you that shit in front of all of us. But as usual, you went right ahead and ignored him. That's what you always do. I mean, you crazy, man."

He said, "So now I gotta keep a loaded gun on me because you got this nigga ready to kill all of us. That was one of his cousins who got shot last night."

BACK AT THE HUDSON HOTEL, Shareef couldn't believe his ears. Trap was way too obvious. But it felt right. It had to be him. Trap knew everything.

Shareef stood with a dazed look in his eyes as he held on to the phone. *So much for old Harlem friends.* He then shook it off and said, "Well, yo, I'm just gon' call Trap and get to the bottom of this. He just made the situation worse than what it had to be. All he had to do was tell me he was involved in some shit, and I would have left his name out."

Polo said, "Whoa, whoa, whoa, horsey, don't do that shit, man. 'Cause you gon' put my name up in it, and he don't give a fuck no more. He don't wanna hear that shit now. I wasn't even supposed to be telling you this, Shareef, you was just supposed to leave."

He said, "The streets is way more complicated than what you trying to make it out to be, man. So even if you left his name out of the book, like he said from jump, other niggas gon' be concerned about *their* names. So you gotta leave it all out. Which means you can't write that fuckin' book."

Shareef said, "But who's to say that Springfield was even trying to drop names on me like that? He was just talking about his story. And Trap knew I wasn't leaving. He know me better than that. I ain't no bitch-ass out here, man. I'm from Harlem. All he had to do was talk to me about it. I'm standing right here."

BACK INSIDE POLO'S BATHROOM, he burst out laughing and pulled his black pistol from out of his robe pocket. He looked at himself in the mirror while holding his gun out.

He said, "That's just what the hell I'm talking about, B. So now you got me up in the middle of this shit, and I still gotta live here. But it don't matter to you. As long as Shareef Crawford is after what he wants, he don't give a fuck about nobody. He just a straight, hardcore, Harlem nigga, straight out the mansions and condos of Florida."

Polo added, "If you wasn't my nigga, man, I'd have to leave your ass out on the line to dry for this shit. But I love you, man, so I gotta help get you out of this . . . and hope I live through it."

SHAREEF THOUGHT ABOUT POLO'S WORDS, and they finally stung him.

What the fuck am I doing, man? he asked himself. *I'm not just put-*

ting my life in jeopardy, I'm putting everybody's else life on the line with me. Damn! Polo got a point.

"Yo, you still there, man?" his friend asked him through the silence.

"Yeah, I'm still here. I'm just thinkin' man. You right," Shareef answered. "I gotta stop thinking about me so much."

"That's what I'm sayin," Polo agreed. "But don't call that Trap nigga, man, I'm telling you. I'm gon' have to lay low from him myself now."

That made Shareef think about the safety of his friend.

"Yo, you think he gon' come after you for real?"

Polo said, "Why wouldn't he? And if not him, then all them niggas who know about it. I mean, you done put us on the other side now. They not gon' let me stay neutral. He gon' say the shit is my fault. You my boy."

"Man, my actions are not your fault," Shareef told him.

Polo responded, "The streets don't care, man. Either I'm with you, or I'm with them. That's how they gon' look at it. And you know I'm not gon' get down with Trap's niggas over you. You family. Trap knows that shit. So he gon' put me in the same boat you in and sink both of us. So, I mean . . . I don't have no choice at this point. I gotta keep my gun on me."

Shareef fell silent again. "Damn, man, my bad," he whimpered.

Polo said, "It's too late for that shit now, B." Then he chuckled and added, "Just make sure you put my family in your will."

That one didn't sound like a joke. Shareef shook his head, thinking it all over.

He said, "Yo, I'm gon' make all of this shit work out, man. I just need a couple minutes to think."

Polo told him, "This ain't no novel, man. You can't just think about it and type the shit in. I mean, what are you gonna do? Them niggas gon' be after us now, me included."

Shareef nodded and said, "Let me call you back in a few minutes." He couldn't concentrate while still talking to Polo on the phone. He needed quiet time.

"Aw'ight, son, I'ma be right here with my lady and my kids. So call me back. Let me see what you come up with."

Shareef ended the call and took a seat on the edge of his hotel bed. He stared into empty space, toward the small office desk and swivel chair, while he thought about his dilemma. He felt like he needed a pen and a pad to write it all down.

"Shit!" he cursed himself.

He stood up and grabbed a black, ballpoint pen from the desk table and found a small, hotel notebook next to the telephone on the night-stand.

He told himself, "I'm gon' work all this shit out. I'm gon' work it out right now." And he wrote the word "Solutions" on a clean page at the top of the notepad.

"Okay, first off, I can't call Trap and let him know what I know because that puts Polo in trouble," he told himself out loud. Then he wrote it down under "Problems" on a second clean page.

He said, "Now, I could have Baby G and his boys to knock Trap off and get it over with, but what would I owe them if I did that? And how would I feel about that?"

He started to pace the room again.

He said, "The cops already think I had something to do with last night, but I didn't. So how would having Trap killed make me look? And what if somebody dimed on me. I would be a real accomplice to a murder. That's premeditated."

He wrote those notes in the small pad below their proper headings.

"Now if I leave New York altogether, then Polo has to deal with Trap trying to get revenge for his cousin, and Baby G and his boys look at me like I'm a bitch."

He thought about that and shook it off.

"I don't really know them guys like that. I have no idea what he wants. I mean, does he really want me to write a book about him? And if he does, and they link him to last night's murders on my behalf, then I write a book about him, how will that make me look?"

Shareef thought about it and wrote more notes in his small pad. So far, his notes all added up to a dead end. He had more problems than solutions.

He tapped the pen into the palm of his left hand and said, "All right, what if I make a deal with Trap to let this shit slide? What would he want from me to do that?"

He wrote that idea down.

"Then again, if that nigga's already sheisty, then there's no way of knowing if he would leave Polo and his family alone," he argued. "And if Polo is right that other guys are involved, then doing a deal with Trap may not include them.

"Shit!" he cursed again at his dilemma. "How 'bout I just move Polo and his family the hell out of New York? Or at least move them to a safer spot."

Before he wrote that note down, he added, "But that would really make Polo a target."

He shook his head and mumbled, "Damn! I might have to break down and move his whole family out of state then. He did tell me his girl's people are from Jersey."

Then his conscience started to speak to him.

Fuck that! I thought you said you wasn't no punk. Well then, you handle this shit yourself. You go back up to Harlem, you get yourself a gun, you wait for these motherfuckers to make their move, and you hit 'em off with some Clint Eastwood shit. Then you can call it self-defense and you'll look like everybody's hero. That's how you handle it.

You can't run from this shit. You gotta make your stand like a grown-ass man.

Shareef heard his radical conscience speaking to him and smiled it off.

He shook his head and said, "Nah, that's crazy." Yet he continued to think about it. It would put all of the weight back on him. And his decisions would be all his own responsibility.

"Man, I never even shot a gun before," he admitted to himself. He didn't want to do it, but what other options did he have? Would he tell the police that someone was after him and let then handle it?

"Fuck no!" he told himself. "I'd look like the bitch of the century if I did that. Niggas would revoke my whole Harlem card. They already think I'm a book-writing playboy with no heart."

As he continued to think things though, his cell phone went off. He looked at the screen and read Jacqueline's number calling him from Florida.

He grimaced and muttered, "Shit. I don't have time for her right now. I gotta figure this shit out." He ignored her call, only for Jacqueline to ring him a second time. He looked at his phone and ignored it again. Exotic pussy was not on his mind at the moment. He had much more urgent issues to deal with.

When his cell phone stopped ringing, Shareef got on the line and called Cynthia back.

"Hello," she answered.

He went straight to the point. "Yo, you still got them things from yesterday?"

"Things? What things?"

"Those heaters."

Cynthia paused for a second. Then she asked him, "What are you planning to do?"

He backed her down and said, "I'm just asking about them. I mean, you know, I may need to have something with me. Just a little something for protection," he told her.

Cynthia responded, "No, Shareef, what you need to do is go back home to your wife and family. And I'm really sorry, again, for getting you involved in all of this. But I know that I still have time to make it right. And this is wrong. I don't want you out here like that."

Shareef was already shaking his head in defiance. He was a man of conviction. Once he made his mind up to do something, that was it. He figured he had to face the mess he had started.

He said, "Look, it's too late for that now. Too many moves have already been made for me to just walk away like nothing happened. I gotta make things right."

Cynthia became hyper. She said, "No you don't, Shareef. I'm serious. You don't have to do anything but keep writing and keep breathing."

He ignored her and asked, "So, you don't have them anymore?"

"I'm not giving them to you," she answered.

"I guess I'll just go out here and get all shot the fuck up then," he told her with a chuckle.

"This is not a game, Shareef."

"Well, give me what I need then."

"Why? You don't need to do that. I was wrong. I should never have even did that. And I'm glad you turned me down yesterday."

"But what if I had gotten shot up last night?" he asked her. "Then what? Then you would have been blaming me for not taking them."

"But you didn't get shot. And if you had them on you, then maybe you would have done something stupid instead of running. Maybe you would have had a shoot-out and gotten yourself killed. So you did the right thing last night. Just run away from it all," she warned him.

Shareef still had time to think. It was only a little after ten o'clock in the morning.

He said, "Sometimes, running is no longer an option. This thing is more complicated than that now."

He was thinking of his friend Polo and his family. Who knows what kind of guys Trap was involved with?

Cynthia said, "Trust me, it doesn't have to be that serious, Shareef. You guys are forever beating your chests."

Shareef shook his head and grinned. Cynthia was making a complete about-face from her earlier position.

He said, "You were the one who called me a pussy for backing down from this shit in the beginning," he reminded her.

"I know, and I was wrong. I'm admitting that now."

"Well, that don't change the fact that niggas were shooting at me last night."

Cynthia stopped arguing and got to the point. "Look, are you trying to get yourself killed now or what? Because I would never be able to live with myself if something happened to you. I mean, you are really a good person, Shareef."

She said, "I admit, you're a little headstrong, but you're still a good brother."

Shareef didn't know what else to say to her. She wasn't helping his problem. Running wasn't part of his solution.

He said, "Aw'ight, well, let me get some breakfast up in here and I'ma call you back later."

"Shareef," Cynthia addressed him before she let him go.

"Yeah."

"Don't do anything stupid. Please. I'm begging you. Go home."

He wasn't attempting to ignore her plea outright, but he was interested in exploring the rest of his options. So he called Jurrell Garland for his opinion. And he assumed that Jurrell would have an opposite perspective from Cynthia.

Jurrell answered his cell phone as if he had been waiting for Shareef's call all morning.

"Hey, player, the word on the street is that you had a rough night last night. Are you cool, man? Everything all right with you?"

Shareef was caught off guard by it. The speed of street news was still alarming to him.

He answered, "Yeah, man, somebody tried to make a move on me last night. What you hear about it?"

Jurrell laughed and told him, "I just heard you showed niggas some football skills and took off running."

Shareef chuckled with him. He said, "Yeah, and then your boy Baby G picked me up and took me out of there. He just popped up out of nowhere. At first I thought he was another carload trying to kill me."

"Oh yeah? What he talk to you about? What he want?"

Jurrell seemed interested in it. Shareef took note of that. He said, "He was just talking shit, basically. Seem like he wanted to be cool with me to write a book on him or something."

"To write a book on him?" Jurrell laughed again and responded,

"Man, what's up with all these kids wanting book deals all of a sudden?"

Shareef said, "That's what I'm thinking. And ain't nobody gon' even read it when I'm done. They gon' all want the movie instead."

Instead of laughing it off, Jurrell went silent for a spell.

He said, "Why not? You think you can get a movie deal out of this?"

He sounded interested again. Shareef wasn't counting on that. He fumbled and said, "I mean, um, I haven't been able to get no film deals done, man. Hollywood don't respect us like that. It seem like only white authors get film deals."

Jurrell said, "So you telling me the only way to make a black book into a movie is through white people, with all the fuckin' money we got out here now? I mean, yo, get some of these hip-hop niggas involved with your shit. You need to write a book they'll relate to."

"That's what I was trying to do with this Michael Springfield story until all of this other shit started happening," Shareef explained.

Jurrell said, "Yeah, I see what you mean. These street niggas are out here getting in your way."

On that note, Shareef asked him, "So you still think I should face this situation I'm in head on? I mean, this running shit don't feel right."

Jurrell answered, "Look, man, you let somebody else handle that shit. What you 'sposed to do is keep writing them books. These niggas can't write no books, but they can pull triggers all day long. So let somebody else do that. And you don't know nothing about it. You hear me? You don't know nothing."

It was another moment of truth. Shareef knew exactly where the problem was coming from, but if he voiced it, he could never take it back, and he could never control what was coming next.

He said, "If any blood is spilled, I'd rather it be on my hands in self-defense then on somebody who didn't have anything to do with it. I mean, at least I can tell myself that it was right that way. But if somebody else do it . . . it'll just feel like I bitched."

He was thinking more about squashing his personal beef with

Trap on his own instead of making things more complicated with rival crews.

Jurrell heard him out and said, "Yeah, I see where you coming from, man. We both old-school that way. You wanna handle your shit like a man. But at the same time, you got too much shit to lose, Shareef. That's like Puffy going to jail instead of Shine. Shine wasn't running no multimillion-dollar company, Puffy was. So it made sense to give the young blood up for the time. You hear where I'm coming from?"

He said, "And whether you like it or not, there's already been blood spilled that's not on your hands. It had to be blood spilled for you to live last night. And the truth is, you don't know who spilled that blood. So that's what you tell the law."

Shareef no longer had an argument. Jurrell made all the sense in the world. Nevertheless, the old-school writer was hesitant to cosign the next action. So he nodded his head with caution and said, "Yo . . . let me think about this and call you back."

"Aw'ight, take your time, B, just don't do nothing hasty," Jurrell advised him. "I mean, 'cause, you an important nigga to me, man. Word."

He said, "Books is long money, Shareef. All this other shit is temporary. But them book ideas stay on the shelves forever. And all it takes is one guy with money to read it and wanna do the movie. And then you making money all over again. So now I'm startin' to see why everybody want a book deal. The shit just makes sense, man. It makes a lot of sense."

When Shareef ended the call with Jurrell, he felt more pressure than he had before he had made the call. What was the right decision to make? He had rarely experienced writer's block, but he had it now. So his pen no longer touched his pad.

He nodded his head and said, "Okay . . . what now?" Then he remembered there was one last call to make.

"Spoonie called me."

With his cell phone battery running low, he made yet another call.

And as the line rang before being answered, Shareef wondered whether Spoonie knew that Trap was behind his recent problems.

Spoonie answered, "Yo, I was trying to get at you last night, man. Hold on a minute."

Shareef paused and said, "Aw'ight."

AT ANOTHER HARLEM APARTMENT COMPLEX, Spoonie left an occupied room for more privacy out in the hallway. He wore only a wife-beater tank top and black jeans. He looked tired and worried as he leaned up against the wall. He then covered the phone with his hand and whispered, "Yo, I heard what happened to you last night, son. But you gon' have to squash this beef shit before it gets out of hand. That's for real."

"That's what I'm trying to do," Shareef told him. "I'm trying to figure it all out. I been thinking about it all morning."

Spoonie listened to him and said, "Well, I know the people you need to talk to. So you need to meet me back up in Harlem."

He listened again to see how Shareef would respond to him.

"Who you talking about?" Shareef asked.

Spoonie answered, "I found out who's behind it all. And they wanna squash this shit as bad as you do. So I had to tell them what kind of nigga you are, man. I told them you from the 'hood, and you know how everybody get down. You wouldn't snitch on nobody. But these kids was like, 'Yo, we gotta see him face-to-face.' So I told them you would do that. 'Cause I know you, Shareef, you ain't no bitch nigga like that. You'll tell a motherfucker to his face what time it is. So they said, 'Look, that's the only way it's gon' get done.' "

Spoonie stopped to see how Shareef would respond.

Shareef responded with a pause. "So they wanna meet up with me to squash it?"

"Yeah, that's what's up. That's what time it is. They know what position you in as a writer. And ain't nobody trying to stop your hustle,

B. They just gotta have your word, face-to-face, that you not trying to put them out there like that. I mean, you not, right?"

Again, Spoonie waited for the response.

Shareef answered, "Nah, man, you know me better than that."

"That's what I told them," Spoonie said. "And it took a lot of fuckin' talking for me to make this shit happen, man. So you need to meet up with me, and we'll go over there together in broad daylight."

He said, "And you can bring Polo with you if you want. I told them you probably would. And they said it's cool. So just let me know what time you wanna meet up to squash all this shit."

Spoonie continued to hang on to Shareef's every answer.

Shareef told him, "Aw'ight. Where you wanna meet?

Spoonie took a deep breath as if a heavy load had been released from his shoulders. His lean body drooped against the wall and looked ready to slide down to the floor.

He explained, "Aw'ight, this is what's up . . ."

WHEN SPOONIE RETURNED to the occupied apartment, Trap was sitting on an old beige sofa with a pistol in hand. He was fully dressed and flanked by three heavily armed men, all brandishing menacing assault weapons. They all looked red-eyed, angry, and hungry, as if they had no sleep or any food in a while. Cigarette ashes were all over the floor. And across from where Trap sat on the sofa, was a nervous young woman sitting in a matching lounge chair. She was an exotic, local stripper dressed in only her black panties and bra. While she exhaled with heavy breaths, she couldn't help staring at the menacing-looking guns that the men carried. She figured maybe she should have gone with her gut feeling and left Spoonie alone when he had asked her to stay over the night before. Then she wouldn't have ended up in the middle of this mess.

Trap looked up from where he sat on the sofa and asked Spoonie, "What he say?"

Spoonie took another deep breath and nodded. "He said he'll do it."

The other angry men looked surprised. But Trap didn't. All he did was nod.

He told Spoonie, "You did the right thing, man. You did the right thing." Then he looked to one of his soldiers. "Ay, Pee, call everybody else."

His soldier pulled out a cell phone, stepped aside, and made a phone call.

"Yo, it's on. Meet us at the spot."

Trap started to grin and spoke to his crew while waving the black pistol in his hand. "This nigga must really think he untouchable. I guess he 'bout to find out now. Ain't he, Spoonie?"

The young woman looked into Spoonie's worried face as he answered. He breathed deeply again and forced out a slight smile. He said, "He should have just left the streets alone, man, like you told him. But some people just don't know when to walk away."

Showdown!

SHAREEF STARED AT HIS CELL PHONE and exhaled inside the tiny Manhattan hotel room. He finally had his solution.

"This is it," he told himself and made another phone call. When the answering service clicked on at his lawyer's office in Atlanta, he left a clear message. "Hey Preston, this Shareef. It's Saturday morning, August fifth, two thousand six, and I'm leaving a very important change to my will. I want you to include 'Polo,' aka Shelton Matthews, and his family to my will with a ten percent stake. So if anything happens to him, his girlfriend and two kids get it. I'll talk to you about it all with the details on Monday. All right? So make sure you write this all down."

That was it. End of message. But when Shareef hung up the phone after leaving it, he chuckled to himself and mumbled, "I *hope* I'll tell you all about it on Monday." Then he wrote down his final notes under his "Solutions" column:

Spoonie / Trap / Harlem / St. Nicholas Park . . .

And he left the notepad open and out on the small desk as evidence.

AT THE SOUTHEAST CORNER of 127th Street and St. Nicholas Avenue, across from the foot of St. Nicholas Park, T, who was now recognized as one of Baby G's most alert young soldiers, bobbed his

321

head to the latest southern hip-hop music with earphones on. He wore a white T-shirt, blue jeans, and sneakers, while he watched all of the Saturday afternoon activity on the streets. It was nearly one o'clock, and the streets of Harlem were buzzing as usual.

After another twenty minutes or so, he eyed Shareef Crawford, now identified as "The Book Writer," heading toward the park with a tall and rangy friend. That's what T was waiting for. So he paid attention to report everything he saw.

As Shareef followed Spoonie north toward St. Nicholas Park, Spoonie asked him, "So, Polo had some runs to make today, hunh?"

They were both dressed in bright, summertime clothes. Neither one of them wanted to look suspicious. Shareef had even bought a new outfit to wear before catching the subway north.

He told Spoonie, "Shit, we all grown men now. We all gotta do what we gotta do. This ain't Polo's problem. This is my problem."

Spoonie nodded. "Dig it. I understand." And he forced out another smile. But he wasn't as talkative as he usually was. He was more interested in watching the streets for any curious eyes that might notice them as they walked.

Out of the blue, three young women spotted Shareef as they strolled up the sidewalk.

"Shareef Crawford?" one of them addressed him. "Oh my God, I love your books so much. When is the next one coming out?"

The other two girls awaited his answer. They all looked in their late teens.

Shareef asked them, "Have you read my latest book, *The Full Moon*?"

"Yeah, we shared that one already," the second girl answered with a chuckle.

Spoonie looked irritated. He wanted to move on and get things over with. He continued to eye everyone up and down the street.

"Can we like, have an autograph or something? We didn't expect to see you just walking around up here," the third girl commented.

Shareef looked hesitant. "I mean . . ."

Spoonie cut him off in haste and answered, "Look, we got a meetin' to make right now. Won't y'all catch up to him at his next book signing or something. You know he's from Harlem, right?"

"Yeah, but he's right here, right now. I mean, all it's gon' take is a second," the first girl argued. They were already pulling out pens and pieces of paper from their pocketbooks and purses.

Shareef smiled and said, "Look, maybe not right now, ladies. I mean, my man is right. We late for a meeting already."

The second girl crossed her eyes at Spoonie and sucked her teeth. If his ass wasn't in the way, they all would have gotten their autographs.

But the first girl persisted. "Come on, Shareef, it's only gonna take you a second. We take *weeks* to read your books, and you can't even give us a *second* to sign an autograph. I mean, that's just *wrong* if you ask me."

Spoonie was ready to snap on her, but Shareef remained diplomatic. He continued to smile. He said, "Maybe next time," before he walked forward with Spoonie.

"Aw, man, that's fucked up," the second girl commented.

Shareef shook his head and ignored it.

Spoonie responded, "That's life," and kept walking.

When they made it across the street to the park area, Spoonie spotted the first familiar face to their left, and he gave the man a nod. "It's all good, man," he commented.

The man nodded back to him and said nothing. He didn't appear to be armed from the front, but who knows what he held behind him. He stood stiff and forward and he barely moved.

Spoonie and Shareef walked past the playground area full of kids, and then past the basketball courts where brothers ran ball before they made their way up the hills of St. Nicholas Park.

Shareef seemed deadly calm, but Spoonie was more apprehensive.

Finally, he told Shareef, "You a brave-ass nigga, man. I gotta give it to you." St. Nicholas Park wasn't exactly the safest place in Harlem to set up a meeting.

Shareef shook it off and said, "I'm not as brave as you think I am. Sometimes it's braver to admit that you're scared. But I be so focused sometimes, man, that it's like I'm inhuman."

He chuckled and said, "That's probably why my wife won't fuck me no more. I'm too damned focused to give her the attention that she needs."

That comment threw Spoonie for a loop. He looked at Shareef and said, "What? Your wife won't fuck you? Nigga is you crazy? Does she know how many girls out here are wide open for you?"

Shareef said, "She don't care. If they're willing to sleep with a married man, then she considers all of them whores."

Spoonie laughed and said, "Yo, that sounds just like a woman. Instead of them giving you what you need without bitching, they'd rather cuss out every other woman that gives you some."

He shook his head and said, "That don't make no damn sense. These bitches is crazy, man. I mean, I'm not calling your wife a bitch, but you know what I mean."

Shareef smiled it off. "Nah, I don't sweat that." He wanted to keep their conversation light and friendly. But the next thing he knew, they were surrounded by four mean-faced men that Shareef had never seen before. And not one of them was Trap.

Shareef didn't like the look of that. He immediately became alert and nervous.

"Yo, let's head up the hill to the car," one of them stated.

Shareef didn't know if Trap was up in the car or not, but as soon as he spotted the first assault weapon in plain view, he wasn't willing to allow anyone to line up behind him. That was part of his game plan.

"Aw'ight, we'll follow behind y'all," he told them. He made sure he stayed close by Spoonie.

"Nah, we'll follow behind you," the ringleader told him. Two of the men attempted to line up behind Shareef and Spoonie with their guns anyway. And when Shareef looked around the park, it became obvious that they had cleared the area of any pedestrian traffic.

Yeah, these niggas are trying to get me in broad daylight now, Shareef told himself. *And I don't know if we're gonna make it to this car or not.*

He used his peripheral vision to search for the edge of the small hill they stood on without turning his head and giving himself away. Before he realized it, he heard Baby G's words repeating in his head from the night before:

"You gotta be willing to die out here, player. And if you ain't ready to die, then they don't take you seriously. But you ready to die, player. That's why I respect you."

In a flash, Shareef took that "ready to die" stance of the streets to heart, and he made his bold move. He had loosened Spoonie up enough with his conversation and remained close enough to him to grab him by his shirt and pants and spin him around like a shield.

"Yo, what are you doing, man?" Spoonie hollered, struggling against Shareef in vain. It was too late. Shareef already had him. It was another part of his plan.

The ringleader saw what was happening and had no patience for it. They were gonna kill Spoonie anyway. So he shouted, "Fuck it! Shoot 'em both!"

Shareef waited for them to aim and shoot before he shoved Spoonie right into their line of fire.

Baa! Baa! Bop! . . .

Juu! Juu! Juu! Juu! Juu! Juu! Juu! . . .

Spoonie's tall, lean body was ripped with bullets before he even had a chance to scream. Shareef then hit the ground and rolled liked a man on fire toward the edge of the hill. The first bullets missed him high.

Baa! Baa! Baa! Bop! . . .

The next line of bullets missed him as he rolled.

Juu! Juu! Juu! Juu! Juu! Juu! Juu! . . .

They were shooting at the spots where Shareef was rolling from instead of shooting where he was rolling to. By the time they corrected their aim, he had rolled over the edge of the hill and took a fifteen-foot fall into the rocks and grass below.

"Shit! Get that motherfucker!" the ringleader shouted.

It was too late again. As soon as the first bullets had been fired, the squad of armed young bloods from the basketball courts quickly made it up the hill with guns they had pulled out from under their tennis shirts and backpacks at the bleachers.

A reckless shoot-out was ready to go down in the middle of St. Nick's Park in Harlem, all over a dispute with a writer.

Pop! Pop! Pop! Pop! . . .

Baa! Baa! Bop! . . .

Juu! Juu! Juu! Juu! Juu! . . .

Pop! Pop! Pop! . . .

Guys were drooping on both sides as bullets ripped into shirts, shorts, pants, and brown skin of all shades.

Pop! Pop! . . .

Baa! Baa! Baa! Baa! Bop! . . .

FROM UP ABOVE THE HILL in two parked sedans on St. Nicholas Terrace, Trap hopped out of the first car with his loaded gun in hand.

"What the fuck?" He started to make his way down the hill to see what was going on. Several more armed soldiers followed behind him.

FROM THE GRASS BELOW the hill, Shareef climbed to his feet with shoulder, rib, hip, and thigh injuries from his long fall. But that damn sure wouldn't stop him from running for his life. So he ran through the pain

"Shit!" he cursed himself while he hustled his way through the park with a limp.

• • •

TRAP SPOTTED SHAREEF running away from the grass area below. He yelled out his name to stop him just long enough to shoot at him.

"Shareef!"

On instincts, Shareef looked up, just like Trap knew he would.

Trap yelled, "You should have went the fuck home, man!" and took aim.

Pop! Pop! Pop! Pop! . . .

Shareef dove to the grass again and avoided more bullets as Trap continued to fire.

BACK ON ST. NICHOLAS TERRACE above the park, Baby G pulled up in a plain, white sedan, his bodyguard driving. Truth sat in the passengar seat up front, and another soldier was in the back next to Baby G. A second car of four soldiers followed right behind them.

A lone driver from Trap's crew was left to ward them all off. But one man with a gun was no match for eight.

Baa! Baa! Bop! . . .

Pop! Pop! Pop! . . .

Trap's driver was hit several times in the chest, and his life quickly came to an end. When Baby G made it into the park with the rest of his soldiers, Trap's crew was easily outnumbered. So he stopped shooting at Shareef and took aim at Baby G's guys.

Baa! Baa! Baa! Baa! Bop! . . .

The beefy bodyguard was the first to take a bullet.

"Ah, shit!" he hollered, falling backward.

Baby G immediately dropped to his knees to aid him.

"Get down, man! Get down!" he yelled. Bullets were flying everywhere.

"Where you hit?" he asked his bodyguard. They were both dressed in all black for the war, including black leather gloves. Shareef had called them that morning to arrange the whole set up. Baby G agreed to it on the strength of becoming famous through his own book deal. That was on Shareef's word.

"He got me in the stomach," the beefy bodyguard whimpered.

Baby G looked down at his bodyguard's stomach, and the damage looked bad. Major organs had been hit, and blood was pouring out of him like a water fountain.

The bodyguard grimaced and mumbled, "Get that ma-fucker for me, man. Get his ass."

Baby G looked into his pained face and nodded. "I got him. He ain't gettin' out of here alive. I promise you that."

The bodyguard nodded back to him and took the pain like a man. Baby G remained with him until he took his final breath. And once he realized that his main protector was gone, he yelled, "Roll up on them!" to the rest of his soldiers. They looked hesitant to continue. Trap's crew were beginning to show their age and experience with better aim and sharper shooting.

T told his leader, "Yo, sir, we takin' too many losses and the cops is coming."

Baby G looked at him with two pistols in his hands. He screamed, "You think I give a fuck? We gon' end this shit right here!"

He hopped to his feet with both guns raised and started charging toward Trap and his men below.

"Aahhhhh!"

Baa! Baa! Baa! Baa! Baa! Baa! Baa! Bop! . . .

Like a madman, Baby G shot down two of Trap's men by himself. But his soldiers moving behind him took bullets and went down themselves, all but T, who remained untouched.

Trap saw several of his men fall to their deaths before he took cover and jumped down the hill. However, he landed on uneven ground and twisted his ankle, falling forward in agony.

"Fuck!" he cursed himself. He climbed back to his feet, ignoring the pain, and limped ahead while he eyed a tree to hide behind. He took a bullet to his left side just as he had made it.

"Aahhh!"

Baby G found his way down the hill and stayed right after him.

• • •

ON THE OTHER SIDE OF THE PARK, hearing all the gunshots in the short distance, kids and parents started scrambling to escape the playground.

"What in the hell is going on?" a grandfather asked as he gathered up his grandkids.

The first of Trap's soldiers, who Shareef and Spoonie had passed at the front of the park earlier, remained calm with his gun still concealed inside the back of his pants. That's what he was told to do, remain a lookout. But when he spotted Shareef making his way out of the park alive, he drew his pistol and aimed at him.

Shareef spotted him dead-on and froze. His instincts told him that ducking was not going to work this time. The guy was poised and stable at point-blank range, and Shareef was already injured and too exhausted to move quickly enough to get away.

Shit! he told himself. *This is it, man. This is the end of my life. But where the fuck are the cops at?* he pondered. And he awaited the bullets to hit him.

Baa! Baa! Bop! . . .

Shareef shook in his stance and closed his eyes, bracing himself for the bullets. He curled his arms in front of his chest and ducked his head inside of his hands, falling to the ground in complete darkness. And after a minute on the ground, he wondered where he had been hit. He couldn't feel anything, but he could hear everything.

People were still screaming and running from the park. Finally, Shareef heard police sirens approaching in the background. Yet before he could open his tightly closed eyes to find out where he had been hit, someone grabbed his arm and barked orders at him.

"Shareef, get the fuck up, man! Let's go!"

He slowly opened his eyes and looked up at Jurrell Garland in dark blue sweat clothes, black leather gloves, and a pistol in his right hand.

Shareef was still confused and hesitant. He hadn't even called Jurrell back that morning.

Jurrell told him, "Look, you not shot, nigga. Let's go!"

Shareef rose back to his feet, found himself still in one piece, and started to run toward another section of the park behind Jurrell.

"This way, man," Jurrell directed him.

They both ran in the opposite direction of the police sirens until Jurrell heard more gunshots nearby and stopped.

He paused and listened. "Hold up," he told Shareef.

Shareef looked at him and wondered why.

He asked, "For what?" He figured they didn't have much time left to get away. And since he was injured, he could no longer run at full speed.

Jurrell ignored him and ran toward the gunshots anyway.

Shareef shook his head and paused a minute before he followed him. "Shit!"

NOT FAR AWAY in the open grass below the hills, Baby G laid face up with his chest littered from bullet holes. Blood poured out from under his tattered black shirt while he wheezed for his last breaths. He could no longer hold his two guns in his hands. He was more concerned with trying to breathe.

Trap limped out from behind a tree with his gun and kicked Baby G in the leg as he stood overtop of him.

"Now what, nigga? You wanted to be ghetto fabulous, hunh? Well, you should have minded your fuckin' business then." And he kicked him again.

Baby G coughed up blood and responded defiantly. "Fuck you!"

Trap had a bullet wound on his left side, and a swollen and twisted ankle. He didn't appear to be concerned about the cops who were now surrounding the park. He laughed in the face of the handsome Baby Gangsta, who was wounded and dying on his back, and he raised his gun to his head.

"Well, take one to the face then, nigga."

Bop!

Instead of being shot in the face by Trap's gun, Trap was struck in the back and fell across Baby G's chest, making it even harder for him to breathe.

"Unh," Baby G grunted under the weight.

Trap laid across his chest, shaking and wondering who had shot him in the back.

Jurrell Garland reached over and pulled him up.

"Is this what you wanted to do?" he asked Trap while he stared into his terrified eyes.

Baa! Bop!

He shot Trap twice in his face and ended his life.

When it was over, Baby G smiled at Jurrell and muttered, "Old-timer . . . make him write that book."

When Shareef stood behind Jurrell, he saw that Baby G was beginning to choke on his own blood. All he could do was stare up at them helplessly.

Jurrell tried to lift him up, but that only made the bleeding and choking worse.

"*Shit!*" Jurrell cursed up to the clouds. He obviously had a lot of feelings for the boy. He said, "Don't worry, man. He gon' write it. I'm gon' make sure."

By that time, T had made it down to them with tears in his eyes. He was still untouched.

Baby G could only blink at them, Jurrell, Shareef, and T, as they all stared down at him. Then he started to shake violently before dying.

Jurrell hollered, "*Aaahhhhh!*"

Shareef pulled at him and said, "Let's go, man. We out of time now." There was no sense in them all being arrested out there. Baby G was dead, and standing around him was not going to bring him back.

So Jurrell dropped his gun and jumped back up to start running.

He told T as he ran, "Hold them off for us, Shorty. Get them guns out."

Shareef ran behind him, still ignoring the pain as best he could.

When they were gone, T grabbed two of the remaining guns and started firing in the opposite direction to divert the cops away from them. He shot both guns in the air with tears running out of his eyes until a half dozen police officers approached him.

"Put the guns down, son. We're only asking you once."

T did as they said and raised his hands up high with no struggle. And when they forced him down and put the handcuffs on him, he continued to cry while staring at the demise of his charismatic leader, Baby G, aka Greggory Taylor, who rested in peace on the grass.

THERE WERE ENOUGH INJURED and dying soldiers on both sides, all desperately trying to escape from every direction of the park for Jurrell and Shareef to make it out to a waiting SUV just before the police converged on them.

They both slipped inside the back of the black Ford Explorer where the seats had been adjusted forward to make room for them to lie across the bottom of the back.

"Ah, shit," Shareef whined from his injuries as he made it inside.

Jurrell ignored him and squeezed down as low as he could in the back. Meesha, his lady friend from the night Shareef had met up with him at the Harlem Grill, was behind the wheel.

Jurrell told her, "Just drive real easy, baby, like nothing's going on. Just remain calm at the wheel." He started to slip off his black leather gloves.

Meesha nodded and told him, "I got it."

She drove past the sirens of the police cruisers on 129th Street right before the NYPD began to block off traffic to and from the park. And when they were several blocks away, Jurrell looked into Shareef's pained face and said, "We got a lot of talking to do, man. This shit right here was a fuckin' mess."

Explanations

MEESHA DROVE Shareef and Jurrell to a single-family home on the northwest side of Harlem between Riverside Drive and the Sugar Hill area. It was a two-story, stone-built home with a private driveway. They drove up and parked in the driveway before making it to the front door where Meesha used her key to let them all in.

Shareef looked around and was impressed with the place. The home wasn't fully furnished yet, but it was still nice to look at.

He nodded and said, "This is a nice place. I've never been to this area before."

Jurrell ignored him and headed straight toward the kitchen in a huff. Once inside the kitchen, he reached to the top of a tall cabinet and pulled down another automatic pistol.

"Yo, come on in here, Shareef."

As soon as Shareef took another step, it seemed that his injuries were getting worse by the second. He grabbed his left side and moaned as he struggled forward.

"You need some ice?" Meesha asked him on cue. It wasn't hard to tell that the man's body was fucked up. His nice new clothes looked as if he had been run over by a truck.

Shareef grimaced and said, "Yeah, I need a whole bucket of it."

She smiled at him. "I'll see what I can do."

"Nah, don't do that shit. He need to feel the pain for when the cops get to him," Jurrell barked at her.

Meesha looked at him and stood silently. Jurrell was the boss, so there was no sense in even asking him about it. And by the time Shareef had made it into the kitchen, Jurrell had his pistol pointed at him.

"Sit down at the table."

Shareef did as he was told and sat at a circular, wooden dinette set for four. It was positioned in the middle of the kitchen dining area. There were dark-colored shades covering all the windows to stop anyone from peeking in.

Jurrell sat on the opposite side of the table with the pistol out. He then sat the barrel of the gun on the table and aimed it directly at Shareef's heart.

"So, how come you ain't call me back this morning, man?" was his first question.

Shareef stared down at the barrel of the pistol and realized his troubles were not over with yet. Jurrell Garland was still dangerous.

Shareef answered, "I . . . I didn't want to get you involved like that, man. I thought it looked like you were trying to lean away from this life."

He looked into Jurrell's hard eyes and asked him, "Was I wrong? I thought you were getting into the cell phone and gadget business."

Jurrell continued to eye him scornfully as he spoke.

He said, "Man, this cell phone shit ain't no real money for me. That's a front business. And everything I tell you in the house right now is off the fuckin' record too. You hear me? Matter of fact, take that fuckin' shirt off so I can make sure you're not wearing a wire. That shirt is all fucked up now anyway."

Shareef looked into Jurrell's eyes and began to peel off the light blue and orange tennis shirt that had been stained from the dried up blood of his injuries.

As Shareef winced at the sting of his bruises, Jurrell looked into his naked brown chest and was satisfied with what he already knew. Shareef was no snitch. Jurrell just wanted his old nemesis to know how serious he was at the moment.

He said, "You just fucked up my money, man. You know that shit, right?"

Shareef sat there and thought about it. Two plus two equals four.

He said, "So, um . . . Baby G was working for you?" It all began to make sense to him. No wonder Baby G and his boys had shown up to protect him outside of his hotel. Jurrell had set it all up. But he was so incensed about how things had turned out that he had to stand up from the table to express it all.

Jurrell stood up with the pistol in hand and said, "Not only was he working for me, but I *liked* the motherfucker, man. The nigga had that *gift*, Shareef. You met him. He a once in a lifetime nigga. He was making me good money. But I kept telling his ass, 'You don't need a hundred motherfuckers from Harlem following you. That shit ain't good.' I told him, 'You just keep your small squad of soldiers, make this money on the low, and keep shit moving.' But this young ma-fucker kept talkin' 'bout the eighties, and how shit used to be when we were shorties, Shareef. And I kept telling his ass, you can't be shinin' in the streets like that no more. Nobody let you live like that on the streets unless you a rapper or an athlete now. And them niggas ain't really *in the streets* like that. That shit ain't nothing but urban marketing."

As he continued to talk, Jurrell began to round the table with the pistol. Shareef sat still and listened to him. It was all key information.

Jurrell said, "But these young bloods out here don't wanna listen, man. So no matter how much I tried to keep him away from doing dumb shit, he would walk right into it. Like, before you even got up here this summer, Shareef, this nigga executes a ma-fucka in an empty storefront. And I'm like, 'For what? I know his ass was talkin' shit. But you let *me* handle that.' But nah, this ma-fucka wanna show off for his li'l crew to prove that he gangsta, right? Stupid shit!

"But I couldn't really stop his ass 'cause niggas liked him too much, and he was smart enough to get away with it. So then he had *more* of these niggas following him," Jurrell explained. "Then people started asking who he was. Even you asked me. And you ain't even been up in Harlem a week.

"So since G was so much into that starlight shit, I tried to set him up with some producers and studio people I know to see if he could rhyme."

Jurrell smiled and shook his head. He chuckled and said, "Man, this motherfucker couldn't rhyme if he had a nursery book sittin' out in front of him. I mean, certain people have certain gifts and certain people don't. It's a whole lot of rappers who wished they could command the streets like he do. But they can't. So he started meeting all these rap niggas and athletes whenever they came up to Harlem, like with that basketball tournament shit. I mean, man, this nigga had his mind hooked on being famous. Everybody wanna be the American Idol now. That's why he ended up meeting your ass."

He said, "He wasn't supposed to give you no ride and start talkin' 'bout no book shit. All I told him to do was to make sure they protected you."

Jurrell stopped circling Shareef with the gun for a minute and said, "But obviously, you must have made an impression on him, because the next thing I knew, he start talkin' 'bout writing a fuckin' book on his life. And I'm thinkin', *Is this nigga crazy?* You don't write no fuckin' book while you still involved with the shit. I'm feeling like them other niggas about that. We still living this shit, man. But at the same time, I was curious."

He said, "This book business has done well for you, so why can't it work for us?"

Shareef just stared at him. "Street books don't work like rap music and drug money, man," he said. "I mean, you know how hard it is for a female in rap or sports to make her money? Well, that's how hard it is for a guy to make his money in the book business unless he's writing about what women want. So most of the people making money from street books are women; Sister Souljah, Teri Woods, Vickie Stringer,

Nikki Turner. That's just how it is, man. They get to write that street shit from a woman's perspective, because that's who's reading it all. Young women. And then they pass it on to their men."

Jurrell studied Shareef's face for a minute and said, "Well, you gon' have to figure out how to make that shit work then, nigga, 'cause you just fucked up my money and got my young blood killed. So I don't wanna hear that shit."

He said, "You owe us your fuckin' life now. *Twice!* So you gon' write something about this shit and give us some dividends on it. And you gon' say, 'This book is dedicated to the life and times of Greggory Tay-lor.' "

Jurrell sat back down across the table and aimed that gun barrel right at Shareef's heart again.

He calmed down and said, "I kept thinking about how I could get involved with you on the business level, man. And I could see that you was still hesitant around me. You got all the reason in the world to be. I'm still a crafty-ass nigga, just like you. And we both from the streets of Harlem. That's why ya' ass was crafty enough to get away. But you know what? Some things in life you ain't gon' get away from, Shareef. And whether you like it or not, you connected to my hip now. That's for real."

Jurrell sat back and smiled and added, "Just like old times in grade school." Then his smile quickly disappeared. He looked across the table at Shareef and said, "The bottom line is this, man. I'm fighting for my life to get the fuck off these streets. I did ten years in jail and I'm not goin' back. We still got niggas who hustled in the eighties who just getting the fuck out of jail. And now these white ma-fuckers got condos coming up in *Harlem,* and we can't get in that shit, because of co-ops and tenant organizations and shit like that, frontin' on us?"

He shook his head and said, "Nah, nigga, fuck that. They not lock-ing me out. This ain't South Africa. Harlem gone stay home for me. And I ain't goin' no-fuckin'-where. So now I just found me a new part-ner in business, and we going legit."

Jurrell continued to stare across the table at Shareef to make sure he understood everything. For the moment, Shareef was still silent.

Jurrell looked down at the pistol on the table and said, "I hate to come at you this way, Shareef, but just in case you forget how serious I am when you leave Harlem, you gotta remember that you got a public access website." He looked back into Shareef's eyes and warned, "I know where you live. I know who your wife is. I know who your kids are. I know where your next book signing is gon' be. I mean, you got a open-fuckin' book on your life, Shareef. And like I said, man, I'm not try'na come at you that way, but . . ."

Meesha happened to walk past the kitchen door when Jurrell revealed how much information he was hip to. Shareef figured that any girl who was a fan of his could log on to his website and tell Jurrell everything he needed to know.

Jurrell sighed and said, "I'm just try'na live my life on the straight and narrow now, man. I ain't had to kill nobody with one of these things in years. But today I had to kill somebody for you, and then I had to kill somebody for G. But what if I ain't find out about this shit today, Shareef? Where would you be then? Where would *we* be?"

Shareef began to shake his head defiantly. All he could think about was the threat on his life and his family.

He looked back across the table and said, "Jurrell, there's a lot of ways out here for you to make a honest living without threatening me and my family, man. I mean, I can't let that shit fly."

Jurrell looked across the table and grilled at him. But Shareef didn't budge. He meant that shit, and he was ready to go to the grave for it.

That's when Jurrell broke out laughing. He stood back up from the table with the gun in hand and said, "You're the same fuckin' Shareef, son, after all these years. A nigga threaten you and you jump the fuck up and start swinging. That's just what G said. He told me last night, 'That boy Shareef a real-ass nigga!' I said, 'I know he is. I went to grade school wit'' em. And he was the only li'l nigga hard enough to fight me. He a beast!' "

Then Jurrell became serious again. He said, "But we ain't kids no more, man. And we not gettin' no younger. I can't sell drugs on these streets and stick niggas up no more. I'm out of time for that shit now."

He held up the gun and said, "I'm not try'na hold on to this for the rest of my life, Shareef. You gotta believe me, man. So here's what I'm gon' do. I'm gon' give *you* the gun. And if you don't think my word is bond on this shit, then kill me right now and your family'll never have to worry about me."

Jurrell actually sat the gun down in front of Shareef at the table and walked back over to the other side to take a seat.

Again, Meesha showed up at the doorway to the kitchen. She couldn't believe what she had just heard. Jurrell had lost his damn mind!

Shareef looked at the gun sitting out on the table in front him, and he remembered all the fistfights they had had in their youth. Despite how brave everyone thought Shareef was, he remembered fighting Jurrell more because he hated the feeling of being so afraid of him. Jurrell had always been terrifying. And Shareef had always wondered how a young boy could be without morals or common decency. Shareef couldn't understand him, so he chose to fight off his insanity. Now they were face-to-face again, and he was being forced one more time to deal with Jurrell's challenge.

Shareef thought to himself, *This motherfucker! I hate this motherfucker! I don't wanna have to deal with this nigga again. I had nightmares about having to fight this boy. He's probably the reason why I'm so fuckin' kamikaze now. I always had to deal with his crazy ass! So if I shoot his ass in the head right now, I'll never have to deal with him again. And I'll just leave Harlem the fuck alone and never come back here.*

Shareef was thinking about it. He was thinking about it strongly. And Meesha had no idea what he would do. Based on what Jurrell had told her about Shareef, she figured he was brave enough to actually pull the trigger. But all she could do was breathe and wait. They were two type A men with a gun out between them. She realized that any interference could prove deadly. Neither man budged at the table while the oxygen in the room seemed to evaporate.

Finally, Shareef came to his senses and shook his head.

"I don't deal with guns, man. That's not my thing."

He didn't even move to touch it.

After he said that, Meesha was able to breathe again.

Jurrell left the gun out on the table and didn't touch it himself. He said, "What are you gonna do then? You wanna fight me? We too old for that shit now, too."

Shareef looked at him and cracked a smile. He said, "It takes a lot of heart for you to put your life on the line like that."

Jurrell responded with no smile. "That's how serious I am about this shit, man. This ain't no fuckin' game. I'm try'na get my life right."

Shareef joked and said, "Is it real bullets in that gun?"

Jurrell eyed him before he grabbed the gun off the table and pulled the cartridge of bullets out the back in one quick movement.

He answered, "Like I said, I'm dead serious about my life. I got a lot of shit I still wanna do, and I don't want my prison record to stop me. So maybe it was divine intervention that G got killed today."

He said, "He was my last line to the streets. I wasn't really dealing with anybody else. I ain't have to. G did good business. I'm gon' have to square his sisters away now like they're my own."

Shareef nodded and wondered how anything would work with Jurrell. What exactly was his plan?

"I mean . . . what do you want me to do?" he asked. He was still confused by it all.

For Jurrell it was simple. He said, "First of all, fuck Michael Springfield. That was divine intervention, too. You didn't really need him anyway. So first, you want to write a book about a young blood trying to be famous on the streets of Harlem, and how that shit led to his end. And that's all based on G. I'll give you more of the details on him. Then, after that, I'll talk to the people on the streets who got the hot stories to tell—I mean, and I got a lot of them myself—and then I'll sit down with you about the best way to tell them, and you write the books and kickback my percentages. Then I'll hook up with the street and prison niggas to make sure these books sell. Or at least up in Harlem."

He said, "But if you buy off them hip-hop magazine niggas—and you can buy them off if you know the right people—you can get them to do full-page ads on our shit. And once these rap niggas get used to seeing our shit selling in their magazines, we can step to them about getting these film deals poppin'. You feel me?"

Shareef cracked another smile.

He said, "You make it all sound like clockwork. But it ain't that easy."

Jurrell didn't budge. He said, "Let me ask you a question then, Shareef?"

"What's that?"

"Do you consider yourself one of the best writers from the black community right now?"

Shareef smiled again and started laughing.

"Come on, man, don't fuck with me like that. I'll write circles around most of these clowns out here."

Jurrell said, "Exactly. Now let me ask you another question."

Shareef paused and waited.

Jurrell said, "Would you consider me one of the most gangsta-ass niggas you ever met in your life?"

Shareef looked and grinned. There was no question about it. Harlem was one of the most vicious communities, not only in America, but in the world. So if Jurrell Garland could scare other criminals half to death in Harlem, then he *had* to be one of the toughest street gangstas alive. Shareef could see exactly where he was coming from.

Jurrell told him, "Real recognize real. We could be that next level shit out here." He stopped with excitement in his eyes and asked Shareef again, "So, what are you gonna do, man? Are you in or what?"

Shareef looked down and thought about it. Then he looked back up and asked, "What would you call this first book?"

Jurrell didn't hesitate. He answered, *"To Live and Die in Harlem."* That's the only title I want for this first one. 'Cause that shit is real. That's how gangsta-ass niggas think. Either we livin', and that mean's living how we want to, or we dying out this motherfucker. Because we won't have it no other way. That's why Baby G was so fuckin' hardheaded."

Jurrell sized up Shareef and said, "That's why *you* so hardheaded. And that's why *I'm* hardheaded. 'Cause I'm not lettin' no motherfucker tell me I'm not gon' have one of those Park Avenue condos. Fuck that! I will be up in that ma-fucka with my feet kicked back."

Meesha smiled from the kitchen doorway. Jurrell caught her and said, "Yeah, and I might let you come over, too."

She finally spoke out loud. "Whatever. I'll be more than your *maid,* I know that much."

Jurrell joked and said, "Yeah, you'll be the maid, the cook, the door girl, the sex slave. And it's all good."

Meesha shook her head and grinned. Her good-natured loyalty was what Jurrell liked about her. Otherwise, he would have never trusted her in his inner circle. A girl had to be more than just pretty. She had to know when to respect the world of the man she chose to be with.

Shareef smiled for a minute, but then the pain from his left side reminded him of the violence they had just escaped from.

He asked, "So, how do we clean up this mess that we're in?"

Jurrell became serious himself. He said, "Well, you know the cops are looking for you. But they don't know I have shit to do with it. And that's how it needs to stay. So you tell them the truth about what you can, make up some shit when they get too close to the truth, and whenever the truth gets too complicated, then you tell them you don't fuckin' know. It's that simple."

Shareef tried not to grin across the table, but he couldn't help it. Jurrell sounded like a much smoother criminal now. So Shareef nodded and said, "I'll keep that all in mind."

Interrogations

MEESHA DROVE Shareef back to 125th Street alone, while Jurrell remained behind at the house. There was no sense in Shareef trying to run. Every finger pointed back to him, and there was no way the NYPD was not going to catch up to him for questioning. So the plan was to allow them to capture him. Then it would be up to Shareef to handle himself accordingly.

Meesha stopped and looked at him before he climbed out of the Explorer. He was wearing his ragged, bloodstained, light blue tennis shirt again.

"Are you okay?" she asked him.

He nodded. "Yeah, I'm all right. I've had bruises before. It ain't no biggie. So let me get back out here and go take care of business."

Meesha placed her hand on his left knee with care and told him, "Be safe."

"You too."

When Shareef climbed out of the black SUV, Meesha made a U-turn and headed quickly away from him. Shareef walked back toward the hotel on 124th and Frederick Douglass. He passed the Hue-Man Bookstore and the Magic Johnson Theater without much notice. He didn't look like a superstar author at the moment, he looked more like a down-on-his-luck panhandler who had fallen off the back of an eighteen-wheeler on the highway. So no one bothered to notice him.

However, when he arrived at the entrance of the hotel, the NYPD knew exactly who he was. They ran right up behind him with their guns ready.

"Shareef Crawford, we need to take you in and talk to you at the station. You have the right to remain silent . . ."

Shareef turned to face them and slowly raised his hands. "Can y'all get my luggage from the front desk of this hotel. I was just coming back to get it."

They put handcuffs on him and responded, "Yeah, sure, somebody get his luggage."

All of a sudden, all of the pedestrians' eyes on the sidewalk were on Shareef as the police led him into a squad car to take him to the station. Fortunately, the Harlem police station was right around the corner, literally one block away, near St. Nicholas Avenue, and less than five blocks south of the park.

Imagine that. Harlem life was that bold. The police station was right there in the thick of things. Nevertheless, desperate people did what they felt they needed to do.

Once Shareef was secure inside an interrogation room on the second floor of the precinct, he sat in a lone chair behind a small table. Then he watched as the arresting officers went through his luggage. But unless someone at the hotel had tried to frame him for something, he was clean.

A plainclothes detective walked in next and asked the uniformed officer, "Did you find anything in there worthwhile?"

He was a large black man in an ugly, dark sports jacket. What the hell did it matter when you were dealing with violence, despair, lying, stealing, murder, and criminals all day? Twenty-five years of that would make any man glum. So his wardrobe matched the mood of his business.

His partner walked in next, a smaller Latino man with a cleaner, sharper dress code. At least he looked like he tried. But he hadn't been in the profession as long.

The two of them were the same tandem who had investigated the execution-style murder at the storefront on Adam Clayton Powell that week. And that case hadn't led anywhere yet.

The uniformed officer shook his head. "Nah, he's clean." He left the room and closed the door back.

Shareef looked up at the black and Latino detectives and immediately thought about a million cop movies and television shows that he had watched since he was a kid, including his all-time favorite, *Across 110th Street.*

Okay, here we go, he told himself.

The Latino partner started on him first. "So, ah, Shareef . . . what do you have to tell us today?"

Shareef sighed and said, "About what?" He figured it would be a long, grueling interrogation, so he wanted to pace himself and take it all slowly.

"Oh, I don't know. I guess we can start off with fourteen homicides in two days, including a stripper who was just found raped and shot to death inside of an apartment building leased by a guy named Spoonie, aka Wallace Lattimore, who I believe was seen walking with you toward St. Nicholas Park earlier today, before we found him dead on the scene at the park. And this is after two armed men were found dead after shooting at you just up the street last night. Now I know you have something to tell us about all of that, Shareef.

"I hear you're an, ah, writer of some sort," he added.

The older black man, who was the lead detective, corrected him.

"He's a *New York Times* bestselling author. That's the big leagues in the book world," he noted. He said, "That's equivalent to a platinum-selling artist in music, or a blockbuster actor in a film."

The partner nodded. "Oh, is that right? Well, Shareef, I like stories. So let's see if your story on this matches mine."

Shareef nodded back to them. He wanted to start off with the truth.

He said, "It all started after I went to visit a guy named Michael Springfield in prison about writing his life story. And I still didn't know if I wanted to do it or not, but then all these people I never saw before started asking me questions about it. And them two guys last night tried to shoot me over it. So I took off running before they got in a shoot-out with somebody else."

Then he began to mix his truth with lies. He said, "And I didn't look back behind me to see who it was. I didn't know what the hell was going on. So once I made it to Adam Clayton Powell, I jumped into a cab and told him to take me downtown. Then I got down there and checked into the Hudson off of Broadway."

So far it all made sense to the detectives. Shareef hadn't said anything to alarm them. But they were far from finished with him.

"So, why did you come back up to Harlem, to get your luggage?" the lead detective asked him.

Shareef dropped his head. He had to look remorseful. Then he raised his head back up and said, "Spoonie called me up and told me that he knew who was after me. He said all they wanted to do was make sure I wasn't planning on putting their names in anything. And he said they wanted to see me face-to-face."

He said, "Now at first—I mean, I'm not no fool, man—I figured they gon' try to kill me again. They were just shooting at me last night. But at the same time, if they really wanted to meet me face to face—I mean, I know I'm not no snitch—so I told myself, 'Look, I'm just gon' tell them I'm not trying to do that and get it over with.' I mean, I'm from Harlem, man, I know how it is. And I figured if they looked me in the eyes and met me, they could tell."

The two detectives looked at each other. They didn't expect Shareef to talk so much voluntarily. They expected to have to pull every bit of information out of him. But maybe he was a good writer. His story was longer and more detailed than expected.

The partner nodded and said, "Okay, so then what happened?"

Shareef sighed and slowed down to get everything just right.

He said, "We get to the park, and we meet up with four guys on the hill, and they got guns with them. And this is in broad daylight. I mean, I figured they wouldn't try no shit like that in broad daylight. That's why I agreed to meet them there."

"Okay, then what?" the partner asked again. This guy Shareef was amusing. His story all added up so far.

Shareef answered, "Then they started talking about going to the car to take a ride. So at that point—I mean, I'm not jumping in no fuckin' car, man, and they already got guns out—so I told them I would follow behind them, 'cause I didn't want nobody behind me, while I tried to figure out which way I wanted to run."

He said, "Well, they didn't like that too much. So we got to arguing about who gon' follow who. In the meantime, I figured out I didn't have anywhere to run, but since we were right near the hill, I told myself, 'Look, I'm just gon' roll off this hill and take my chances.'"

As he spoke, he turned slightly in his chair to the right to show them the injuries to his left side.

He said, "So once we got to a stalemate on the hill, their main guy said, 'Fuck it. Kill 'em both.' Once I heard that, I hit the ground and started rolling. That's when the bullets started flying."

He looked up into the faces of both detectives with remorse. He said, "And you know, rest in peace to my man Spoonie, but he just wasn't thinking as fast as I was. So I made it off the hill, took the fall like a man, climbed back to my feet, and started running for my life again."

Again, the two detectives stopped and looked at each other. Either this guy was an undercover super hero, or he was lying his ass off.

The detective asked him, "Whose idea was it to meet at St. Nicholas Park?"

Shareef didn't hesitate. "It was their idea."

The partner said, "Okay, so what about the other guys?"

"What other guys?" Shareef asked him.

The lead detective looked again to his partner. Was Shareef claiming he knew nothing about anyone on his side. Incredible.

He asked him, "Let me get this straight. You come back up to Harlem by yourself, knowing that these guys are trying to kill you, and you don't bring a gun or anything, and nobody's around trying to protect you? Is that what you want us to believe?"

Shareef opened his empty palms and said, "That's just what it is. I mean, you don't see no gun residue on my hands. It's just dirt, sweat, and blood."

The Latino partner began to get impatient. He said, "This is bull-shit. You're sitting over there . . ." He stopped and told his partner, "This guy could pass the lie detector test. He *is* a fuckin' writer. He set this whole thing up and now he's trying to get away with it. Fourteen people were killed on account of him, and he claims he doesn't know anything about it."

He looked back at Shareef and said, "What are you, *Angel Heart* over here?"

Then he looked back to his partner. "You remember that movie with Mickey Rourke? That's the one where people end up dead every time he leaves the scene, and he claims he doesn't know anything about it. Then he finds out that he sold his soul to the devil."

The lead detective nodded. "Yeah, with Robert De Niro as the devil. I remember that one." He looked back at Shareef himself and asked him, "Did you sell your soul to the devil, Shareef?"

Shareef played it seriously and frowned. "Come on, man."

"Well, let me ask you something else," the detective followed up. "Do you know a guy by the name of Baby G, aka Greggory Taylor?"

Shareef was as straightforward as he could be. He said, "Of course I know him. He's the most popular guy in Harlem right now."

The partner corrected him and said, "You mean *was* the most popular guy in Harlem."

Shareef looked confused by it. "What are you sayin'?"

The partner squinted his eyes in concentration. "Okay, so I guess you don't know anything about his death at the park, either."

"I mean, I don't know the guy like that, I just know who he is," Shareef told him. "I haven't been in Harlem long enough to know him like that."

"Well, how do you know him?" the detective questioned.

"I saw him at the basketball tournament. The Kingdome. And people were talking about him. So, you know, I listened, like anybody else would. I didn't know his real name though. Most of the time when they say G they mean like, 'gangsta,' like in Baby Gangsta."

"Yeah, we know the street lingo. We don't need lessons from you," the partner responded.

The lead detective asked, "So, you never had a conversation with him?"

"About what?" Shareef asked.

"About him and his boys protecting you," the partner interjected.

Shareef shook his head and said, "Look, man, this whole situation is crazy. You say fourteen people were killed on account of me. For what? For writing a fuckin' book? A book that I ain't even started yet. I just got off tour, man. I'm not even near a computer up here. Black men don't read my books no way. I got an audience that's ninety-five percent women. So why would these guys be chasing me over some book? I'm still try'na understand that myself. Do y'all have any answers for that?"

Shareef was trying to turn the tables on them using his own frustrations, steering them away from the Baby G subject. But at the same time, he didn't understand it. What did Trap and his guys have to hide? He knew Shareef wouldn't write anything about him. Was it all about ego? Were Trap's feelings that hurt that Shareef wouldn't back down? It was all insane?

The black detective responded, "You tell us. What did you plan to write about in this book?"

Shareef said, "It was a prison love story," just out of spite. Then he told the truth again. "Come on, man, the guy wanted to tell his life story, but I didn't even get to talk to him about it yet."

"Yeah, and then *he* ended up dead. That just happened a few days ago. So that makes *fifteen* bodies now," the partner responded.

"And I had something to do with that, too, right?" Shareef asked him.

"Did you?" the partner asked him back.

Shareef shook his head and remained silent. He didn't even bother to answer that.

The lead detective asked, "So, how did Michael Springfield get in touch with you?"

Shareef looked up and said, "Believe it or not, he was reading my books. That's where the majority of my five percent of reading men come from. Prison. You believe that shit? That's fuckin' sad, man. But it's the truth."

The partner said, "Look, we don't want to hear your damn politics."

The lead detective countered with a thoughtful nod. He said, "Yeah, but if you think about it, it makes more sense to me now. So if you say that most of the men who read your books are in prison, and these guys who were after you are one foot in, one foot out of jail anyway, then it makes the most sense in the world for them to want to stop you. You're writing directly to their peer group. And all of these jailbirds know each other."

Shareef had never thought of it that way. Male prisoners were indeed a niche group of readers. They just weren't able to buy many books. But they read them when they got them.

Shareef said, "But I don't even write those kind of books."

"Yeah, but this book would have been that kind," the detective noted.

Shareef agreed with him. He said, "Yeah, I guess you're right." He ran with that discovery and tried a brand-new approach to get himself quickly out of guilt.

He eyed both detectives and said, "But here's what it is, Officers. At the end of the day, I have no criminal record whatsoever. Not even for jaywalking. I got a wife. I got two kids. I make my living writing romance books for women. I'm a college graduate, and I just got caught up in some crazy-ass bullshit back home in Harlem—because that's what this shit is—and I can guarantee that I'll never get caught up in this street shit again. I can promise you that. 'Cause all this right here is ridiculous. I can't even believe I'm sitting here."

The partner said, "But you are sitting here, Shareef. And we have *fifteen* homicides to solve."

Shareef snapped, "Well, solve them then. Y'all know who pulled the triggers. And it wasn't me. Not one of them. Y'all know that shit already."

He said, "All I did was run for my fuckin' life up here. So at this point, I've said about all I'm gon' say, and y'all know how the story go; you can talk to my lawyer. And I'd like to make my phone call now."

All of the conversation in the room just stopped. No one knew what else to say. But Shareef looked heated and was still irritated by the pain of his injuries that still had not been tended to.

The lead detective sighed and told his partner, "Let me talk to him for a minute."

The Latino partner nodded and left the room.

Okay, here we go, Shareef told himself again. *Now he wants to make his personal statements to another black man.*

The detective sat on the edge of the table while Shareef prepared himself to hear whatever.

The detective stated in low tones, black man to black man.

He said, "I know your type, Shareef. You all think you're above the law. And I'm not talking about a black or white thing here, because I've been around white boys, too. Matter of fact, the white boys are the worse. So I celebrate with a drink every time one of you assholes gets sent off to jail."

Shareef stopped him and asked, "What exact *type* are you talking about?" He had an idea, he just wanted to hear the detective say it.

The detective answered, "You know what the hell I'm talking

about. You smart enough. Ain't you? You give a man a little bit more money than the next man, and he starts thinking he's smarter than everybody, and that he deserves some type of special privilege. So when he fucks up real bad, he thinks he's smart enough to get away with it. But he don't want to be treated like some average street con. Oh, no, this nigga got lawyers working for him. The best lawyers in the business. And he's on top of the pecking order. So he never do his own dirt, nor does he want to clean up his own shit afterward."

Shareef shook his head and said, "You don't know nothing about me, man. I'm no damn criminal. I'm not stealing from the stock exchanges. I'm not robbing the poor. I'm not taking old people's pensions and overcharging people who don't have health insurance for medicine. You got the wrong guy, man. I'm not him."

The detective leaned back and nodded. What could he hit Shareef with that would stick?

He said, "You say you got a wife and kids, right? And you write books for women?"

Shareef just stared at him. "What's your point?"

The detective asked him, "You got a girlfriend or two you see on the side?"

Shareef didn't flinch, but he was caught off guard by it. He thought to himself, *This motherfucker's just looking for anything to get under my skin with.*

Then he had a question of his own. He said with an honest face, "Well, let me ask you a question, Detective. Are police officers jealous motherfuckers before they take the job, or is that just a part of your training?"

The detective cracked a smile, chuckled and nodded.

He said, "You may get away with your bullshit in this life, Shareef, but it's gon' catch back up to you when you approach the gates of heaven. You just remember that somebody told you that. And all this after the community made a decent effort to clean up St. Nick's and keep it safe."

When he finished his private conversation, he stood up from the table and slapped his heavy hand against Shareef's left shoulder.

"Ahh, shit," Shareef whined and winced.

The detective stopped and told him, "Oh, I'm sorry. I forgot. You hurt yourself there, didn't you?" And he walked up out of the room.

Shareef rubbed his badly bruised shoulder with his right hand and stared into the empty space of the room. The detective had gotten his point across. How did heaven look down on him? Shareef had to think about that himself. And he felt guilty, as if the gates would not open for him.

Nevertheless, while Shareef was still on earth, his intentions were to remain a free man. So he planned to stick to the script.

Tough Decisions

C HARLES PICKETT ARRIVED at the Harlem police station, pronto, to pick up his grandson and to make sure he was safe. He expected a fight to do so, and he was ready for it with his active NAACP membership card. He had in his mind to let the officers know that he would be back with a well-publicized lawsuit if he experienced any problems. But when he walked into the station and let the desk clerk know who he was and who he was there for, they responded with unusual speed.

"We'll have him right out for you, Mr. Pickett."

"Thank you," he told them. And he waited patiently at the front for his only grandson.

Inside of a second interrogation room on the second floor, the lead detective and his partner were asking questions of T, who had been arrested at the scene of the shoot-out, while firing two automatic pistols into the air.

"So, you say you had no idea why you were there?" the lead detective asked him.

T looked up at him from his chair behind the interrogation table as if it pained him to answer. He was still pretty spotless as compared to everyone else who had been picked up at the scene.

He answered, "Yeah, like I said, we had beef."

"Beef over what?" the partner asked him. "You had to be beefing over something. How did you all end up at the same place?"

T shook his head and muttered, "When you down for your team, you down for your team. It don't matter what the beef is. So that's how it went down. I just went in for my team."

The two detectives continued to look at each other to try and figure things out.

The lead asked, "Have you ever heard of Shareef Crawford, the book writer?"

T looked up and grimaced. "Who?" It wasn't as if he had read any of his books or anything.

The two detectives looked at each other again and shook their own heads.

The lead asked him, "So, you're ready to go to jail for assault, illegal possession of a handgun, reckless endangerment, and murder, and all you have to say about it is that you were down for your team?"

T looked him in the eye and didn't flinch. He answered, "All I know is that my man was killed in the beef. But I didn't shoot nobody. I was just there for backup."

The partner asked him, "You were only there for backup? Well, who shot the guy named Trap in the back?"

T shrugged his shoulders and said, "I don't know who shot him. A lot of people got shot out there today. And they were both dead when I got there."

The partner said, "And didn't they find you with two pistols in your hands, firing away like a madman? That's what we heard?"

T looked down at the table and said, "I just took the guns and started shooting them in the air after I got there."

"Why?" the lead detective asked him.

T looked up at him as if he was crazy.

He said, "Because I was mad. My man had just got killed."

Again, the officers looked at each other before they were interrupted by a knock on the door.

"Yeah," the lead detective answered it.

A uniformed officer stuck his head into the room and said, "We got a pickup here for Shareef Crawford."

"Who is it?" the detective asked him.

"His grandfather."

The detective looked at his partner before they both walked out of the room to see for themselves.

WHEN SHAREEF STRUGGLED to walk down from the holding room with his one bag of luggage, the Latino partner spotted him heading toward his grandfather, and he asked the lead detective, "So we're not even gonna try and hold him for a day? What if someone else ends up dead when he leaves here?"

The lead detective shook it off. "We still don't have enough to hold him with. We know he was at both places, and we know that he ran both times. But everything else that we *think* we know, we still have to prove. So we have to gather up more of the guys out here who are still alive and willing to talk to us about it. And so far, that hasn't happened."

He said, "Now if we could charge him for being stupid and for getting involved with these people in the first place, he would definitely be staying here tonight. But until we have more concrete information, we let him go, and when we have something, we'll go get him and bring him back."

He added, "He's definitely gonna have to stand trial. So he's not going anywhere. All we need is time."

The partner sighed. He still didn't agree with letting Shareef go that easily, but what could he do about it? The older, veteran detective knew better.

WHEN SHAREEF CLIMBED into the back of a cab with his grandfather, he grimaced again from the stinging pain of his injuries.

His grandfather looked at him and asked, "Do I need to take you over to the hospital first?"

Shareef shook it off. "Nah, I just need some ice and some bandages. That's all the hospital is gonna do. So I'll be all right. I don't have any broken bones, just bad bruises."

His grandfather nodded to him. And as much as he admired his grandson's adventurous nature, there came a time when enough was enough, and that time had come.

So his grandfather cleared his throat and told him, "Now, Shareef, you gon' need to take some good advice after all of this here."

Shareef took a deep breath and figured as much. He may have been a grown man, but that didn't excuse him from being called out for his bad decisions. A grown man needed correcting just as much as a young man when he was wrong, and Shareef was in no position to argue.

He mumbled, "Yeah, I know."

His grandfather nodded to him. He said, "But knowing it and doing something about it are too different things. See, 'cause a man can know that he has cancer, and do nothing about it until it's time for his deathbed."

Shareef listened and silently nodded back to him. What else could he do?

"Well, I'm not trying to watch my grandson go to his deathbed before I tell him what changes he needs to make in his life," his grandfather told him.

Shareef heard the word "changes" and reacted to it instinctively. He began to fidget and twist up his face as if the word hurt him as much as his left side did. He didn't like to make *changes* unless he was the one deciding to make them.

His grandfather knew as much. You don't raise a boy from his infancy to middle age without knowing what kind of a man he is. Shareef was a bull, a ram, a lion, and a grizzly bear, all rolled up into one. So his grandfather scrambled to be logical before he could raise up on his hind legs, charge forward, claw, and buck his grandfather off of him.

"Now Shareef, I've watched you make decisions on what you wanted to do for your entire life, and it's been mostly a blessing for me. I liked seeing a young man take charge of himself."

Charles Pickett raised his index finger and added, "Of course, your grandmother thought differently on a number of occasions, but I always managed to fight her off so you could be a man." He said, "You know, because sometimes a woman can get involved and mess up the process of a man learning himself. And that's when you end up with these young men who don't know how to take charge and be a man."

The African cabdriver overheard the advice being dished by the grandfather in the back of his car, and he couldn't help but smile. He agreed with him wholeheartedly. There were far too many womanish men in America for his own taste, a bunch of soft men who made too many excuses for themselves.

The grandfather added, "But there have been those times, Shareef, when I had to agree with my wife, and this happens to be one of them."

He said, "Now I've watched you work hard to build yourself into the kind of proud man that other men find it very easy to admire, but at the same time, you still have this reckless shit that you do, every now and then, that you still need to learn how to grow up out of."

He said, "Now maybe you need to learn how to play golf or something to get away from those tendencies."

Shareef heard the word "golf" and began to smile. He just wasn't a golf-playing man.

His grandfather read the smile on his face and asked him, "Now what does that mean? You think golf is a sissy game, don't you? And you don't think Tiger Woods is a real athlete because he hits golf balls instead of people."

Shareef shook it off. "I didn't say that. Tiger Woods is the beast. That's why they call him Tiger. I'm just not into playing golf."

"Well, you're gonna have to do something, Shareef," his grandfa-

ther told him. "Because you can't keep doing what you been doing." He said, "And you know they called your wife up about this,
don't you?"

Shareef looked alarmed by the information. "They what?"

Charles watched as the cabdriver approached his home in the
Morningside Heights area next to Columbia University. He told him,
"Hey, right here."

The cabdriver eased on the brakes and came to a stop in the street.
Charles figured he would finish the conversation with his grandson
once they were out of the taxi. So they climbed out, paid the driver,
and pulled Shareef's one bag of luggage from the trunk.

"Thank you," Charles told the driver. And as soon as he was alone
outside of the house with his grandson, they picked back up on their
conversation.

Shareef asked him, "So you say they called my wife?" That was the
last thing in the world he wanted to hear. It caught him off guard.

"The police called her before you called us. They were looking for
you everywhere," his grandfather answered him. "So then Jennifer
gets on the phone all shaken up, and lets your grandmother have it
with everything. She starts talking about how you left the house, and
all the little groupie girls who've been after you, and how she thinks
about divorce, and what about the kids, and the marriage counseling,
and she just broke down in tears about everything. That's why your
grandmother didn't want to talk to you when you called. She started
looking at me and saying it was my fault, and that it was up to me to
fix it."

Shareef looked into his grandfather's face and let out a deep sigh
before he looked away. What could he say about all of that? He realized he wasn't in the world alone. No man was. He had a wife, kids,
grandparents and friends whom he all loved, and he had to answer to
all of them with his actions and reactions.

Whether he liked it or not, everything he did affected them. So he
nodded his head to his grandfather and said nothing. He still didn't
know what to say.

His grandfather placed a soft hand on Shareef's right shoulder and told him, "There comes a time, Shareef, when a man has to pull his own ideas and behavior into line with those he loves around him. Now that don't mean that you stop going for your dreams and aspirations, but it does means that you have to think first about what that means to everyone else. You have to think more about how you make those things happen in a balance, so that you don't end up pulling yourself too far away from everything that really means something to you. Because, see, I know how much cotton candy is out here, believe me, but I also know how much you love your wife."

Shareef suddenly felt like a little boy again in his grandfather's wise hands. He didn't want to hear the lecture. He didn't want to hear the hard answers. He didn't want to hear about his marriage. Nor did he want to hear the truth about maturity, but he had to.

His grandfather told him, "Now you can have all these people out here who fake like they love you, but they only love you for as long as you're a celebrity in the limelight. They don't love you when it gets dark. They only love you when the lights are on. And they don't love you when you're old and slower moving. They only love you when you're young, slim, and quick on your feet. You hear me?"

Shareef got the point and smiled. It wasn't as if he had never heard it all before, he just needed to hear it again and he appreciated the timing.

He said, "So, Grandmom probably won't speak to me right now, will she?"

Charles laughed and showed his teeth. "Oh, you already know that. You just got *both* of us in the doghouse. But at least you're all right. Now let's go on in here and take care of these bruises."

Shareef followed his grandfather into the house, and he was glad to be back there. But as soon as they walked in, he heard his grandmother's feet moving through the hallway upstairs and toward the bedroom, where she slammed the door shut behind her.

Bloom!

Wilma Pickett had been waiting at the top of the stairs for Shareef to arrive at her home so she could show him her fierce disapproval of his recent behavior.

Shareef took another exhausting breath and shook his head. He was going to have to apologize to his grandmother after he apologized to his wife. He already knew the deal, he just had to prepare himself for it.

"Now let's get you out of these clothes," his grandfather told him.

Shareef grimaced as they took off his bloodstained shirt for a second time. Then they pulled off his blue jeans and shoes. His left shoulder, ribs, hip, and thigh were all purple, black, and blue. His body was stained and sticky from dried up blood, and he was swollen in several places from the lack of ice or care of his wounds.

"Yeah, you took a bad fall there," his grandfather told him.

Shareef asked him, "How did you know?"

Charles looked at the wounds all on his grandson's left side. He said, "Well, that's what it looks like. It looks like you fell off a damn cliff and landed clean on your left side."

Shareef grinned and said, "That's just what happened."

His grandfather told him, "Well, I don't want to know too much about it? Just tell me that you're innocent."

"I am," Shareef told him. "I guess I just didn't realize how serious some people are about protecting their names in the street. And I wasn't even planning on putting their names in anything."

His grandfather stopped and nodded to him. He said, "Shareef, I've lived here in Harlem for a long time now, ever since your grandmother and I moved up here from Georgia in nineteen fifty-nine. And I have never been to a place where people think about their good names as much as they do in Harlem. So if you needed any information on that, I could have told you that a long time ago."

He said, "Now let me go in here and get you a bucket of warm water, ice, Neosporin, and bandages to deal with these wounds." He looked at the injuries again and added, "I hope you didn't damage anything internally, because you may need to go to the hospital anyway. But I'd rather you did it back down in Florida with your family."

Shareef nodded as his grandfather went to prepare for the beginning of the healing. But once Shareef thought about his wounds and checking into a hospital in Florida, he thought about facing his son, and what Shareef Jr. would think about it all.

"Damn," he mumbled to himself. "I just gotta tell Little J that things happen."

ONCE SHAREEF WAS ALL CLEANED UP, bandaged, and iced down, he sat in the comfortable living room chair with his left leg up and only white towels wrapped around him, and he thought about everything. He had made it out of a serious jam alive, but everyone else hadn't, and now he was in debt to his lifelong nemesis because of it.

So he thought of Jurrell Garland and the threat he had made about his wife and family in Florida. Did Jurrell mean what he said? Of course he did. And now Shareef had to deal with that. He would have to play or pray.

He shook his head again and let out another deep sigh. He thought about Jennifer and his kids back home, and whether or not he could ever return to being a committed husband to a woman who had lost her passion for him? Jacqueline Herrera wouldn't hang around long enough for him to decide, that was for sure. She was already mapping out her departure from his life. Shareef would never become that serious about her anyway. In fact, he wondered if he could ever be seriously committed to a woman again. Based on how they changed so much, he didn't trust any of them. A lot of women were simply too emotional for him.

I wonder what Cynthia's up to right now, he pondered. Cynthia seemed to know men a little better than the average girly-girl, because she hung around men. But in hanging around men, maybe she would always be more trouble than he needed in his life.

Yeah, I'll just stay cool with her and keep myself out of Dodge, he told himself.

Then he thought about his friend Polo, and wondered if he should change his will back to normal, since they were both safe and sound.

Ten percent of a couple mil' is a lot, he told himself of his estimated wealth. *Then again, if Jennifer and the kids get half, including the house, then my grandparents get twenty-five to thirty-five percent, and Preston takes care of the rest with a family estate fee, then Polo's ten percent comes out as a nice little nest egg for a lifelong friend to do something with his family.*

As Shareef continued to think things through, he heard his grand-mother walk back out of her room upstairs and into the hallway.

"Shareef!" she called down the stairs to him.

Her yell woke her husband, who had put Shareef back together and had fallen asleep on the comfortable sofa beside him.

"Yes, ma'am," Shareef answered her.

"Have you spoken to your wife yet?"

By that, she meant, *Have you called your wife back to apologize and to beg her for her forgiveness?*

Shareef answered, "I'll call her right now, Grandmom. I just needed to get some ice on my wounds first."

His grandfather immediately climbed off the sofa to go and re-trieve the phone for him.

"Are you okay?" his grandmother called downstairs to ask him.

"Yeah, I'll make it," Shareef told her.

"Good. Then tell your wife."

By the time Wilma Pickett slammed her door back upstairs, Charles had brought the phone over to Shareef to make his call.

"Thanks, Grandpop," Shareef told him. Then he took a deep breath with the phone receiver in hand.

Can I help her to get back her love for me? he asked himself as he made the call. Then he shook it off, doubting it.

That's the wrong thinking to even deal with her, he concluded. *And as long as it's my idea, she'll fight it. That's our problem now; everything she brings up, I don't like, and everything I bring up, she doesn't like. So how do we settle that?*

"Hello?" Jennifer answered.

Shareef said, "It's me. I'm all right," and he got nothing but silence for the first couple of minutes.

"What happened to your cell phone?" she finally asked him. She had been calling it for hours.

"It's a long story," he told her. "But I left it at the hotel in Manhattan this morning. I didn't want it on me today."

"Why?"

Shareef exhaled and told her, "There was too much going on. I just thought it would be a distraction."

"A distraction to what, of you running around in the damn streets of Harlem, Shareef? Is that what you want to do with your life now? I mean, I just can't take much more of this. And if you want to get rid of me so damn bad, then why don't you just get Preston to write up the divorce papers. Why are you trying to stress me like this? *Why?*"

Shareef could see the tears ready to roll out of her eyes without even being there to witness them. He could hear it in the shakiness of her voice. He knew Jennifer just like she knew him. And he knew enough about her to realize that every word he spoke would be countered from her perspective. So he stood paralyzed on the phone. There was no sane thing for him to do but to give in, and even that was insane.

Shareef rarely gave in to anything. But if he had given in a few days ago, a week ago, a month ago, or a year ago, *fifteen* people would have never been killed in Harlem. So he finally made the *sane* or *insane* decision.

He said, "You're right. I need to get a grip on myself. And this has been a long time coming."

Then there was more silence.

Jennifer said, "Please don't patronize me, Shareef."

That was how his wife of ten years responded to him giving in. It was a foreign language to her. She had no clue of knowing how to accept it.

Shareef paused and thought, *Yup, that's just what I thought. There's no way out of this. She's gonna fight me with everything I say.*

He looked over at his grandfather and smirked. How did men and women ever figure out how to get along? It seemed impossible. Shareef and Jennifer had been married for a decade already. His grandparents had been married for more than five decades. How in the hell did they do that?

Charles nodded back to his grandson and told him calmly, "Just hang in there."

Shareef then told his wife, "I guess I have to show and prove more than I can talk at this point. Because talking about it is not gonna do anything for you."

Suddenly, Shareef's grandfather began to shake his head with a face of doom.

He said calmly again, "Tell her that you love her."

Jennifer said, "Whatever, Shareef. I can't trust anything you say or do anymore."

Shareef listened to his grandfather and said, "Well, I love you and the kids anyway. And I'm never gonna stop loving you. That's why I never filed for no divorce, Jennifer. I don't believe in it. And I don't believe we've stopped loving each other. I'll never believe that."

His grandfather looked at him and smiled. He began to nod his head and was pleased with Shareef's words. But did he really mean them?

Jennifer said, "Yeah, well, you have a very strange way of showing it. I wonder how you would act if you hated us." At least she sounded calmer now.

Shareef repeated his wife's words out loud so his grandfather could hear them and help him out again.

"If I hated you? Why would you say something like that?"

"That's how you've been acting, Shareef," she told him.

"She didn't mean to say that," his grandfather told him. Nothing Charles said in the room was loud enough to be overheard through the phone, so it was safe for Shareef to continue.

"You don't mean that, Jennifer," Shareef told her. He said, "You know better than that."

She asked him, "So, what do you plan to do? Are you moving back home?"

That was a tough question. Shareef didn't even want to look to his grandfather for that answer.

He asked her, "Do you want me back there?" It was the safest response that came to mind.

"You're the one talking about showing and proving, Shareef. So, what does that mean? Does that mean you can still have your cake and eat it, too?"

She was backing him up and putting him on the spot. That made Shareef feel powerless, exactly how he didn't want to feel. Nevertheless, he was willing to rest and heal for a minute. He realized that they all needed healing, including his kids, a healing from missing daddy so much.

"Well, let that be the first step then," he told her.

"Let what be the first step?"

Jennifer was playing her usual game of specifics. Shareef had become so vague with her at times that it became necessary for her to ask him exactly what he meant by everything.

"Me moving back in," he answered. He said, "And I'm sorry about all of this."

He no longer needed his grandfather's help at that point. He had his own rhythm going on. He knew what he needed to do to make things right. It just wasn't going to be easy.

Jennifer gave him another stretch of silence. Shareef understood what that meant. She wanted to doubt him again. But even though she may have been thinking it, Jennifer refrained from saying it. She was open to give it a chance herself. She still adored the man. She couldn't deny it.

So instead of her saying something to disturb the progress of their new agreement, she simply asked him, "When are you getting back?"

Shareef looked to his anxious grandfather and nodded with a grin. The situation with his wife and family looked positive. It was all on their shoulders now, and they would try and work things out.

He answered, "My original flight is still scheduled for tomorrow morning. But I have to see how my body feels in the morning. I'm figuring that tomorrow I'll be more sore than I am today. So if that happens, I may have to hang around up here and get iced down until Tuesday.

"Are the kids still up?" he asked her. By then, it was after ten o'clock at night.

"Shareef is, but if you're not coming back until Tuesday, then I'd rather you speak to him tomorrow sometime. At least that'll be closer. And I know he's been wanting you to see him at practice and everything."

Shareef nodded and smiled. "Yeah, I know. Li'l J wants to show me all his new moves."

WHEN HE ENDED THE PHONE CALL with his wife, his grandfather asked him, "So, what do you think?"

Shareef paused. He told him, "It's a struggle, man. It really is. I just wish I could take it back to the beginning. Things were a hell of a lot easier then."

His grandfather chuckled and said, "Well, instead of going back to the beginning, how about starting a new beginning." He said, "So, what you have to do, is court your wife again like you did when you first fell for her. In fact, try this. Don't even think of her as your wife anymore. Think of her as just Jennifer. And then you do everything you can to try and make her your wife again. How about that?"

His grandfather had twinkles in his eyes as if he had just come up with a genius plan.

Shareef chuckled at it himself. He said, "I'll try that. That sounds better than trying to pick up where we left off, because where we left off was nowhere. So I think it's best for me to look at it as starting over."

"Exactly," his grandfather agreed with him.

It took only a few more minutes for his grandmother to walk out of her room again.

"Shareef?"

"Yes, Grandma?"

"Have you spoken to your wife?"

"Yeah, I just got off the phone with her."

"And is she okay?"

Shareef paused and looked at his grandfather again.

"Yeah, she's okay," he answered. He said, "We're planing to start things over when I get back home on Tuesday."

"Tuesday? Why Tuesday?" his grandmother asked him.

Shareef told her, "I'm still healing. So tomorrow and Monday would be the sorest time for me to travel."

His grandmother told him, "Let me see what you're talking about, boy," and she began to march down the stairs.

Shareef and Charles looked at each other. They both knew better. Wilma realized that her grandson was injured a while ago, but she refused to see him until after he had spoken to his wife. So by the time she arrived in the living room in her nightclothes, Shareef realized that he owed his grandmother an apology.

She immediately looked over his left side, all bandaged and iced up. She said, "Are you sure you don't need to go to the hospital?"

"He's going once he gets back to Florida," Charles answered her. "We figure it's better that way. There may be some of those other guys in the Harlem Center. So I'd rather he not go there."

Wilma frowned and said, "Well, take him down the street to St. Luke's."

St. Luke's Hospital was three blocks away, at the foot of Columbia University.

Shareef and Charles looked at each other again and began to laugh. Neither one of them had even thought of St. Luke's.

Charles said, "Well, hell, my mind must have taken a trip. Why was I only thinking about the Harlem Center?"

"Because every time the police are involved, that's exactly where they take people. Now get this boy together with some clothes so we can take him down the street."

She looked her grandson in the face and told him, "And this is what a *good wife* is for, Shareef, not just for jumping in the sack, but taking care of her husband and family all together."

CHARLES GATHERED TOGETHER some of his clean sweat clothes that would fit his grandson, and they called the hospital emergency service to have an ambulance pick them up from the house.

Right as the ambulance arrived, Shareef looked into his grandmother's wholesome brown face and said, "I'm sorry for all of this, Grandma. I'm definitely too old for this kind of trouble."

"Aw, baby, I'm just glad you're okay," she told him. Then she kissed his cheek with a smile before she became serious again.

She said, "Now, what are you gonna do about these street books you wanted to write?"

She had him stuck. Shareef hadn't come to a final decision about that yet, but he knew he still had to deal with Jurrell if he made the wrong one.

He told her, "I don't know yet." That was an honest answer. He didn't know.

His grandmother heard that and turned away from him with a grunt. "Hmmph. Well, you need to make a decision," she advised him. "The right one."

Charles looked on and chuckled again as they both prepared their grandson for his ride in the ambulance.

Out of the Fire

AFTER MUCH NEW YORK MEDIA reporting one of the worst public shoot-outs in recent history, the case of St. Nicholas Park held various court dates from October 2006 through January 2007, with no conclusive evidence that linked Shareef Crawford to any of the murders. To the jurors, Shareef appeared to be an ill-advised author caught between two groups of the wrong people at the wrong time. Behind the scenes, however, Jurrell Garland made certain that no one had any reason to talk. It was not as if a witness would gain much from pointing a finger. None of their friends or loved ones would return from the grave, and unless one of the suspects on the other side were given a deal that included no prison time, going "up north" after snitching was not a safe thing to do. In fact, unless a deal included a new place to live and a brand-new identity, a snitch was not safe on the streets of Harlem. At least not while Jurrell remained desperate to become a legitimate businessman. And his plans included Shareef Crawford remaining a free man to write and promote books. So by February 2007, with Shareef found innocent of all charges, healed from his wounds, and back home safe and sound with his family in Florida, he was free to execute the next stage of his plans.

Back to Normal

IN MID-MARCH of the new year, Shareef tossed a Little League baseball from the pitcher's mound at a recreation center field in Fort Lauderdale, Florida. At the plate, a nine-year-old boy in a red helmet swung his aluminum bat and made contact for a grounder toward second base. He then dropped his bat and began to run toward first.

At second base, Shareef Jr., wearing an Atlanta Braves jersey and cap, made the catch off the second hop with his leather glove, aimed his throw to his left, and zipped the ball toward his first baseman.

Shareef Sr. hollered to the hitter, "Run it out! Run it out!"

But the hitter watched the ball about to beat him to first base, and he slowed down his run before he made it there.

Shareef told him, "Look, man, you run it out anyway. He may miss the catch at first. Or it may be a bad throw. Then you can turn the corner and run to second. You hear me?"

Shareef turned and faced the rest of the nine- and ten-year-olds in the outfield. He said, "I want everybody to finish out their runs to the bases. Nobody slows down. If you slow down, you're giving me a lap around the field. And you're only gettin' this one warning, so make sure you hear me."

He looked them all in their eyes and said, "All right?"

The kids all nodded and mumbled their yeses.

Outside of the baseball field, Jennifer Crawford smiled and shook her head from her foldout chair. Her daughter sat in a smaller foldout chair beside her, with the rest of the mothers who watched their sons at practice.

"Your husband sure is a good coach. He's gon' have those boys *ready*," one of the mothers commented to Jennifer.

"I know that's right," another mother agreed. "He's much tougher than last year's coach. Last year those boys did whatever they wanted to do."

Jennifer knew that wouldn't happen with Shareef. Just as her husband played to win, he would coach to win. There was no other way that Shareef would get involved, no matter what it was.

AFTER WRAPPING UP another evening of baseball practice, Shareef and his family went out for dinner at Red Lobster. Over his giant snow crab legs, Shareef Jr. looked across the table and asked his father, "How long are you gonna be in New York, Dad? For the whole week?"

"Of course not. We have another practice on Friday," Shareef told him. "So I'll be in New York for two business days and back to Florida in time for practice."

His daughter asked him, "Can we go to the airport with you?"

Shareef said, "Girl, you have school tomorrow. And I'm getting out of here at six o'clock in the morning. You wanna be up that early?"

Shareef Jr. responded before his sister did. "No way."

However, Kimberly grinned with shrimp on her fork and answered, "Yeah."

Jennifer chuckled and said, "Yeah, right. If I tried to get you up that early, you'd be kicking and screaming."

"No I wouldn't."

Jennifer ignored her daughter and went back to eating her lobster.

•   •   •

BACK AT HOME THAT NIGHT, Shareef tucked his kids into their separate rooms. His condo near Miami had been sold months ago, and Jacqueline Herrera had faded away months before that.

Little J asked his father, "With you coaching again, Dad, you think we can win the baseball championship like we did in football?"

Shareef chuckled and told him, "We gon' try. We'll see how far we get."

Little J nodded. He said, "I love when you coach, Dad. It's like, everything is better when you coach."

"That's because I coach to win," Shareef commented to his son. He said, "But at the same time, I always want the game to be fun, too. So I make sure we keep it moving and learn to play the right way."

His son nodded to him and was satisfied. His negative attitude had tapered off a great deal since Shareef had been back home. Little J, however, was still no saint. He had an obvious, competitive edge to him, and his father was pleased with it. Shareef looked at it as partially hereditary, and partially training.

When he went to tuck in his daughter, Kimberly had a different idea for him.

"You're gonna sleep in here with me again, Daddy?" she suggested.

Shareef chuckled and said, "Not tonight, girl. Tonight I got a date with your mother."

Kimberly looked alarmed. "You and Mom are going back out? Who's gonna be here with us?"

Shareef laughed harder and told her, "Nah, we're not going back out. We have an in-house date."

Kimberly looked confused, "An in-house date? Well, what are you gonna do? You're gonna watch a movie on DVD and eat popcorn?"

Shareef continued to laugh. He said, "Good idea. I'll see what your mother thinks about that. In the meantime, I need you to close your eyes, relax, and count those pretty, pink sheep."

Kimberly told him, "Daddy, there's no such thing as pink sheep. Sheep are white. And I never see them when I sleep anyway."

Shareef grinned and shook his head. Kimberly would keep him there all night if he let her. So he kissed her on the lips and said, "All right, it's past ten o'clock, girl. Go on to sleep."

Instead, Kimberly wrapped her arms around her father's neck.

"Please, Daddy?"

Shareef stopped smiling and became serious.

He said, "Now Kimberly, when a man says no, that's what he means. Just like when you say no. You hear me? You want a person to stop when you say no. That's when you know that they respect you."

He said, "Now we can't all have what we want whenever we want it. Okay? That's just the way life is."

Kimberly released her arms from around her father's neck and mumbled, "Okay."

"Now go on to sleep," he told her. "I'll kiss you in the morning."

She said, "In my sleep?"

Shareef stood up from the edge of his daughter's bed and smiled at her one last time.

He said, "Yeah, I always kiss you in your sleep."

"Why?"

He wasn't expecting her to ask him that. But he shook it off and answered, "Because I love you, just like I love your brother."

"And do you love Mommy, too?"

Shareef wondered if all little girls could talk forever if you let them.

He said, "Of course I love your mother. But if you don't let me get in there with her, she may start to doubt it. Now you want your mother locking me out of the room?"

Kimberly smiled from ear to ear and said, "You can sleep with me. I won't lock you out."

Shareef paused for a minute. His mind traveled to the wrong place, an adult place. He told himself, *There's always gonna be another woman on that other grass. That's just life, too. But do I want my daughter being like that?*

Her innocent comment stopped Shareef in his tracks. But how innocent was it? Did his daughter even understand what she was saying?

Was he ready to make a big deal out of nothing? Shareef didn't know what to say or do.

Finally, he told his daughter, "That's not right, Kimberly. Daddy was only joking. And you know your mother wants to see me. So don't be unfair like that. Okay?"

Kimberly nodded to him. "Okay."

Shareef turned off her light and said "Good night" as he left her room.

"Good night, Daddy?"

BY THE TIME Shareef reached the master bedroom to join his wife, who was in her nightclothes, he had lost his sex drive. Their bedroom action was still not as steamy as it had been before they were married with kids, but it was much better than it had been over the last few years. And they had come to the agreement that it was best to give a traveling man something to miss at home before he hit the road in the morning. Nevertheless, Kimberly's comment had tossed Shareef for a loop.

Jennifer could tell that something was amiss as soon as she felt her husband's rigid body in bed.

"What's wrong?" she asked him.

Shareef was rarely rigid when it came to sex and foreplay. He only said no in the fourth quarter of a football or basketball game, the last round of a close fight, the ninth inning of a close baseball game, or whenever he was on a roll while working on his latest novel. But none of those things applied that night. So what was his problem?

Shareef sat up straight and shook his head. He said, "I'm trying to figure this out."

"Figure what out?"

He looked at his wife and told her, "Before I came in here, when I was putting Kimberly to bed, I joked with her that you would lock me out of the room if she kept holding me away from you, and you know what she said?"

"What?"

"She said, 'You can sleep with me. I won't lock you out.' And the shit just hit me as a grown-up thing. And she was smiling her ass off when she said it."

Jennifer started laughing. She told him, "That sounds like a guilty conscience to me, Shareef. She didn't mean anything like that. And you know that."

"But how can we be so sure?"

Jennifer sat up straight and said, "I don't believe you. How dare you think that about our daughter?"

Shareef shook his head and immediately felt ashamed of himself. Maybe he shouldn't have even brought it up. But it was too late for that now. He had his wife thinking about it.

Shareef leaned over and hugged her, not in a sexual way, but in a comforting, understanding, please-forgive-me hug.

Jennifer didn't push him away, but after a minute or so, she commented, "That's karma for you, Shareef. Like they say, what goes around . . ." She stopped herself and grunted, "Mmmpt, mmmpt, mmmpt. Now you got me thinking about my daughter for no good reason."

Shareef felt bad about it himself. He thought, *Damn! Ain't this a bitch! Now I feel like I'll become one of those crazy-ass fathers who won't let anyone near his daughter, and that only turns them out more.*

Shit! he stressed himself.

On cue, his wife chuckled and said, "You did it to yourself, Shareef. You did it to yourself."

But she was concerned about the future of her daughter now as well. *And* her son. How would they turn out in their marriages?

Jennifer figured they would both be as creative about life as their father. But where would that creativity lead them when they found things more restrictive than they desired?

Shareef mumbled back to his wife. "They're just gonna have to choose right, that's all. Choose right and fight for it, that's all they can do."

Jennifer thought twenty years ahead and grumbled, "Mmmph. I don't believe you have me thinking about this."

Shareef chuckled about it himself. "I guess I'm finally growing up now, hunh . . . into a scared-ass parent?"

His wife grinned and told him, "Yeah, you need to put that in that new book you're writing."

Shareef told her, "It's too late. I've already finished it."

IN THE MORNING, he climbed out of bed with no sex, took his shower, gathered his luggage, and kissed his family good-bye as they continued to sleep in their separate rooms. Contrary to what many women thought, not every man had to have it every night. Shareef had other things on his mind and they pushed his sexual desire aside for the minute. Not only was he thinking about the future of his kids, but about the future of his writing career.

Jennifer mumbled when he kissed her. "Call me when you land in New York."

WHEN SHAREEF EXITED the walkway from the plane in New York's LaGuardia Airport in Queens, he strutted in his familiar, dapper uniform of a sports jacket, slacks, fine shoes, and a handsome mug. He had a new respect for his audience of women, too, and the lifestyle that their support had given him. So when the first woman noticed and made him aware that he was her favorite author, Shareef was as gracious as he had been when his writing career had first taken off.

He told the young East Indian woman, "I thank you very much for enjoying my work. I know you could have spent that time and support on someone else."

She argued, "No I couldn't have. I'm addicted to your books, Shareef. I love them all. You're just so *real* the way you write, you know. I can really *hear* and *feel* the people."

He thanked her again and laughed at his natural urges as he moved on toward the cab stand outside the luggage claim area. The woman looked too good for comfort.

Yeah, this is gonna be a struggle my whole life, he told himself about his strong attraction to women.

"Where are you going?" the taxi director asked him at the front of the line.

"Times Square."

"Hey, Times Square."

A car pulled up, the driver tossed Shareef's luggage into the trunk, Shareef climbed in, and he was off on his way to his editor's office in Manhattan to discuss the future of his writing career, face to face, with the marketing, sales, and publicity departments.

SHAREEF STARED OUT of the window on the eighteenth floor of the Worldwide Publishing Group building in the middle of Times Square. William Sorenski, his tall, dark-haired editor, sat behind his office desk with a recently published book, a second book in galley form, and a third book still in manuscript. That was three new books in three different publishing stages, all from the same author.

Shareef had been extremely busy working on new projects over the past eight months, and Bill was pleased with the product.

"I must say, you've really outdone yourself, Shareef. I guess all of the stress of last summer bumped you up to a new level," Bill commented. "But, ahh, I wouldn't advise you to follow the same method for next year. I mean, I was really concerned about everything I was forced to hear and read about you in the papers concerning your court dates. We all were."

Bill had even shown up a few times in court to support him.

Shareef chuckled at the window, while thinking how fortunate he was to make a healthy living as a writer. The location of the building, including the view from his editor's office, allowed him a chance to assess his position in life. And no matter what would become of his career in the future, Shareef realized that he was in a special place and that he should never take it for granted. So he nodded his head and turned to face his editor.

"Hey, man, I just want to thank you for going to bat for me on this new imprint and everything else we're doing," he told Bill. " 'Cause you could have backed down and hung me out to dry on this thing," he admitted.

Bill looked surprised. He said, "Are you kidding me? These books are great! I couldn't wait to fight for you. And you've gotten yourself in enough trouble over this new stuff for me to figure you've earned it. I mean, that's what all the true greats do, right? They all find ways to turn their adversities into personal genius."

Shareef smiled at him. He said, "I thought you told me you didn't like me using that word?"

Bill smiled back. "I guess your overzealousness is rubbing off on me." Then he held up the new published book entitled *To Live and Die in Harlem*, by The Street King. It was a trade softback title, with a cover design of a flashy, urban youth holding a pistol at his side. The book was published through a new imprint called The Underground Library. And The Street King was the pseudonym they had agreed on.

Bill said, "I love how you managed to humanize your protagonists no matter how ugly their lives may seem from the outside, you know. You really find a way to get in there. It's like you're using your skills as a romance writer to reveal the true emotions and character of a thug. And that's a skill a lot of these street writers are not able to utilize."

Shareef thought about the real-life Baby G, on whom the book was based, and he figured there was no way in hell *not* to humanize him. No matter how wrong he may have been in his aspirations, Greggory Taylor, in his short Harlem life, was a an interesting young man.

Shareef shook off the praise and asked Bill, "What about the other street book?"

He was being curious, like any creative person would be. And professional, literary opinions were what editors were for.

Bill picked up the three-hundred-plus page manuscript entitled *The Square Life,* a second novel from The Street King. The plan was to publish two paperback books a year, one in the spring and a second in the fall.

He said, "Now this book reminds me of one of my favorite all-time movies, *The Usual Suspects.* This guy is really wheeling and dealing behind the scenes. And you know he's doing it, but what's amazing about it is *how* he's doing it. This guy's like three steps ahead of everything." Bill smiled and added, "He's an urban Keyser Soze."

Shareef thought about it and started laughing. If only Bill knew how real it all was. As charismatic as Baby G was to inspire the first book, Jurrell Garland's inspiration for the second title was even deeper and deadlier. And since Shareef still had to deal with him, his laugh was not as carefree as he wished it could be.

Bill added, "I don't know about this title though. I think we can come up with some better titles for this one."

Shareef told him, "My idea was to have something that leads readers away from the fact that this guy is crooked. Because if I use the original title, *Legitimate Criminal,* then the book is already telling on itself, and that kills the whole fun of the discovery."

He said, "That's like calling *The Usual Suspects Keyser Soze.* If you did that, you would kill the whole buildup of the ending. Then we would start off expecting to meet this person instead of being surprised by him. But with *The Usual Suspects,* we don't know what the hell the movie is about. We only knew that there was a crime involved."

Bill heard him out and frowned anyway. "Yeah, let's think on that one a little longer. I mean, *The Square Life* . . . you know, it just doesn't seem Harlem enough," he commented. Then he asked, "So, Shareef, ahh, how much of this material is based on, you know, real people?"

Shareef grinned at him and shook his head.

"We don't want to know, man. And that goes for both of us."

"So, in other words, you wanna make sure that the media never finds out who The Street King is to protect your sources?"

Shareef wasn't that afraid of it. He knew the plans.

He said, "Well, eventually, if they figure it out, they figure it out. I think the books'll do more good in the long run then bad. Even *The Square Life,* or whatever we decide to call it, has a redeeming quality to it. And that's what I want to continue to do with these books. So after a while, I won't mind if people know. But I do think we need to start off with a little mystery as to who's writing them."

Bill nodded. "I agree."

Shareef asked him, "Now what about the latest Shareef Crawford book?"

Bill had to lean forward and take a deep breath for that one. He picked up the galley book entitled *A Second Chance,* with a mock-up cover of a man sliding a gold ring on a woman's finger. It was the new hardback title for the summer, the bread-and-butter book for Shareef's overwhelmingly female audience.

"Ahh, it's a good book, a great book actually. But how close are you trying to get to your real life with this one?" Bill questioned. "I mean, I would hate to see you open up a can of worms with your most supportive audience that you can never close again. And at the end of the day, you have to ask yourself, 'Okay, how much of my real life do my fans wanna know?' I mean, sometimes they'd rather have the fiction than the nonfiction, you know what I mean?"

Shareef nodded to him and argued, "Yeah, but the whole premise of this book is to redeem the shattered marriages out there that can still be saved. We all deserve to give ourselves a second chance."

Bill said, "Well, since you're bringing that up, how are you and your wife doing in real life now?"

Shareef said, "We're doing great now. I called her up this morning and talked to her for the majority of my cab ride in from the airport."

Bill couldn't argue with that. He leaned back in his tall leather desk chair and shrugged.

"Okay, well, you're the artist. You'll be the one getting all the questions about it when this book comes out. The only thing I can tell you is to get ready for it."

Shareef eyed his editor and said, "Come on, man, you know who you're dealing with. I'm always ready."

Bill nodded and joked, "Well, it's your funeral. Better your wife pull out the gun than mine." Then he looked at his wristwatch. It was nearly eleven o'clock, time for their meeting with the other departments.

"Okay, so, I guess you're ready for the staff meeting, too, then."

Shareef raised his lotioned palms and said, "Of course."

Bill stood up from his chair to lead the way to the conference room. Shareef followed him out of the office.

Working the Plans

T THE CONCLUSION of his meeting with all the publishing staff who would help launch the plans for The Underground Library imprint, as well as for the current and future Shareef Crawford romance titles, Shareef took a taxi straight back to Harlem for another business meeting. His destination was the condominium homes at Park Avenue Number Three. His appointment was with Jurrell Garland, his new partner.

Shareef took a couple of deep breaths when his cab reached Harlem. Returning home caused him spells of high anxiety now. He then called Jurrell on a secured cell phone line as soon as the cab arrived at the building.

Jurrell answered the line and spoke quickly. "Shareef, they know who you are at the front. Come on up."

Shareef paid his cab fare and walked into the condo building carrying a new saddle brown leather briefcase. The security guard inside the building recognized him and gave him the okay to enter.

"The East Wing is straight to the back of the hall on my left," he told him.

Shareef nodded and headed down the long corridor hallway to his right to find the East Wing elevators to Park Avenue Number Three. He arrived and hit the up button, while finding his stomach full of butterflies as he waited. When the arriving elevator opened, he stepped on, pushed the button for the fourth floor, and rode it up.

He got off at the fourth floor and walked to the same split-level condo that Jurrell had gotten excited about when they had given the place a walk-through over the summer. And before Shareef could ring the bell or knock lightly on the door, Jurrell opened it wide and let him in.

Jurrell smiled at him inside the doorway like an overgrown kid. He closed and locked the door behind Shareef and told him, "We doing this shit, man! We doin' it!"

He wore dark green slacks, a lighter green button-down shirt, and brown alligator shoes with a brown leather belt to match. He looked like a rich businessman. And his place was immaculate. It looked as if a professional designer had mapped it all out for him with leather sofas, exotic throw pillows, tall lamps, tasteful bookcases, and quality wood tables. Even the kitchen area looked done up.

Jurrell walked over to the kitchen and strolled out with two glasses of chilled dark wine in small wineglasses.

"We don't need a lot of this, man, just a little taste in your mouth to feel rich with."

He sat down on the dark brown leather sofa in the living room and crossed his legs, taking a sip of the wine. Shareef shook his head and grinned. He couldn't believe it. Jurrell's place looked as if he had spent every dime of his book advance on it.

Shareef sat down on the black leather sofa across from the fine wood coffee table that sat in the middle. Various magazines littered the coffee table from *King, Smooth, W, Essence, Black Enterprise,* and *Vanity Fair,* with several copies of the new book, *To Live and Die in Harlem.*

Obviously, Jurrell had succeeded in turning the place into a show-off pad.

He asked, "So, what they say today in the publisher meeting?"

Shareef took a sip of the wine and nodded. The taste shocked him.

"Damn! That's good wine."

"Nothing but the best, baby," Jurrell told him. "I'm try'na live this life now, you know. So what they tell you, man, anything good?" Despite the looks of lavishness that surrounded him, Jurrell was all about the business.

Shareef nodded and dug into his leather briefcase, pulling out a breakdown of the marketing and PR plans for the launch of The Underground imprint.

Jurrell took the paperwork and looked it over, while wearing a platinum pinkie ring that was all iced out with small multicolored diamonds.

He read the detailed heading slowly and deliberately aloud, "The Street King of urban literature has arrived, with the launch of his debut novel, *To Live and Die in Harlem,* from The Underground Library, a division of World Publishing Group."

He stopped and nodded. He said, "I like that." He read the rest of the breakdown in silence. He nodded again and said, "So, they only want to advertise in women's magazines."

"That's where we're gonna get the biggest bang for our buck outside of what you plan to do in the men's magazines," Shareef answered. He said, "But you have to understand that a major publishing house is not going to get the same rates that you can get on the low. A lot of the big companies can get great deals when they buy a lot of ad frequency, but when they're first coming in, a lot of these magazines see a big company and they start thinking about paying all of their bills with one big paycheck. You feel me? So we have to be careful with who we choose to spend this money with and how."

Jurrell chuckled. He said, "They'll try to give us the inflated Michael Jackson rates, hunh? Well, I got my magazine contacts, man, I'm ready with it. That's when it pays off to know the right people from Harlem who land in the right places."

He handed the paperwork back to Shareef and said, "So they're gonna print ten thousand bookmarks, run radio ads, and everything?"

Shareef took the paperwork back and nodded. "Since I can't really tour for these books, we can use all of the budget for direct marketing instead of them spending the money for me to stay at fancy hotels while eating room service."

Jurrell put two and two together and said, "That's how these record companies get these musicians, hunh? They send them on all-expense-paid world tours and have those assholes a million dollars in debt by the time they get back home."

Then he stood up and began to pace the room. He said, "Well, like I told you, man, we got a nice little program we're gon' start up in Harlem. Then we'll take it down to East Orange in Jersey, Philly, B-More, and D.C. That's all the get-money cities where you can sell books straight off the street. I already peeped things out."

He said, "Now I got this cell phone shit poppin' off at the next level with pretty voiced females doing most of the business for me. I got Meesha runnin' most of that shit. She's a good girl. She helped me get this condo with her good credit. I mean, it wasn't great, but it was good enough to talk some shit to get in. You know, with Meesha and the information you gave me."

He raised his arms up with his wineglass still in hand. He said, "But now I gotta pay for all this shit, man. I got about twenty-five days left on all this store credit, so this first book comes out in perfect timing. And they 'bout to pay us for the second book, too, now, right? I mean, you finished it already."

Shareef nodded to him. "Yeah, that's another fifty Gs each in the next couple of weeks."

"And how long does it take for the royalties again?"

"Every six months, twice a year, as soon as we break past even on the advance money."

"And we earn about a dollar a book on top of the shit we sell ourselves, right?"

"Yup."

Jurrell grinned and said, "Damn, that's sweet. So we buy these books straight from the publisher at five-six dollars each, make ten-twelve dollars back on the streets, plus a dollar every book for royalties?"

Shareef smiled back and said, "Yeah, that's the formula. All the publisher wants to do is keep the books moving. So if you can get the street teams poppin' like you say you can, then it's all gravy."

Jurrell said, "Nigga it's already goin' down. We got them first three boxes up on One Twenty-fifth with the squad of young bloods 'bout to make 'em move right now. We gon' run the three-card monte trick on the crowd. Then we can go after them movie deals you want."

He said, "And yo', thanks for the contact on them lawyers, too, man, to help get the boy the Truth up out that jam for us. So instead of him doing hard time, he got eighteen months probation. So I told him to stay right with this book hustle, and I put him in charge of the shit. That boy trustworthy, man. That's why G called him the Truth. T never even spit your name out in all this shit right here, man. Now that's loyalty. So I had to reward him for that."

With all of Jurrell's fast, hustler talk, and big plan living, Shareef wondered how long it would take for him to revert to something illegal if the book game didn't work as effectively as he hoped it would.

Shareef opened his mouth and said, "Look, man, like we said before, I'll run this thing down with you as long as you plan to keep it straight. But if you start spending up money like this . . . I mean, new books on the market just don't sell that fast, man."

Jurrell started shaking his head already. "Look, you don't understand me, Shareef. I got no fuckin' choice, man, I *gots* to make this shit work, that's why I went out and bought all this to make sure I'm motivated. Now if these books are ready for our next order, then you watch us move these motherfuckers. That's my word."

He sat back down and said, "By the way, I had this girl up in here last night who been running the pimp game since she was seventeen. She twenty-six now. That's our next book idea, Shareef. She had some interesting shit to say, man. So I'ma keep talking to her and give you the story."

Shareef just stared at him. He asked himself, *What the fuck am I gettin' into with this guy? This shit is crazy! He's 'bout to turn into a damn monster. Look how he's trying to live already. I can just imagine what his bed-room looks like upstairs. He probably got silk sheets on a waterbed.*

He asked Jurrell, "You really want me to write a book about a whore, man? I mean, come on, that ain't no new story."

Jurrell's eyes got wide. He said, "Nah, she not a whore, B, she a young *pimp*; a pretty brown-skinned girl with brown eyes like maple syrup. So I told her I was getting in the street book game, and she said, 'I got a story for you then.' And, yo, B, I heard about this girl before. She on the one wit' hers."

Shareef still couldn't believe him. But it didn't matter to Jurrell. He was already sold on the girl's story. *Pretty Brown Eyes.*

He said, "And I know what you thinking, Shareef. You thinking it's another degrading story of black women, and you got a wife and daughter at home. But yo, peep this, right. The first thing that came out of pretty brown's mouth about it, she told me 'I can't see why these girls want to sell themselves short like that. So once I saw that they could be turned out, I just wanted to be the one to protect them and teach them how to be smart about it.' And after she told me that, I was like, 'Damn! My man Shareef could do something with this.' Because if you still look at these videos and movies out here, man, a lot of young girls still need that hard smack in the face to wake the fuck up from the bullshit. And that's real."

Jurrell had so much passion in his eyes that Shareef found it hard to stare at him without believing him. It was like the tempting dance of a serpent. He was forced to look away to break the seduction. All the while, Shareef continued to think, *How the hell can we get all this crazy shit to work? Maybe I need to start thinking about how I can get rid of his ass.*

HOWEVER, on 125th Street, T and three of his helpers stood over a small table full of African-American books from the urban street genre, ready to sell to anyone who walked past them.

A group of four young girls stopped in front of the table.

"I got this book. I got that one. I got that. Ooh, and I need to get that one," the outspoken girlfriend stated as she pointed to the various street titles that she had already read.

T told her, "Nah, what you need to do is get this new book right here. This the one everybody buying right now."

He held up *To Live and Die in Harlem* by The Street King.

One of the other girls read the cover and said, "The Street King? Who he 'sposed to be?" And they began to laugh at it.

T remained calm. He said, "That's what it is. This guy is claiming the street book title like T.I. did with Atlanta rap music. I mean, he statin' it, and he doin' it."

Before the girls could dispute it, one of T's helpers pushed up on the table with three, ten dollar bills out, ready to buy books as if they didn't know each other.

He looked at the book in the girl's hands and said, "Yo, that's that new one dedicated to Baby G, ain't it? That's just what I was looking for? Everybody reading that now. Yo, give me three of them for my squad."

T nodded and collected three of the books from a box under the table.

The girls asked him, "That book about Baby G who got killed last summer? You didn't tell us that."

T counted his money and said, " 'Cause y'all was too busy talking out the side of y'all mouth. I told y'all the book was hot."

"Well, how much is it, ten dollars?"

"If you buy at least two, it's ten apiece. But if you only buying one, it's twelve. I'm trying to move these things to get more out here."

The girls began to negotiate with each other. "Aw'ight, Shannon, well, I'll buy one if you buy one."

T ignored them as if they had fake money. He went after an older sister who looked on curiously.

"That new book is that hot?"

T remained calm and nodded to her. He said, "They call me the Truth 'cause that all I tell."

The older sister frowned and said, "Now that's a damn lie."

The younger girls overheard her and laughed again.

T remained calm. He smiled and said, "It's a good one though, just like this book is good."

The older sister asked him, "It's two for twenty, and one for twelve."

"Yeah."

She said, "Aw'ight, well, give me two of 'em," and pulled out a twenty. "My girlfriend like to read these kind of books."

T got out two more books, and the younger women were ready with their money.

"Aw'ight, we'll buy two. And it better be *good* or we're coming back out here to find you."

T took their money, pulled out two more books, and told them, "Just make sure y'all bring more people who got money in their pocket. 'Cause I know y'all gon' like it."

His understated demeanor was effective. People seemed to gravitate to him without much solicitation.

"What's that book you selling over here?" an older man asked him. He looked to be in his mid-fifties.

T told him, "*To Live and Die in Harlem*. It's about people who ready to live or die for theirs." That was the simple speech Jurrell had told him to make.

Jurrell said, "You let everybody else be your hype man. But you just sit tight, stay calm, and count the money. I notice that people respect young guys like that. It makes it look like you used to gettin' money. That's what you want them to think. When they think you always gettin' money, more people want to give it to you. The shit becomes contagious."

He said, "That's how G did it. Remember? Well, you up next, Truth. You next in line. Just do what I tell you to do."

Right before the older man was ready to turn away and walk off uninterested, T's group of helpers returned to the table with more money out.

"Yo, they just bought up them books we had, son. Give us three, four more of 'em."

T took the forty dollars and dug up four more books for his helpers. He figured they must have sold the books for real. They didn't have that much money on them earlier. They had already given him most of their money to run their sales games for the crowd.

T whispered. "Yo, B, y'all sold them books for real?"

His helper told him, "Yeah. As soon as we turned the corner with them, people started asking what the book was about, and as soon as we said, Baby G, they wanted to buy 'em."

T nodded. "Aw'ight, that's good. This first box 'bout to go then."

When he set more books on the table, the older man had his own twenty-dollar bill out. Young guys selling books inspired him.

He said, "You know what, I need to get my two grandsons to read this book. Now are they gonna learn a valuable lesson from it?"

T had to come up with something on his own to close the deal.

He said, "If you can't learn a lesson from dying too young, then I guess you don't want to learn no lesson."

The older man nodded and agreed with him. "Yeah. If it takes you to die before you learn a lesson in life, then you just a damn fool. Give me two of them books."

Before T knew it, he had a full crowd in front of his table. He had to tell some of his helpers to stay with him.

"Yo, get some more of them books out the box and open up that second box," he told them.

The crowd became real specific about which book they wanted, too.

"That's the book about the boy who was killed last summer in the St. Nicholas Park shoot-out?"

T didn't know if it was a good thing or a bad thing for them to be so specific. The book was not an exact, tell-all story, it was only as much of the truth as they could get away with writing about him. But would reader curiosity lead to another investigation of the case? One thing was for sure, the cat was out of the bag. *To Live and Die in Harlem* was beginning to sell from that table like hot cakes. T's helpers even had a carload of guys pull up in the middle of the street.

The Truth didn't like that idea. Things were getting out of hand.

A guy in the passenger seat of a dark blue Chrysler hollered out the window, "Yo, give me five of them Baby G books."

T looked at him and didn't budge. He whispered to one of his helpers, "Yo, man, go get the money first. Then when you come back with it, you get him the books."

"Does this book say who shot 'em?" someone asked from the crowd.

T spoke up immediately and looked the guy in the face.

"Nah, man."

He didn't like the sound of that question. He even wondered if it was time for his crew to move on and get out of Dodge for their safety. But once he looked the kid in his face, the boy quickly looked away from his glare, and T could tell that he was only being a smart-ass.

So the Truth told the entire crowd in front of him, "Yo, when we say *To Live and Die in Harlem,* this ain't no game. Ain't nobody coming back out here like no Xbox. That was my man who was killed. How many of y'all had friends and family who got killed in Harlem?"

The Truth spoke it with pure heart and a grown-man's character. He had to grow up a great deal in the last year. He didn't need anyone to tell him how he felt about it either. And his truth only made the crowd want to buy the book with more zeal.

His helpers pulled the remaining boxes from under the table and began to sell the books straight from the boxes.

The comedian approached T at the side of the table and told him, "My bad, man. I ain't mean it like that."

T started to ignore him, but instead of doing that, he said, "Yeah, you need to read this book, too, and get something out of it, son. Real life ain't no damn comedy show. Comedians make jokes to get away from the pain. Ask Dave Chappelle about that."

The boy nodded his head in agreement and pulled out a twenty-dollar bill.

T took it from him and said, "Matter of fact, you need to pay me twenty for this book so you'll know how serious it is."

He looked the boy in the face and dared him to try and assert himself. But T already knew that he wouldn't. The boy didn't have the edge in him. He was nowhere near ready to die yet.

So he told T, "Aw'ight, you can have that, man." And he walked away with his book from The Street King, while looking back behind him to make sure he didn't receive a kick in his ass to go along with it.

As T's helpers began to chuckle at it around him, the incident only reminded him of how much he missed the presence, courage, and wisdom of his idol, Baby G.

He thought to himself, *I hope you proud of me, man. I just hope you proud of me.*

What Now?

SHAREEF TOOK A SIP of raspberry lemonade on the second floor of Friday's restaurant in the heart of Times Square. His friend Polo sat across the table grinning with his own drink in hand, a strawberry daiquiri. It was nearing eleven o'clock at night.

"So, they sold three boxes of books in one day?" Polo asked Shareef for clarity.

Shareef set his tall glass of lemonade on the table and grinned.

He said, "Jurrell wants me to order ten new boxes from the publisher tomorrow."

"How many books is that?" Polo asked him.

"Four hundred, with forty in each box."

Polo laughed and took a sip of his drink. He said, "And you was all concerned about how he was gon' sell 'em."

"I mean, selling books and drugs is two different things."

"Is it really though? I mean, it's all about how bad the people want it, right?" Polo suggested. "Maybe the people want this book that bad." He said, "I'll tell you this though, that Michael Springfield book wouldn't have done the same thing. Baby G was the right kid to write a book about. He was still young and on his way up, so people'll miss him. But Michael Springfield? I mean, he been in jail a long time, man. Them young guys ain't feeling him like that. And the young guys are what make shit hot nowadays.

"Jurrell right about that," Polo added. "That's why he only dealing with them young hustlers. And a lot of these young guys wanted to be down with Baby. So now they gon' wanna buy his book."

Then Polo smirked, knowing that Shareef would sweat him over his next revelation.

He mumbled, "And umm . . . I mean . . . you did your thing on this book, man."

Shareef eyed him across the table and asked him, "You read it?" just as his friend knew he would.

Polo started laughing again. He said, "I already know what you thinking, man. I didn't read none of your other shit, but I read this one. But look, man, them other books you write just make me mad about relationships, and then they make my dick hard when you get to the sex scenes. I mean, I tried to read them books, it just wasn't my thing."

He said, "But this book here, it held my interest. What you want me to say? You don't watch no relationship movies. You watch the same crime and action movies as every other guy. So this is the kind of book you always should have written."

Shareef continued to grin and shook his head. He said, "And you know that young reporter I've been beefing with from the *Amsterdam News,* he even gave me a good review on this one. They're publishing it this week. My publicists showed it to me today. It said, 'Finally, an urban book with heart and soul to match the gritty action.' "

Polo agreed with the review. "Yeah, man, we all know you can write. You just gotta write shit that we can read. We not women."

Shareef didn't want to get into another male/female story conversation. What was the point? He would write for both audiences now.

Polo asked him, "So, the next book is based on Jurrell. How you think that one gon' do?"

"I'll let you read it once we have it in galley form. But it's more like a mystery/thriller kind of book than this one. My editor called it the urban version of *The Usual Suspects.*"

Polo's eyes got big. He said, "Now that's what I'm talking about, that was a good-ass movie."

The waitress arrived with their food, Monterey Jack, barbecue chicken, and shrimp for both.

Before she walked off, she smiled and asked Shareef, "I hate to bother you, but . . . could I possibly come back and get your autograph?"

She looked hesitant as if Shareef would turn her down.

He smiled and said, "Of course you can. As soon as you collect the bill, just bring an extra piece of paper for me to sign for you."

"Oh, thank you. I've read several of your books, and I like them all."

"Well, thank you," Shareef told her

When the waitress walked off, Polo asked Shareef, "How are things with you and Jennifer now?"

Polo hadn't asked his friend about his marriage in a while. He understood that his partner was going through enough already.

Shareef shrugged his shoulders. "I mean, so far so good, man. I just learned that you can't get too imbalanced with a marriage. If you expect too much, you settin' yourself up for a letdown. And if you accept too little, then the same thing goes. So I'm just trying to keep myself balanced in the middle somewhere and take care of family."

Polo nodded with his first bite of food.

He mumbled, "That's a good way of looking at it."

"Yeah, writing all these romance books ought'a teach me something," Shareef commented.

"So, what ever happened to that girl Cynthia?"

Shareef took a bite of his own food. He finished chewing and answered, "I talked to her a few times during the whole court process, just to make sure everything was cool. But her idea was Michael Springfield's story, so I couldn't really talk to her too much about Baby G and all that."

Polo sized things up and began to laugh. He said, "Yeah, you couldn't tell her that you fucked up Jurrell's money and he was a lot more dangerous than her. I mean, you don't have to explain it to me, man."

Shareef stated, "Yeah, so, that's pretty much how it went. She gave me the whole idea to write the street book, but now she's out of the loop with me."

Polo sat quietly for a minute while they enjoyed their meals, but he couldn't help thinking about how Trap and Spoonie chose the other side and ended up dying because of it.

Finally, Polo forced himself to mention it. He shook his head with his fork in hand. He stated, "Man, it's just fucked up the way things went down with our people. I mean, you think you know some people better sometimes."

Shareef looked up from his food and nodded. He understood what Polo was getting at. He had been forced to think about it all himself.

He swallowed his food, took another sip of his lemonade, and responded, "What can you do, man? I wasn't giving up my life for theirs. Nor was I willing to give up your life. So, I wrote the shit down and came up with my options. And the shit may sound insensitive to some people, but that's just how life is. Sometimes you gotta write niggas off."

Then he looked Polo square in his eyes. "But like you said, some of us get to that point where we become family. And you ended up having to put your neck out there for me, man. All on account of me being hardheaded," Shareef commented.

Polo shook it off. "Man, you dun' put your neck out plenty of times for me. I don't know where I would be all of these years without you. Whenever I needed something, you was there for me. And that's love."

He grinned and added, "Yeah, but if you didn't come up with what you came up with, they damn sure was coming after me next. I ain't even gon' front. But like always, Shareef, you found a way to handle that shit."

Shareef couldn't argue with that. He had been overachieving his entire life, and he'd become comfortable with figuring his way out of jams.

Polo asked him, "But now, how you really feel about this Jurrell shit you involved in? I mean, I know you, man. You don't like a ma-fucker telling you what to do. And he already acting like he your boss now, so imagine how he gon' act if these books become bestsellers. Or not even *if*, but *when*. Because I know everybody gon' feel this book."

Polo hit the nail right on the head. The forced partnership with Shareef's childhood nemesis, of all people, looked like a slow cancer that was sure to kill him.

Shareef took a deep breath and tried to explain things as best he could.

He said, "My grandfather had to remind me after all this shit went down that I'm not alone in this world, man. And no matter how independent I like to be, or we *all* like to be for that matter, we still owe allegiances to people whether we like it or not. So, with that in mind, it's like this whole thing has become a life lesson for me. I gotta look out for my family. I gotta look out for my grandparents. I gotta look out for your family. I gotta look out for the women who read and support my books. And now I gotta look out Jurrell and his family, and all the street niggas who need to understand more about the consequences of that lifestyle."

He said, "So, if this Underground Library imprint ends up employing another ten, twenty, thirty people, and giving them a better way to live, then who am I to complain about having to write these books. I mean, don't get it twisted, I'm still getting paid from all this, and that's good money for all of us. Because if I got more money, and I know who I'm responsible to, then we all in good shape. The same thing goes for Jurrell. As long as he's connected to people like he is, then he got money to get, and he can't chance not getting that money. So he knows how much he needs me, if just to get this shit started. But if he finds someone else to write shit for him, or to do business with him, then we'll have to make a decision of where we go from there."

Polo nodded his head and cracked a slow smile. Then he extended his hand across the table. When Shareef took it in his, Polo told him excitedly, "Shareef, you my nigga, man. That's word to my whole fuckin' family. You know why? Because you always figure the shit out. No matter what it is."

He said, "And niggas can hate on you all they want, B, for going for yours. But at the end of the day, we need niggas like you. Straight up and down. Because if we don't have anybody of our own, who can figure shit out, then who do we have? You know what I mean, Shareef? Who else can we count on?"

Polo released his hand and added, "For all them people who like to front on you, man. 'Shareef think he the shit. Shareef think he know everything. Fuck Shareef!' Nah, fuck them niggas, man! Fuck everybody who think that way. Because if we didn't have no Michael Jordan, no Puff Daddy, no Damon Dash, no Spike Lee, Suge Knight, or Martin Luther King and Malcolm X, then who would the people look up to to be inspired by, man? Fuckin' Muhammad Ali was important out this bitch.

"And I see you in the same way that I see them, man. You just doing it in the book world," Polo told him. "So, no matter what, Shareef, you just keep doing you. Don't slow your roll for nobody. Make them catch up. And if they can't catch up, then that's their problem. But if you slow down . . ."

Polo looked at him intently and pointed with his index finger. He said, "If you slow down, on *purpose*, and know you 'sposed to win, and you *don't*, then you just fucked up for all of us, man. That's how I see it."

He said, "If you got a gift in this world as a black man, then you 'sposed to *use* that shit. Don't stop your shine for nobody. 'Cause what niggas need to understand, man, is that, as long as one black man is shinin', then we can all shine by supportin' him. But if nobody's shinin'. I mean, like, *nobody*. Then what the fuck we get out'a that?"

Polo stared across the table for Shareef to take it all in. And when he did, Shareef just shook his head. He was surprised by it all. Polo had his back, all the way to the graveyard.

Shareef looked at him and said, "Damn!" He paused for another minute and said, "Damn!" a second time. Polo had blown him away with his words.

Polo laughed and decided to help him out.

"Yeah, B, I picked up a li'l something from being around you all these years. You ain't expect me to say something like that, right? You think I been sleepin' all these years?"

Shareef laughed and said, "Obviously not, right? But, um, I thank you for saying that to me, man. Word. 'Cause sometimes I start to feel like I'm wrong for pushing forward. I start to feel like I'm wrong for wanting more, for *all* of us. You know? Sometimes I ask myself, 'What's wrong with what you have right now? What's wrong with just getting by?' "

Polo shook his head before he even finished. He said, "Man, fuck that just-gettin'-by shit. That's for them other niggas. You a winner, Shareef. You always been a winner."

He chuckled and added, "I wanna be on a yacht in five years, and you the only one who can get me there. You feel me? And I want my son to be right there with your son."

He said, "But all jokes aside, it's not just the material things, man, but aspirations, *period,* that you go for in life. For most successful people, it's not really about the materials anyway. They got 'em all. You already got shit down there in Florida. So shut up, man, with all that everyday-black-man-struggling shit, and tell me your big plans for tomorrow. 'Cause see, that boy Jurrell ain't gon' let you slow down anyway. He ain't try'na hear that shit. That ma-fucka gon' want a private jet off ya' ass next year. So let me get you back home and back to work."

Polo looked over and yelled, "Hey, waitress, my boy Shareef is ready for the bill now and that autograph you want."

Shareef smiled at him and laughed it off. He was ready to pay another bill, as the weight on his brown shoulders continued to increase.

But it was all right. He had been gifted with enough energy and smarts to deal with it. And even if others failed to understand him, he realized that he was born to do what he had to do and be who he had to be, and there was no turning back from it. The game of life goes on with more wins to get.

About the Author

New York Times bestselling author Omar Tyree is the winner of the 2001 NAACP Image Award for Outstanding Literature in Fiction and the 2006 Phillis Wheatley Literary Award for a Body of Work in Urban Fiction. His books include *What They Want, Boss Lady, Diary of a Groupie, Leslie, Just Say No!, For the Love of Money, Sweet St. Louis, Single Mom, A Do Right Man,* and *Flyy Girl.* He lives in Charlotte, North Carolina.

To learn more about Omar Tyree,
visit his website at omartyree.com.